Zombie
An Old

Mark Tufo

Edited By: Joy Buchanan

Dedications: To my wife - She gets me!

To my hard working beta readers, Vix Kirkpatrick and Kimberly Sansone, I hope you know how much I appreciate your input.

As always to all the men and women in uniform and the first responders, I appreciate all the sacrifices you endure to ensure our way of life. I will always be a fan of yours!

Special Shout-Out: This is for a brave little boy named Raiden Quinn P. may you be granted the strength to overcome all that has been set in your path. The Tufo family will hold you in our thoughts and prayers.

Table of Contents

Book of Talbotisms: My life would be easier if I were dead.

Eliza

It is hell. Unending darkness would have been a more welcome void. Each second is dragged forth into a hopeless eternity. My self is being seared away even as I am forced to remember who I was, who I am. Each sin must be paid for in its own way. Tomas, help me!

Prologue

"June, do you really believe what they say about him?" Will asked as he pulled himself away from the microscope he was peering through.

"You're looking at the evidence right there in front of you," June, his lab partner and sometimes bed partner, replied.

Will was a little too skinny, and his nose too large for her liking; but the end of the world had severely curtailed her choices. She'd been chosen for this project because, even though she was a brilliant biochemist and was near to the top of her field, it was her gambling addiction that had ultimately paved the way. She would have been on a short list for the Demense Group anyway; it was her large debts to some shady characters that had forced her hand, so it was she hopped from one evil to the next. She knew enough about her flaws to realize that she may have accepted the Demense Group's offer even without them paying off her crippling debts. That was just the icing on the cake. The rub though, was they owned her now; she couldn't leave this facility even if she wanted. And where would she go? The world had gone to shit. The only thing worth doing now was Will.

They'd not directly come out and told her, but she'd learned through her research that the zombie virus came from this facility. They just had too much information on it, literally hundreds of documents on the virus. As if that weren't bad enough, they were now experimenting with animals to see if a crossover could happen.

June had done all in her power to thwart Will's progress, sabotaging his experiments as subtly as she could. Whenever he got close to discovering the truth, she would reach her hand into his pants and he would forget pretty much everything else on the planet. Discovering a vaccine for a zombie bite had fallen squarely on her desk, and she'd done it. It was the brilliance of Doctor Baker's work that had pushed her to the results she'd been striving for. She'd used her experimental vaccine on the large black man known as BT and the Talbot son, Justin. She'd warned everyone that she wasn't sure if it would work or if there wouldn't be horrific side-effects. She didn't want them to yet know she'd been successful but she couldn't let the man and boy die. If there was any way to salvage her soul she was going to try.

She was warring within herself over how much she wanted to give these old cronies who would wield this vaccine for their own devices, making a world of have and have-nots from who was left. The "haves" in this case would have more power than they already did and that was what it always came down to for those small-minded, small-dicked men. Power was a drug much like gambling, she mused. She admonished herself for giving grief to someone else's vice.

Will was hunched down, his eye nearly connected to the microscope. June smiled. She couldn't figure out why he didn't just look at the thirty-two inch monitor that showed the exact same thing he was looking at through the eyepiece.

"Evidence? I don't see anything except some strange thing that may or may not be a virus. One thing for certain is that it's dead, not dormant."

"Are you sure?" She got up from her chair.

"Here...look." He pushed away from the scope.

"I'll look here. Thanks." She was standing in front of the monitor.

"Oh yeah, right." He grabbed his laser pointer. "See the edges here? If this were dormant, and not dead, they would not be this blackish color and frayed like they are on the edges. This virus, and I'm hesitant to say that, is not viable for an injection."

"All the vials are like this?"

"I just pulled this sample out of the cryo-freezer."

"Could the freezer have done this?"

"It was dead before it got in there."

"How long was the virus outside the host?" June was

reaching over Will, looking for the paperwork, her breasts pressed up against his nose, his glasses pushed askew.

"Umm, what were we talking about?"

June had grabbed the log and was pulling away, hardly noticing the flustered flush to her partner's face. "Two minutes? Two minutes from extraction to freezing. How could it have died that quickly? Can we possibly bring the host here so he is closer to the freezer?"

"Oh, I don't think that would be wise," Dixon said from the doorway. He was the senior member of the Demense Group.

"Mr. Hawes, it's good to see you!" Will got up quickly. June put her hand to her mouth when she noticed that, much like a pimply faced high-school freshmen who could not control himself, Will was housing a tent in his trousers. How he could *not* notice she didn't know. Dixon did, though, avoiding the oncoming scientist's handshake as best he could.

"Sit, sit," Dixon urged Will. "Show me what you've got. It's imperative that some headway is made with these samples."

The talk of work got Will back on track. "Right, right." He turned back around. "Well, sir, I've taken slide after slide, and on every one of them, the agent you are asking me to isolate and replicate is dead…not dying or dormant…just flat out dead."

"That's good, right?" Dixon asked; coming closer, but not too close.

"If we were trying to make an antidote, I'd be more inclined to agree with you. But when you want this virus to thrive and be suitable for infection, it needs to be healthy and alive. Something like a flu virus or hepatitis can live outside the host for hours, and in some cases up to four days. That's why they can be so easily transmitted. This looks and acts more like rabies. It dies within seconds, if not instantaneously, of being outside the vector host. The only way to pass that from person to person or mammal to mammal is through a bite. And given all I know about the donor, that fits." Will had a shine in his eyes, hitting his stride and talking about things that fascinated him.

"So you're saying I could have him drained of blood and it wouldn't make a difference?"

"None at all," Will said matter-of-factly.

Internally June winced. She'd known the moment that Dixon Hawes had extended his hand, when they'd originally met, that she was about to make a deal with the devil, but her options had been entirely too restricted to refuse. Now, however, upon reflection, how bad would broken kneecaps really have been? She would have died in the outbreak, and her unremarkable but mostly upstanding life could have drifted off peacefully into the sunset. Now, though, she had a gnawing pit in her stomach that future annals would someday record her acts as grievous and traitorous to all mankind. It was the tarnishing of her legacy that scared her the most.

Will's nonchalance didn't surprise her in the least despite the fact that they were talking about killing another human being. It was all about the possibility of doing something unique and revolutionary—not what it took or who was going to get hurt to reach to that point.

"Would I be able to see the host?" Will asked.

"You could see him, although, I would not recommend getting near him. What he has makes rabies look like scabies."

"Is there a chance he would bite someone that would be more compliant?"

Dixon thought about it for a moment. "It's possible. I have leverage."

Dixon turned and left, now with the unenviable task of thinking who would be trustworthy enough with that sort of power. He wanted it to be himself, but he'd no sooner get in that cell with Michael than he would a pit viper. He could feel the malice radiate off the man even from the monitor he had in his office.

Chapter One – Mike Journal Entry 1

Here I sit, locked up in a cell again. It's not like there isn't some reason out there I shouldn't be here for. Lord knows I've done enough stuff in this lifetime and probably a few others that merit me being caged. Not my family though, they're the innocents in all this. I came here (well maybe not *here* per se, but somewhere) with the express and sole purpose of getting help for Justin and BT and to also help Doc Baker in any way that I could. Had I known how far over the edge the Doc had been pushed, I would have struck out earlier or tried harder to get to him while we were still out on the road. The man lost everything and was holding me responsible for the bulk of it. And some of the fault was mine; I'd had a lot of time to replay everything that had happened thus far in this new, fucked-up world we found ourselves in. Could of, should have, would have…those are all the stupid words I come up with.

I *should have* shoved a stake in Eliza's heart the very first time I laid eyes on her disease-ravished body. I *could have* left Tommy up on the Walmart roof. I *would have* done both had I known a tenth of what I do now. I've risked everything to keep my family safe and made the choices at the time that I thought would further that cause, and where has *that* gotten me? I'm in a cage, next to one of my best friends, and nearly my entire family is in this same facility. Safe for now, but at some point, that will change; whether it's when they get what they want from me or realize that they can't. Either way, it's a razor-sharp and ultra-thin rope I'm now balancing on, and at any moment, I could fall to either side or be split right down the middle from it.

"How long have I been asleep?" Dennis asked, sitting up and rubbing his eyes. He'd had the unfortunate luck of hopping a ride with what I could only describe as the anti-Christ, Mrs. Deneaux. I'd seen cats with fewer lives than her. The woman probably had a wing in hell named after her.

"Long enough that I ate your dinner," I told him.

For the last couple of days, we'd had no visitors except for a guard named Hiccup, who delivered our meals. I don't know if he was on any particular schedule or just dropped off food randomly. I didn't have much to go on in regards to the passage of time. We had no sunlight and no clocks other than our internal ones, and without some sort of way to calibrate those, it was nearly impossible to say how long we were down here for sure.

"Was it good?" He stood up and stretched.

"The usual. Filet mignon, garlic mashed potatoes and a nice Pinot Grigio."

"Dammit, no wonder I drooled in my sleep."

"You drool in your sleep anyway, who you shitting?"

"Have you slept or have you been pacing the entire time?"

"Six thousand, seven hundred and twenty six-steps since you fell asleep."

"You should get a hobby. Hear anything about your family?"

I shook my head.

"I'm sorry about this, man."

"Not your fault," I told him. "In all honesty, I could say the same to you. There's at least a half dozen times I could have left Deneaux on the side of the road with a fork lodged in her throat."

Dennis shrugged his shoulders. "Got a feeling it would have turned out like this no matter what you did."

"Probably right."

"Just my luck to hitch a ride with the Demon Queen."

"Yeah, the horns should have given it away."

"I was in a bit of a pickle when I got in the truck, didn't have time to ask for her stance on basic human decency. Any ideas?"

"Yup, as soon as some idiot gets within my grasp, I'm going to pop his head off like a champagne cork."

Dennis involuntarily put his hands to his throat and gulped hard.

We both turned as we heard a door open down the end of the corridor. We couldn't see from our angle, but it sounded like more than one individual was headed our way.

"Where is he?" a voice bellowed out.

My heart soared—it was BT; and if the volume with which he spoke was any indication of his health, then he was doing pretty good.

"Geez, he's right down here. You sure you don't want any chicken? It might keep you from being so angry. It keeps me from being sad." It was Porkchop, BT, and hopefully a key…and a machinegun…and a helicopter. No, scratch the helicopter. If we had one of those, chances were we'd need Trip to pilot it. That would probably not work out well.

"Who's with you?" I asked down the corridor.

"That you, Talbot? Who the hell am I kidding? Who else would they feel the need to throw into the slammer?"

"The slammer? What is this, 1940?" I asked Dennis.

"Why are you asking me? Ask him…oooh…I see why you didn't ask him, he's huge. He's your friend, right?" Dennis was subtly moving away from the bars and deeper into his cell.

"He's mostly a friend, although I think he'd kill me if he had the chance." I was smiling like the village idiot right now. A lot of things were wrong, but BT looked good, and that counted for more than a little.

"You look like you just got your first handie. You alright, man?" BT asked as Porkchop rolled him up to my cell. BT's legs bumped into the steel bars as Porkchop let go of the wheelchair in an effort to lick his fingers clean.

"I'm mostly fine. You look good, man. You alright?" I had my hands wrapped around the bars.

"The kid has rammed me into three doors, a wall, two armed guards, and now your cell. If I survive him, I think I'll be okay. I see they have you locked up. Your craziness finally caught up with you."

I nodded. "Hey, I keep my insanity cloaked in normalcy."

"Keep telling yourself that. You know it was only a matter of time, right, Mike? I mean society, even as screwed up as it is, has to have some sort of rules and regulations. They can't just let someone like you keep wandering around." He was grinning as he spoke. "It's pure anarchy with you loose."

"You like this shit? This funny for you?"

"Yeah, pretty much. Who's the cracker?"

"This is Dennis."

"He cool?"

"We grew up together. He's cool."

"So what, then? Is he just guilty by association?"

"Good one. No, he had the unfortunate luck to cross paths with Deneaux."

"Holy shit. You're lucky you're still alive. She makes black widows seem decent."

Dennis gave BT a waning smile.

"How is everyone?"

"Everyone is fine for now." BT got serious. "Trip keeps talking his crazy shit to me and I'm going to have to plant him, man. I just won't have a choice. I mean, I know you like the guy and all, but he keeps telling me I must be from another planet or at least a crossbreed with an alien. He thinks I have half Genogerian blood running through me, whatever the hell that means.

"He scares the hell out of me, Mike. I mean, I thought *your* type of crazy might be catchy, but his just radiates off of him like plutonium. I don't want him to make me sick." BT kept going on like this. "Help me, man!"

He pulled himself up from his chair and wrapped his hands around the bars much like I was on my side. I'm still not sure how a man with fingers as large as his could manipulate them so deftly. I felt him smoothly shove a folded-up piece of paper under my palm. Even the security camera, if it had super slow motion capability, was not going to pick up the sleight of hand.

"I cannot tell you how good it is to see you," I told him.

"Got a plan?" he asked. He already knew the answer—it was a long running joke between us. I'd yet to have a fully formed or functioning plan since this shit-fest started. Why break the trend now?

"Just going to wing it, I think."

"They said I could only have a few minutes down here. I just wanted to make sure you were doing alright, man, and…and I wanted to thank you."

"This must be hard for you," I said to him.

"You have no idea. I had it all thought out, but now, looking at your smug smirk is making me debate letting you know how I feel."

"I get it. It's all good."

"Just…Mike, stop for a sec. I just need to tell you how appreciative I am. I know you had Justin's health in mind as well, but you risked everything for me. Not that I would have ever forgotten the thousand other things we've done together. But this, man, this I will hold above the rest. I don't know how I'm ever going to repay you, but I will."

I made sure to safely palm the note before I wrapped my hands around his. Well, wrap is a stretch. But you get the idea. "You keep our family safe, BT. That's all I ask, and we're more than square."

He opened his mouth.

Before he could speak, I cut him off. "And yes, that includes Trip."

"Dammit."

"Let's go." A guard was heading toward us.

"You take care," he said to me. "Nice to meet you, Cracker," he said to Dennis.

"Umm, yeah, likewise, I guess." Dennis held his hand

up weakly.

"Come on, BT. I know where they keep the jars of peanut butter." Porkchop was struggling to maneuver the chair around. BT's knees whacked into just about every bar.

"You're going to break my damn kneecaps. Just get me back to my quarters. You get a hold of peanut butter, and I'm going to have it all over me like the chicken grease." I could hear BT complaining all the way down the hallway and partly down the next before the door to the cellblock closed.

"He's your friend?"

"Yeah. When he doesn't want to kill me, we get a long pretty well."

Getting completely out of view of the cameras was no easy feat, but I needed to know what BT had risked getting me in that small, folded-up square of paper. I decided to feign sleep. At least I'd been provided with a blanket for warmth, although it seemed to be made of burlap. I turned to the wall and pulled the covers completely over my head before unfolding the note. The print was tiny, which I thought kind of funny given the massive fingers used to write it.

In military installation of some sort, family safe. Doc is lying or was told to. Justin and I were guinea pigs for a whole keg full of experimental drugs, apparently we're clean now. When you get out...(He had much better faith in me than I did.)*...take a left down the corridor to Quarantine area. Once inside there, go to Blue Wing. I'll have a beer waiting.*

"Thank you for that," I said, barely audible.

"You taking a nap?" Dennis asked.

"Not really." I folded the piece of paper up and stuck it in my pocket. I thought about eating it, but who knew what germs BT might have had on his hands at the time that he wrote it.

We sat there a few more hours, reminiscing about our earlier, much less complicated lives. We would invariably come around to Paul, as he was a large part of just about any story we could conjure. We'd laugh for extended periods of time; only to then have equally as large moments of silence and reflection.

Human life, in relatively normal times (if such a thing truly exists), is rife with change, loss, and gain. It is the nature of life itself. The thing with loss, though, is that it is generally incremental, and this gives us time to accept, grieve, and mourn for the passing away of a life, a relationship, maybe our innocence, or even a job—whatever it may be. As human beings, we need to work through this time of adjustment. Some never do or require the guidance of therapists, or a myriad of drugs—whether prescribed by a doctor or self—to each their own. I'm entirely too guilty to point a finger at anyone else.

During this shit—this zombie invasion, apocalypse, or just plain zombie cluster-fuck—change and loss have come at such a rapid pace that my mind has not been able to keep up with it. I have not been able to give every bereavement its due. A day of reckoning will come when the accumulated weight will crash down upon me, and this balancing act of surviving and coping will implode. If I still had a soul, I'm pretty sure it would be fairly threadbare and riddled with holes. Someday, I will be sitting on a porch with my family safe and secure, and I will toast everyone I lost. Odds were that I was going to get pretty shit-faced that day.

"Oh, man, do you remember—" Dennis was cut short as we once again heard traffic coming our way.

"I feel like we're at the zoo and we're the damn exhibits," I said grumpily.

Dennis nodded.

"Oh, shit." I placed my head in my palm.

"What's the matter?" Dennis asked with alarm.

"Ponch! Ponch is that you? Hey, man, could you bail me out, I'm in jail again," Trip said as he grabbed the bars. "I told Don Carlos that guy was a cop, but he didn't listen, sold him three kilos of Arabica beans, and now I'm here, man!"

"He sold a cop, coffee?" Dennis asked me.

"Just go with it," I told him.

"How are you doing?" Stephanie, Trip's wife and I'm sure a person up for sainthood, asked.

"I'm good. My family?"

"They're okay." Her gaze slid away from mine. That was enough to let me know that danger might not be present at this very moment, but it was lurking like the insidious little fuck it was.

"Oh, Stephanie, they got you too?" Trip asked, seemingly seeing his wife for the first time since they came to visit. "Ponch, man, you got to get us out of here. I've got some money stashed in an old Chevy down by the mall."

"Trip, it's alright. I'm the one in jail."

Trip looked around; I guess finally noticing he was in an open hallway. "How did that happen? Were you with Don Carlos?"

"It's good to see you're both doing well," I told them honestly.

"What's going to happen to us, Mike?" Steph asked. She already knew, and she'd know if I was lying.

"We need to get out of here." That is what I told her. Seemed much better than, "They'll eventually kill us."

"I'll get you out of here. I've got money, Ponch."

"I know, I know, in an old Chevy down by the mall."

"What? Who keeps money in abandoned vehicles on the side of the road?" he asked almost indignantly.

Stephanie shrugged behind him. Dennis may or may not have lightly dinged his forehead against his bars. "I've seen you make more sense passed out, Mike."

"Oh, you have company. I'm sorry, man, we didn't mean to intrude." Trip grabbed Stephanie's hand and quickly pulled her down the hallway.

"Bye." She waved over her shoulder.

"What the fuck was that all about?"

"That was actually pretty lucid for him."

"He another friend of yours?"

"You know, I'm pretty sure he doesn't even remember my real name, but yeah, he's another friend of mine."

"I thought it was a fairly select group I was in. Seems you'll let just about anyone in."

"Anyone that saves my life gets a free pass."

"Him? Really? You are kidding, right?"

"No. He's saved me three…four times at least."

"How is that even possible?"

"Luck of the Irish, or he has a platoon of guardian angels. Take your pick. Sometimes I think there is way more going on behind that burn-out façade, but then he'll come out with something like, 'Did you know you can snort jalapeños?' and I'm not so sure anymore."

"Do you chop them up first?"

"What?"

"The jalapeños…does he chop them up first?"

"Not you, too. I don't think I could take two of him."

"And Stephanie?"

"That's his wife."

"I figured she was his caregiver. They're married? How does she deal with him?"

"Beats me, because she sure as hell doesn't do drugs. Anything that got near their household would get sucked up by him. Oh, here's another fun-fact. He's loaded."

"Why are you screwing with me?"

"Serious, like multi-millionaire loaded, invested in some stock that went through the roof. Knowing him, he probably walked into Merrill-Lynch to request a dime bag and instead bought the first shares of Apple."

We kept talking. I was hoping that this parade of fellow captives would finally lead to my family. Tracy, my kids, Gary, and Henry had yet to show. If my captors were attempting some form of psychological terror, they were succeeding. They must have known I'd ask BT and Trip about them. Why not just let me see them as well? I knew the answer—it was a way of control and potentially a way to soften me up for whatever they were trying to get from me.

"Mike, Mike," Dennis was shaking my shoulder through the bars. I don't know if I was sleeping or contemplating; either way, it took me a second to figure out what was going on. "Someone is coming."

I sat up, my fingers crossed in the hopes that it was Tracy or the kids. It ended up being one of my kids in a sense. I could just make out Henry's massive head from my angle. Something looked wrong, though, as he looked entirely too tall. And then I knew why. The guard walking him had pulled his leash taut and Henry's front paws were a good six inches from the ground. Henry was breathing heavy, trying to get in enough oxygen as his airway was being restricted. If I had the strength to rip those bars off I would have.

"Henry!" I yelled.

He heard me and was able to get enough thrust with his back legs to pull the leash from the guard. The guard kicked out, nailing Henry in the side. He yelped in pain, his back legs nearly sliding out from under him. He righted himself and kept coming my way.

"This fucking sausage yours?" the guard laughed as he followed after my Henry.

Henry was running down the corridor toward me. Running might be a gross exaggeration, but you get the idea. His jowls were flapping like an eagle's wings, drool was spraying to the floor, and I'd swear he had a grin on like we'd both been caught raiding an off-limits birthday cake. The guard picked up his pace just as Henry was getting to the bars. I reached through and quickly stroked his head and chest, Henry was in bliss. I got the feeling that the guard was supposed to let me see but not touch and now had to quickly correct his mistake. I moved to the far side of my cell, closest to Dennis and furthest from the cell door. Henry followed, as did his leash. The guard was just reaching down for the trailing rope when I moved with only a speed I'd been granted.

Even as the guard's hand was clasping around the rope, mine was clamping around his forearm. I yanked him in so hard that his forehead slammed against the bars. He'd have a decent sized knot that was going to be the least of his troubles. I positioned his upper arm halfway between the elbow and shoulder between the two bars before I forced it backwards, shattering the bone. He screamed in abysmal pain.

"You ever fuck with my dog again, I'll rip this arm off, shove it up your ass, and then parade you around like a fucking puppet. We clear? And, oh yeah, he's not fat he's just big-boned." I pulled the man's arm toward me, the bone fragments grinding together as I did so. He passed out from the shock and the pain.

"That's fucking gross, man." Dennis had paled considerably and had one hand close to his mouth in case he spewed. I pushed the guard away hard enough that he came to rest on the far side of the hallway. I knew my time was limited, so I took advantage of it. I squished Henry's face like it was made from Play-Doh.

"Who's my good boy?" I was face-to-face with him, scratching behind his ears as he gave me a tongue lashing.

"Fuck, man, that's worse than you breaking that guy's arm. Ever think about getting a room?"

"Got one," I said as Henry moved his hindquarters into position for a good old-fashioned rub down.

The door opened again. It was Grand Central all right. "Move away from the bars," an authoritative voice shouted out. It was punctuated by the ratcheting of many rounds into many chambers.

"You keep an eye on Mom," I told Henry, gripping his large head between my hands.

Henry barked, but to say it was a bark would be like saying I could sing like an angel. And trust me, I sing worse than I dance. I'd once been asked to leave the floor of a father-daughter dance after I'd stepped on a third set of feet. It was more like the bark of a seal, so imagine that sound and roll with it. He seal-barked three more times, hopefully in understanding of my words.

"Is he dead?" the new guard asked as he approached cautiously, at least four other soldiers coming with him. I stood and moved back from the front of the cell, as did Dennis.

"He's not dead, but if he ever fucks with my dog again, he will wish he was by the time I'm through with him."

"Come here, pooch," the lead guard said, not wanting to get any closer to my cell than he had to. Henry seal-barked at him.

"It's alright, boy, go ahead. Just do as I ask." Henry looked to me and seal-barked again. He walked over to the guard on the ground, lifted his left rear leg and let a warm stream coat the man's thighs, then went to the guard who had asked him to come.

"I'll take care of him," he promised me, and I believed him. "Milts, Jonesy, get Samuels. I'll cover you."

Milts and Jonesy did not look overly thrilled with their new duties as they each grabbed one of Samuels' shoulders and dragged him away from there. He moaned loudly in his lifeless state.

"Mike, shit, man," Dennis said as the cell block door once again shut and the men were gone.

"What? I would have done the same if they kicked you. Don't look at me that way. You spent most of your time locked up with your dad. Now I'm not saying you had it easy, so don't go getting all butt-hurt. I'm just telling you that I've been back and forth across the states, and I've met some of the worst assholes imaginable. This is the way of the world now…it's swift justice or get screwed. I'll dole it out any day before I'm the recipient."

"You're not quite the easy going guy I knew."

"We're not in our teens trying to feel up chicks and smoke weed any more, bud. Or even in our twenties out to just have a good time. This is survival, and not necessarily of the fittest, but more the ones that are willing to do what needs to be done."

"At what cost? At what point does it become too much?"

"Don't pontificate on me. If someone threatened your dad no matter their reasons what would you have done?"

"I don't know, man. I don't know what I would have done."

"That hesitation would have got you both killed. Trust me."

"What else did Tommy take away from you with that bite?"

"Don't you dare. Just don't. I don't care who I have to go through for the safety and lives of my family and friends, you included."

"I just don't know," Dennis said as he moved to his bunk and sat down.

We sat that way for hours, maybe minutes, I don't know, felt like a damned eternity. All I could think about was my family and getting them out of this latest jam we'd found ourselves in.

The door opened once again. I pressed my head as hard as I could against the bars in a hope to get an early view of my wife coming toward me. Unless she was in wing-tipped shoes, this wasn't her. An older man with three armed guards was heading my way. Well, here came the answers.

"Hello, Mr. Talbot, my name is—"

"I don't give a fuck," I said as I went to the rear of my cell and lay down on my cot. I placed my hands behind my head and stared at the gray ceiling.

"Right." He looked to his guards and back down the hallway. "I had planned on allowing the rest of your family to visit before your last demonstration."

"He got off light. If he'd actually injured my dog, it would have gotten pretty messy. The cleaning staff would have probably charged you extra to get the stains up." I noticed the three men with him were a little antsy.

"We need something from you, Mr. Talbot."

"Refer back to my opening statement."

"I don't think you understand the precarious situation with which you find yourself in. Your family—"

He had not even finished the word "family" when I had sprung from the cot and slammed into the bars, my outstretched arm inches from grabbing the front of his suit jacket and pulling him toward me. He jumped backwards once he was able to catch up to how quickly I had moved. "You saw what I did because some asshole kicked my dog, what do you think I would do if someone so much as gave my wife a bad bruise?"

He swallowed hard and smoothed back his hair in an attempt to compose himself. I had to give him credit—he recouped quicker than I expected. "Um…impressive." There was a healthy dose of fear in his eyes but something else as well. Greed maybe, desire?

"You touch my family and I will rip your head off with my hands."

I could see one of the guard's hands gripping his weapon so tightly that his knuckles were the color of ivory.

"No…wait…hold that thought. First, I will pull the skin from your face while you're alive. You'll be screaming so loudly at first, and then it will kind of taper off to this whimper of the insane, and then the hitching of one who is in shock. THEN I will rip your head off. I'll most likely stick my left hand into your mouth and my right will be on the back of your skull, kind of where it protrudes, then I'll twist it back and forth a few times. This has the added benefits of breaking your spine and loosening up those pesky muscles and tendons. Next, I'll step on your feet. That's to hold you down while I yank up on your head. I'm not sure if you'll still be alive or at least cognizant of what is going on, but your mouth will forever be open in this voiceless scream-looking thing. And I'm sort of OCD about these kinds of things, so I'll have to do it to all of you. I'm kind of forced to…horrible disease that it is."

The guard who was already attempting to grind his weapon into dust was imperceptibly moving the barrel of his weapon upwards. I don't even think he consciously knew he was doing it.

"Enough, Mr. Talbot. I had not wished to force your hand, but I have your family. I will do whatever is necessary to secure the resources I desire."

"What exactly is that?" I growled.

"Your blood, your incredible blood."

"I found the needle holes. I would imagine you have more than you could possibly need for whatever you're trying to do. But then again…I guess not, because if that were the case, I'm sure I'd be dead. What's the matter? One of your clumsy lab techs drop the tray and it spilled all over the floor?"

"No, nothing quite so mundane. It appears that the vampiric virus will not sustain itself outside of its host…which is you."

"How fortuitous of me."

"Quite. We need you to bite someone."

"Come closer, I'll do it now." I opened my mouth.

The man before me stretched his neck, gulped and rubbed his right hand along the side of his wrinkly skin.

"Oh, no, not you. Right? You'd never risk your aged ass. I'm sure you've got a bunch of lackeys you can toss in here with me. Why don't you get one of these fine upstanding men to come a little closer?"

The guards looked amongst themselves, unsure what

each would do if he did indeed order them to do just that.

"You will give me what I want, Michael, if it takes the blood of your family to make it happen."

"I have no soul. What makes you think I care?"

The man looked long and hard at me. Here was an adversary to be wary of. He was intelligent; I'm sure in orders of magnitude more than me. He was cagey and would be able to lie without a momentary pang of regret for doing so. Plus, he projected an air of authority and fearlessness. I knew in the span that it took my heart to contract and expand that he was a politician.

"You're lying, Mr. Talbot. I have been around some of the most adept liars this country has ever known. You're not even in the same league."

"I think I should be honored by that."

He had a small laugh. "Perhaps. Let's start over, you and I, shall we?"

I nodded. "Whatever floats your boat."

He pursed his lips ever so slightly, but like the good little voted-in liar he was, he did not let it show any more than that. He was practiced at this routine. Showing one caring, trusting face to the populace while simultaneously devising optimum ways to screw them and further himself. He was a lot like the scum I'd been happening upon these last few months, only, he had much more power.

"My name is Dixon Hawes."

"That's a nice, southern name. Where is your drawl? Or did you get rid of that because it made you sound stupid?"

His lips pursed again. No matter how much he wanted to deny it, I was beginning to ruffle his feathers. I would think that normally he would just ignore me or, if the need necessitated it, he'd just have me killed. But he couldn't— not yet anyway. I had something he desired, shit, coveted might be a better word.

"Mr. Talbot, you are in a cell. I have three armed men with me. I am holding your family. *I* am in control here."

"You keep telling yourself that."

"Bring the youngest one in." Dixon was speaking to the camera on the far side of the hallway.

"Hey, dipshit," I whispered to the guard whose weapon was about midway up his thigh. "When I get out, I'm going to save you for last. First, I'm going to round up all those you care for, starting with the goat and then—"

"Fuck you!" The rifle came up, the first bullet striking the bars and ricocheting off the back wall. The second round caught me square in the side. The third burned up my arm as it traveled down the length of it. I had wrapped my hand around the barrel and was pulling the gun and the gunman toward me.

"NO! You fool!" Dixon was screaming as he turned back around.

I snapped at least two of the guard's fingers as I twisted the rifle up and away from him. I quickly pulled the rifle through the bars and had two rounds in the guard's head before he had a chance to wrap his undamaged hand around his broken fingers. The other two guards were bringing their weapons up.

"Drop them or I'll drill your boss."

I now had muzzles pointing to my midsection, even as mine was trained on Hawes'.

"Mr. Hawes, I'm sure I can take another bullet or two before I'm incapacitated. Can you?"

"Drop them," Dixon said with force.

His guards seemed reluctant but, ultimately, did as he ordered and put their weapons gently on the floor.

"Now, if you could be so kind as to push one of those over to my friend, that would be much appreciated." One of the guards was shaking with impotent rage. "I asked nicely, now hurry the fuck up." I put my rifle up by my shoulder. "You two are dismissed." They looked to Dixon but left before he could agree or order them to stay.

"You can't get out of here, Mr. Talbot."

"Maybe…maybe not, Dixon. But if I don't get out, then neither do you."

He laughed, it was forced, but he laughed. "I am merely a cog in the machinery here. My bosses may mourn my passing, but business will go on as usual, I can assure you of that."

I watched him intently as sweat formed on his brow, beaded up, and sluiced off the side of his head. Dennis was checking his weapon to make sure it was loaded and the safety was off.

"Wow, you know, I really didn't think karma was going to come into play this quickly, Mr. Hawes."

"What are you talking about?" he asked haughtily.

"You see, I've raised a daughter, and in her teenage years she was about the most skilled fabricator of the truth I have ever seen. I mean, Mr. Hawes, it was amazing. I would have indisputable evidence to some minor crime of hers, and she would never waver in her declaration of innocence to whatever the offense was. I mean, it got to the point where I would begin to doubt myself. It was amazing, it really was."

"What does this have to do with me?"

"I was getting to that if you hadn't so rudely interrupted me," I said angrily enough that the two guards put their hands up in a placating manner. "What I'm saying is that, you, Mr. Hawes, are lying through your ass. Funny that I should now be thanking my daughter for all those years of torture she put me through. I don't think you're some indispensable cog—I think you run the show here. You're just cocky enough to come down for a visit in the slums. I saw the lust in your eyes when you thought about the immortality that my blood could offer you. Funny thing is, I'm pretty sure you wouldn't even need to give anything up to get it."

"What exactly does that mean?"

"Your soul. I don't think you have one. That's what I'm saying."

"This is irrelevant. Kill me or don't, but like I said, I'm mid-level at best. All I could really do for you is get you a better pillow for your cell."

"Is that true?" I asked one of the guards.

"Of course it is!" Dixon answered.

"I was talking to him. Interrupt me one more time, Dix," he bristled at the abbreviation, "and I'm going to put one in your kneecap while I get this figured out. You want to talk about painful? Shit…it's bad, and I'm thinking that, at your advanced age, you probably won't be a good candidate for a replacement. You'll never walk right again. You'll have to kiss babies in a wheelchair. Although, what God-fearing mother would ever let your lizard-looking mug touch their most precious commodity is a mystery to me. So I'm asking again, Mr. Guardman, how replaceable is my guest?"

The guard looked from me to Dixon.

"If I even get a whisper of a hint that you are telling me anything but the truth, I will shoot you in the scrotum."

"Dude, the scrotum?" Dennis asked.

"I want him to live long enough to regret his decision."

"But the scrotum?!"

"I know, man, but harsh times call for harsh measures." I turned to the guard. "Well?"

"You're right. He runs the show."

"Purdoch!" Dixon yelled.

"Fuck you! He killed Nelson, and he's threatening to kill me. I'm not dying for you."

"See how quickly they turn," I said to Dixon. "Your money and influence will only go so far. If he cared about and respected you, he would have taken that bullet for you. And shame on you," I said to the guard. "By definition you are supposed to guard him with your life. Get out of here before I kill you."

"You're going to let him go? Just like that? He'll go and get help," Dennis warned.

"Buddy, we've got at least three cameras on us that I know about. They're well aware of what is going on down here, the only reason they haven't busted down the door and blown us to shit is because of our new best friend."

"I told you this would happen, you stupid shit!" a voice came over the loud speaker next to the camera.

"Hello, Mrs. Deneaux," I said. "You should come down here. We could have a little reunion."

Her cackling sounded much like what I figured a mule's bray would, if shards of glass were being dragged down its back. "Oh no, dear, I'm much too frail for this kind of confrontation."

"Frail my ass," Dennis mumbled.

"I was going to say that." I glanced over at him. "That battle-axe is going to outlive all of us."

"Your concern is overwhelming," she replied.

"Vivian, I could use a little help," Dixon said, looking toward the camera.

"I warned you about him. I even suggested that you not go down there. Just kill him and be done with it. Do you remember that conversation?"

Dixon looked like he had just stuffed two lemons into his mouth. I don't think he was used to being admonished, probably hadn't been talked down to since he was five. He wasn't taking it well.

"Vivian," he entreated.

"What did I say? I told you he was resourceful and that your best course of action would be to end his existence."

I looked up to the camera.

"Well, what did you expect, Michael?" she replied. "It's a sign of respect that I wanted to get rid of you that quickly, seeing as you're a huge threat to my continuation. Nothing personal."

"Nothing personal? You say that like you didn't pick me for your volleyball team at the company picnic. You wanted to murder me."

"Pfft, you're so dramatic."

"Vivian, get me out of here."

"How do you expect me to do that? Should I just ask Mr. Talbot to politely let you go? How about it, Michael, will you let him go?"

I placed one hand on my chin for a moment. "I'm going to say… no."

"There, Dixon. I did my due diligence."

"Bitch."

"What was that?" Vivian asked. Obviously it was impossible to tell from this side of the camera, but I would swear she said it with some mirth. "Mr. Talbot, it appears there is a small stand-off taking place right now. I have over a hundred troops waiting on the other side of the cellblock door at the end of this hallway. Even as imaginative as you are, I do not see this as being a happy outcome for you or your friend. What was his name…Denard?"

"I hate her." Dennis was shaking his head back and forth.

"Easy, buddy, she's messing with you. If I know her at all, she knows your social security number and who you screwed in high school, if you did anyone at all."

"Still doesn't mean I don't hate her. And hey!"

I thought about it for a second. "Sorry, and yeah, I guess I agree with you on that." We'd been talking in whispers.

"I don't like all the soft-speak, Michael. Makes me feel like you're plotting against me," Deneaux said.

"Paranoia will eat you up. Never figured you for that type. Alright, let's talk, Deneaux. I've got the big cheese here so what do we have on the table?"

"You have nothing, Michael. You've actually done me a great service here. Had not my dolt of a husband been a philandering fool, I would have been ruling here by his side all along. Mr. Hawes there, with my now-dead-husband's presence and mine missing, had decided that all of this was his. Partly he is right, but mostly he's wrong. And now, with him firmly in your grasp, you've given me the opportunity to ascend to my destined seat."

"Is she saying I just helped her with a coup?" I was asking Dennis and Dixon.

"Vivian, you can't be serious? I would have given you a seat on the council."

"Why should you have *given* me anything?" she said with disdain. "I earned my spot. It was mine all along. To be honest, Dixon, I don't trust you."

"Well, isn't that the wheel calling the hubcap round," I said. Dennis looked over at me. I shrugged. "Sounded right, the whole kettle calling the pot black thing is overused."

"You were always more ambitious than smart. This latest, and last scrap, you find yourself in is proof of that."

"Wow, she turned fast even for her. Dennis, can you get the camera to your side?" I had a difficult angle, but two shots later I was able to send pieces of the electronic equipment I could see spiraling to the ground. Dixon flinched at every shot.

"I think I can get the one at the end of the hallway as well," Dennis said. Eight shots later and all of our ears ringing, he did it. "Sorry about that."

"Dixon, open these doors," I told him once I was relatively assured we no longer had an external audience.

"What makes you think I have the key?" he asked as he backed up a step.

"Because you're just that arrogant. And I'm thinking that you would trust no one else in this entire facility with it."

He looked at me, momentarily stunned at how fast I'd caught him. He was already thinking of a way to cover his bases.

"Listen, before you come up with what you think is a great idea, if you don't open these doors, you're useless to me, and I'm just going to riddle your body with bullets. Do I look like I'm lying?" I kept my gaze steady with his.

His head dropped a bit. "No, Mr. Talbot, you do not look like you are lying." He reached into his pocket, looked from the key to the lock, to me and to the door that led to freedom, before coming forward and sliding the keycard against the locking pad. Sirens from mythology could not have made a more beautiful sound than those tumblers made as they released me. He quickly stepped back as I nearly flew through the opening.

"I think the air is better out here!"

"Any chance you're going to let me out?" Dennis asked.

"I suppose it could be arranged. Mr. Hawes, I do hereby pardon Dennis Waggoner."

Dixon unlocked his cell as well.

"Now what?" Dennis asked as we looked down to the end of the hallway where at least three guards were fighting for viewing space on a small eight-by-eight metal-threaded glass port in the heavy steel door.

"Can she take over just like that?" I asked Dixon.

"If I'm dead, sure. There will be no one to oppose her."

"I guess that makes us allies. It's that whole *Art of War* thing, the enemy of my en—"

"I'm familiar with the reference. What assurances do I have that you will not kill me when you get exactly what you want?"

"None, Mr. Hawes. What assurances did I have from you that you weren't going to kill my family, my friends, and me when you got exactly what you wanted?"

He looked pissed; impotent might be a good word for someone his age, although I wasn't going to say that out loud. I wouldn't wish that on my worst enemy. Which, funny enough, he wasn't as that honor currently belonged to Mrs. Deneaux.

"We're both alive right now at this very moment, Mr.

Hawes. That is really the best I can offer. Are you in or are you out? It's going to be much more difficult if you're dead, but I'll still try."

'Mr. T?'

"Oh, shit!" I spun, putting my left hand to my head.

"Are you okay?" Dennis asked, placing his hand on my shoulder.

"What? Did I say something out loud?"

"How long did you hang out with that Trip guy?" Dennis asked nervously.

'Mr. T?'

'Tommy, are you close? I'm in a bit of trouble.'

"Mike?"

"Hold on, man. Just thinking." I didn't want him to know I was communicating telepathically with Tommy; first off, because he might not believe me. Shit, I wouldn't if the roles were reversed. And secondly, I didn't want Dixon to know anything.

'When aren't you in trouble?'

'You sound like BT.' He was silent, waiting for me to elaborate on my predicament. *'That not funny to you? Fine, I'm in a stand-off with a hundred or so armed men and Mrs. Deneaux at the helm.'*

'How are you still alive?'

'I have one very important card-slash-hostage.'

'Important to Deneaux? Are you sure?'

'Not her, the facility.'

'That makes more sense.'

'Are you close to the building?'

'I'm inside.'

"Holy shit."

"What?" Dennis was looking around for some new sign of trouble.

"I said that out loud, too?"

"Mike, what the fuck, man?"

'Do you know where I am?'

'Not yet, but I'm sure I could follow the steady stream of people heading your way.'

'Screw me, Tommy! Find my family...our family. Find them and get them the fuck out of here.'

There was hesitation on his side. *'She'll kill you, Mr. T.'*

'I know that, you know that, she knows that, my hostage knows that. We're most likely a lost cause, but if you can get them out of here, I would consider it worth it.'

Again with more hesitation. I was going to force his decision. *'They are OUR family, Tommy. You have to do everything in your power to get them to safety.'*

'I KNOW that," he stressed. *'I'm just trying to figure out a way to do both.'*

'Don't! The longer you delay, the more opportunity Deneaux has to play this out however she wants. Tommy?'

'Okay, okay...I'll get them out of here, and I'll come back.'

I was going to tell him no, that it would then be his job to get them back to safety—all the way to Maine safety. I had a feeling he wouldn't listen to me.

'Alright then, works for me.' Best guess was that Deneaux was going to have someone throw about ten or twelve grenades down here long before he ever got the chance for a return visit.

"We're good. I mean, I'm good," I said to Dennis.

"You sure? Looked like you checked out for a few minutes."

"Yeah, yeah, I'm good. Come on; let's get back in the cell before someone tries to see if they can shoot through that glass."

"Damn, didn't even think of that."

"It's alright, buddy. I've had way more people trying to kill me than you have. Lead the way, Mr. Hawes."

"You want me in there?"

"You're a politician—you should have been in one

years ago." I shoved his shoulder.

"Now what?" he asked as I sat down next to him on the bunk.

"You tell me."

"You don't have a plan?"

"Oh, how little we know about each other. A plan? No, not so much, plus, Deneaux sort of throws a wrinkle in the whole thing, don't you think? I was merely going to march your ass around with a gun to your head until I got my family a safe distance from here. Then, more than likely, I would have let your ass go where you then would have relentlessly pursued me until I had to forcibly remove you from the planet's ecosystem at a later date."

"You would have never gotten away with it."

"You seem pretty sure of yourself."

"We have control over satellites. It would have been nothing to have tracked you down and then sent drones to dispatch of you."

"You say that like you're giving up. Come on, what kind of dastardly foe gives up that easily?"

"Deneaux has me by the balls here."

"Aren't there some men you can trust who can hold her power in check?"

"I'm sure she's rounding them up right now."

"Fuck, she's smart. If she used half her evilness for good, the planet would be a utopia." I sat back, my blood-sticky back cooling against the concrete. As I reached behind me, red stained my hand, and I pulled it back to look at it.

"Shit, you're shot. Dude, are you alright?" Dennis asked, concerned.

"It's merely a flesh wound."

"Are you really using a Monty Python reference right now?"

"Stop sounding like my wife, it's freaking me out."

"Mike, you're shot."

"Dennis, did you not listen to any of the story I've

been telling you for the last three days?"

"I just…I mean…I just figured some of it was bullshit, you know."

"Look." I pulled up my shirt. Blood was oozing out of the closing wound.

"Where's the bullet?"

"I'd imagine it's lodged in the wall behind me somewhere. Thing went in and out."

"Does it hurt?"

"Like a bitch."

"But, you're fine?"

"Mostly."

"Fascinating. Can we try and figure out what we're going to do here?" Dixon asked. "The more time we give Vivian, the worse for us."

"Can you stop calling her that?" I asked him.

"What? Vivian?"

"Yeah, makes her sound almost human."

Dixon actually laughed a little. "She was always a difficult woman. I've never met a more driven person, and I've personally known three presidents, a king or two and multiple heads of nations. Viv…Deneaux wanted something and she got it, end of story. She was a sight to behold back in the day."

Dennis shivered so violently that the bunk shook. "Sorry. Just having visions of a naked snake."

"Why didn't you two end up together? Seems like you wanted to, and you have, apparently, succeeded in life. I mean, up until now anyway."

Dixon eyed me. "I'm not quite dead yet. Anyway, her husband was a much more pliable individual than me. In the end, I think that is what it came down to, who she could, and could not, manipulate with more ease."

"Where is the man now?"

"She killed him. Walked into his house, sat down, had a conversation with him. Pulled out her gun, put a bullet in his chest and then one in his forehead. She then walked out of that house and into her car like she merely stopped by for a spot of tea."

"Why the hell isn't she in jail?" Dennis asked.

"The body wasn't found until after the zombies came. The police and the military had bigger problems on their hands. My man, Captain Najarian, found the surveillance tapes and brought them to me. Her husband was an idiot. He was merely the face for the genius, no great loss as far as I was concerned. The calmness she dispatched him with, though, that gave me pause. When she showed up here, I probably should have just put her in the cell next to your friend. I...I just couldn't. I thought there was a chance we could rekindle what we once had."

This time, *I* shivered violently. "Sorry, pain racked my body."

"Obviously, that was a mistake. Whatever she'd had for a heart was burned out long ago."

"I'm not sure she ever had one. I just think she was better at hiding it," I said.

"Perhaps." Dixon let his head hit his hands. He was sitting on the edge of the bunk.

"You hear that?" I asked, standing and going to the edge of the cell. "I think they're getting ready to come."

"And what of me? If they storm this place, are you going to kill me?"

"I've got to figure that, if Deneaux is sending them in, they have orders to eliminate all of us. Much cleaner that way, and at least one less stain to put on my soul. The door is opening, here we go." I quickly checked the chamber in my M-16.

Chapter Two – Tommy's Story

"What is happening?" Tommy questioned out loud when he finally got free of the zombies that had surrounded the snowplow.

The fall had cracked three of his ribs and shattered his left femur. Even as a vampire, he had nearly succumbed to the pain. They weren't life-threatening injuries, not in and of themselves. If he could have just lain where he had fallen even for a few moments, he would have healed sufficiently to continue on. With the zombies, he was not going to get that respite.

He'd crushed four of them as he landed, driving their necks straight into their skulls, killing them instantly. Tommy had cried out as he collided with their outstretched hands and then into the bed of the truck. It was that last part that had broken his leg and sent red, finger-thick tendrils of pain through his brain. The only thing that saved him at that point was that the zombies were so thickly packed together they could not bend down to get at him. Tommy quickly turned over and began to pull himself hand-over-hand until he got to the edge of the truck bed. Even now he could feel the bones beginning to knit together, but he had no delusions that he was not about to suffer and suffer greatly as he put his full weight on a broken leg.

With his undamaged left leg, he quickly pushed up, grabbed onto the lip of the truck body, and hurled himself over. He did his best to make the zombies absorb the shock of the jump. Still, he thought the possibility of passing out was higher than he could ever remember it being in his long existence. He flung zombies out of his way with impunity, to the point where they looked like they were being repelled instead of forcibly removed. He was not more than ten feet from the vehicle when he felt the wash of heat hit his back from the rocket propelled grenade's explosion. His shirt was on fire, his skin was burning, and still his leg dominated with its blinding pain.

When he reached a house on the far side of the street, he was able to pat down the areas that were still aflame. Charred sheets of skin fell from his back and arms. He leaned against the house, tears of pain cascading down his cheeks, and still the zombies came at him. He wanted to keep running to find a safe haven where he could heal, but the zombies were not going to be so obliging. They were already within striking distance when he realized there was a window above his head. He reached up, smashed out the pane, and pulled himself in, screaming in agony as a zombie pulled on his trailing broken leg. He was out before his head hit the cold tiled floor.

Tommy awoke a few minutes later to the smell of burnt flesh; his stomach turned. He pulled himself completely into the house, and when his ankle caught on the windowsill he grimaced. He turned over onto his back, fresh spikes of pain radiating through his body as his new pink skin came in to contact with the tile.

"I think I pulled a Mr. T." He tried to smile. "Should have thought that out a little better."

He sat up with a grunt. His leg itched furiously as the bones were knitting together. His body was in hyper-drive working on its multiple injuries. The gnawing hunger was already stirring in his stomach. He needed to replenish the major stores that were being used to get him back to top predator functioning ability.

Machinegun fire erupted outside. In the lull of bullets being shot, he could hear the frenetic talk of men under duress. Engines began to get louder as they were put under load.

"They're leaving!" He used a moth-eaten couch to pull himself up. He knew he needed to follow them if he was to have any hopes of finding his adoptive family. "I'm coming," he grunted. He meant what he'd said; that was, of course, until he looked outside and saw that he was completely encircled by the enemy.

"Going to need some weapons."

He started with a shuffle as he began to move through the dusty house. The main floor yielded nothing more than two steak knives. Desperation was beginning to set in. When he opened the door off of the kitchen, he was immediately assailed with a smell he knew all too well.

"Zombies," he said as he stared down into the murkiness of the basement.

He would have just closed the door if not for the white, cowhide-covered ball at the foot of the stairs. Where there were baseballs there were bound to be baseball bats. "I don't really like zombies," he said softly as he descended down the stairs, still favoring his right leg.

Two zombies, a male and a female, were both staring out a small window set high in the concrete wall. Soft groans emanated from each as they watched their brethren walking back and forth outside. Small piles of various animal bones littered the floor. Tommy thought it would be better if he didn't try and figure out what they once belonged to.

He sighed when he realized the two zombies were right next to the shelving that housed all manner of sporting goods—from tennis racquets to bocce balls. In addition, two wooden bats and one blue-painted aluminum one were hanging from a frame specifically designed to hold them in place by the handle. The male zombie was so close that he could have handed it to Tommy, if he was so inclined. Tommy was eyeing the route to the bat that would allow him to grab it without any further conflict when the female sniffed the air. She turned quickly, her lips pulled back in aggression as she moved. Her hands came up and she growled as she ran toward Tommy.

"It's just a girl," he said sadly as the teenager ran at him.

As her foot caught the first step of the stairs, she fell over, her head and mouth coming dangerously close to

Tommy's feet. She was pushing up with her arms as Tommy brought the heel of his foot down on the base of her skull. The noise of the bones snapping got the attention of the male. Tommy's heart sank, even through the purple and blue hues the disease caused in the skin; it was easy enough to see the familial relationship as the boy ran toward his sister's killer. In a normal world, he may have done this to avenge her death. In this world he cared little as he stepped onto her still flailing limbs. He wasn't sure where the zombies ended up when they were finally killed. He could only hope that this boy ended up with the rest of his family. It was impossible to tell if they still had their soul in this state. Did it move on when their consciousness was taken? He hoped so, otherwise did they have to pay for the sins this reanimated puppet performed?

Tommy waited until the boy had made it up the first couple of stairs before he moved quickly to the side, grabbing the side of the boy's head as he did so. Then he smashed it against the cement wall three times. On the third attempt he was rewarded with a spraying of black matter on his lower arms. He let the body drop, the boy falling protectively over the body of his prone sister. Tommy quickly went to the bat rack. One of the wooden bats had a longer reach, but he knew that it would eventually crack and splinter. He grabbed the aluminum bat, smacked it against his hand once, and headed back upstairs.

His leg wasn't quite a hundred percent, and his ribs still ached—not to mention his tender skin—but it was now or never. He debated getting onto the roof and jumping down past the zombies, but he wasn't sure if his leg could take it, especially before he got a feeding. He did a quick three-sixty around the house to see where the zombies were least concentrated and decided his best bet was to head out the back door. Zombies were in the backyard, but once he fought through them and over the privacy fence, he should be free of the main herd. The back door swung inwards and the storm door out. The thin, steel-framed door bent as he pushed two zombies off the small landing. Three more behind them kept them from falling completely backwards.

The bat rang hollowly as he brought the meat of it down on top of the closest zombie's head. The skull wrapped around the bat almost like it had been made for it. Tommy pulled back, blood, hair, gristle and brain clinging to the metal death-dealing device. He had just enough time to swing the bat into the side of the second closest zombie as he stepped out onto the landing. The victory was small; he was outside, but the fence seemed to move further and further away as more zombies came to investigate what the pinging sound was in the back. It was as if they were remembering summers past, watching their kids play in little league games, the sun shining bright and warm as parents talked to other parents about upcoming parties or their jobs. It was the bond that all suburbanites shared before they would occasionally yell out to their kid some words of encouragement.

Tommy could barely hear the roar of engines as they moved further and further away from this desolate spot. The groans of the damned began to dominate. The bat was a blue blur as he smashed it back and forth and up and down, depending on where his adversary was. The heavy viscosity blood covered him from head to toe, if not for the fact that the zombies were converging on him, it would have been impossible for a passerby to not believe he was one of the undead. He kept as much of his weight on his left leg as he pivoted and swung, which wasn't always easy. It was now his ribs that were beginning to cause him the most pain as his constant shifting made it difficult for them to set properly.

Tommy's energy levels were flagging as his body pulled resources from everyplace it could in a desperate bid to keep him healthy enough to continue on. He'd killed a dozen zombies and had only made it halfway across the yard. Now he had the added danger that the zombies could attack from any angle. *Lizzie, help me,* he pleaded internally. A cool breeze swept across the yard, and whether or not it was his ill-fated sister he wasn't sure. By the time he got to the six-foot fence, his arms felt leaden. He was thankful to be on the side of the fence that had the mid-rail as he wasn't so sure he would have been able to pull himself up without it. He had a split second as he was swinging his leg over where he almost lost his balance when the zombies slammed into the pickets. He didn't think he would have just given up, but it would have been much easier; and then maybe he could search for his sister in earnest.

Unlike Heaven, which he could never enter, Hell had an open door policy. Unfortunately, once through the door it was nearly impossible to get back out. To him that didn't matter, he would have chased after her in that realm forever if that was what it took. If only the fate of the living wasn't resting so precariously on a certain set of sarcastic shoulders. He'd known for a lot of years it was going to be a Talbot; he'd just not known specifically which one. Mike had his pluses, but he also had a list of negatives that would span pages. Of all the Talbots Tommy had come in contact with, Mike would have probably ranked in the lower half in terms of who he thought would have the best chance of actually succeeding. It wasn't that Mike was not honorable or brave. No, his biggest detriment was his willingness to run headlong into trouble without so much as a cursory glance at all the ways that it could go wrong and invariably did.

He smiled even as he thought such a thing. Whoever was overseeing the entire event liked threading needles with wet thread in heavy winds. Tommy got over two more fences before he felt secure enough to get onto a roadway. He cut through one more yard before he was finally on the main thoroughfare heading out of town, just catching a glimpse of reflecting sunlight as the Humvee he was chasing crested a small rise in the distance. Tommy followed at a pace he felt he could sustain without too much difficulty. He'd been so lost in his thoughts as he ran that he nearly exposed himself to the military men. They had pulled off to the side of the road and were talking. Something had happened to one of their own.

"He's been bitten."

"Sorry, man, I am," one of the soldiers said as he pointed his weapon at the stricken man's head.

"Don't do this, Cortez, please," the man pleaded, his hands outstretched as if his weak flesh could stop the lead projectile. "I have a wife…a kid on the way."

"I'm sorry, man, you're dead already. You don't want to become one of them, you don't. We talked about this, and we both said we'd do what was right if it happened to either of us."

The pleading individual put his hands down. Sobbing, he said, "I…I just figured it would be you." The tears turned to laughter as he accepted the insanity of a zombie virus coursing through his body and his best friend pointing a high-caliber weapon at his head.

"Me too, man, me too." Without warning Cortez pulled the trigger. His friend's head whipped back, followed immediately by the rest of his body as he fell to the ground. "I'm sorry." He leaned down and closed the man's eyelids.

"Let's go," a man standing to the side said as the remainder of the vehicle's occupants got back in and headed away.

The deeper into the night Tommy ran, the further the men got from him. It mattered little; he was starving, and he had their scent from the onset. In a world so devoid of food, he would be hard pressed to lose their trail, no matter how much they might wish that. Had they known they weren't just being followed, but stalked…

He reached out with his mind. *'Tommy?'* Mike asked. *'You're still alive? I thought I'd lost you.'* The relief within Mr. T was palpable, Tommy's hope surged as he felt the good tidings emanate from the man. He thought he might never feel that again, not after his treachery.

'You alright?' Tommy asked.

'I'm almost as hard to kill as you are.' Even though the words were not being spoken orally, those last ones came across with some mirth.

'When we were going up in that helicopter, I was just happy that all of you were safe. And then I saw everyone unconscious and you had just been given a shot. I hit the release on the winch. Crashing down onto the zombies bought me the time I needed as I jumped out of the truck and ran for cover. I got the distinct impression that, if they couldn't catch me, they would attempt to kill me. I wasn't wrong. They shot up the truck until it finally caught the fuel on fire.'

Tommy wasn't sure why he lied about that last part. He thought part of it might be that he didn't want to unnecessarily burden the man any further with how close he had come to dying. Another more significant part was that, if Michael showed any signs of not caring other than because it would lessen his and his family's chances of survival, Tommy wouldn't be able to bear that right now. He was weakened, tired, and hungry. He needed all the hope he could garner. Maybe even part of it was that he could already feel the strain in Mike's thoughts and didn't want to overstrain him. Whoever the people were that had saved him, it appeared they wanted something in return.

'How'd you get away from the zombies?' Mike asked.

'I can move faster than they can react.' That part at least was the truth, well, partially the truth, but not in the condition he had found himself at the time. *'Just think about you walking around normally and everyone else is in super slow motion. That's what it's like for me with the zombies. What's this got to do with women's locker rooms?'* Tommy asked, picking up on some of Mike's stray thoughts.

'Ah...nothing...sorry. I'm glad you're here,' Mike changed the subject.

'I'm not quite there. I'm following the ground unit

back. I just picked you up a few miles ago. How's everyone else doing?'

'Good as far as Porkchop says.'

'Porkchop's there?' Tommy asked. It was a mixture of anguish and thankfulness.

'Doc's here too, Tommy,' Mike informed him. The airwaves between them went silent, only to be filled with imagery of horrific detail. *'He may have found a cure for BT.'*

'That's great,' Tommy said with true appreciation for that fact, but thoughts of Doc's family dominated his attention.

'Tommy, he said he knows a way to kill you.'

'I would imagine,' Tommy said.

'I'm telling you this so you'll be careful,' his adoptive father admonished.

'I've got it, you don't want me to die until I help you get out,' he said with some bitterness in his voice.

'Tommy, would it help if I said I don't want you to die at all?' Mike asked.

'It would, Mr. T, it would.'

'Get us out of here, kid...all of us.'

He pushed his darker thoughts down. *'I'll see you soon.'*

'Looking forward to it.'

It was as the sun was coming up the following morning that he found his quarry's lair. A large building some two miles off was set-up to look as if it had been abandoned and dilapidated. To an untrained eye Tommy thought it might look that way, but the fence with the razor wire was the key detail many would overlook. It sparkled in the sun where everything else looked drab and dreary; and where something so unused and vandalized should have had holes, this had none. It was erected in such a way as to make it look like sections were leaning unsteadily, but there were cross-sections that held it fast in place.

Even had he missed some of the visible cues, he would have been hard pressed to miss the smell of his food. His mouth watered just thinking about it. The cherry of a lit cigarette mostly behind a gouged out cement pillar caught his eye as he approached. He instinctively knew the building would have security cameras around it; the question was how far out were they watching. He kept about a thousand yards away as he encircled the entire structure, always staying as hidden as possible. There were at least two entrances that he had discovered. One was near to where the smoker had been patrolling. On the far side, he found a ramp wide enough to fit a large truck heading down into the structure. He was confident that no men were in the three levels above ground, which meant that whatever this place was, the important things were underneath.

"The government sure is going to great lengths to keep this place secret. I get saving some civilians, but why knock them out first? Was it to protect where this place was? That's not true though, I *saw* the cell Mr. T was in."

Tommy got the distinct impression that Mike did not yet completely know why he was in a cell but whatever the reason, it was not good. Tommy knew he had to get in, but first things first. He loped off into the distance as a Humvee came out from the ramp.

Chapter Three – Mike Journal Entry 2

"Mr. Hawes?" a voice called down the chamber.

"That's Captain Najarian," Dixon told me.

"Ally?"

"Should be, can't imagine he'd flip over to Deneaux that quickly. Not sure how he eluded her."

"Sir?" the question rang out.

"I'm here."

"Are you hurt, sir?"

"No."

"But he could be if things don't go down the right way," I added hastily to make sure he wasn't planning anything nefarious.

"Mr. Talbot?" the captain asked.

"Mike is fine."

"Mike it is then. I wouldn't recommend harming Mr. Hawes. His being alive is the only thing keeping this facility from breaking down into a civil war."

"Okay, so what's the downside?" I asked.

"Your family."

"Is that a threat?" He'd angered me to a point that I almost walked out of the cell to confront him, where I'm sure I would have met a bullet head-on.

"Not directly…at least not from me. Deneaux is starting to ratchet down the screws. My guess is that your family would be one of the early casualties. I have men loyal to me that I trust implicitly who are watching them right now, but they only number eight strong. If Deneaux wants them gone, they will be able to do little to stop her."

"I am going to kill the bitch." I was seething. "So now what?"

"I don't suppose you'll let Mr. Hawes go?"

"Not a chance."

"Every minute he stays down here, she will be marshaling her strength."

"You're not giving me an out, Captain. Feeling very much like a caged animal."

"I'll let your family go."

"You don't have that authority, Captain," Dixon shouted.

"What would you have me do, sir?"

Dixon was quiet.

"I noticed how I was left out of that equation, I get it. I have your word as an officer and, presumably, a gentleman that you will let my family go, to not be hunted down or rounded up at a later time?"

"You do."

"You believe him, Mike?" Dennis asked nervously.

"I have to, my options are limited. Captain, the big guy, BT…he's not going to want to leave and neither will my wife. And don't let her diminutive size fool you into thinking she doesn't have a hell of a right cross. I don't give a shit if you have to sedate them both to get them into a truck and out of here. My boys and brother will understand. I want you to take Dennis as well."

"No fucking way." Dennis turned to me.

"Yes fucking way, you're going to look out for my family while I'm here."

"Mike, I can't abandon you."

"You're not abandoning me. Your survival helps in the survival of my family. I'd much rather you were with them than with me, my friend."

"This sucks, Mike."

"If you stay around me long enough you'd soon realize that this is pretty much how it always is. Captain, now it's not that I don't trust you…wait…no, that's a lie, I *don't* trust you. I'm going to need proof of their release, like a live video feed as they're being put in a truck, and then I'm going to want to see satellite surveillance of the truck as it's leaving and up to a hundred miles from this place."

"Satellite?"

"Yes, satellite. Do you think I just made that up to trap you?"

"I can do that."

"Captain Najarian! You are usurping my authority."

"Sir, your authority was usurped the moment he took you hostage. I'm doing everything in my power to rectify this situation before it gets further out of hand."

"Burn," I said to Dixon.

"Mr. Talbot, I don't know if I'm going to have the time to get them at the distance you requested before Deneaux makes her move."

"Better get cracking then," I told him.

"Cracking?" Dennis mouthed.

I shrugged my shoulders. "Oh, and make sure they are all armed and can hear me when I talk."

"Armed like firearms?"

"No, I meant fucking yo-yos. Of course firearms."

The captain may have sighed as he exited. He was back in less than ten minutes. "May I approach?"

"Any weapons?" I asked.

"Of course, but I don't have them out."

"Well, at least you're being honest. Come on down. Just know that if you even look at me funny, I will rip Dixon's larynx out. Believe me?"

"Implicitly."

"See, man, why can't my wife say that when I ask her?" I asked Dennis.

"I don't know, man. Do I look like a marriage counselor?"

Captain Najarian came down the hallway cautiously but with a purpose. He was slightly taller than me and had a build you wouldn't necessarily call buff, but you could tell he had accumulated a fair amount of strength from his years in the military. He was not nervous as he looked down the barrels of our rifles, which let me know he'd seen more than his fair share of violence. He was not a man I would take lightly. I had a feeling that, if he thought he had any chance of successfully taking us down, he would do so without a moment's hesitation.

"Dennis, stay to his back."

"What?"

"He can't see you that way, and lower your weapon to his torso. If he were to move quickly, there's a good chance you'd miss his head. He's not quite a zombie yet, so he can die by ruptured internal organs."

"Can I get on with the quick lesson here?" the captain asked as he put the laptop down on my cot.

"Come here, Dixon," I told the man who was slowly pacing around the cell. He did as I requested. I gripped his throat in my right hand. "You move away and it's the last dry breath you will take. It's amazing the amount of panic you will begin to feel as blood clogs your airway. Your feet will start tapping violently, your eyes will grow wide, and your face will turn all of these unnatural hues."

"I get it," he struggled to say.

"Anything funny, Captain, and it will be his throat, then yours. Clear?"

"We're clear. I gave you my word nothing was going to happen. Let me power this thing on. Your family is already on the move."

'I SEE THEM!' shot through my head as Tommy yelled.

"Fuck!"

Dixon's hands clawed at my arm as I had involuntarily squeezed his throat shut.

"You okay?" Captain Najarian asked. He could have meant his boss or me, but either way, it had the effect of me loosening my grip.

Dixon pulled in some raggedy breaths.

"Get the picture up," I said curtly. *'Next time, Tommy, use your indoor voice.'*

'Sorry. I see Mrs. T, Justin, Travis, Gary, Trip,

Stephanie, BT, and Henry.'
'You see them? Is everyone alright?'
'They seem fine.'
I about hitched.
'They're surrounded by about ten men, but they appear to be looking for outside threats rather than inside.'
'That's their escort out.'
'BT looks pissed.'
'I figured as much.'
'Do you want me to do something?'
'No, if this works right, they should be a good long way from here soon. You should get going as well.'
'You want me to leave? What about you?'
'I can die happily knowing my family is safe.'
'We'll see about that.'

And then there was silence even as I reached out for him. Did he mean I might not die happily or that he was going to try and get me out? I mean, I was pulling for the latter, but he really wasn't all that clear.

"Here we go, live feed."

My heart skipped a beat as I was looking at my wife.

"Could you get that thing out of my face please?" Tracy looked pissed. She'd always hated posing for pictures, even when we got married she'd seemed annoyed at the photographer like he was intruding on her space. I had to remind her more than once that she'd hired him.

"Hi, hon!" I touched the screen as I said the words, hoping that somewhere in those pixels I would feel the warmth of her skin.

"Mike?" She was looking into the camera. "Are you alright?"

I might have cried if not in the presence of so many other men. As it was, I had to swallow a couple of times before I felt confident I could speak without my voice cracking or having a giant lump in my throat. Which is kind of funny considering the predicament I was in. I had been holding a rifle to a man's head while simultaneously holding the throat of another. I wonder if I asked nicely, would Dennis have wiped my nose for me when it started to run from the cry I was on the verge of. Yeah, probably not.

"I'm…I'm fine."

"Where are you?"

Captain Najarian nearly had me inadvertently rip his boss' throat out when he quickly reached over to the laptop and hit a button.

"Sorry, the only way I could convince them to leave was to tell them that you were waiting for them in the truck." He then hit the button again. I noticed it was labeled "mute."

"I'm waiting for you." I did my best to sound convincing.

"You're lying to me, Mike. Why?"

"I made a deal."

"What kind of deal?"

"Can BT hear this?"

"What kind of deal?" his heavy voice asked.

"Fuck." I wanted to pinch the bridge of my nose. "Well, this went south in a hurry."

"Is your honky ass staying?"

"Honky? Does your friend know what era he lives in?" Dennis asked.

"I heard that!" roared through the tiny speakers, pushing them to the edge of their specs.

"Oh shit." Dennis backed up.

"BT, I'm staying—"

"Then so am I!" He stopped.

"No, man, you're not. You're going to get my family the hell out of this place."

BT's eyebrows were so furrowed that he looked like he'd dug grooves into his forehead. "What about you?"

"I'm going to catch up on some missed episodes of *American Idol*."

"What the fuck are you talking…" He trailed off

when he figured out my roundabout reference.

I'd just let him know Tommy was in the mix. When I'd first met Tommy, I didn't know whether he was truly channeling Ryan Seacrest for help or just using his name as a way to keep me distracted from what was really going on in his head. I still wasn't sure what Tommy's intentions were, but I needed BT to go.

"Fine, I'll watch your family. I'm not picking up after your dog."

"That's fine; I wouldn't do it either without a HAZMAT suit."

"Hey, Dad." The camera angle changed and I was looking at my youngest, Travis.

"Good to see you. You need to look out for your mom; you're the man of the house now."

"Dad, I'm still around." The camera swung to Justin.

"Um, sorry, I meant men! You're both the *men* of the house. You look good, kid. Best I've seen you since the day before you went to Paul's."

"I feel good too, Dad. I almost forgot what it felt like to be healthy."

"I'd appreciate if you and your brother don't fight too much."

"You got it," he answered.

"You coming home?" Travis asked off-screen.

"What do you think?"

"Yeah, that's what I thought." He was grinning when the camera finally got back to him.

"Mike, they're getting close to here, I'd like to take Dennis to meet them out in the hallway. You'll have communication via a link from this laptop to a radio in the truck."

I knew implicitly it would be worlds better if Dennis went to meet them rather than the other way around. Without a doubt at that point I would not be able to get them out of here, and we'd be involved in a hellacious firefight that could only end one way with the odds so stacked against us; especially with an adversary in Mrs. Deneaux that wanted nothing from us but our deaths. I nodded.

"Let's go," the captain said to Dennis.

"Mike?"

"I'll be fine, get your ass out of here."

I watched as Dennis and the captain left. Dennis kept turning around to look at me, as if he couldn't believe his act of betrayal.

Dixon's hands again raked on my arm as I was once more choking the wind out of him. This time I completely let go. The sense of loneliness I felt as I watched Dennis join with my family and they left the building was profound. My heart thudded in my chest; it felt like I was absorbing a mid-strength punch to my chest with each beat. Whatever chemicals are responsible for depression were working overtime to worm their influences throughout my brain.

"I promise when we're done, we'll make it as humane as possible," Dixon said in a comforting tone. If my family was not still in striking distance, I would have just repeatedly slammed his head into the wall until there was nothing there save the leakage that would seep into the porous material.

"Are you really trying to make me feel better about the death you want to force upon me? I can see you're not much of a people person. Why don't you just shut the fuck up and let me enjoy my family for a minute?" I'll give him credit—he did just that. Seemed more like one of those people who needed to get the last word in, and he was sort of right in that aspect. If he had spoken, it would have indeed been his last words.

Tracy waved back to the camera as she got into the front passenger seat. BT gave me the finger. Trip was kissing his hands and waving á la a Miss America pageant winner. Travis picked up Henry and placed him into the back of the military truck. The rest got in with various gestures. I loved each and every one of them and hoped I'd be back to see them again. The truck pulled away, and the camera followed until they took a turn and were out of sight. In this case, out of sight did not nearly equate to out of mind. Unless I added one little pronoun and said out of *my* mind, because then, yeah, I definitely was.

There was a second or two as the picture on the monitor turned to that of a satellite image hovering hundreds of miles in the sky. It wasn't difficult to find the truck, as it was the only thing moving in the whole city block the camera was focused on.

"How do I know it's them?" I asked aloud.

The camera was zoomed in from a remote operator. Inexplicably I saw an insanely large black arm come out from the back of the truck, followed immediately by the revealing of a large, black middle finger.

"Fucker," I said. BT's other eagle-gestured arm came out as well. I had no idea the cameras on those things were as powerful as they were. I probably could have been able to tell if he had a hangnail if I looked hard enough.

I kept watching, the camera panning back out to reveal what looked to be about a square mile. If somebody was following, they were staying safely out of the shot. They'd traveled not much more than ten miles when I started to see people, at least what I originally mistook for people. Maybe "hoped" for was a better word. But no, it was a horde, and it was massive. I hadn't seen that kind of amassing since Eliza.

"Operator, zoom back to the truck, please." There was an urgent tone to my voice. "BT, can you still hear me?" He must have picked up on my distress because he didn't flip me off this time. "Better yet, can everyone hear me?" Waving arms came out of both windows and the rear. "Operator, please pan out with a few square miles showing, please." I could still just make out the truck, the roads, and the horde—which was enormous. If I hadn't seen if from closer up, I would have assumed it to be a body of water.

"Gary, I'm pretty sure you're driving, at least I hope to God it isn't Trip. You have a horde straight ahead. You keep going the way you're going and you'll see what I'm talking about soon enough." I was frantically looking for an alternate route for them to take which did not involve coming back this way. "Gary, there is a right in about a half mile. Take it for maybe a mile, I can't really tell, and then take a left. That should get you going back in the right direction and avoid the zombies." The truck was slowing as it came up to the turn. "I'll let you know when to take your next turn."

"Satellite feed loss in thirty seconds," the operator's voice came on.

"That's not the deal! Captain Najarian!" He had come back after getting Dennis to the rendezvous point.

"I'm sorry, Mike. I can't alter a satellite's trajectory."

"What else did you lie to me about?"

There was silence until the operator came back on. Ten seconds to feed loss."

"Gary your turn is coming up. Ditch the fucking truck when you can. I'll catch up."

Static filled up the screen.

"Catch-up, Mr. Talbot? What did *you* lie about?" Captain Najarian asked over the computer.

"Yeah, I'm pretty much thinking I'm going to get away when that horde gets here, because I guarantee they're headed this way."

"Zombies can't get in here. This facility is sealed."

Tommy got in, I thought. *'This your doing?'* I asked Tommy.

'Not me, but it'll help. I saw Tracy and the rest leave. Everything looked on the up and up.'

Rifle shots immediately snagged my attention.

'Not at me,' Tommy responded when he caught my concern.

Chapter Four – Mrs. Deneaux

She'd known the moment the arrogant bastard had
walked out of his office and grabbed three armed guards that
everything was about to change…and not for the better. At
least not for Dixon's better—she would do everything in her
power to make his loss her gain.

"I'll be back shortly." He'd let the corner of his
mouth pull up in a wry smile. She thought that perhaps this
was some sort of display of masculinity on his part, a 'going
to face the wild beast' sort of thing. It was one more reason
she was happy she'd never been cursed with a penis. Men
would do the most idiotic things in an attempt to sway a
woman into opening their legs. "Please wait and I'll break
out the Cognac upon my return."

Shit, she thought, *he really does think he's going on a
safari or something. Oh, I'll stay, but only because I want to
see how you die. Idiot.*

Mrs. Deneaux went over to the other side of Dixon's
desk, sat down, and adjusted the posh chair to her liking
before settling in for the show. Dixon walked into the
cellblock and smiled up to the camera. Did he know she was
watching, or was it for the sake of posterity?

She leaned forward as Dixon went closer to Mike's
cell. She swore she could hear Mike's rattle of warning
before he was about to strike.

"Stupid, stupid, stupid," she mumbled. "Kill him."

She threw her head back and laughed. She wasn't
sure whom she was rooting for. Dixon, in some odd fashion,
cared for her; but he cared much more for his power, and just
her being here threatened that. He was just as likely to kill
her as woo her. If Michael killed him, she would become the
heir apparent to whatever new world she decided to build in
her image. *Oh, it would be grand.* She cupped her hands
together.

If Dixon wised up and stopped poking the tiger and

just shot Michael repeatedly, her biggest, non-duplicitous enemy would be dead. She could maneuver with Dixon, but if Michael ever got free, she knew he would crush her skull in his hands, as no words would ever smooth over the betrayals she had inflicted upon him. She'd assuredly been the main reason for his best friend Paul's death, and she'd also done her best to deliver Michael into Eliza's arms. And she had nearly succeeded, although, upon reflection she was not sure what ground she would have gained from the vampire's victory. She would have had to work that one out later. All she'd known at that point was she didn't want to be on the losing team when the end came.

"Backed the wrong horse in that race." She laughed again, and then took a sniff of her sleeve. "And I still smell like roses!" She grabbed Dixon's half-smoked cigar and lit it, taking a large drag from the Cuban.

She'd been so busy making sure she was getting the cherry lit properly that she'd nearly missed Michael getting the rifle away from the guard. The part where the guard was shot and folded in on himself—*that* she saw in vivid detail. She coughed as she pulled too much smoke into her lungs. Even she didn't think it would happen that fast. The other guards were dropping their weapons. Dixon had his hands up in the air. Mrs. Deneaux moved closer to the screen. Watching this was better than anything that had ever been "produced". Michael had the man trapped, and even though he might not be the smartest man on the planet, he was savvy. There would not be much Dixon could say that would warrant Michael letting him go. Desperation was its own motivation.

Dixon was ensnared and Michael was still locked up, although that would change soon. She knew in a moment that neither man could be allowed to leave that block. She spoke when Dixon got caught and had been enjoying herself immensely until the savage Talbot and his sidekick Dennis had destroyed the cameras. Then she realized her mistake for what it was—time. And she'd wasted it playing around. She hit the silent alarm on Dixon's desk even as she cursed herself for slipping.

Dixon's office door exploded open.

"Sergeant Merts, we have an emergency in the holding cells."

The sergeant took note that Mr. Hawes was not sitting at his desk. Dixon had told the sergeant to treat Mrs. Deneaux with all the courtesies afforded to her station, but if he noticed any suspicious activity, he was to contact him immediately. As far as Sergeant Merts thought, this would constitute suspicious.

"Stop looking at me like I stole a baby's rattle. Your boss is being held hostage. Come here if you don't believe me." She had replayed the dvr and was pointing to the monitors that were playing back the footage.

The sergeant came around, his eyes growing big, barely believing what he was watching. "This is Sergeant Merts, get a detail down to Cellblock B now!" he spoke into a small radio attached to his shoulder. "Are you alright, ma'am?" the sergeant asked.

"I could use an ashtray, but other than that I'm fine, thank you."

Sergeant Merts paused to look at her.

"I'm fine, I'm fine. Go save the day, Sergeant."

"Ma'am." The sergeant was out the door so fast that he created a breeze.

She would have a small window in which to consolidate her power. Best case scenario, Michael and Dixon would both be pushing up daisies soon. She couldn't count on that, though. Michael could not afford to kill the man, and Dixon's men obviously would not shoot him. She needed to force one of their hands. She smiled as she thought about it. Michael's family—that was the key. If they were dead, Michael would wish he was as well, and he would attempt to tear down the walls of this facility around them all.

"Will an RPG kill him? I do hope he's in a section with video surveillance when it happens. I would really like to see it."

She pressed the alarm again. This time a corporal came in—Dowery she thought his name was.

"Corporal Dowery, how good it is to see you."

"Is there another emergency?" he asked, looking around.

"Well, there is, not necessarily here, though. Do you like being a corporal?"

"Excuse me? There's really a lot going on right now, and I need to be doing other things."

"Relax, my boy, we'll get to that. I asked you a question."

The corporal debated answering the question and, realizing that this mysterious woman had Dixon's ear, thought better of it.

"It's better than being out there, I suppose."

"Oh, it is. You can trust me on that. Now I don't know much about the military rank structure, but corporal...that's pretty low down there, isn't it? Excuse my ignorance."

The corporal looked at Deneaux, realizing she was playing for something. He could tell by the way she'd said it that she was full of shit. "Umm...yeah, pretty low down there." He agreed with her, as it seemed the safest route.

"How would you like to be a captain? No...let's say major?"

"I'm not sure what you're asking."

"Oh, I'm not really asking. I'm about to give you a task that, if you complete it successfully, I will promote you to the rank of major."

"Who would I have to kill?" he laughed.

"Now you get it." Her eyes narrowed, her face becoming severe.

"I can't kill Dixon Hawes if that's what you're

saying."

"Don't you worry about that, it's already being taken care of. There are about to be some sweeping changes here, and you can either remain on the bottom where you currently feed, or you can rise to the top and be the officer I know you can be."

"I'm a soldier, Mrs. Deneaux, not a mercenary. I don't kill for personal gain."

"Oh how quaint, an assassin with morals. Have you been to war, Corporal?"

"Every man in this facility has been. Mr. Hawes only wanted seasoned personnel. Soldiers that wouldn't run at the first sign of trouble."

"Don't you realize that every war is predicated on gain? Perhaps not personal gain, but most definitely gain. Sometimes it is for money, gold or other valuable resources. Sometimes it is for the advancement of one country's religious beliefs or ideals. Sometimes it is just to gain precious land. But make no mistake; every soldier who has ever killed another human being has done so for gain in one manner or another."

"Mrs. Deneaux, part of the reason I'm here, that all of us are here, is that we're trustworthy."

"Wonderful, but I'm not asking you to break that trust. I'm asking you to start forging new relationships…ones that will further advance your livelihood. Your previous boss, Mr. Hawes, has got himself into a very compromising situation, one I do not believe that he will be able to extract himself from. I'm sure you already know what is going on. That madman Michael Talbot will probably tear him to shreds before this is over. When Mr. Hawes is gone, there will be a struggle for control of this facility. Perhaps it will be that idiot Harry Wendelson, the man giggles like a girl and somehow he is the Third Member of the Triumvirate, or more likely Captain Najarian. At some point, you are going to have to choose an allegiance, and I can guarantee you will not be in a position of potential strength like you are now."

"I'm still listening."

"Dixon is a dead man. I do not see a way he can escape the clutches of Michael Talbot. It is imperative that Michael die as well."

"I would think that would take care of itself the moment he killed Mr. Hawes."

"One would think that…and why not? However, I need to force Mr. Talbot into doing something rash, and this is where you come in."

Corporal Dowery said nothing.

"I will take your silence as a possibility that you are entertaining my idea."

"You haven't told me what it is yet in order for me to agree or not."

"I need you to kill Michael's family."

The corporal laughed. Mrs. Deneaux did not. "Wait, you're serious? You just want me to barge into their room and mow them down? There're two kids and two women in there."

"I know who is in there. And I want the dog dead as well. Come, come, Corporal. I'm sure you've seen your fair share of death and destruction."

"It was during a war," he replied.

"This IS a war. Make no mistake. Michael Talbot is a threat like nothing this place has ever seen, and you must kill the roots if you want to take him down. You're wasting my time with that slack-jawed look. If you are going to say no, get out of here and I will find somebody that will. But be warned, Corporal, my memory is long I will remember those who did not help me. For two minutes of distasteful, but necessary deeds, the rest of your life will be secured."

"I cannot do this alone."

"Of course, of course." She waved her hand.

"I will need to be able to promote four or five individuals that I bring with me."

"Gladly…if they help you, they will be helping me as well."

"This is going to take a minute. I will have to track down men I can trust."

"Not too long, Corporal. Michael Talbot has never been blessed with the gift of patience. Rest assured, he will act soon…whether to his detriment or ours."

Chapter Five – Mike Journal Entry 3

"Who is shooting?" Dixon stood up.

"I would imagine Deneaux has launched her coup," I told him.

"You have got to be kidding me!"

"I've only had the displeasure of knowing the lady for the last seven or eight months, so it's not really that big of a surprise to me. But what is, is your thinking that she's not capable of it."

"These are my men. Most of them hand-picked."

"I've already shown you that money doesn't buy respect, Dix. Fear and power maybe, but not respect. There's no guessing what the hell she's offering. It might just be that she won't kill them."

"Never have I been so simultaneously happy and sad to see someone as I was when she showed up here."

"At least you had some reason to be happy, I'm just usually depressed. People just continually die around her. The Reaper probably sends her a thank you card ever year."

"What of our deal?"

"You in a rush to go out there? I say we let them sort it out, and I'll do my part." I was splitting hairs with my words, not promising at all that I planned to be his lab rat. If Tommy could get me out of here, then I was going. I'd perhaps spare his life, but even that wasn't a foregone conclusion at the moment. We'd have to wait and see what the captain had to report when and if he came back from his fact and support finding mission.

Chapter Six – Tracy

"Is this Woodstock?" Trip asked, looking out the front windshield of the truck at the seemingly endless expanse of zombies.

"I wish," Tracy said. "And I don't even like most of that music."

Trip had come up front to sit in between Tracy and Gary. He'd told his wife that sitting in the back reminded him too much of the teacups ride from the carnival, and that was just too traumatic an experience for him.

"How are there that many?" Gary asked. He'd taken the road Mike had told him to before the signal had been lost. They'd been driving parallel to the zombies for the last mile and still there was more of the horde to pass. "And where are they going?"

"I think that's obvious," Tracy said, referring to the secret underground structure.

"Spokane? Why would they be going to Spokane?" Trip asked.

Tracy wasn't sure if it was even worth correcting the man. She'd been around him long enough to realize that he was so firmly entrenched in his own world that, no matter what she said, it would require further and further explanation.

"Mike said get rid of the truck, and I'm sure he had his reasons, but I really don't want to until we can't see them anymore." Gary was pointing out the window as if anyone needed a clearer explanation.

"I wish I had my tinfoil hat, it keeps the signals out that the government broadcasts to keep us all in line. They use the fluoride in the water as a conductor for it. The fluoride gets in our bones and makes them act like antennas. So I've got an antenna here," he said as he held up a finger. "And here." He held up another finger and repeated this for every digit on his hand before moving on to his toes. He was undoing his belt when Tracy stopped him.

"We get it."

"I just wanted to show you my radio tower."

Gary busted out laughing. "Sorry," he said when he saw Tracy's glare. "Wait, I think he's got something there."

"Of course I do, I'm not a eunuch."

Gary would have placed a palm to his head if it didn't take both hands on the steering wheel to keep the truck from plowing into the various obstacles strewn on the roadway. "No, I don't mean the...erm...radio tower. I'm talking the signal. Not really that, but I think that's what Mike meant. They probably put a tracer on this thing so they can find us."

"And get us back," Tracy finished. "Hurry up and find something else we can ride in."

"You're welcome," Trip said.

"Don't," Tracy told Gary when she saw he was about to ask what for.

They drove a few more miles before approaching a sign that announced they were entering Hallowell City Limits, population 26,732. Gary stopped the truck after they crested a small rise looking down at the city.

"There will be a car there," he said.

"Along with everything else."

"I saw the Dead here once." Trip had awoken from a short power nap.

"Got a feeling we're going to see them again," Tracy replied.

"I think he meant the band," Gary spelled out.

"Is it always going to be the job of Talbots everywhere to drive me crazy? I know what he meant."

"I was just helping out. Because your dead are not the same as his Dead."

"Got that, too."

"Well, how could I be sure?"

"You're right, you couldn't. Could you park for a second? I'd like everyone to know what we're doing and to keep a lookout." She didn't want to add that she also needed to get away from them for a moment. Gary, God love him, had been doing his best to keep her from worrying about Mike with his constant chatter. Who knows, maybe that's what Trip was doing as well. But she wanted to reflect on what Michael was doing, and to dwell at least for a bit on how he was going to get out of there. "Michael, this has got to stop happening," she muttered.

"You alright?" The words could have only been delivered from one person as the majority of sky was blocked out.

"I'm doing alright, BT. Thank you for asking."

"You know he'll get out of this, right? Tommy will get him out of there. Do you believe that?"

"I have to believe that. What other choice do I have?" She looked up at him.

"Do you mind?" he asked, extending his arms.

"Of course not," she said as he stepped forward. She was completely enshrouded within his grasp. She felt like a butterfly within a protective cocoon. "Now I know why Mike likes this so much," she said as she tapped BT's chest.

"Mom? Dad will be here soon. Don't you think you could show a little respect?" Travis had come out of the truck and had seen his mother within the massive confines of BT's grasp. He was smiling.

"It's...it's not what it looks like!" BT looked horrified.

"The boy is screwing with you, big man. And thank you," Tracy said as she extracted herself from BT.

"Justin, Mom is cheating on Dad," Travis called, turning to his brother.

"I'm surprised she waited this long," he replied.

"Justin!" Tracy yelled. She wasn't mad, she was actually quite happy to see him feeling better. Since the day of Paul and Erin's rescue, and the subsequent scratch he'd gotten, she'd watched, wondering and worrying when he would finally succumb. A large piece of her would have died with him as well. And his death would have been for nothing. Paul and Erin were both dead and they'd almost taken her son with them. She knew in her heart that she would never have forgiven them; even if there were such a place as Heaven and she was to get there and run into them. She was certain she would have carried the grudge even to that most hallowed of places.

Justin and Travis were smiling as they came up to her. She reflexively joined them. They had so much of Mike in them. That was both a comforting and disheartening thought at the same time. She ached as she looked upon them. They'd both grown so much in such a relatively short time. They'd both gotten much leaner from their restricted diets and hard life. Justin was a few degrees too gaunt as the virus had been consuming him internally. His pallor, which had been a sickly yellow hue, was not vastly improved, but it was better, and that was a huge comfort to her. Victories were short-lived in this new time though. She'd no sooner got her son back, and now her husband was in trouble. She wondered if there would ever come a time where she could stop to take a breath.

As Gary was telling his nephews, Dennis, and BT the plan, Stephanie was walking with Trip, who kept stopping to pick up cans for the nickel redemption. No matter how many times Steph told him that the can return centers were no longer open, he insisted on doing it.

"They collected the nickel extra when the people bought these, so they have to pay it back when they are dropped off," he'd told her.

Henry had a long expression on his face as he sat in the middle of the roadway, looking back the way they had come. Tracy was about to go over to the dog and rub his head, maybe giving each of them some much needed mutual comfort, when she heard the rustle of small growth off to her right. Henry heard it too as he came up next to her. His bark startled her to attention.

"Zombies," she heard herself say, not nearly loud for anyone else to hear. She cleared her throat. "Zombies!" That did it.

"Mom, get back here!" Travis yelled from the rear of the truck. He had flipped his safety off and was looking for a firing line clear of relatives, specifically his mom.

Henry was barking, his massive chest heaving. He stood squarely in front of Tracy who had yet to move.

"Mom, come on," Justin said, going over to grab her.

"Henry," Tracy said calmly as she let Justin guide her back, flipping her safety off as well.

BT brought his rifle up and fired just as she got passed him. His first round hit the zombie high in the chest, shattering its collarbone and sending white fragments of bone spinning into the air.

"Nice shooting, Tex," Travis told him, placing his first round neatly in the zombie's forehead.

"Listen, I already have your father to deal with, I don't need another Talbot riding my ass." BT fired again as a line of zombies began to emerge from the side of road.

"Let's go!" Gary shouted.

"I'm pissing!" Trip yelled from the opposite side. "Be there in a couple of minutes!"

"Couple of minutes? Get your ass over here!" BT shouted.

"He really likes to take his time when he goes," Stephanie offered as an apology as she went to get her husband.

"Can he not hear what's going on here?" Travis asked his brother.

Justin shrugged which sent his round low. The zombie's head fell forward as the bullet blew out the front of its throat.

"That's just gross. Can't anyone hit a head anymore?" Travis nailed the zombie on the top of its now fully exposed cranium. It fell hard to the ground.

Stephanie had grabbed Trip and was physically manhandling him out of the ditch he was in.

"Why are his pants down?" BT asked as he was muscling Henry into the back of the truck. "I thought he was peeing?"

Stephanie smiled sheepishly. "This is an improvement. He normally likes to take them completely off—"

She was about to elaborate. "I don't want to know." BT put a hand up and bowed his head. Henry gave him a large slurp on the side of his face. "Fucking Talbots," he grumbled, before wiping away the goo.

Justin and Travis were holding the line as everyone got back into the truck.

"Just like old times!" Travis said to his brother.

"I liked it better when we were playing video games, and the zombies weren't real" Justin told him.

Trip was struggling to move fast with his pants around his ankles, nearly falling over before BT bear hugged him and literally tossed him into the back of the truck. He stopped sliding when he smacked into Henry.

"Whoa, that was fun!" he said to Henry.

"Oh, for fuck's sake." BT shook his head. He pushed Stephanie in as she climbed up. "Boys, let's go!" The closest zombies were within ten feet and more were coming out every second.

"You first," Justin said to Travis.

"No way, you're older, you run slower."

"We don't need another pissing contest. Both of you get your asses over here, or I'll launch you into this truck. I'll make Trip's flight look like the Wright Brothers' first attempt compared to what I do to you two!" BT yelled.

"Big man seems angry, we should go," Travis said calmly.

"You first, I insist."

"BOYS!"

They both ran. Messing with BT was one thing, angering him a complete other. He cuffed them both on the back of their heads as they climbed in. "Fuck with me, will you? Just because I endure your father doesn't mean I'll suffer you as well! This isn't a game." He climbed in.

Tracy waited until her boys had gotten in before she climbed into the passenger seat. No sooner had she closed her door than the first of the zombies slammed into it. A snarling face and clawing hands reached for the glass of her window.

Gary was still outside the truck, right by the door, frantically patting his pockets down, a look of sheer panic on his features.

"Gary, get in the truck!"

"Get this thing moving!" BT bellowed as zombies were attempting to get into the rear. Shots rang out as they fought to keep the zombies from climbing in. Tracy spun quickly as she heard the door mechanism click open.

"Shit, I forgot they've been getting smarter." She grabbed the handle and yanked it back, ripping two fingernails clear from the zombie. He groaned, not in pain, but in yearning, as his meal eluded him for the moment. She slammed her forearm down on the lock just as she got the door shut. Zombies were now in front of the truck and would soon be over by Gary, who had not yet entered.

"Gary! Get your ass in here!"

"Tracy, I can't find the keys!" He was still checking his pockets while also spinning around looking perhaps for where he had dropped them.

Tracy would have berated him if she'd had the time. "There are no keys, it's a military truck!"

"Oh, yeah." he said serenely. "I knew that." He pulled himself up and in.

Tracy wanted to slap him in the side of the head, she was just afraid she would do it so hard she might knock him out. Barring that, a good tongue-lashing might be in order. She wouldn't do that either; unlike Mike, Gary had a much kinder soul and would take it to heart, no matter the heat of the situation they had been in at the time. Mike, in most cases, would blow it off or come back with a speedy retort and then not think on it again. Gary, on the other hand, would hold on to that hurt, and she just couldn't do that to him as he looked so relieved over there.

"Umm, now might be a good time to drive, Gary," she said, biting back the list of things that came to the tip of her tongue—none of them good.

The truck lurched forward as it hit a line of zombies. Tracy grabbed handholds while the truck rocked back and forth as it ran over zombies. "They should call you Rut!" she shouted, nearly biting her tongue off for the effort.

Gary was looking at her, and not the roadway, for long seconds. "OH! I get it…because of the rough ride," he answered before once again focusing on what was in front of them.

"And I thought Mike was a bad driver," she mumbled, still holding a minor grievance for her Jeep he'd ruined on day one. More than once, Gary launched Tracy so high in her seat that her hair had scraped the roof of the cab. She couldn't even imagine what was going on in back of the truck.

"When did we rent a bouncy house?" Trip asked as he landed roughly on BT's stomach. He was laughing hysterically.

Justin had an arm wrapped around Henry and an iron grip on a strut from the small wooden bench that ran down the length of the inside of the truck.

"You need help?" Travis asked him.

"I got him, just hold on." They were both sitting on the floor.

Travis would never admit it, but he was thankful his brother was back and looking out for him.

"Trip, honey, come over here and hold on with me," Stephanie pleaded as she saw the angry look BT gave Trip every time he went airborne and somehow, like a magnet, found his way back to land on some part of BT.

"Hold on? Why? I haven't had this much fun since I went up in that plane and experienced zero-gees."

"He's serious," Stephanie told BT.

Zombies kept spilling out from the woods.

"Where are they all coming from?" Tracy asked.

Gary kept nervously looking down at his speedometer, the needle slowing with every contact. If they didn't get past the zombies soon, they were in danger of being stopped. The road ahead was filling up rapidly.

"Gary?"

"I see them. I don't know what to do though." To the right was brush and then trees, to the left was a drop off he had no chance of navigating as the truck would roll over long before he got to the bottom. He stomped down on the gas and became alarmed when the large machine did not gain speed but only held steady. "We're in trouble."

The zombies nearest the truck took notice, but the ones up ahead seemed completely oblivious as they crossed over the road and down the ditch. Some were even heading off into the field.

"They look like they're going to meet up with the rest of the group," Tracy said. The bumps and jostles had slowed down considerably, but surprisingly enough, that was not a good thing.

"Why aren't they in stasis?" Gary asked. Their speed had dropped to under ten miles an hour. Any slower, and the zombies would be able to outpace the truck with a power walk.

A valid question for which Tracy did not have an answer.

"Tracy, I'm not going to be able to push them out of the way much longer."

"I know." She was busy slamming bullets into her magazine.

The trucked rocked to the side.

"What the hell was that, Mom?!" Travis asked. He had to shout over the cacophony of the zombies snarling and the whining of the engine as it fought harder and harder, only to move slower and slower.

"Oh, God, it's bulkers!" She braced for impact, the side of her door dented inwards as a behemoth of a zombie thumped into it.

"Bulkers?" Gary's face got long as he thought on that one word. The last time he'd heard it, his father had died. The truck took another direct hit. Tracy wasn't sure, but she would have bet money that her side had raised up off the ground. Loose bullets fell from her lap as she came back down.

"Round two!" Trip yelled joyously.

Bulkers were crushing regular zombies as they hurtled themselves into the truck. One had impacted the front tire guard and pushed the heavy metal into the tire, making it shred like an apple corer. The front dipped down as the tire lost air and dropped down onto the thick rubber of the "run-flat", a modification specifically designed for military vehicles to be able to keep moving should the tires ever be shot out.

The ride, which had already felt like a teenager's first go with a clutch, was quickly devolving into something more along the lines of a rider-less stagecoach being pulled by rabid horses. The truck somehow was being nearly imperceptibly moved a fraction of an inch at a time to the precipice on their right.

"I think they're trying to roll us." Gary kept looking from the front to his side.

"I know this goes without saying, Gary, but do something." Tracy was doing her best to try and stay calm.

Gary cut the wheel hard to the right and was standing

on the accelerator. The truck was moving as much forwards as it was sideways. "This can't be happening," he murmured. "I'm trying, Tracy."

Tracy was just about to roll down her window and start blasting when she saw a subtle shift in the zombies—something she didn't think Gary had quite taken note of yet. The zombies directly in front of them were quickly moving to the sides of the truck, leaving an opening directly ahead. The truck leapt forward when it came free. It was with horror that Tracy realized what had just happened. The wheels of the truck were cut so far over that, when it began to move again, it was headed straight for the trees.

Gary had not eased up on the gas pedal yet, but was frantically trying to right the ship; he was having about as much luck as the Titanic when it had tried to dodge an iceberg.

"Shit." Tracy braced her legs against the dashboard as the tree line dominated their view.

The truck swung to the left just as the wheels dropped off the side of the road and on to the soft shoulder, nearly ripping the steering wheel from Gary's grip.

"Shit," he echoed Tracy.

The hard rubber dug deeply into the gravel and dirt, making it impossible for Gary to regain control. The rear wheels dropped off the roadway as well, brush scraping along the side of the vehicle with larger and larger branches thwacking the front end and windshield.

"Brace for impact!" Gary hadn't finished the word "impact" when they struck something solid enough to crumple the front end. Tracy's body lurched forward. She was pretty sure she was going to be sore for days if they survived. That was a problem she would have to deal with later...if she got the chance.

"Everyone alright?" Tracy yelled out over the groans of the engine. In truth, it was a low-velocity impact, punishing to the body to be sure, but not deadly—at least the initial part of it. What happened after was very much up in the air.

"We're good! What happened?" BT yelled from the back.

"Gary had a Mike moment!"

"Can we get out of here?" Travis asked.

Tracy looked to Gary who shook his head. He was too embarrassed or disappointed with himself to answer with words.

"Engine is dying." And as if Gary was the second coming of Nostradamus, the truck shuddered and lay still. The hissing of zombies overtook the popping protests of the heated cylinder block.

"Everyone up top!" Tracy shouted as rifles began to fire behind her.

"Up top?" Justin was looking at the canvas covering the truck bed. The canvas was plenty strong to hold their accumulated weight...the thin metal supports holding the canvas up...well, that was potentially a different story.

"You heard the lady, let's go!" BT was crouched over and had shoved a blade through the canvas, opening a hole wide enough for a person to fit through. "You okay?" He looked to Travis and Justin who were holding the encroaching horde at bay for the moment.

"We got this, get them up," Travis told him.

"I feel like I'm being born again!" Trip said as he was pushed up through the breach.

BT could only shake his head. They all looked up for a moment as they saw Trip's outline on top of them.

"That going to hold?" Travis asked.

"Sure," Justin told him.

"Is that like a Dad "sure", where he's really trying to figure it out himself, or do you know for real?"

"Sure," Justin repeated.

"Thought so. Five more shots and I need to reload."

"Do it now, I have ten."

"Boys, one of you needs to come up," BT said after he got Stephanie up and handed Henry to her.

"Trip, NO! This is not still the bouncy house!" Stephanie shrieked. Justin looked up and could clearly see Trip's feet outlined above his head as the man had stood and was preparing to jump.

"Justin, I've got a full mag, go," Travis said hastily as he shoved the last bullet in.

Justin would have argued but they didn't have the time as zombies were at the edge of the truck with some even pulling themselves in. "Hurry up." And with that Justin let BT propel him into the air.

"Your turn."

Travis turned when BT spoke. A vise-like hand wrapped around his ankle and pulled him to the ground. His gun went skittering away as he landed on his hands.

"Travis!" BT roared, moving to grab the boy's outstretched hand even as he was being pulled toward the rear of the truck and out.

Justin poked his head through the hole, and without a moment's hesitation, dropped back down. BT dove and wrapped his hands around Travis.

"Please don't let me go," Travis said as he looked at BT.

"You go, I go, I promise," BT told him as he reached out and grabbed onto the seats.

"No one's going anywhere, especially without inviting me," Justin said as he reached down, grabbed a magazine from the bed of the truck, and shoved it into his magazine well. He quickly pulled the charging handle back and roared rounds through it, the first ones coming dangerously close to Travis's ankle.

Justin was nearly leaning outside of the truck, placing the barrel of his weapon directly against the skulls of the zombies. He kept pulling the trigger until he heard BT tell him Travis was free.

"Come on, boy!" BT was yelling, it could have been at him or his brother.

"FUCK YOU!" Justin was shouting to the zombies as bits of brain and blood splattered up and on to him. "NOT NOW, NOT EVER!" His bolt slammed open as he fired his last round. The trigger was impotently frozen.

"AHHHHHH!" he yelled as he flipped the rifle around and started pounding on the zombies' skulls, who seemed to clamor for more and more of the damage he doled out as if they were masochists thriving on the punishment.

"Just got you back, boy, not going to go through this again." BT physically removed him from his spot and ran to the front of the truck.

Trip was poking his head through. "You two coming? It's such a beautiful day!"

"Trip, move!" BT was already sending Justin up. Dennis grabbed the boy and moved him to the side in preparation for BT's ascent.

Gary's side had thankfully been clear as he opened his door. He wrenched his sister-in-law over and somehow got her through his door before he actually exited. She stepped onto the roof of the truck and then onto the canvas, Gary quickly following her.

The truck swayed as zombies and bulkers ran into it. Gary, Stephanie, Dennis, Justin, Travis, Tracy, and BT, who was holding Henry, sat precariously on the thin cover supports. They all held on for dear life as the truck moved. Trip had been walking on the canvas, wondering why he wasn't getting the bouncing sensation he desired until BT's glare made Stephanie reach out and pull him down. Zombies had now entered the cab and the open bay, fingers and hands attempting to push through the thick, green fabric. At first they'd moved their feet every time a zombie had touched them through the canvas, but now it happened so often that they would have had to keep their feet constantly in their air. That would have been fairly impractical given the width of the area they were perched on.

Zombies still flooded past to the front and rear of the truck, going to an as yet unknown destination, but at least a few hundred had stopped for an afternoon snack.

"Maybe they'll move and try to catch up with the other zombies," Justin said hopefully.

Nobody answered. It was what they all desired, but there was no way to tell if it would happen or not. Once zombies got fixated on food, they were rarely persuaded to leave it. BT was closest to the hole in the canvas, far enough that the hands poking through couldn't reach him, but close enough to feel a certain level of anxiety as those plague-filled extremities sought purchase. He wasn't too concerned initially, as the zombies' fingers had been sticking straight out. Then, something subtly changed as those same fingers began to curl, and not only curl, but do so with a purpose as they gripped the lip of the fabric.

"We've got to go," BT said. He'd thought about standing, but the bulkers were still ramming the truck and he was afraid he'd pitch off to the side.

"Go? Go where, BT?" Tracy asked. "I think Justin is right, maybe we should just wait them out." Anything more she had to say was cut short by a tear in the very fabric that held their existence in place.

Travis moved closer to BT to see what was going on. He then did a quick look around him. "The trees—we can make it to the trees," he said, looking at the large one the truck's front end was resting against.

BT saw it as well and hastily glanced down to the package in his arms. Unless Henry became a jungle cat and quickly, his short limbs were going to be an extreme hindrance to climbing. "Everyone give me whatever clothing you can spare." In a normal situation, such an odd request might generate a half a dozen questions. But questions meant time, and that was something they had little of. The next few moments had everyone pulling off various articles of clothing, most of it socks, although Tracy and Stephanie both had a top on under a heavier shirt. Trip, for whatever reason, handed BT his pants. He was now proudly standing there in his underwear.

BT wanted to tell him to put his damn pants back on, but unfortunately it was exactly what he needed. He fashioned a harness for Henry who seemed none too pleased to be donning anything extra. Everyone had quickly figured out where this was going and were doing their best to ensure that the knots would be sufficient to hold Henry's heft. And, at least for the moment, Henry seemed content with everyone paying him so much attention.

"Let's try this out," BT said as Travis and Justin got Henry up onto his back. Stephanie and Tracy were adjusting the makeshift knots. BT was cinching the knots in front as tightly as was humanly possible, which in his case was nearly superhuman.

BT stood slowly, getting used to the added weight on his back. Henry was breathing on his neck and even once or twice let his thick tongue get a taste. "You keep doing that, dog, and I'm going to leave you here." BT shivered.

Gary had been eyeing the tree. "It's at least seven feet from the top of the hood to the lowermost branch." Like everyone else that had survived this far his body had gone through immense changes, but he still couldn't forget the little kid he'd been who had not been able to climb that rope back in grade school. His friends—and the gym teacher for that matter—had teased him mercilessly. He was now getting the cold sweats just thinking about that climb.

Trip moved past them all, with his ghost-white legs and untied shoes.

"Honey, what are you doing?" Stephanie asked as Trip jumped over the outstretched zombie hands and onto the roof of the cab.

"Looking for coconuts," he told her as he dropped down onto the hood and within mere inches of zombies scrambling to get at him. "I could really go for a Mounds." Trip reached up, grabbed the branch, jumped, placing his feet against the tree, and effortlessly pulled himself up. "I think I see some!" he said, looking up and shielding his eyes. "Come on! I could use some help when I knock them down."

If not for the sound of more fabric tearing, they may have stayed there and looked at him for a much longer time.

"Go," BT said to Travis who was next in line.

Trip reached down and helped Travis up, who quickly moved to another part of the tree. The closest call thus far had come when Stephanie and Trip had locked arms. He had swung her around like they were playing on the monkey bars at a playground.

"John, please!" she'd pleaded. It was safe to say that none of them had taken a breath as they waited to see if Trip would venture back from whatever dimension he had traveled to.

"I'm sorry; I was just trying to lighten up the mood. These people are SO serious."

"I get it, honey, I do, but could you just maybe not do it with my life?"

"Your life? I'd never jeopardize your life," he said in all seriousness as he hoisted her up.

"Alright, Gary, just you and me. We've got to go." BT and Gary were standing on the cab roof, the canvas tarp now pretty much relegated to salvage as the zombies had torn half of it down.

"You go," Gary urged.

BT stopped to truly look at Mike's brother. "You're scared."

"Me? Naw. This way I can keep an eye on Henry when you climb."

"Now normally that sounds like a good idea, but I'm thinking that if I go up that tree you won't."

"Pssh...come on," Gary exclaimed. "You think I want to stay down here with the zombies?"

"I don't think you *want* to, I just think you don't want to climb that tree more. What's going on?"

Gary paused. "I've had, umm, issues with climbing before."

"FUCK!" BT roared, "What is it with Talbots and past events? Get your ass up there or I'm going to put you in the sling with Henry!"

"Something is going on!" Travis shouted.

During BT and Gary's conversation the zombies had vacated the truck, leaving some room around the perimeter.

"Are they leaving?" Tracy asked.

BT looked around, "I don't think so, they're just standing there like they're expecting something."

"I think I know what it is." Justin was pointing. A line of bulkers was forming.

"They're going to try knocking the truck over. You guys need to get moving!" Travis shouted. He brought the barrel of his gun up to rest on a branch so he could get some stability for his shots. Justin was doing the same. The bulkers were moving forward with as much speed as they could generate in fifteen feet. The truck rocked violently from the impact, Gary steadied BT as his footing slipped.

"Gary, you have to go. If you don't go, I don't, and if something happens to Henry, Mike is going to flip the fuck out."

"Yeah, he'd probably be more pissed about that than anything else."

"That's a fair assessment. Come on, I'll help you out. Fear of heights?" BT asked tenderly.

"Not at all...fear of climbing."

BT shook his head. "Is that even such a thing?" he asked as he pushed on Gary's ass to get him into the tree. The zombies had now pulled back even further, giving the bulkers more room to gain momentum. Trip was hanging down like a bat, his head nearly even with BT's, his legs wrapped around the branch.

"Hello, good sir. Going up?"

"Get out of the way!"

"Second floor, women's apparel, candles, small household electronics," Trip announced as BT launched himself into the air.

He grunted heavily as he pulled himself up and past. "Thanks for moving," he said sarcastically.

"No problem, man," Trip said as he moved to sit upright.

The truck groaned as the bulkers slammed into it, the tires coming up nearly eight inches before crashing back to earth. They hadn't succeeded in turning it over, but it was safe to say that they would have dislodged at least a couple of the previous inhabitants from the top with their efforts. The zombies now looked from the truck to the tree, unsure of how their food had moved.

The group could only watch as the bulkers repeatedly hit the truck, caving in the side and finally getting it partially tipped. The truck came to rest against another tree, the passenger's side wheels off the ground and the truck balanced at a forty-five degree angle. The only perch that would have been afforded to them then would not have been wide enough by half to hold them all. BT shuddered; he wasn't the only one to do so.

"Well, at least we got rid of the truck," Gary said. His attempt at lightheartedness was not met with overwhelming results. The day was warm, although thankfully not hot as the sun made its journey across the sky. The tree was safety, but it was safety without comfort. The only one who was not constantly adjusting in order to find a more easy sitting position was Trip. He looked as if he might be performing meditation he was so still. Henry had been good thus far, but at some point he was going to want out of his restrictive harness.

"We have to keep moving," BT said. The massive horde had finally passed them by leaving only their dinner guests, which numbered in the hundreds.

"You're serious?" Tracy asked. "What are we going to do? Pretend we're Tarzan? No, Really!?" she asked as she looked to the trees next to them. Some were within reach while others tantalizingly close.

"We can't wait them out, Mom. They'll never leave," Travis told her.

She knew he was right, there was no question he was right, but she hadn't liked climbing trees when she was young, and doing it now to save her and the lives of those around her wasn't making it much better…if at all.

"This is insane," Stephanie chimed in.

BT had wanted to tell her the only thing that was insane around here was her husband. He used an extraordinary amount of restraint to refrain from issuing those words, though.

Again Trip took the lead, appearing as if he wasn't even cognizant of the conversation that had been going on around him. He leaped as if he were the Sugar Plum Fairy in a classic remake of *The Nutcracker*, his legs already a shimmering white as if he'd been wearing tights. As he was in mid-air, his left shoe spiraled off and hit a zombie square in the nose. If the zombie minded, he said nothing in protest.

It was a long second that Trip floated in that air before his body came down onto a branch, a loud crack heralding his arrival. The group held a collective breath as they waited to see if Trip would go plummeting to the ground. The branch held, although it was clear to those looking at it that the limb was suffering a catastrophic failure.

"Honey, you should move to another branch," Stephanie urged.

"Why? Will this bank not let me withdraw money?" he asked, clearly confused.

"What is he saying?" Dennis questioned.

"Allow me," BT said. "I'm starting to understand Tripanese. See, he thinks when his wife said 'branch' that she was referring to a bank."

"Well, why not? Makes perfect sense." Dennis was looking down at the zombies that, for the time being, were mostly silent, though the way in which they gazed upon the tree-dwellers was unsettling. He had the feeling they were like crocodiles in a marsh waiting for the hatching birds to fall so they could get a quick meal. Trip, in the meantime, had moved higher up the tree he'd jumped to.

BT looked around desperately; with Henry on his back he knew he was well over three hundred pounds of combined weight. He'd need a branch somewhere close to the thickness of his arm before he'd feel safe enough to make a leap of faith.

"You guys coming? If you don't hurry, we'll never beat the Nottingham Sheriff to Robin's lair," Trip called out.

"Guys, there's another tree over here that looks sturdy enough." Gary was gauging the distance. "I think I can make it." He was pushing against the tree he was on, looking for some extra propulsion.

"You go from scared of climbing trees to Batman?" BT asked him.

"I said I was afraid of climbing, not afraid of heights," Gary replied. He leaped and missed.

"Oh shit." Travis reached out to grab the shoulder of his uncle. He came up empty.

Gary's arms were flailing as he tried to grab onto the bark. He came down hard on the tree's lowest branch, crotch first. The only thing saving him from jewel-crushing defeat was that his feet came down on the tops of the zombies' heads. Even with the cushioning, he turned pale as the pain erupted from his privates and cramped his stomach. Breakfast, part of last night's dinner, and some unidentifiable thick, brown liquid spilled from his mouth in a torrent.

Travis quickly made the jump, landing softly on the branch above that his uncle had been originally shooting for. He reached down and steadied Gary's swaying form. Gary had both of his hands in front of him on the branch trying to keep from rolling off.

"Don't feel so good," he looked up.

"I get it, Uncle Gary, I do, but you need to stand up," Travis said sympathetically.

A half gurgle half grunt came out of Gary as he flexed his arms and pulled his legs up from the zombies that were now reaching for them. "Might puke again."

"I would expect nothing less, but how about you come up here and do it." Travis' grip was tenuous at best, and if Gary fell over, he would either fall over with him or have his hand wrenched free. Gary moved with slow and deliberate movements, his legs shaking as they finally got on the loin-crunching wood. Travis was concerned the outcropping might not support his weight. His uncle hugged the tree as he stood taking in deep breaths.

"You alright?" Travis asked as he gently clapped his uncle's shoulder.

"Maybe never," Gary replied, his forehead resting against the tree.

Travis gave his mother the thumbs-up.

Some of the zombies had moved so that now all three trees they were perched in were completely surrounded.

"We can't keep doing this," BT said aloud what they were all thinking. "We can't move fast enough to get by them, and someone is going to eventually fall." BT's tree shook minutely as a bulker crashed into it. None of them were in any danger of being shaken loose, but it was still disconcerting.

"Hope he crushes his skull doing that," Justin said.

"Can we fight our way out?" Tracy was looking to BT.

He shook his head. "Not enough rounds."

"What if I jumped ahead by myself and got in front of them? I could either lead them off or maybe find some help," Dennis said.

"And just who do you think you could find that will be willing to help a group of strangers stranded in trees surrounded by a shitload of zombies?" BT was uncharacteristically cross. Part of it was the dire situation they found themselves in, the other was that the doctors had told him he would be extremely tired for a few weeks while the concoction of medication they had administered to him took hold within his system.

"I'm listening for your better ideas!" Dennis pushed back. "Oh, that's right, I haven't heard any."

"Don't mess with me, little man! I'll squeeze you like a zit, Mike's friend or not!"

"Don't let the fact that I'm Mike's friend stop you from trying. I've never beaten up a half-giant."

"Giant? Who the hell do you think you're talking to?" BT was looking up at the next branch, obviously wanting to climb up to get closer to Dennis.

Dennis had not once in his life backed down from a fight, and he knew in his heart that a fair amount resided in the fact that he was shorter than most of his friends. He'd always felt the need to constantly prove himself to them. The term was Short-Man's Syndrome; to him it was a matter of pride.

"Don't come any higher, or your elephant ass will topple the tree. I'll come down to you!" Dennis told him.

"BOYS!" Tracy interjected. "You're making a horrible situation worse!"

"Tracy, I'll only fuck him up a little," BT growled, rising up from his branch.

"You're just lucky you're holding Henry."

"Yeah, I'm sure that's the only reason you don't want to mess with me. I could be holding Gary in my arms and still take you down a rung from that lofty ladder you think you're sitting on."

"Fuck it," Dennis said, getting closer.

"TRIP!" Stephanie cried out; the potential fight

forgotten for the moment.

"He's gone!" Stephanie was looking around desperately for some sign of him in the surrounding trees.

Travis was searching the ground for the more likely alternative, but the zombies were still patiently waiting for their food to fall from the skies. If one of them had landed it would be a feeding frenzy down there.

"We have to find him." Stephanie had tears falling from her eyes.

"Oh, honey," Tracy said, wanting to move closer but afraid of her precarious positioning.

"Damn fool. And I'm talking about Trip, not you, so don't go getting your locks all in a twist," BT said to Dennis.

"Kiss my ass," Dennis said without much vehemence, their dispute on hold at least temporarily.

"What do we do?" Justin asked.

"What can we do?" BT sat back down. "Yeah, this is real comfortable. He probably forgot we were with him and took off to see if he could find Jerry Garcia."

"Jerry Garcia is dead." Gary finally twisted his head from its resting spot to speak.

BT gave him a look as if to say, "That's what I meant."

"Any chance either of you could think before you speak, or are your male minds just not capable of such higher functioning?" Tracy chided them.

BT just looked away, the sour expression on his face nearly matching Gary's one of induced pain.

The sun blazed across the sky, indifferent to the plights of the inhabitants residing on the small blue jewel. Travis found a small crook in the elbow of the tree and managed to get into a position that was marginable better than the others. For the time being though he was in no danger of getting comfortable enough to fall asleep.

"Gonna be night soon," Justin said as he watched the sun begin to set behind a distant ridge of hills.

"Captain Obvious strikes again," BT grumbled.

Tracy was close enough to hear. "Listen, I know you're not feeling well, and carrying Henry can't be easy, but I need you, BT. We all need you. Whether you want the position or not, you are the leader of this small band."

BT glared and then softened. "I'm sorry, Tracy. I know. I know that I'm supposed to be keeping us safe, and I couldn't even make it a couple of hours out on my own without Mike. We're like a treed fox up here with the hounds circling below. We'll be lucky if we make it through the night, and then what? Eventually someone will fall asleep and roll off. Oh and those fuckers down there, they'll wait 'cause they got nothing better to do."

"When in the hell did you become such a defeatist? This is a side of you I wouldn't have dreamed you were capable of."

"Fuck, Tracy, for all your husband's idiosyncrasies, he brings out the best in me. And now, when he needs me the most to protect all those he loves, I've failed. I've failed miserably." BT's head hung low.

"We're still alive, BT. I will not have you talk that way to me, especially in front of my sons. We will make it out of here—all of us. Mike would expect no less."

BT could not manage much more than a satisfactory grunt; and that above all scared Tracy. If the strongest link in their chain was already getting ready to break, it could set a dangerous precedent.

Tracy, reaching down and over, grabbed his ear and twisted it violently.

"Fuck, woman!" BT bellowed.

"Stop feeling sorry for yourself and start thinking of a way to honor your promise!"

"You need some help?" Dennis asked, wrongly thinking that BT and Tracy were now in the midst of a battle. They sort of were, but this one was a much more one-sided event.

"What are you going to do? Jump up and punch my thighs?"

"BT!"

"Sorry, sorry. Let me just work through this a little. I'll be fine. I promise."

Henry took that most opportune of times to deliver a thick, wet, drool laced lick to the back of BT's neck.

"See? Even he has faith in you," Tracy said as she went back to her previous place.

The mosquitoes came out in full force as soon as the sun was completely down. Gary had nearly fallen as he swatted the pests away. He had used two hands at one point, forgetting that they were the only thing keeping him rooted to his spot. He had pin-wheeled his arms for twelve butt clenching seconds as he fought to regain his balance.

"I think you'd be better off letting the bugs bite you than them, Uncle," Travis said, pointing to the zombies when he realized Gary was once again settled.

"Probably right." Gary had turned as pale as a Winter's moon. He was grateful that it was too dark for anyone to see the transformation.

Stephanie would periodically call out for her husband and cry. If Trip was out there, it would have been impossible to see him. The night was pitch dark, a thick layering of clouds covering even the meager amount of light the stars and a crescent moon could have offered. Each person was stuck in his or her own personal misery. Tracy asked how each of them were doing in turn and would then encourage them to tell a favorite story of theirs. All had participated save Stephanie, who was too far lost in concern and grief. Tracy couldn't help but be reminded of Erin, Paul's wife, who could not cope with the prospect of facing the world any longer without her husband and had simply walked off into the night, never to be heard from again.

Tracy hoped the woman had found a peaceful way to exit; however, the odds were extremely stacked against it.

There were not too many easy ways out anymore. Growing old and dying in one's sleep had grown out of favor, much like eight-tracks. Even Tracy, whose reservoir of optimism had seemed depthless, had her moments of doubt during the night. It was not hopeless—not yet anyway. She had to count the pluses, which in this case were only positives because they weren't negatives. It wasn't cold out, it wasn't snowing or raining, and they weren't being eaten.

The group had hoped that out of sight would equate to out of mind for the zombies. Not so much. Tracy's eyes watered and burned as the morning sun made its entry. The dawn showed the dead in all their horrified glory. The only thing she knew was that they could not stay there another night. BT was in the same position and still looked as dour as he had when Tracy had seen him last. The only thing moving was Henry, who Tracy was concerned had to take care of some personal business and most likely wanted to stretch his legs. The dog might be the epitome of a lounge lizard, but even he liked to move around occasionally.

"BT, I think Henry has to go," Tracy said calmly.

"He already did," BT answered without looking up.

Gary had turned so that his back was now against the tree. His eyes would shut for a moment and then pop open in alarm when he realized where he was exactly and that he was in danger of falling off.

Travis and Justin looked tired but she knew before the zombies came the two were famous for pulling all-nighters on their Xbox systems, running campaigns of one sort or another through a gaming world. They could go for a while longer before crashing. Dennis was staring off into space, remembering a better time Tracy figured. How hard could that be? Right now sitting in a dentist's chair getting a root canal would be preferable to their current situation. Stephanie looked washed out; hope had been drained from her the previous evening. She was already beginning to look like a shell of her former self.

"Gary, wake up!" Tracy said, startling them all.

"They're just cups, Mom!" he cried, coming out of whatever fugue state he'd entered.

They needed to make a plan. This inaction would be just as lethal as any action. Mike would not be riding in on a white horse—or preferably a coast guard helicopter—any time soon. If they wanted to survive, they were going to have to find their own way out. She was just so exhausted that it was difficult to think clearly.

"Mom, I think there're a few less zombies," Travis told her as he looked around.

A hundred and fifty was marginally better than two hundred, but still too many by about a hundred twenty.

"Yeah, we can take them," Justin chimed in.

They couldn't, not really. There was a chance with some great sacrifice that some of them would make it, not all though. The numbers were just too greatly stacked against them.

"BT, what if you and I move over a tree and jump down?" Tracy asked.

Henry and BT both swiveled their heads to look at her. BT and, she thought, probably Henry, discerned the true message in her words. She wanted to get down and kill as many as she could to give the others a potential chance to get away.

BT began to stand with no small degree of difficulty.

"Both of my legs are asleep!" He was holding on tight to the tree, but then grabbed the branch above his head, waiting for the slicing of a thousand tiny daggers to pass as the blood circulated in his system.

"Then what?" Travis asked. He could smell something worse than the zombies below brewing.

"Then we kill a bunch of the bastards," she told him.

"I'll go," Stephanie intoned. "I've got nothing left to live for."

"What?" Justin asked. "Mom, I think you've been

watching Dad too much. Even with his half-baked ideas, he would see how bad of a strategy that is. You'll drop down right on top of them, probably won't even be able to get a shot off."

"That's not really the point," BT told him.

"Wait, you two are just planning on getting eaten?" Justin asked. "That's unacceptable, I won't allow it."

"It should be me," Gary said. "Those are speeders down there. I won't be able to outrun them; I might as well make my death worth it."

"NO! Dad told me I was the man of the family; I forbid any of this crap. Trip made it somehow, I know he did. Maybe we should just follow his model," Justin insisted.

"Oh, and what model is that? Fly through the trees like a monkey and forget everything else?" BT asked.

"Sort of. We leave one at a time. It doesn't look like the zombies will leave the main group. You'd only need to go five or maybe six trees over then jump down and make a run for it. One of us could find a car or something, pick the others up…" Justin was fumbling trying to think it through before his mother hit desperation mode and went ahead with a plan she could not come back from.

"Worth a shot." Dennis had been watching a bird circle high overhead.

"Travis, you've got the youngest legs, so give it a go. I've got a pretty good angle to cover you," Gary said as he stood.

"Mom?" he asked.

Tracy choked back a sob. Her son was in mortal danger and she could do nothing to prevent it. If he didn't fall to his death, there was a high likelihood she would never see him again.

"Try it. WHEN you make it, you have to promise me you won't come back here. That you'll go to your uncle's, you'll live out your life, and maybe when this is over find a special girl, raise a family."

"Have kids? Mom, what are you talking about?" He wanted to smile, but the pain in his mother's face prevented that.

"How do we decide who's last?" BT asked.

Again Stephanie spoke. "I'll stay."

The answer was right there, and BT wanted to take it. It could have been so simple. It should have been so simple.

"I'll do it," BT said instead. "I can't make the jumps, especially with this big dog on my back. We'll wait for you to come back."

BT didn't know what he was expecting—a few protests, some crying, perhaps a couple of other people stepping up to volunteer. He got none as Tracy spoke before anyone else could.

"Do you believe we'll come back for you?" she asked.

He looked over and into her eyes. He saw a determination and fierceness there and maybe even a promise if he looked hard enough. "I do."

"Travis, go. And I swear if you hurt yourself I will kick your ass."

"Mom, that doesn't even make sense," he told her as he rolled his eyes.

"Did you just roll your eyes at me?"

"You can't even see me from there."

"Then you don't deny it?"

"Trav, you'd better go," his older brother said, trying to shield him.

Travis was preparing for his first jump.

"STOP!" Dennis yelled out.

"It's not your turn. What are you scared about?" BT asked him.

Dennis didn't reply to the barb as there were bigger things going on. "Look," he said, pointing down.

The zombies were, at first, looking away from them into the woods. If the term curious could be used, then that is what seemed to appear on their features. Then they abruptly turned the opposite direction and started to move away from the treed victims.

Tracy half sobbed in relief. "Is this possible?"

"They're leaving!" Justin shouted.

"You have a gift, brother. No…really, you do." Travis was poking his brother.

"What are you doing?" Tracy asked Travis.

"I'm getting down, Mom. I used to think climbing trees was the best thing in the world. Now I only want to chop them all down in the hopes that, if I ever need one again, there will be none left standing."

"The zombies—"

"Looks like they're heading to greener pastures," BT said as he dropped down on the ground. Henry was squirming around, BT had no sooner let him down when he squatted and left a present that rivaled the smell of the zombies.

"Thank you, dog, for not doing *that* on my back." BT took a couple of steps away.

Henry had a look of concentration as he finished up. It must have been particularly brutal, because he didn't even do his usual turn, sniff and back leg thrust to cover it up. Like BT before him, he moved away. Justin and Travis had gotten down and were making sure the zombies were really leaving. Tracy helped Stephanie down, who was almost a ghost of her former self. Dennis had also dropped down and was staring up at Gary's form.

"Is he asleep?" he asked, shielding his eyes.

"He has to be. Why would he stay up there?" BT was also looking up while he stretched out his back. Henry was walking around with a distinct limp as he worked the circulation back into his extremities.

Dennis reached down and grabbed a stick. He started poking Gary on his legs.

Gary moaned out. "Mom, is Glenn with you? He says

it's not as light out as it should be, he also said something about the Four Horsemen of the Apocalypse. Never did like horses, Mom."

Tracy unexplainably shivered as Gary was apparently seeing two of his deceased family members.

"Gary, get your ass up." Dennis was jabbing Gary with the stick. Tracy figured he was poking him with it harder than he needed so he wouldn't have to hear what else Gary might have to say.

Gary was forgotten for the moment as they heard a horse whinny in the distance. Tracy looked to BT. He shrugged.

"Coincidence, right?" Dennis asked BT.

"I hope so." That didn't stop him from checking his rifle. "This mean we're friends now?"

"For the time being. I figure you're marginally better than pestilence," Dennis told him.

"Travis, Justin, come on back," Tracy said, loud enough for only them to hear. At least that's what she hoped. The boys were off watching the zombies retreat.

"What's going on?" Travis asked.

"We either have some biblical characters coming...or dinner," BT told him.

"What?"

"Horse, BT? You'd eat horse?" Tracy asked him.

"I'd eat the saddle right now," he told her.

"I don't want to eat horse." Justin came up alongside his brother. "The zombies are heading out. Not even looking back."

"This can't be good," Dennis said to the group. "Whatever is scaring zombies away should be bad enough for us to be leaving as well."

"I was going to give you shit for wanting to run, but I think I'm on your side with this one," BT told him.

"Not that it matters but thank you, I guess."

"It's not Revelations, I think...but we can't follow the

zombies and I believe avoiding whoever is coming would be wise. We either go up that way and follow the tree line or down the other way. When we think we've skirted around them we should go deeper in until we can find a car or something. Sound good?" Tracy asked.

"Might be too late for that." BT was urging everyone to get lower. "There's definitely more than one horse out there and right now there's no way of telling which way they're going."

Each member of the group had picked a tree to hide behind. Rifles out, they waited to acquire a target. The only thing that broke the silence was Gary's rhythmic snoring.

"Someone should probably get him." Tracy was looking directly at BT.

He started grumbling about always having to do the dirty work.

"Gary, get your ass up." BT could just touch Gary if he reached up and jumped.

"Hornets!" Gary screamed before rolling off and into BT's arms. "Well, this is awkward," he said as he looked at BT.

BT immediately put him down.

"Where are the zombies? What's going on?" Gary asked as he looked at everyone.

"Horses," Tracy told him, putting a finger to her mouth. Although she was pretty certain that whoever was out there would have heard his earlier outburst.

"Horses?" he asked, a look of confusion on his face like he was remembering that he had just forgotten something but for the life of him couldn't figure out what it was.

"I just need to let all of you know that if I see a skeleton riding one of those things, I'm going to have to leave," BT told the group.

"Don't worry, we'll all be behind you," Tracy told him.

"Yeah, definitely behind BT, because if we were in front, there would be the possibility that he would run us down. It would be like a semi hitting a VW Bug—he probably wouldn't even know he'd done it," Travis told the group.

"You know, sometimes being around a father, especially *your* father, too much can be detrimental."

"Shh," Tracy said, putting her hand out. "I think I see one." She was whispering now.

The woods got quiet as everyone trained their rifles on where they figured the horses and potential enemies from the bible would manifest themselves. The only thing that could be heard was the adjustment of leather as men sat in their saddles and the barrels of rifles as they rested against tree bark.

"Please don't be a skeleton, please don't be a skeleton," BT mumbled over and over again.

"What are you talking about?" Gary had asked at one point. "Why would there be a skeleton? Do I want to know?" He looked over at Travis who shook his head. "I liked sleeping better. I guess I'm running too if there's a skeleton."

"You're the one that puts the idea in my head and then doesn't remember? All you Talbots suck. I just want you to know that."

"What is he talking about?" Gary turned to Tracy.

She looked over at him with a gaze that said if he didn't shut up and right quick she was going to twist his nipple until it fell off. He got the hint.

"It's around here somewhere. I remember that tree, reminded me of a guy I used to hang out with."

"Trip?" Stephanie said as she stood, her rifle dropping down by her waist.

Chapter Seven – Mike Journal Entry 4

Gunfire intensified and then abruptly stopped.
'Tommy, what's going on out there?'
'Can't see much from inside this closet.'
'Big help.'
'Me being dead isn't going to do any wonders.'
*'I have really got to tone it down. I had no idea
sarcasm was contagious. Alright, when you have an
opportunity could you please let me know if you find anything
out?'*

"Any idea what's going on out there?" I asked Dixon.

"Well, she either won or she lost."

"That's about as helpful as…ummm, forget it."

There was knocking on the door. "Mr. Talbot, Mr.
Hawes, this is Captain Najarian."

"Captain, could you please enlighten us on the
situation?" Dixon asked.

"May I approach?"

"Of course," Dixon said.

I arched an eyebrow. "You unarmed?"

"Same as before."

"Then like, Monty Hall used to say, 'Come on down!'
"

"I'm curious, Mr. Talbot, were you already insane
before the vampire bite?"

"Careful, Mr. Hawes, we're not quite friends yet. Just
because we've survived this far doesn't mean both of us still
will."

"I have honored my part of the agreement; your
family is miles from here. If, however, you decide to renege
on your part, I still have the capability to pick them up at any
time."

"I knew you'd put a tracking device on that truck."

"Of course. I had to make sure you would comply and
wouldn't try an escape, kill me, or kill yourself. If anything

happens except your complete complicity, I will butcher them like livestock. Are we clear, Mr. Talbot?"

To say I wanted to snap his neck would be like saying I only wanted to be friends with Farrah Fawcett when she came out with that now famous swimsuit poster. Come on! I was thirteen, and I don't think there was a straight pubescent male on the planet that didn't fawn over that picture. It sort of lost its luster that next year when Paul decided to lick the poster in an oft-viewed portion of the portrait. I'd had to take it down because his dried saliva had left a telltale sign of his defacing. If I remember correctly, Cheryl Tiegs had taken her spot. Oh, if you only still had Google to see what I was talking about. Fantasy doesn't even begin to cover the stirrings she, erm, "aroused" in me. I hoped Dixon hadn't seen that far away dreamy look I sometimes used to get when I thought about that pink bikini.

"We're clear, Mr. Hawes, but I believe you need to rethink your stance before you go spewing at the mouth. Going to be extremely tough for you to give the order to get my family if I shove your femur down your throat first. Don't you think?"

Captain Najarian appeared just as my words had been processed in Dixon's head and he had the opportunity to realize precisely how dangerous I still was.

"What was...?" Dixon coughed to clear his throat, his voice an octave or two higher than he wished. "What was the commotion about?"

"I was right to put guards on the Talbots. Deneaux sent a team to kill them, but luckily they were long gone. We planted the room with my soldiers, so it was a pretty big surprise for them."

"The threat has been quelled then?" Dixon asked, wanting to be as far away from me as possible.

"Not quite, sir. She still has a fair number of personnel at her disposal, and she has control of the nerve center."

"Nerve center?" I asked. "It's not like this is a spaceship. What's the worst she can do? Turn off the lights? Make the temperature go up past eighty degrees? Oooh *that* would be atrocious."

"It's a little more involved than that," the captain said.

It was easy to see I'd irked him a bit. Good. Why should he be any different?

"This base runs off of nuclear power, so if she got creative, she could turn this entire facility into a thermonuclear device. That would create temperatures in excess of eighty degrees," he said sarcastically.

"Our Viv is entirely too narcissistic to blow herself up. What else can she do?" I asked.

"If she figures out Mr. Hawes' security code, she can open up the doors. That will leave us vulnerable to attack. Or she could activate the automated security system."

"Oooh, alarms!" I shook one of my hands in the air.

"I don't consider fifty caliber machineguns pivoting on a turret using laser targeting systems as something to think so casually on."

I stopped. "Yeah, me neither. Where are those things located?"

"Every hallway. She could cut down every person in this place twice before she ran out of ammunition."

"Can't they be disabled? Cut off the power or throw down a grenade? Something like that?"

The captain shook his head. "They sit behind two inches of hardened steel, and the only thing that shows is the barrel muzzle."

"What about smoke? Blind them I mean?"

"Infra-red back-up I'm afraid," Dixon said.

"You really left this woman alone in your office? What is wrong with you?" I was pacing back and forth. I never broke stride as I spoke. "Captain Najarian, you keep reaching for that Colt 1911 you have tucked in your waistline, I'm going to kill you both by repeatedly slamming your skulls together." He stopped, I kept pacing. "Okay, so your password for a place like this has to be something stupid hard, right? Like 1028-bit encryption or something. I mean, how is she going to get past that?"

Red lights began to spin on the wall as a powerful klaxon wailed three times.

"Well, it would appear she got past my security."

"So I take that to mean it wasn't some huge encryption then."

"It was her birth date."

"This is the guy you let lead you?" I asked the captain.

"The pay was good," he replied. "We should probably stay put in the cell. Once she figures out how to activate the guns, they'll be online in ten seconds."

Tommy, you'd better stay wherever you are. Deneaux all of a sudden has an army.'

'I can think of no scarier thought,' he replied in earnest.

'I'm serious—don't move. She has the ability to activate machineguns in the corridors.'

'What's wrong with this place?'

'I don't know, Tommy, I don't. I wish I did.'

'You alright?'

'Sleeping with the enemy right now, but they need me as much as I need them at the moment. So I'm okay for a bit. Would really like to get out of here soon though.'

'I don't feel too bad for you. I'm next to all the mop buckets, and I think the janitors must have had to clean up the bathrooms after a tainted chili dinner.'

'Yeah, I'll talk to you later.'

I exited out of that conversation faster than when Tracy asked me if her new jeans were slimming. I mean, honestly, the jeans looked fantastic and I could not think much beyond how I was going to get them off of her. The problem was, had I answered with, "Yes, honey, they are indeed slimming", I would have been immediately nailed with, "So I was fat-looking beforehand?" Oh, and if I had been so wrapped up in a World Series game watching the Red Sox in, like, game seven and they were up by a run in the ninth inning and I just hadn't been paying all that much attention and said, "No, they're not", well, that has its own inherent dangers built in. Men, by nature, are built for win or lose. We can deal with either scenario, sometimes poorly, other times with dignified grace. But we need to win or we need to lose. Why do you think guys are so competitive with each other? It's because we *understand* that. I beat Paul four games to three in darts, he beat me four games to three in pool. It makes sense. When cavemen would go out and hunt, they either struck gold, and brought a mammoth home, or they starved. It's win or lose, plain, simple, easy. Then women were thrown into the mix, and men have been clueless ever since as they constantly, and repeatedly, put us into situations where we can never win. The outcome is always a loss. Even when we think there is a possibility of a bright outcome they will change the rules of engagement.

I mean, honestly, can you imagine if you were playing basketball with your friends and you scored the final points and then your buddy on the opposing team says you need to hit a home run to win? I mean, where do you go from there? That's what women do to us, and it means nothing that we know this. We're still powerless to defend against it. Maybe genetically we got the brawn, but they're so beguiling that they win, hands down. Where the hell was I? Oh yeah, Deneaux has machineguns and I'm stuck.

"Dixon, honey," Deneaux's voice grated over the PA system. "Can you hear me, my darling? Has Michael killed you yet?" She cackled. "I think it's so sweet you used my birth date as your password."

"I thought they didn't make years before Jesus?" I asked, unfortunately knowing that Deneaux would not be able to hear it.

"I might not have ever guessed that, thankfully you kept it under your keyboard on a handy sticky note." She cackled again.

"You might as well have just said, 'here' when you walked out of your office," I berated him. "New World Order my ass, you're as stupid as the Old World Order that got us into this mess to begin with."

Dixon stood defiant; he wasn't a meek man, that was for certain. I wouldn't have thought him trusting either, yet he might as well have handed the keys to a Lamborghini to his fifteen-year-old son and told him not to drive it while he, himself, was out of town on business.

I turned my attention to someone who actually might have an answer. "Captain Najarian, any answers?"

He was thinking about it. "Well, she's effectively got us pinned down, and she'll be able to allow whoever is loyal to her the ability to move around. She can go on the offensive at any time. She has us divided and will be able to strike at will at each pocket of defenders."

"Move around how? Will she have to monitor their progress, shut down the gun in each corridor and then bring them back up once they're clear?"

"That's one way but it's cumbersome and not very practical in a battle situation. No, more than likely they'll have remotes."

"Like for a TV?"

"It's a little more high tech than that. It has codes that are ciphered and change every few seconds. It will automatically send out a pulse that controls the gun in whatever corridor the wearer of the remote is in, effectively shutting the gun down."

"How big is it?"

"About the size of a pack of cigarettes."

"I could go for a cigarette right now." I may have started to daydream. "Sorry...so we need to get a hold of this remote. Probably going to have our chance soon enough."

"We can't go out there." Dixon looked a little pale. It was easy sending others off to die in the name of one cause or another. It was a completely different sensation when you discovered you were being sent to the front lines, although in this case the front lines were coming to us.

"Don't sweat it," I told him. "We're not going out there." He seemed to relax, although it was easy enough to see he didn't trust me. And why should he? "They'll be coming for us soon enough."

"I suppose you're right, she can't really afford to let either one of us walk away from this."

Machinegun fire was repeatedly ripping through anyone foolish enough to test the system. Up to this point, cold, calculating steel and lead was winning every time. Yeah, so which of you reading this journal thought machines taking over the world was a far-fetched plot? Not me. Not then, and certainly not now. Here was something that held no emotion, cared for nothing or nobody. It had been created for one purpose, the destruction of life. It had been given the power and the instructions to do so. It would not be riddled with guilt. It would not suffer PTSD. It would just do its job; not happily, not sadly. Man had been trying to create the perfect soldier since at least the Spartans in ancient Greece. The perfect soldier could not contain flesh and blood, or the capacity to think. Machines take over the world? Absolutely.

"So how does this work? Do they have to get some poor bastard to stick his arm through the doorway and click the remote?"

"The opening of the door will automatically trigger it, shutting the gun off. If you don't mind my asking, why will Deneaux bother with us at all? I mean, I get why she'll have to attack some of the troops, as they will be in the way of areas vital to the operation of this facility. But we're locked away here, we can't go anywhere we can't do anything. She could just starve us out."

"Dixon, you want to answer the young captain's query?"

"Wouldn't be dramatic enough," Dixon said. "She'll most likely put our heads on spikes and parade them around as a way to deter any future trouble."

"Hadn't thought about the spikes part, but that seems fitting for her," I said. "What's the reaction time on the gun?"

"From the time its laser guiding system acquires a target and the bullets are fired." He paused to think. "It's at just about two seconds. Give or take the beat of a hummingbird's heart."

"You figure the door to this hallway at what, fifty yards?" I asked, not intending to stick my head out.

"Forty-five."

"That's pretty specific."

"I'm paid to know this place. And no, you can't make it to the door before that gun cuts you in half. It would take a world class Olympic sprinter somewhere in the neighborhood of four seconds to make that. No disrespect, but you don't look like a World Class Olympian."

"I'll have you note that I took third place in the Beer and Bong Olympiad 1987. Fucking Bennie Jacobsen, I swear the dude had an iron lung. Nobody takes a full hit from an Apogee bong and stays standing. It's just impossible."

"I don't see the relevancy."

"Oh, there's none really. I just like to say inane things right before I try stupid things."

"I've already told you that you can't possibly make this."

"Just tell me what I'm looking for."

"I would imagine the white light."

"Humor me, Captain."

Captain Najarian shook his head. "The second or third guy in the column will have a bright yellow device, most likely adhered to a special Velcro strip on the left side of his chest."

"Most likely?"

"He could just as easily have it in his pocket. It will work just as effectively from there. Mr. Talbot, I have to say it again…you cannot make it."

"Let him try," Dixon interceded as if he were doing me a favor.

I knew better. His chances of survivability increased with me out of the picture. Not great mind you—he still had Deneaux to contend with, but any percentage points of an increase was better than nothing.

"Aw, Dix, I think we've had a breakthrough," I said, touching my heart and then caressing the side of his face. He didn't share in the merriment. I could feel him shake from within. I'd like to think it was more terror than anger.

The guns had been silent for a few minutes. Whoever had thought to test their strength and resolve had either thought better of it, or was more likely dead. The time of our reckoning was coming nigh. Satan was around the bend, so to speak.

"What about Satan?" Dixon asked.

"I really said that shit out loud? Weird. Be quiet, I have to time this right."

"It's suicide." Captain Najarian was next to me, doing his best to look down the hallway at the door like I was.

"Shh. I think they're here." They really weren't trying to be all that quiet about it, and why should they? The victorious and over-confident were always boisterous. "Do not get in my way, and don't let Dix over there slide the cell door shut on me."

Dixon barely looked up from the bed he was sitting on. "Stuck between a pit viper and a mongoose."

"Pit vipers will strike out against anything. Mongooses, is that how you say the plural? Is it mongeese? Naw, that sounds weird. Whatever, a mongoose only attack the snakes. I'm assuming in your analogy that Deneaux is the viper?"

Dixon looked over at me. "I can see why she's wanted you dead."

"Are you talking about my wife or Deneaux? I just want to be clear."

"They're getting ready to open the door so whatever idea you had, you might want to put into action soon," the captain warned.

"Well, they're never really ideas," I told him as I gripped the bars to either side of me and took in three rapid breaths before pushing myself out into the hallway.

I misjudged my shove off and hit the far side wall. My heart pounded hard, blood pulsing through my system at supersonic speed. I heard the thump of it as it flashed by my eardrum. My chest vibrated from each heavy contraction. A squirt of pure adrenaline was injected into my blood stream as I watched a small slit open up in the wall directly in front of me. To the rear I could hear a series of beeps as one of Deneaux's men was keying in the entry code for the door. I looked forward and backward, lining myself up as best I could.

My legs felt simultaneously wooden and feathery. Would they fail me when the time came? My heart thudded again. Time had perceptibly slowed down. To Captain Najarian, seemingly no time had passed since I'd left the cell. To me, I think I could have read the *Iliad* and caught up on all those seasons of *Lost* I'd missed. He looked to be in slow motion as he was getting his arm in place to urge me back with a wave. We might be enemies on paper, but that didn't mean we still didn't need each other's help to deal with the bigger threat. It was safe to assume Dixon wasn't going to get his hands dirty anytime soon.

Red lasers flared out from the hole, the entire corridor was bathed in the iridescence. I simultaneously heard the sound of a round being primed into the machinegun, and the bolt being retracted in the door behind me. It was this hummingbird's heartbeat that was going to be the death of me. The walls of my heart had just contracted. I pivoted and was launching myself back into the cell. Captain Najarian was getting to the side of the door. I was halfway back when the first round exploded from the gun, the bullet close enough to burn the outer layers of my shirt, as it traveled by. It was followed by eight or nine of its buddies. The gun had followed me all the way back to the cell where Captain Najarian had helped to pull me in a fraction of second quicker.

As soon as I was in, I gripped the bar on the inside to stop my forward momentum and pull me back so that I could see if my gambit had worked. A pool of blood and the upper torso of a man who had been cut down from bullets meant for me, clogged the open doorway. Another behind him had been hit as well; this I could tell from his screams. I grabbed my rifle and started running down the corridor. Probably should have waited to make sure the remote hadn't been hit, but it was too late now as I brought the M-16 to bear and raced down the corridor. Five or six men were still trying to come to grips with what had just transpired when I opened fire. I caught two of them completely unawares. The rest were quick to recover, and by recover I mean retreat. I'd killed another and wounded a fourth, his leg leaving a marking of his trail in blood.

"Get down!" Captain Najarian was shouting as he was running up behind me, his pistol in his hands.

At first I thought it was an attempt to apprehend me. That was, of course, until bullets started to slam into the wall next to me. I dropped down to the ground as fast as gravity and commands to my muscles would allow. I let my rifle go as I braced for impact. I could hear the air around me as it was violently parted from the assault of the bullets.

Once the whine of echoing bullets died down, I rolled my head to look up at the approaching captain. "What now?" I asked. His pistol was down by his side, more or less pointing at my head by default.

"Kill him!" Dixon shouted from the cell. He'd just gotten brave enough to poke his head out.

"Pecker," Captain Najarian mumbled. As far as I knew, he could be talking about me *or* Dixon. He got closer and leaned down, extending his hand.

"I ordered you to kill him, Captain!"

"I heard you loud and clear. You want him dead so badly, take my gun and do it yourself."

I grabbed my weapon as I got to my feet. "Thanks," I told him as I stood up.

I hope that covered all the instances it was directed for. He had saved my life when he told me to duck, he had not killed me—which was a bonus—and he had helped me up. Yeah "thanks" should be fine. I walked through the door and to the man that had the remote I was looking for. His head had been completely removed. You'll note I did NOT use the adjective "neatly". Flaps of skin and skull were still holding on, and his spine was jutting up from the hole; but yeah, other than that, his head had been vaporized.

The men who had retreated from our small battle had walked right into an ambush. Another fifty cal had eviscerated them before they realized they didn't have the all-important remote. I'd seen a lot of death since this began, and to say one death was worse than another kind of trivializes the whole thing; but holy shit, what that round will do to a human being is beyond description. It was tough to tell where one body ended and the other began. It looked more like a human spare parts factory—a tooth there, a nose over there, a femur chunk in the corner. A swallowed grenade wouldn't have done as much damage.

"So we're pretty much good to go now?" I asked the captain as I slipped the remote into my pocket.

"Mostly. She can still have workarounds, but the chance that supporters of hers will know how do to it are slim. I designed the system and the back doors within it."

"That's only sort of what I meant."

"Me and you? We're fine. If we make it out of this, and Hawes is still alive, I'll have to make a show of trying to recapture you."

"How good of a show?"

"I was never a very good actor."

"Okay because that wasn't abundantly clear. I'll ask a different way. We make it through this, you'll let me go?"

He laughed a little. "Yes, Mr. Talbot, we survive and I won't lift a finger to stop you."

"But," I raised my own finger, "you also won't lend a hand either, right?"

"Correct again, I will still need plausible deniability if that should come to pass."

"Is he dead yet?" Dixon asked without looking this time.

"He seems fine to me," I said as I patted the captain's chest, looking for any bullet wounds. "Come on, Dix, we've got a coup we need to quell."

"Our deal, Mr. Talbot, is it still in effect?" Dixon asked as he walked out of the cell, nervously glancing back at the gun station that was quiet.

I'm not going to lie. I thought about tossing the remote away from me and watching Dixon get pummeled by high speed projectiles. But the man was still useful.

"I promise not to kill you, Dix, but I want to renegotiate the rest of the terms. And I swear, if you bring up my family again, I'm just going to shred your face like pulled pork. I'll help you get your little boy's club fort back, and then I think we're more than even. Wouldn't you agree?" I asked this as I casually rested my rifle barrel on my right arm, conveniently pointing at him.

I had no doubts Dixon Hawes would play the penultimate politician and promise me exactly what I wanted to hear, and when the time came, he would do exactly as he'd always intended. Odds were he was never going to truly let my family go, not with their knowing where this facility was, and also with possible thoughts of revenge on their minds.

"Even? I guess that I am inclined to believe that we are. No harm shall befall you or your family." The smile he gave me would have made a shark proud. He approached with his hand outstretched.

"I'd rather shake hands with a reptile."

"Excuse me?" he asked as we clasped grips and shook.

Here we were, two men lying to each other face-to-face, hands clasped in a sign of friendship and honor. How many times had this most basic of agreements been broken since the dawn of the gesture? I would kill him whether I got out of here or not.

"Nothing. Sorry. Any ideas, Captain?" I asked. It was easy enough to see the glares Dixon was leveling at his underling who was doing his best to ignore them.

"Yes, Captain, what should we do now?" Dixon asked sarcastically.

If body language was any indication of intent, Dixon was in more danger from his captain that he was from me at the moment.

"Reinforcements, we need to get more of my men. We'll have to be careful. Deneaux's men still have the ability to travel unhindered. And now she's going to know we've made it through," he said, pointing to a camera.

I pulled the remote from my pocket and waved to the camera, a huge grin on my face.

Chapter Eight - Mrs. Deneaux

"Son of a bitch," Mrs. Deneaux said, staring at the monitor. "I would really like to have met his mother. She probably could have showed me a thing or two." She cackled, but it was not nearly as full of mirth as it had been a few moments earlier. "Again, Michael, you have escaped what I would have thought was an unwinnable position. Why are you constantly making me feel that I have chosen the wrong side? Oh well, try and try again as my old pappy used to say."

Mrs. Deneaux pushed down on the PA system. "Michael Talbot has escaped. He is with two other fugitives outside of Cell block B. The first to kill him and his companions will be given one pound of gold."

Chapter Nine - Mike Journal Entry 5

"Wow, does she have that kind of payment lying around?"

"Yes, Fort Knox contents now reside here…or really, in actuality, always did."

"That's enough, Captain!" Dixon shouted.

"Does it really matter if he knows or not?"

"I knew those conspiracies on YouTube were right. My wife thought I was crazy, staying up all night and watching them. Said it was going to rot my brain. I think I'm just fine.

"Umm, yeah," the captain muttered. "I think we should leave. Just because there really is nowhere to spend a pound of gold doesn't mean they won't kill us trying to get it."

"I'd kill me for a pound of gold," I said.

"That can be arranged," Dixon said.

"I wonder what your hide is worth." I asked, grabbing him by the shoulder. "Wait, if you can't spend the gold what's the sense in having it here? What does it matter?"

"I'll give you the condensed version, Mr. Talbot, since you seem like a *Reader's Digest* type of person," Dixon said.

"Is that a slight? I've always liked the 'Humor in Uniform' section."

"Me too," Captain Najarian added.

"Every country since the dawn of man has collapsed. It's an inevitability. The average citizen did not think this could happen, especially modern day Americans who were lulled into a false sense of security. On average, this country was tested to its limits every fifty years—the war of 1812, the Civil War, WWI, and WWII. It was after the Second World War that the government recognized the pattern and started to design ways to keep its people in line. A big part of that was television news. Fear mongering were the words they used. The easiest and most effective way to control a populace is through fear."

"Come on, you're going to tell me that Walter Cronkite helped usher in the modern era of trepidation?"

"He was handpicked by the CIA because of his perceived trustworthiness as an individual. Fear of the Communists, fear of drugs, fear of terrorists, fear of your pedophile neighbor—this keeps people in line. They are too busy and concerned with all these other threats to give their government, who supposedly protects them, much more than a secondary glance. Our goal had always been to show the government for what they truly were."

"And replace it with what? What you have here? Oh, you've done brilliantly. Can't tell you how much better this is, as opposed to sitting at the DMV all day. I hope you guys really focus on cleaning up bureaucracy."

"We really should get going," Captain Najarian urged.

I wanted to tell him that I was just going to need a moment while I picked up a smug Dixon by his ankles and then kind of swung him around until I smashed his head against whatever got in the way. Instead, I nodded and let him lead on. The stealth with which we moved seemed relatively pointless, because at every new corridor we entered, Deneaux would announce our location over the PA.

"I don't know which of you two assholes I want to kill worse," I said after Deneaux made her newest broadcast. "I mean Dixon or Deneaux. Not you," I assured the captain when he turned to look at me.

'Tommy, where are you?'

'Heading your way.'

'How do you know that?'

'I joined in with a column of armed men running. I've been around you long enough to know they're most likely going toward you in an attempt to kill you.'

'That's sort of funny in a strange way.'

'I thought you might like it.'

'You catch the part about the remote?'

'Working my way past each man, haven't seen it yet. Might have it in a pocket or something.'

"Oh, this is going to be good," came over the public address system.

I had to think Deneaux had pushed the button inadvertently. Maybe, maybe not. It would sort of be like her to torture her victims first but unlike her to give advance warning.

"I'm going to shove a cigarette in her eye the next time I see her," I said as the captain and I took defensive positions. Dixon was behind the captain as we tried to hug the walls.

'Tommy, you'd better be careful. If you come through the door, there's a good chance you'll end up shot.'

'I haven't found the remote.'

'Get out of there then. Wait...first tell me how many there are.'

'Thirteen.'

'Well, at least it's a nice lucky number.'

'Not for them.'

The door to our corridor was just opening when the rifle shots rang out. The captain looked to me, but I was already on the move and heading to the door. Tommy was firing on the group he was traveling with; he had the element of the surprise, but once they regrouped, he'd be in some serious trouble.

I've got to give the captain credit—he didn't so much as furrow his eyebrows trying to figure out what I was doing. He followed quickly. Dixon didn't; no surprise there. Tommy had taken four down by the time I got to the doorway. The rest were all in various states of turning to look for their attacker, so none of them had the good fortune to be looking toward my doorway. The first man was so close I didn't even need to aim. I just pressed the barrel against his side and let loose a three round burst that I'm sure tattered his insides.

I was firing again as he fell away and was three deep in death by the time the remaining four realized they were in a crossfire.

"Drop the weapons!" Captain Najarian shouted, his M-16 pointed at the head of one of Deneaux's troops.

"Pathetic!" Deneaux shouted.

The man Captain Najarian had dead to rights sealed the fate of those with him when he attempted to swing his rifle around. The captain didn't hesitate as he shot him in the head. Those left knew they were going to face a firing squad anyway and opted for another way out. I didn't blame them for their decision. Who wants to sit in a cell waiting for the inevitable? I'd rather take my chances in the heat of battle rather than in the cold realization of execution.

Tommy had taken some hits; one to the leg and the other to his side. If he was in pain, he hid it well.

"You alright?" I asked him, looking at the blood on his stomach.

He nodded.

"Thank you," I told him.

He nodded again, looking grim. For all the death he'd seen over his entire existence he had never gotten used to it. In fact, if anything, he was probably getting more sensitive to it as he got older.

"Come on, let's get Dixon and get out of here." I turned to go back the way we'd come.

"Two pounds of gold for Michael Talbot's head!" Deneaux shouted, upping the ante.

"Wow, that's just about a pound for pound payment," Tommy smiled.

"No it's not, an average head is like fifteen pou—oh, I get it. Fucking hilarious. Maybe you and BT can go on the road with your show."

"Dixon's gone," the captain said after checking the corridor.

"How is that even possible?" I asked and then it dawned on me. "Bastard had a remote on him, didn't he? He must have shut it off hoping I'd get killed out there in that hallway. Why are people with power so corrupt? Does the power do it? Or are the people that seek it out already infected with an inherent flaw?"

"Usually a little of both." Tommy had come up beside me.

"You're Tomas?" Captain Najarian asked a bit of trepidation in his voice.

Tommy nodded.

I could see that the captain had more questions but just then Deneaux spoke over the p.a.

"Did your fearless leader abandon you?" She asked.

I would have flipped her the finger, but she would have taken that as a sign of victory, and I wouldn't give her that satisfaction. I instead turned away from the camera, quickly undid my belt and dropped my pants, bending over to give her a view I hoped she wouldn't soon forget. I was rewarded with a scratchy cackle that quickly devolved into a coughing fit.

"Oh, Michael, I will sorely miss you when this is over. You make the end of times a hoot," Deneaux managed to get out during her choking fit.

"Someday, if we have more time, you're going to have to tell me how you met," Captain Najarian said as I quickly fastened my belt back.

"*That's* what you want to know if we survive? Fine. Where to?"

"The plan is the same, we have to get some help and then we have to get to Deneaux."

An alarm tore through the complex, lasting a good long two minutes before it was silenced.

"Michael, we have a problem," Deneaux said.

"No shit!" I yelled back. I think she could hear me, but you didn't need to be a lip-reading genius to pick up on what I'd mouthed.

"I'm talking about something besides this little stand-off you and I are in the midst of."

"Stand-off? You call trying to kill me repeatedly and then placing a heft bounty on my head a stand-off? Sure…okay." I shook my head.

"Are you done now? I've seen Hollywood starlets less inclined to drama than you."

"Is she kidding?" I asked Tommy. "You're trying to kill me. How should I be acting?"

"Was."

"Was what?"

"I *was* trying to kill you. Now I'm not so inclined."

"Prove it, call off your men."

"Such little faith, Michael," she sighed. "Anyone trying to kill Michael Talbot or those he travels with I will rip their testicles off with my bare hands. Happy now?"

"Better, but that visual is going to haunt me forever. Why the sudden détente?"

"We're about to have a bigger problem, one that you and your cohort are better equipped to handle."

"And what would that be?"

"Zombies. Thousands of them, in fact."

"In here? How is that possible? Didn't I tell you to lock up after letting the dog back in?"

"Zombies can't get in here. It's impossible." The captain was pacing. "Nothing can get in here without passing through at least five security measures."

"I got in," Tommy told him, quieting the captain immediately. However, it did not stop his pacing.

"Maybe that's possible. I mean, you're basically superhuman and you can think. But a zombie? A mindless eating machine can't possible get through."

"Zombies think," I told him, probably ruining what was already a bad day for him. "I'm not sure they'll ever get to the point where they could work their way through a standard tax form, but they can think. They're learning and adapting, that I know for sure."

"Any reference in the whole world you could have come up with, like maybe the theory of relativity or building a rocket and you use taxes?"

"Ever done taxes, Tommy?" I got him to clam up almost as fast as Captain Najarian had.

"How are they getting in?" the captain asked Deneaux.

"Someone has opened all the doors. They're flooding in."

"How is this possible?" The captain whipped his hat off and was running his hand through his short hair. "Mrs. Deneaux, you have to shut them!"

"I would, sonny, and I probably wouldn't even have bothered you three with this trivial matter if not for the red lettered override message that keeps flashing over the monitor."

"Override? How is that even possible? Can I have safe passage to you?" He was already walking before she could answer.

"Are we going with him?" Tommy asked me.

"Better to see what our enemy is up to, don't you think?"

"This could be a trap, Mr. T."

"Potentially. But this isn't really the way Deneaux operates. She's much more into the theatrics of the kill. I don't think she'd enjoy it half as much if we just walked into her snare."

"You sure about that?"

"Not really, I'm making this up as I go. I believed her implicitly when she said zombies were coming, but I guess it really could be a trap. What the hell is wrong with me? The woman has been trying to kill me and now I'm going to drop everything and see if I can help her. Well, I guess not so much her. All of us."

"Have you convinced yourself yet?"

"I'm getting there," I told him as we followed the captain. I kept a vigilant look out for anything unusual. But just by the definition of a trap I most likely wasn't going to notice anything until it was too late. "Any tingling going on? Can you sense anything?"

"I'm not Spiderman, Mr. T."

"Figured it was worth a shot."

"You ready?" Captain Najarian asked as we approached a rich mahogany door that seemed completely out of place in this military installation.

I didn't even need to see the nameplate next to the door to know whose it was. Only a pompous ass like Dixon would need to have this door specifically put in.

The captain knocked.

"Help!" Dixon shouted out.

I shrugged to Tommy. "At least we know where he went."

The captain pushed the door open quickly and then scanned the room, his pistol pointing wherever he was looking. I followed immediately behind. Deneaux was sitting behind a huge, most likely mahogany, desk; an impossibly large revolver sitting in front of her on a blotter. She had a cigar in her hand, a large plume of smoke encircling her head. Residual smoke leaked out from a wry smile.

"Hello, Michael," she said, rising. "Good to see you." She extended a hand, which I avoided. "Oh, come now, we can be civil about this, can't we?"

"Civil? Are you shitting me?" I advanced.

On all that was holy, I should have just raised my rifle up and blown her into whatever realm she belonged. My abject fear was that the bullets would pass right through her as if she were ethereal, holding no more substance than the smoke swirling around the room. That would be when the ambient lighting would turn red and she would begin to laugh at me in an unnaturally deep demon spawn sound. I hadn't crapped my pants since I was an infant, but if that happened, all bets were off.

"I need help!" Dixon yelled.

I'd been so focused on Deneaux that I hadn't even seen the man. He was sitting in an over-sized chair facing Deneaux, his hands clamped over a wound in his thigh. A pretty messy one if the blood leaking past his fingers was any indication.

"She shot me!"

"Stop being dramatic, darling, I barely winged you. Really it's your fault anyway. You come in here ranting and raving, screaming and shouting. You made me nervous with your threats to seek retribution. What did you expect me to do when I felt that my life was threatened?"

"You shot me as soon as I opened the door!"

She paused and looked at him. "Would those things not have happened?"

"Preemptive strike? That sounds about right," I said. "Why bother dealing with words when you can get right down to the meat of the problem by shooting it?"

"Oh, come now, Michael. Please tell me you are not crying for this man. Given the chance, he will kill you and feel nothing. I, at least, will have a momentary pang of guilt."

"A momentary pang? Would that be because of the half dozen or so times I have saved your ass?"

"We do not have time for verbal sparring, Michael. This facility is quickly being overrun with zombies, and we have either got to defend against them or find a safe way to exit."

"I'm sure Tommy, myself, and the captain here, if he wants, could get out of here just fine. But I can't think of any reason why I would want to saddle myself to you again."

"No reason at all, Michael? Strange—I can think of nine."

"That's a pretty specific number, Deneaux. What are you getting at?"

"It is the number of loved ones you have that left this facility."

"If you do anything to them—" I surged toward her. Tommy held me back.

"Don't be so crass. I would not hurt them. But Dixon here, he would…without a moment's hesitation. Isn't that right?" she asked as she came from behind the desk. She stroked the side of his face with her palm. He pulled away and winced as the movement caused him pain in his wound.

"Just spill it, Deneaux. We don't have time for you to play out the drama and intrigue in your little soap opera performance."

I looked over at the wall of monitors. Zombies were beginning to dominate the cameras that were trained on entry points. Soldiers were effectively repelling them, but it was only a matter of time. The outside shot showed a horde that made the last stand at Little Turtle or even at Carol's farm seem like child's play. No, this was a coordinated, directed attack. But who could wield that much power? Eliza's name screamed across my brain, enough so that Tommy recoiled.

"Did I ever tell you I did a stint on *As the World*—"

"Villain, right? Had to be. Come on, Deneaux, I really just want to kind of kill you both and get back to my family."

"I was actually the twin sister of one of the stars, which was funny, because we looked nothing alike. Yes, I was the villain. I shot her husband after we slept together and he realized I wasn't his wife. He said he'd known because we'd done things he'd never done before."

"Gross, just gross." I had a crappy taste in my mouth.

"Handsome man, unfortunately he was a lemon squeezer." She was looking off to a far-gone time.

"Yes, horrible. Agree with her, Tommy." I smacked him on the shoulder.

"Horrible," he said, looking at me. "What's a lemon squeezer?"

I shrugged.

She whipped back to the present in less than heartbeat. "The satellites, Michael. He will track your family and you, should you escape. He needs what you carry inside, and no matter what he promises, he will do everything in his power to attain it. As for your family, they are now collateral damage. Had you not taken him prisoner, they would already be dead. I saved them."

"You?"

"Yes me. I called back the drones."

"You launched drones!?" I asked Captain Najarian. I was in his face. Any closer and I might have to take him out for dinner.

"I had my orders." He stood tall under my withering gaze.

"Funny, that's the same defense the Germans at Auschwitz used. It wasn't adequate then, and it sure as shit isn't adequate now. I thought you were one of the decent ones." I grabbed him by the throat and immediately applied enough pressure to cut off his air supply.

No one moved, not even Tommy. Deneaux looked on with a smug sort of satisfaction and maybe the tiniest of glints in her eyes like she was either excited or scared; or more likely both from what was going on. Captain Najarian wrapped his hands around my arm as I lifted him off the ground.

"Mr. T, he could still help us get out of here." Tommy took a step closer but, as of yet, had not interfered.

"Are you saying I shouldn't crush the life out of him?"

"I'm not saying he isn't worthy of a cruel death, I am merely saying that, much like Mrs. Deneaux wants to use us for her own means, we can do the same with the captain."

"Looks like it's your lucky day, Captain," I said as I rattled him about a couple of times and unceremoniously dropped him to the floor.

He drew in great ragged breaths, his hands caressing his neck. I stepped over him and to the shrinking form of Dixon. "So much for the deal," I said to him as I moved his hands aside to see the bullet wound Deneaux had put in his thigh.

"What...what did you expect me to do?" He was near to crying. "What are you going to do...!" It trailed off into a scream as I stuck my index finger up to the second knuckle in his wound. "Man, who knows where my hands have been today. A good chance this is probably going to get infected." I was wiggling my finger around. I laid my right arm across Dixon's chest, holding him down like a vise as I probed deeper. "Damn, I'm almost all the way through."

Even Deneaux winced. "Really, Michael, is that necessary?"

"Don't you even start!" I pulled my finger out from Dixon's wound, it made a large satisfying sucking sound as I did so. I was now pointing that blood covered digit at Deneaux. She stared transfixed at the fat droplets of blood as they fell from it. The bat was something—she didn't so much as flinch.

"We kill, Michael. All of us in this room, we kill. Don't be so shocked by it, and don't even try to deny it. I know what you're thinking, that you killed them all to ensure the safety of your family. Can you honestly hold that truism for each and every one of them? Weren't there at least a few times where it wasn't directly related to self-defense or family preservation but rather it was more advantageous if he or she were dead?"

"This is different, Deneaux. He was going to kill my family in cold-blood, my innocent family."

"Innocent?" she scoffed. "They knew about this place, he was protecting his own by eliminating them. Would you have let a hostile force leave your brother's home to get reinforcements? He was defending what is dear to him. Look at that wheel spinning in your head; it is a sight to behold."

"You've muddied the waters enough, Deneaux. What point are you going to make that changes my mind about your and Dixon's fate?"

"This deal is for me, he is on his own."

Even through his misery Dixon took the time to shoot a glare at Deneaux. "How did your husband put up with you for so many years?"

"As long as he did what I told him to do, we got along fabulously. I warned you not to go down to Michael's cell. I told you when I found out he and his family were here that you should kill them immediately. No offense," she said to me.

I waved it off. I was offended, but she would not have cared.

"How did not listening to me work out, Dixon?"

"Fuck you, Vivian."

"You wanted to, didn't you? If you had played your cards right this all could have been yours."

I'm pretty sure if she'd had a skirt or a dress on she would have pulled the front up. Tommy turned away, embarrassed. I was wondering if I could make it to the waste bucket in time to launch my lunch into it. "Wow, how did that become the most disturbing thing the day has yet to offer? Deneaux, out with it, we're running short on time. Why am I not going to kill you along with my buddy Dix here?"

If his wound in his leg didn't hurt so much, and wasn't gushing blood because of my ministrations, I think Dixon would have taken this time to make a run for it.

"I can disable the computer system in this facility...forever," she added at the end when I didn't immediately react.

I was about to tell her "big fucking whoop" when I finally figured it out. "No computers, no satellites."

She touched her nose. "Exactly."

"You can't!" Captain Najarian said as loudly as his

tortured throat would allow, which wasn't much above a hoarse, whispered yell. "You'll be condemning the lives of thousands."

"Pity," Deneaux said. "What of it, Michael?"

"If I kill Dixon what does it matter?" I asked.

"Do you truly believe that someone else, perhaps even the captain here, will not immediately take hold of the throne? There are always more idiots. Isn't that one of your lines?"

"Could be. Sounds vaguely familiar."

"As much as I'd like to tell you to take your time, we can't, Michael. The zombies are on a different timetable than us."

"Mr. T?" Tommy asked. Was he asking for my decision, or why I was even contemplating it? Who the fuck knew?

"How many times can one make a deal with the devil before something gets firmly entrenched up an anal cavity or two?" I was looking straight at Deneaux, but if I was looking for some sort of a "tell" from her I was barking up the wrong tree. The woman could look a crying baby holding a kitten, in the face on Christmas day, and not show a lick of emotion. Unless, of course, maybe if a snake was trying to eat the baby, then she might crack the corner of her parched and withered lips.

Eliza was evil incarnate, you knew where you stood with her at all times. She wanted you dead, always and at any cost, pretty easy to figure her out. Deneaux, on the other hand, well it all came down to what purpose you could serve to better her life. She was a constant shifting sea of ambitions and conditions. You were safe if that suited her and dead if not. Trust was not something you could ever hope to achieve with Deneaux, the best you could hope for was a platform of mutually assured destruction.

"Kill the system. I'll take your ass out of here, but once we're safer…we part ways. I am not bringing you with me."

"Those are acceptable terms."

I grabbed Captain Najarian's arm, as he seemed like he wanted to jump over the desk and stop her as she performed a set of keystrokes. The lights in the room flickered, and the monitors behind Deneaux got grainy, went to complete white static and then blackness. While I was watching all of this transpire, I took note that the captain's struggle against my hold was now lackluster at best.

"How do you know I won't just kill you now?" I asked her.

"How long do you think I've been dancing this dance, Michael? No matter the state of your soul or lack thereof, you still have a moral compass."

She let that comment sink in. I've got to admit, hearing her say it out loud hurt a little more than I figured it would, and I'm not talking about the part about the compass. Although if she truly knew how far out of whack it was now that I was no longer moored to a soul, she might not be so smug. Sometimes that needle spun like I was going through the Bermuda Triangle.

"We need to leave. I suggest you finish Dixon off so that we can."

"Bitch," Dixon heaved out.

"And perhaps the captain if he doesn't want to join us."

"Wow, you are something special," I said sarcastically.

"Coming from you, my dear, I will take that as a compliment. Well, I do believe it is time to go."

"Naw, not quite yet. Something stinks here, and I know all about bad smells; I have an English Bulldog after all. See, you might be a world-class deceiver, Deneaux. Shit, you probably taught the devil a thing or two to hone his craft. But the captain here, well, he's a different story. He should be a lot more distraught about you having just destroyed their safe haven. I mean, I would imagine this is one of the last bastions on US soil. And like he said, there are thousands here who rely on this place. Not only for food and shelter, but also for research and obviously for the grand designs of taking over a crippled planet and ruling it as any normal sociopath would. For all I know you just changed the channel."

"I can assure you I have wiped the computer system clean," she said calmly as she smoothly produced a cigarette from who knows where. I hadn't even seen her put the cigar down.

"That's it? No redundancies? Even at home I had an external hard drive in case my system crashed. Got to be a room full of servers that will have this thing back online and up and running before we can get halfway out of here."

"How would I know? Do I look like a member of the Geek Patrol?"

"Squad," I corrected.

"Squad, Patrol, what's the difference?"

"Well, the fact that you even know about them lends credence to my argument. Look at you, my little liar," I cooed. "Playing both ends against the middle. You get me to take you out of here, but always leaving the option that Dix here will be able to track you down and save you or, if he was smart, put a cruise missile up your ass. I'm going to need more proof that this place is shut down, or I'm not leaving, and I'll gladly kill everyone in this room, save Tommy, to get the answers I want."

"Appreciate that, Mr. T."

"No problem, Tommy."

"I need medical attention." Dixon grimaced.

"I bet," I said to him as I pushed the captain down into the chair next to him.

We all looked to the door as gunfire erupted down the hallways.

"We really should be going," Deneaux said to me. I

don't think she was overly nervous, but she did have an air of concern about her.

"Where are the servers?" I asked Captain Najarian.

"I don't know what you're talking about."

I squeezed his shoulder so hard I thought it was going to pop. He was a tough one, though; I didn't get much more than a slight groan from him, and he never tried to pull away.

"How about you, Dix?" I asked as I extended my still bloody finger.

"I can't tell you."

At first I thought it was because perhaps somehow he didn't know, but he surprised me with his honesty instead.

"If you destroy them, I will lose my chance to rule the world."

"I can't say I was expecting you to say that. Most people who are attempting to rule the world really don't just come out and say it. Must be the pain clouding your judgment; because I don't know how you think I would possibly let this place stand after you admitted that."

"You stupid, little man, Dixon," Deneaux seethed.

"Are you on my side now, Deneaux, or are you just admonishing him for taking one of your options away?" I asked her.

She smiled and, as she took an impossibly long drag from her cigarette, I think half of it disappeared with that one intake. Almost like she was using an iron lung to get her nicotine input.

Once again I jabbed a finger in Dixon's wound, he howled in excruciation. I got to give it to the old bird—he didn't crack. I wouldn't have thought he had it in him.

"Mr. T, time is running short." Tommy was peeking out the door.

"Not for Dix here. I'm sure it's stretching into an unbelievable eternity every time I wriggle my finger."

"Michael, you should heed the boy," Deneaux said.

"Viv, Viv, Viv. In the short time we have gotten to

know each other, have I never done what I said I was going to or at least attempted it?"

"You will promise me that you will do everything in your power to assure my safety while we escape this place."

"Is that more of a statement or a question?" I asked her.

"Answer me, Michael, and I will give you the information you want."

"You can't!" Dixon shouted, attempting to stand.

"Oh, I assure you I can, Dixon. Michael has an uncanny ability to follow through."

"I don't fucking believe this, I'm going to get stuck with Deneaux again."

"That is your word, you will honor it," she said.

I tipped my head.

"It's two corridors down, third door on the right. Door says, 'RAID Servers One through Thirty-Six.' "

"Tommy?" I asked. He was keeping an eye on the corridor.

"It's clear for now, but whatever's coming is close."

"What are you going to do with these two?" Deneaux asked, attempting to separate herself from her former allies.

"You bitch," Dixon hissed again, seemingly stuck on this one word. Couldn't blame him, maybe vary it up a bit though, I'm sure she'd heard that word so many times before that it had lost its impact.

"This?" I asked. "You're mad about this? She does this shit all the time. Gotta tell you, it's nice not being on your end for once."

"I'm sorry, Dixon. A girl's got to do what a girl's got to do."

'Girl?' I thought-sent to Tommy. 'I'm thinking that ship sailed a long time ago and probably ran on steam as well.'

Tommy laughed, that in itself was funny because it was so out of context.

"You'll need to kill him, Michael," Deneaux said, pointing to Dixon. "He will not stop until he has exacted his revenge. I may be cunning, but he is ruthless. You must remember, he has killed over ninety percent of the world's population in an attempt to rule over the remainder. His hands are not simply wet with blood, they are stained with it."

I knew he needed to be killed. This was the kind of shit that always got me in trouble. Good guys (okay, perceived good guys) always let the bad guys go when they have them dead to rights. It's one thing to kill a man in combat; it's expected. But the first thing a bad guy does when he is losing is plead for forgiveness, because he knows there's a good chance he's going to get it. Obviously, if the roles are reversed, the good guy is going to get drilled in the forehead; that's why the bad guy is the bad guy. Being the good guy, always encumbered with morals and mercy, can be a pain in the ass. It's tough to shoot a man with his hands in the air, no matter how much you want to. And yeah, Dixon's hands were technically not in the air but rather protecting his wound, still…it's the same thing.

"I'm not going to kill him in cold blood," I told her.

"For Christ's sake, aren't you supposed to be the one without the soul?" she asked as she picked up her revolver. Dixon didn't even have time to beg for his life or even attempt to stop the bullet with his hands as she placed one pretty much center mass in his sternum.

"What the fuck?!" I had backed up.

"He would have become a problem, Michael. I fancy myself a problem-solver."

"I thought maybe at one time you had loved him."

"*Love*? *Him*? Don't be so naïve. You do know that love is merely a chemical reaction within the brain, right? The mingling of pheromones? It is no more the connecting of souls than basket weaving is to fine art."

"Huh? I thought I was the one that made the bad

analogies."

"I am saying that I love a good butter cookie. That has use to me as I let the taste and texture melt on my tongue. Love for people is a myth. It is a weakness that allows us to be exploited. Even in a happy relationship, Michael, did you not feel that your love was used against you?"

"I'm pleading the fifth." But when I thought about it, how many home projects had I undertaken, how many errands, how many crappy obligations had I lost a weekend to, all in the name of love? "Fuck if I'll ever admit you're right."

"You don't need to," she replied as she opened up her revolver and exchanged the spent round for a fresh one.

"I have got to stop talking out loud. You've got it wrong though, Deneaux. I do believe some people are destined to be with others. Do I have to occasionally do some shitty stuff? Sure, but those nights when Tracy and I could just share them between the two of us with no outside distractions—that's when the magic happened. And I'm not just talking about sex, some of the best nights I've ever had are when we just laid there in each other's arms. Love...it is a tangible thing that you can feel. It's a powerful feeling to know that someone always has your back."

"That's a lie!" she shot back. "When things are at their worst, individuals will always choose themselves over another. We are programmed to survive! Altruism is a fable. People save others so they can feel good about themselves."

"I don't know what happened to you that set you down this path, Deneaux, but your bitterness has caused you to miss out on some of the best things this life has to offer."

"Pssh." She waved me off as she closed her cylinder. She pointed the revolver at Captain Najarian. "What of him?"

"Captain?" I asked, truly hoping he would come along for the ride. Deneaux would plant him in that seat if he so much as flinched in the negative.

"A vampire, a half-vampire, and a crazy bat. Of

course I'm in."

"Splendid," Mrs. Deneaux said as she lowered her weapon.

"We really should be on our way." Tommy pulled back into the office.

"Can I have my weapon back?" the captain asked.

I was about to tell him sure when Deneaux spoke. "We'll just wait a bit on that."

"She's about as trusting as a mole," Tommy said.

"What?" I asked him.

"Moles are known as one of the least trusting animals in the animal kingdom."

"You're kidding, right? Forget it; let's get to that server room so we can get out of here."

As we moved out, constant gunfire reverberated throughout the hallways. Whenever there was a lull, it was punctuated with the screaming of men being devoured alive. More than once, the ground would shake as if someone was pulling pins on grenades or launching handheld missiles.

When the echoes from those large explosives would die down, you could sometimes hear the moaning of the undead as they seemed to mourn the passing of their humanity. That might be a little bit of an embellishment, as I'm sure it had more to do with the pit in their stomach caused by the endless need to eat the flesh of living beings. I liked the "mourning" theory better, though. It meant there was still some shadow of a person left. Well, shit, maybe that was worse. What would that shadow think as they were tearing out the throat of a child? Yeah, maybe the gnawing hunger thing was a better angle.

We saw a total of five soldiers as we headed to the server room. They were hauling ass. It was impossible to tell if they were heading into or away from the fray. Two of the men had expressions on their faces like they'd just caught their mother with their uncle in a compromised position and couldn't get away fast enough. Two of the others looked like

Mark Tufo

they'd just caught their wife with their best friend and were going to kill both. I think the other was probably a professional card player back in his day. He could have been going out for a turkey sandwich with the expression he wore.

"We're here," Tommy said as he gripped my shoulder. I'd been so intent on looking for imminent danger, I wasn't even paying attention to the doors we were passing.

I twisted the handle, it didn't move. Captain Najarian sidled up next to me and swiped a card he had hanging from a lanyard around his neck.

"Pretty good idea you didn't shoot him now," I said to Deneaux.

"Why? I could have just taken that card from his dead body."

"Shit, she's cold," the captain mumbled.

"Yup," I said as I opened the door.

I don't know what I was expecting to see. I guess I was hoping for one large computer in the middle of the room that had a sign above it reading, "Back-up machine 1001" and I could put a couple of rounds in it and be gone. The room was massive—maybe forty by forty—and just flat out crammed with black boxes with varying lights blinking in greens, reds and the sporadic yellow. I could empty all my rounds in here and not feel confident I'd taken out the beast.

"Maybe we can snag a rocket launcher."

"No time, Mr. T."

"Shit." I was rubbing a hand through my hair. "Everyone in. We're going to tear each one of these down and smash the hell out of it."

"That'll take hours, Mr. T. I think we have minutes."

"I don't give a shit; I'm not leaving here as long as I know this place can come back on line. Dixon might be dead, but there's never a limit on power-hungry assholes, and someone will want revenge. I get that, but they're not going to have this advantage to do it. I will not allow my family to be in this degree of danger. Look at that, Deneaux. I am doing a selfless, sacrifice for my family because I love them."

She sneered. "It's not doing you any good, you'll be dead." She turned her attention to the captain. "Initiate the Data Dump."

"What?" he asked.

"Do you believe I will shoot you in your balls?"

The captain moved over to a small workstation set in the corner without saying so much as a word. "I believe you would," I told her.

"So does he." She motioned with her gun.

"What the hell is a Data Dump?"

"I've yet to come across a clandestine group that didn't have one. It is the ability to effectively and permanently destroy all data housed on the hard drives. And more importantly it's much quieter than smashing."

"And you can tell if he's actually doing it?" We were both watching the captain and the monitor he was staring at, a stream of code flashing by the screen.

"Would you attempt deception if your manhood was on the line?"

"Good point. I hate to admit it, but sometimes having you on my side has its bonuses. I can't believe I just said that. I really need to think before I talk." I walked away. I took note that the lights on many of the servers began to blink rapidly and then one by one began to turn off.

"It's done," the captain stood, "I killed them all. Looks like you and I can be bunkmates in hell," he said to Deneaux.

"I like my privacy," she said.

I knew what was coming next.

"NO!" I tried to make it back to her. Fucking Deneaux—I'm pretty sure she was a faster draw than Doc Holliday, and she'd already had her gun out. The shot sent the captain spinning into the workstation. One of the legs collapsed on the table as he landed on it. The monitor shattered as it crashed onto his head. He died in a shower of sparks.

"What are you doing?" I skidded to halt at the captain's feet.

"He programmed most of this, I'm sure he had some sort of retrieval code built in," she said as evenly as if she'd just ordered a salad for lunch.

"Are you sure?"

"No, I'm not *sure*," she spat, saying that last word with a nasal pitch; I think just to get my goat. Who am I shitting? Of course she did it to ruffle my feathers. "Did you really want to take the chance, Michael? What do you think the captain would have done once he came across some of his men? Do you believe he would just let us go? He might not have been as power hungry as Dixon, but he was most certainly not going to let this prized jewel slip into the night."

I knew she was right; instinctually, I knew the hag was right. It's just that her methods went so against the grain of everything I believed in. "When can I expect my own bullet?"

"It's not like I'm going to tell you, Michael. Let's go." Her cylinder clicked closed a moment after the tinkling of an empty brass casing hit the floor and bounced into a spreading pool of Captain Najarian's blood…where it would most likely reside for all eternity. I couldn't help but think it looked a lot like the sap that covered the mosquito in *Jurassic Park*. Who knows, maybe some advanced humanoids or possibly aliens would unearth this structure someday far in the future and clone the captain. My guess is that he would go hunting for Deneaux as soon as he was able. The fucking bat would probably still be around.

We weren't more than ten feet from the server room door upon exiting when the first of the zombies rounded the corner from a side hallway. Eagle Eye behind me drilled him in the forehead from twenty-five yards. My ear rang from the explosion. I felt the heat from her barrel as the bullet left the chamber, that's how damn close it was to my head. A few more inches and she could have just separated my brain bucket from the rest of me. I grabbed her arm and pulled her flush with me.

Tommy looked like a commando as he fired controlled rounds into the oncoming storm. It wasn't going to be enough, not by a long shot as the corridor was flooding with zombies. The damn had broken, and the ground was wet with them.

"Ready to run, Deneaux?" I asked as I tapped Tommy on the shoulder and pointed behind us.

"That's why I have my tennis shoes on."

Tennis shoes, who calls them that? This I thought, as there wasn't enough time to verbalize. Speeders, deaders, bulkers, skullers (the ones with the extra thick skull plating) were all in front us, so thick that their forward progress was being hampered by their sheer volume. Had to have been fifteen feet from wall-to-wall in the passageway, and they were wedging themselves in tight trying to get to us. Did the ones in the middle even know what they were chasing or were they just being pulled with the tide? In the end, it really didn't matter much. When we got what I figured was a safe enough distance away, I would stop and quickly pop off some shots. Wound or kill; I didn't care as long as I could potentially make a choke point.

"How big is this friggin' place?" I asked as I once again caught up to Tommy and Deneaux. I let my empty magazine fall to the ground as I shoved in a new one. "Two left," I said, more to myself.

Deneaux was keeping a pretty decent pace, but even demons get tired. She had most likely been one of the ringleaders who had wanted to cast stones at Jesus's Mary. Her age was catching up to her and she was beginning to flag. Why, why, why couldn't I just cut her loose? She'd served her purpose. She'd shut this base down and gotten rid of two viable threats. All I had to do was basically…nothing.

Just keep running. The zombies would overtake her, and it would be over.

But nope, no it wouldn't, the thought dawned in my head. She'd shoot us both. Sure as shit she would. If she couldn't make it, nobody would.

"Tommy, you want to shoot or carry?"

"What?" He figured it out as soon as he looked at Deneaux. I was wondering if he was thinking the same thing.

'Why won't her fucking heart just burst? I thought to him. *'Something that small, shriveled and underused can't be of much good. And her damn lungs have got to be bits of charcoal by now, don't they? She must have smoked three packs a day for something near to three thousand years...that's like a billion coffin nails. But no, not this one, the cigarettes are too scared to give her cancer.'*

'Hate has its own power.'

"At least I didn't say that out loud."

"Perhaps he should carry you." Deneaux took in a big breath. Looking down to her pocket, I knew what she was thinking. She was wondering if she could get a drag from a cigarette before the zombies caught up.

Tommy quickly handed me his magazines and scooped up an indignant Deneaux. "You are more solid than I would have thought," Tommy told her.

"That's not an appropriate thing to say to a lady." Now that she realized she had the time, she dug for that cigarette she'd been pining for.

I laid down another ten rounds to give us a little breathing room between the deadly tide and us. We could still hear fighting going on around us, I couldn't make up my mind if it was worth going toward or away from the sound. Both paths had their own inherent dangers built in.

"What about the labs?" I shouted out in question.

Tommy's shoulders sagged, as he knew what I was asking. We had to do our best to find Porkchop and Doc.

Chapter Ten – The Lab

"I thought we'd have those new blood samples by now," June commented as she once again peered up from her microscope.

"You know, no matter how many times you look at those slides, that virus isn't going to reanimate," Will replied, smiling.

She hated that he'd used that word. Since the zombies had "reanimated" people, her life had devolved into nothing more than work. There wasn't a family out there that she pined for, but she mourned for the loss of her social life and her friends.

"Now take this zombie virus. It's not much hardier than our vampire virus, but with some bonding agents, we can at least keep it stable enough to get a live virus into a host." Will jumped rails, something he was oft prone to do. "Don't you think it strange that these two monsters are created by a virus? How strange is that?"

"I don't think it's that strange at all. A virus is a living organism, and what is the primary directive of any living entity?"

Will looked at June as if she were trying to trick him. "Survival?"

"Survival," she answered as if he was in grade school and she was giving him affirmation. He seemed pleased with himself. "What would be a virus' biggest threat? Think, Will. There's a reason other than the Demense Group's involvement as to why the zombie virus is so prevalent."

Will sat there for long minutes. June prodded more than once to see if he wanted the answer and each time he'd held his hand up to stop her from giving it. Finally he looked up. "It can't be? How would that even be possible? It's man and Vira-stat, the anti-viral drug! It has to be."

June nodded. "I don't know for sure, but we were so close to having a drug that would attack the proteins in a virus, taking away its fuel to replicate. We were months away from wiping hepatitis, AIDS, mumps, measles…all of it off the face of the planet. It would have taken minimal effort to change some of the genetic markings the Vira-stat needed to look for in each virus, and we would have finally cured the common cold. We were on the edge of a dawn for a new age of man."

"This place is a conspiracy theory, June. I don't think you needed to go to a cellular level to look for one as well. Maybe someone here knew how close your work was and unleashed this before you could destroy something they've been working on for decades."

"Maybe there's just something about a disease that has a one hundred percent transmission rate and a one hundred percent fatality rate."

"It's man-made, so of course it's going to be more virulent, it's designed to."

An alarm klaxon went off, causing June's arm to flinch, sending her coffee mug full of herbal tea crashing to the ground. Chunks of ceramic littered the floor. "Damn it, I just made that."

She got up to get the broken pieces. Will went to get some paper towels to soak up the still steaming liquid. She thought she was done until she saw the handle some ten feet away. She debated asking Will to get it, but he was still bent over sopping up the tea. The handle sat up on the two broken ends, looking as if you pulled on it you could find a trap door underneath that would lead away from this insanity. Iggy, the five hundred pound male silverback mountain gorilla, looked from the cup handle to June.

She'd hoped the milky white cataracts that covered both his eyes would somehow obstruct her from his view. Iggy was the result of Will's genetic tampering. Up until two days ago, the zombie virus was exclusively a homo sapiens malady. The virus scared her like no other, on some level, though, she thought the world would most likely be a much better place when the virus had run its course and removed its biggest threat from the face of planet. But her lab partner may have changed all of that. If she had the courage, she knew the right thing to do would be to slit his throat while he slept and destroy his research.

Will had found a way to bridge the one-point-six percent genetic difference between ape and man. That he'd found this relatively extraordinary leap before the point-nine percent difference between monkey and man was just a testament to his perseverance or luck. True science usually was a decent combination of both. The monkeys, no matter the species, would die almost instantly when the virus was introduced into their systems, despite how many modifications Will had made. It was Iggy who somehow had the strength to survive those first few agonizing hours. The poor beast had screamed in pain and clawed at his body in an attempt to rid himself of what he'd been infected with.

A line of drool hung low from Iggy's mouth as he watched June approach cautiously. His silence was unnerving. He didn't bang against the cage, nor did he uselessly attempt to poke a hand out knowing she was too far away. He just watched and waited for an opportunity, his gaze never leaving June's. She broke the handle into two smaller pieces as she stepped on it, not daring to take her eyes from Iggy.

"Don't be ridiculous. He's five feet away, he can't possibly reach you."

She verbalized her fear in the way she had during her childhood in an attempt by making it auditory to make the imagined fiends go away. But Iggy wasn't imaginary as he cocked his massive head to her words. As she peered at the gorilla, she wondered how much trouble she would get in once they found Will's body. They might do nothing, seeing as how her work was vital and it didn't look like there were any replacement candidates coming any time soon. Even if they did throw her in a cell, or even the extreme of execution, so what? Her small sacrifice would pale in comparison to what she was saving.

Now that Will had discovered how to mutate the virus to make it transferrable to other animals he wouldn't stop until he'd gone as far as he could. Dogs, cats, emus, rats. He'd never stop and his reasoning would be just to see if he could. Once the first zombie rat escaped the facility and oh yes it would, they always did, the world would be devoid of nearly all life. Maybe not the insect or plant variety but within a few short years everything else would not even be a memory for there would be nothing left with the power to remember. It was even possible that the insects would adapt as well. June shuddered at the thought of a zombie mosquito.

The only thing that moved on Iggy was the drool that was nearly touching the floor and his eyes. His unblinking, watery, unwavering gaze stayed steadfast on June as she bent down and cautiously reached around to pick up the broken pieces. She was rewarded with a painful skin-tearing slice for her efforts.

"Got it all," Will said as he tossed the paper towels and came toward her to see if she needed any further assistance. He stopped when he saw what she was looking at. What she was looking at with abject fear he was staring at with unbridled pride. Iggy was his greatest achievement. "Beautiful isn't he?"

June didn't answer; Will didn't seem to notice or care. She figured the trumpets going off in his head were loud enough anyway. She stood, the modest heel on her boot twisting slightly from an unyielding piece of the handle she'd missed. She would have been able to make the necessary adjustment if not for the explosion that made her lose her balance. Will spun in an attempt to get his hands under her arms and keep her from toppling over. He was quick enough, but did not have the stability to keep them both upright as he was twisted to the side. June fell over, knocking Will off-balance toward Iggy.

Iggy was lightning fast, his hand shooting out, completely enveloping Will's neck. June was still recovering from her near fall and did not realize what was happening. She was smiling in embarrassment and about to thank Will for saving her life when she looked up. Will's face was cherry red and his eyes were bulging out from the pressure Iggy exerted on his neck.

Will had one hand tearing at Iggy's in a destined-for-failure maneuver. With his free hand, he was reaching out to June for help. It was a dead-heat for which one was a more useless gesture. June backed up, one hand on her throat as if in sympathy, the other reaching around to make sure she didn't walk into anything.

Iggy was crushing Will's airway. He couldn't even manage a strangled cry from the vice-like grip the large primate had him in. Will slowly slid to the ground as Iggy loosened his hold.

He's still alive, June thought; although she moved no closer. She was transfixed as she watched the events unfold before her. Iggy reached his other hand through the bar underneath the cross bar that was about midway high on his cage. *He obviously doesn't want Will to potentially slide out of his reach.* They had three tranquilizer guns in the lab, all of them loaded with darts. She knew if she put the gun up to the bars it would be impossible for her to miss. She could save Will—she had that power. She could also save the planet. There was a very good chance that the Medical Sciences lab would perfect the vaccine they'd been working on so diligently. Man could recover from this but not with Will's work running loose.

"Please," Will pleaded. He could not manage much more than a broken whisper and a half-hearted attempt at raising his hand. Iggy had him pulled tightly up against the bars.

"I...I can't."

Betrayal, hurt, and resignation showed on Will's face.

Iggy reached out with his free hand and yanked on Will's shoulder until his arm was within reach. There was a nauseating cracking of bones as Iggy pulled Will's arm backwards and through the bars. By the angles of Will's arm, June figured that he'd at least had his shoulder wrenched from its socket and his elbow broken. There was also a good chance that the ulna was broken as well. Will's screams were cut off as he passed out from the pain, thus saving himself from having to hear Iggy tear through his lab jacket to the soft flesh and tissue below. He did not eat though; puddles of drool were dripping onto Will's exposed arms, and Iggy's teeth were bared, yet he did not eat.

June jumped back as Will's body was slammed up against the bars repeatedly. Iggy was savagely jerking on Will's catatonic body until the arm came free with a shredding sound. In comparison, once he had torn the arm loose, he was almost tender as he pulled the meat away from the bones getting at all of the protein.

June was swallowing back gorge as she watched Iggy clean Will's arm much like a bar-goer would a chicken wing at happy hour. Blood poured from Will's wound; yet, incredibly, he was still alive. Iggy switched hands so that he could get at Will's other arm. Thankfully, an explosion nearby masked most of the sounds of bones being traumatized. Iggy didn't waste any time pulling Will's other arm off, and once again he ate.

June could not tear her eyes from the beast. At first, she thought that perhaps Iggy was tearing Will limb from limb because of reach and perhaps that was part of it, but then she thought there might be more to it.

"He's trying to not infect the rest of him. Oh, my God."

And this time her splayed fingers were no match from the volume of bile that leaked through and around them from her mouth. Will had turned an ashen gray, but not from becoming a zombie. He'd died sometime during the assault.

They knew from enough trials that human zombies would eat a non-infected human only for a certain amount of time before becoming disinterested in the carcass. Many of the scientists had argued that, by stopping at a certain juncture, this allowed the host to repair the damage done by the zombies and let the virus replicate in the new host, thus adding to the numbers of the infected. This angle never made a great deal of sense to June. If the zombies were merely trying to swell their numbers, why do all that damage to begin with? She'd told them as much.

It was her research that proved, without a doubt, that the zombies became disinterested in their victim when, and only when, the introduction of the virus had reached a certain threshold; and without fail, they would leave the tainted meat. She acquiesced that, in part, this could be a built-in function of the virus' need to sustain itself. But, more importantly, and she'd laughed when she'd discovered it, zombies weren't cannibals. They would not eat their own. In that, they were actually more civilized than man, whose history had been wrought with that particular affliction.

Will had clearly bled out by the time Iggy had torn off his lower left leg. He was digging at the bone with his dexterous fingers, making sure to get all the marrow free.

"I've got to get out of here."

June was looking from Iggy to the door, where sounds of fighting were intensifying. Iggy was watching her carefully even as he slurped up a particularly long string of muscle. He had also quickly learned that, by killing his meal first, he did not allow the virus to replicate upon the host's own cells.

"If only the first zombie thought the way you did, Iggy. This thing would have been contained in a couple of days with only a few hundred deaths," June muttered.

Will had somehow luckily stumbled upon how to disable the trigger that had been engineered in the original weapon. This version of the virus wasn't as concerned with affliction as it was with consumption.

"You could be the key, Iggy, but somehow I don't think we're going to get the chance to find out."

The lights were flickering; the only thing keeping Iggy in his cell was the magnetic door lock. If the power went out, he would be free. Mr. Hawes had assured her that this could not happen as there were redundancies set in place to make sure that power flowed uninterrupted throughout the facility at all times.

"For God's sake it better. We're using nuclear power," he'd quipped when she'd first come aboard.

Iggy would occasionally glance up at the lights as if he knew. "No, he knows," June said.

Whatever Will had done, in addition to getting the virus to spread, also instilled more intelligence. Iggy had been fairly average as far as apes go. Intelligent when compared to the rest of the animal kingdom, but he was about the equivalent of an eight-year-old human child in terms of smarts—generally innocent and wide-eyed. But not Iggy 2.0. The only thing that shined behind those obscured irises was an abundance of aptitude, adaptability, cleverness, and worst of all, cruel, cold, calculating intelligence. And, oh yeah, one more thing, endless hunger. That part burned brilliantly.

Will was now down to his core, and Iggy didn't look like he'd even touched on the outer edges of his needs. This was the point in which the beast did something completely unexpected; he turned what remained of Will so that they were now facing each other, although Will's head was lolling to the side. Iggy began to move Will closer to the door to his cage.

"No it can't be." June was frozen in terror.

Iggy had manipulated Will so that the dead man's chest was about even with the card reader locking mechanism. They'd had the old locks changed after an accident last year. One of the technicians had been walking by a cage and her keycard, swinging on a lanyard, had come within a foot of the card reader and allowed the mechanism to unlock. June had watched the video surveillance the following morning to ascertain how Petey, the Guinea Pig, had escaped. Not that he'd gone far or done any damage other than make a small mess outside of his cage, but if this could happen with his cage, then it could occur with the much more dangerous animals housed in the next room. The readers had been calibrated to make them not nearly as sensitive. The cards that the techs wore had to now be physically placed on the reader before it would change the locking light from red to green. It would also give an audible alarm much like the chirp a smoke detector would when its battery began to die. June had just turned and was heading for the door when she heard the telltale tweet.

Too late, she thought as she heard the cage door crash open. Her screams were swallowed up in the maelstrom of battle.

Chapter Eleven – Tracy

Trip sat atop a horse, a thick, woolen white robe with a heavy red cross emblazoned on the front enshrouding his body.

"Trip, I've been so worried!" Stephanie sobbed as she ran toward him.

"Hold off, ma'am." Another rider came up next to Trip. He was riding a great brown stallion that nearly dwarfed Trip's gelding. He was wearing the same robe and had a brilliant ornamental scabbard hanging down by his side, which was not nearly as threatening as the Israeli Uzi he had slung in front of his chest.

"I've got this," Trip said to the man.

Stephanie stopped short as Trip held his hand up. "What doth the lass request?"

A look of confusion swept across her face.

"I should just shoot him," BT mumbled to Tracy. "What the hell is he sitting side-saddle for?"

"Mom, I know that symbol. It's for the Knights Templar," Travis said.

"Trip, it's me, honey. Your wife, remember?"

Trip held his hand up to the side of his face like he was going to deliver a stage whisper. Instead, it came out a few decibels short of a full out yell. "Of course I remember you, honey. I have to play it good for these guys. This Renaissance Festival stuff is a hoot. If I knew how much fun they had, I would have joined up years ago. If I do it right, they'll let me stay."

"Um, I see," she replied.

The man on the horse wiped a hand across his face and sighed.

"I guess he's been around Trip too long. Imagine that," BT said surly.

"My name is Joseph DiPaolo," he stated before getting down from his horse. At six feet two, he was nearly as imposing a figure off the horse as he was on. Closely cropped hair hinted to a past military career, as well as the demeanor with which he strode to Stephanie. "Ma'am, honored to finally meet you. After listening to John, err, I mean Trip, I wasn't sure you truly existed."

"Yes, he has a way of skirting around reality."

Trip slid off the horse. "Holy shit," he exclaimed when he touched ground and turned around. "Where'd we get elephants?"

"Honey, are you alright?" Stephanie asked nervously.

"I know there are more of you out there. My men are close, but not too close. I didn't want to mistakenly touch off a small battle. Those things seem to happen in abundance in these End of Times," Joseph seemingly spoke to the forest. BT stepped out from around a tree. Joseph's eyes grew momentarily big. "I…umm, sorry. I thought he was kidding when he said you were traveling with a grizzly. You must be BT, the traveling bear." Joseph approached with one hand extended, the other loosely gripping the Uzi in case not all went as planned.

"What are your intentions?" BT asked, ignoring the man's outstretched hand. He hadn't brought his weapon to bear but he was in a much better position to do so if the case was warranted.

"With you folks it's nothing more than to lend some assistance. Trip told us about your group camping in the trees."

"He called that camping?" BT looked like he wanted to rip Trip's arms off and beat him with them.

"I told you he was ornery," Trip said in between kisses from his wife.

"He's just being cautious. I understand the sentiment during these difficult times. I'd appreciate it if perhaps you put that weapon down some and we talked, friend."

"The last person that called me 'friend' when we first met nearly knocked me out with the handle to a broken hockey stick and stole my brand new sneakers I'd been saving up for all summer."

"Someone knocked you out?" Gary asked.

"I was nine." BT turned to answer and then directed his attention back to the front. "So, we're not friends, Joseph, because I don't have new shoes and even if I did, I don't think you'd be capable of taking them from me."

"Okay, let's start over," Joseph said, raising his hands up off his sub-machinegun, which hung from a tactical harness. "We are just here to see if everyone is alright and perhaps needs anything before we move on. We are not in the business of harming others, at least those who are not deserving."

"Who determines who is deserving?" BT growled.

"Well, this is going nowhere fast. You keep going like this, BT, and we're going to be in a firefight in the next couple of minutes." Tracy came out from behind the bush she'd been hiding behind. "My name is Tracy Talbot," she said as she approached Joseph. She took note that part of him was dwelling on her name like he'd heard a song from yesteryear but just couldn't remember the title. "My friend means well here, but he's a little overprotective. We appreciate you coming when you did. We've been in the trees for quite some time now and didn't think the zombies were ever going to leave. It seems something scared them off."

"Not scared...driven."

Now it was Tracy's turn to look confused.

"This is going to take a second, and you might not believe a word of it."

"Does this have to do with the Knights Templar robes?" Travis asked, still hidden behind a tree.

"Why don't you just paint a bulls-eye on your forehead, boy?" BT grumbled.

"Oh shit, you made him mad," Justin whispered.

"Now I know why Dad wanted to get on his good

side. Damn." Travis shrunk back a bit.

"When I was back in the Naval academy, I was approached by my commander who was a Freemason. We talked for hours, most of it sounding like crap to me. I'd honestly thought he had lost his wits."

"You talking to me?" Trip was looking around.

Joseph continued. "I'm not going to go into a long drawn out history of the Templar order except to say we were created as an elite fighting force back in the eleventh century, which was most famously known for the Crusades. When we were officially disbanded in the fourteenth century, we went underground. We went from fighting for Christianity to preserving its relics. When that mission was completed, we strove to find another higher purpose."

"I can't help it, I need to know," Travis said to his brother as he exited his hiding spot.

"Boy, I am going to string you up by your toes!" BT said, getting in between him and Joseph like a human shield.

That same searching for an answer expression came over Joseph's face as Travis found a way around BT. "So you're saying you found *all* the relics?" Travis asked.

"All of them," Joseph answered.

"The Ark of the Covenant?"

"Yes."

"The Holy Grail."

"Of course."

Travis stopped to think.

"I'll save you the trouble. We have the real Shroud of Turin, the Seamless Robe of Christ, the Veil of Veronica, the Crown of Thorns, the Holy Lance and the True Cross among others that might not be as famous. When we'd completed our mission, our jobs became different. We were now protectors of the origins of Christianity. We decided to take that one step further and protect all of humanity."

"From what?" Travis asked.

"From itself, unfortunately. But to do that, we soon

realized we needed to expand. Not so much to put distance from our earlier roots…but to be more adaptable. This was too big for just one sect, thus was formed the Illuminati."

"The Illuminati? But you guys are supposed to be taking over the world."

"That's what others would have you believe. The ones that truly wield the power and have been amassing it for ages want the attention on anyone but themselves."

"Why not just come out and squash the rumors?"

"Not a bad idea, but we're not even supposed to exist."

"So what are you doing here?" BT queried.

"I think you already know. According to our friend here, you just left their building. The Demense Group, while relatively new in the world domination scheme at a hundred years old, has had some serious technological and monetary backing that has thrust them to the forefront."

"Like you, he is not my friend, either." BT made a point to let him know his status with Trip.

"Very well, but neither am I your enemy."

"We'll wait and see on that."

"Is he always like this?"

"Pretty much," Tracy responded. "So…the zombies?"

"That was our doing…wait, wait, I don't mean creating them. No, the Demense Group can take credit for that. We missed stopping the spiked flu shots by hours. Could have stopped all of this and brought them down at the same time. For that I will ultimately have to answer for, as it happened on my watch."

"Not completely your fault, Jopesh."

"It's Joseph. For the forty-eighth time, Trip, it's Joseph."

"I know, Jopesh, I know. For the forty-eighth time you don't need to keep telling me. I think he really likes his name," Trip said to Stephanie. "I just think you ought to know that parts of this contest are being played out on vastly higher levels and the outcomes there have great influence on what happens here."

"Trip, I do not know how you go from Chong to Descartes within the same sentence." Joseph stroked the side of his horse's head as he'd whinnied loudly.

"Do you think I can ride the llama again, Jopesh?"

"Okay, getting back on track, we fortuitously stumbled across some plans in a white panel van full of cheap beer."

Tracy placed her hand to her mouth. "I think you're talking about Mad Jack's truck. Was it full of air-soft guns?"

Joseph laughed, his face seemingly lighting up as he did so. Tracy looked at him. The laugh was genuine, and he enjoyed it. She could also tell it was not something he did often, at least not recently.

"I guess perhaps laughing is not the best thing until I know his fate." Joseph had let the smile dissipate.

"He's fine, at least he was the last time we saw him." Tracy eased his mind.

"My men and I just thought it was one of the funniest things we had come across. In the midst of an apocalypse, someone was running around with toy guns. We stopped laughing the moment we took a look at his plans. It had to be a sign, just another indicator that perhaps Trip is right. If we had come out of the woods a hundred yards further up or back, we would not have bothered to see what was in it. We have some pretty technical personnel within our group, and they were able to shrink down his original design somewhat."

"You have the zombie repeller boxes?" Travis came closer.

"Huh? I guess we never thought of it that way, but that works as well. We thought they were constructed for herding."

"Is that what is going on here?" Tracy asked.

"Yes, we've been assembling the largest army of zombies we could in order to send them into the Demense facility and take it down. We have a person on the inside who should be opening the doors right about now." Joseph looked to his watch and then the sun.

"All the doors?" Tracy asked in alarm. "You're letting all those zombies into that building? BT, we have to go back!" She turned.

"Ma'am, there are over twenty thousand zombies going there. You can't get through them."

"My husband is in there!"

Another confused look came across his face and then a light dawned. "Your last name is Talbot? And your boy is a dead ringer. He about this high?" Joseph held his hand up close to his chin. "Mostly mouth and bad decisions?"

"That's him," BT answered.

"You know my husband?"

"I do. I was his Unit Commander, and for a while I thought I was his principal, he was sent to my office so many times. Boy, I liked him. I couldn't let him know that, though. He dressed down more of my officers than I care to remember. Although, in fairness, they all deserved it. I could have perhaps gone for a little more compliance out of him."

"Couldn't we all," BT stated.

"Hell of a soldier, and not much would stop him if he was determined to get through it. I'm truly sorry for your loss."

"Shove your loss up your ass and call your zombies back!" Tracy got up in Joseph's face.

"Ma'am—"

"It's Tracy. Do I look seventy to you?"

"No ma...Tracy. Like I said, there are twenty thousand zombies there. It has taken us over a month to assemble that kind of herd, and I've lost a dozen men in the process. Even if I wanted to stop them, which I don't, I couldn't anyway."

"Oh, you've gone and done it now." BT was moving close, not so much to pull Tracy off of Joseph as to protect the man from her wrath.

"Your husband was—"

"IS!"

"Is…um, an interesting man, and I liked him greatly, but this is bigger than any one person. That facility is attempting dominion over what little of humanity is left. And they have the ways and means to accomplish that. We have an opportunity to stop that now. We may never get another chance like this." A radio on Joseph's hip squelched. "Hold on, I have to take this." He grabbed the radio and moved away.

"When did I get a job with the Red Cross?" Trip was looking down at his chest. "Are there doughnuts?"

"I know what you're thinking, Tracy, and I'm with you all the way. We just have to send everyone else away. Especially him." BT was pointing at Trip who was searching his pockets desperately, looking for the doughnut that wasn't there.

"You do know that, for all his faults, he just saved us, right?" Tracy asked.

"Yup, and I'll have to live with that every day for the rest of my life, which probably won't be that long anyway when we go back for Mike."

Joseph came back a few moments later, clearly confused about the news he'd just received.

"What's going on?" Tracy prodded.

"The computer systems are down inside the facility."

"That good or bad?" BT asked.

"It's good, it's means their satellite surveillance is down as well as their defenses. Now coordinating a strike or any future attacks would be extremely difficult for them."

"Wasn't that part of your plan?"

"I'd like to say so, but our plant was fairly low level. Plus, the man could barely operate his cell phone, so I'm pretty positive that he could not have hacked the main frame and shut it down."

"This has Mike written all over it." Tracy turned to BT.

"How is it that Mike is in there? Are you, or were you, part of the group?" Joseph asked. "Near as I could get from John was that you had been staying at the Holiday Inn and he seemed agitated that the pool wasn't open."

"I can assure you we weren't guests. We were…" Tracy paused. There was only so much information she could trust this man with, and she wanted to be careful to not give him anything more than the bare minimum.

"Out scavenging." BT picked up the thread. "We got surrounded by zombies, probably part of your horde now that I think about it. Was looking pretty grim until some military guys showed up. Dropped some explosives and then we were rescued by a helicopter. Next thing we knew, we were all in cells."

"Why go through all the trouble of rescuing you folks just to deposit you in cells?" Joseph asked, clearly fishing for more information.

"I…I think they wanted to use us for human experimentation for their vaccines," Tracy answered when BT stalled. It probably would have looked more convincing if BT hadn't shook his head in response as if to say, "good answer."

"Makes sense, but why then are you out here?"

"The leader, Hawes."

"Dixon Hawes? I knew it was that wily bastard. Figured it couldn't be Deneaux, too egotistical and, to be honest, too stupid and obvious. Seemed he was more of the front man."

"Man? Oh, I thought you were talking about Vivian Deneaux."

"Vivian? Is *that* spawn still alive?"

"She may be running things now," Tracy said.

Joseph took in a sharp intake of air. "Holy crud. She's actually still alive?" Tracy nodded. "Kind of surprised she hasn't fired off a nuke yet then. I'm sorry...so how are you out here and Mike's still in there?"

"Mike got a hold of a weapon and held Hawes as a hostage until we were released."

"I told you he was a damn fine soldier, could have made a career out of it if he found a way to stop his mouth every once in a while."

"Might as well ask the sun not to shine or the wind not to blow," BT said.

"He gets it, BT," Tracy said.

"Or an animal not to shit in the woods, or—"

"BT!" Tracy nearly stomped her foot.

"Sorry."

"Or a pope not to be Catholic," he finished quickly.

She glared at BT before talking to Joseph. "We're going back regardless of whether you help or not. All I ask is that you don't try to stop us. However, we do need more bullets."

"Yeah, lots more," Travis agreed.

"Honey, those are not magic mushrooms!" Stephanie shouted a few feet away.

"I know that look, Mom," Travis said. "Don't even bother trying, if you're going back, I'm going with you."

Tracy wasn't sure if she should be absurdly proud or terrified.

"I'm going, too," Dennis said, walking up. He had just returned from picking through the destroyed truck with Gary.

"Where we headed?" Gary asked, lugging up an ammo box. "Oh, to get Mike," he said as he looked around at the group. "I'm ready when you guys are."

"I could stop you from this futile act," Joseph told them.

"Yes...but will you?" Tracy asked. "I understand you not wanting to help, but would you actively attempt to prevent us from going back?"

Joseph actually pondered the question. Ultimately they were free citizens to live and die as they chose. "I will not. As for ammunition I will have some trucked up here for you. The help I will give as long as it does not place my men in harm's way. They have sacrificed enough for this mission."

"Thank you," Tracy said. "One more thing?"

"Yes?"

"Can we get a new means of transportation? Ours seems to have met with an untimely demise."

Gary weakly raised his hand as the guilty party.

Joseph nodded and, once again, walked away so that he could speak into his radio.

"I see smoke!" Justin had gone back up a tree and was trying to get a glimpse of the outlying area.

"Where are you?" Tracy shielded her eyes to look up. "Get down from there!" she shouted when she realized just how high up he was.

"I'll get him as soon as I find my jet pack," Trip said, looking up with Tracy. "I know it's around here somewhere."

Tracy paced restlessly, waiting for their ride to come. Right now she wasn't sure if she was more concerned for Mike's safety or Justin's as he descended from the tree. She cuffed him behind the ear when he touched terra firma.

"Damn, Mom. You do know I'm an adult, right?"

"Doesn't matter—you'll always be my kid."

"Damn," he said again as he walked away, cupping his smarting ear.

"Stephanie, I can't ask you to go back. I'm sure Joseph will watch over you both while we're gone." Tracy had said it in such a manner that Joseph, even if he wanted to, would not be able to decline the offer.

"Of course. We'll be staying here for as long as it takes to make sure that the Demense group is no longer and can never be operational again. If...um, I mean *when* you return, you could join back up at that time. If something should happen that would make that an impossibility, we would surely escort your friends to a safe location."

Trip had found a backpack and was securing the front fastener. "Almost ready," he said.

"For what?" BT asked.

"To get the boy. Where have you been? Just hope I have enough fuel in this thing to get up there and back down."

"God loves fools and children." BT walked away.

"I am not a child!" Trip shouted at BT's back. BT flipped him the finger over his shoulder. "Rock on to you, too!" Trip stuck out and waggled his tongue.

"You have got to be kidding me," Tracy said as their vehicle pulled up. "A Prius? You truly think this is a one-way trip, don't you? How could I possibly get Mike back in this thing when it's already going to be over-filled?"

"I'm sorry, we don't have very much else to spare." Joseph was apologetic.

"Where are they going?" Trip asked as Tracy, after browbeating Gary, took the driver's seat. BT sat in the passenger seat, nearly taking up the entire front as Travis, Justin and Dennis crammed into the backseat. Gary had popped the trunk and was about the only one sitting with any semblance of comfort.

"They're going to get Mike," Stephanie told Trip. When she realized he didn't have a clue who she was talking about she added, "Ponch."

"Why aren't we going? Or should I just avoid the eight hundred pound gorilla in the room?" Trip asked.

Chapter Twelve – Mike Journal Entry 5

The smell…I don't bring it up because it was any worse than it had ever been, it was just so prevalent. It was that, almost above all, that made me realize just how much of a world of stink we were in. Oh shit, that's kind of funny; I made a pun and hadn't even intended it. There was no sense on dwelling where all the zombies had come from. That they were here was enough to deal with right now. Finding a corridor that was not flooded with them was out of the question.

"Mr. T, I think we need to find a room quickly! There are soldiers running this way. And to be honest, I don't think they're looking for us."

"Well, that's good isn't it?" Then I figured out that was because they were being chased. "Locked," I said, trying the closest door. In fact, all of the doors I could see probably were as they all had a card reader square out in front of them.

"Let me down, you oaf." Deneaux got a proper hold on her cigarette, took a decent puff, and then fished around her neck.

"Looking for where you placed your heart?" I asked.

"Always the kidder," she said as she pulled out a lanyard with card on it, a picture of the newly deceased Dixon Hawes emblazoned on it.

"Who's kidding?" I was being completely serious.

Deneaux pushed the door open and I immediately followed. I swear I could smell the deceit on her. If she could have shut that door on us, she would have. Maybe it's inherent; like a whale needing to surface every hour or so to breathe, she needs to fuck someone over every once in a while just to make sure she hasn't lost any of her skill. I held it open for Tommy. I was just about to shut it when I saw the soldiers Tommy was talking about. There were five of them. That quickly turned to four as a speeder dragged the slowest of them down.

"Come on!" I waved them on. Good idea…bad idea…I have no idea. I hadn't thought it out. All I knew was that they were in trouble and, oh—they had guns. I was hoping that their enemy was my enemy thus making us some sort of allies. The man in the front looked relieved as he darted past me and in. The four little Indians became three as another soldier was dragged down. Well, not so much pulled down as suffering a mechanical failure. I'd seen the expression enough during my football days to realize he'd just pulled a hamstring. His eyes clamped shut as his mouth pulled back. His right hand shot down to the back of his right leg as it seized up.

He was less than twenty feet from safety as he started dragging his bad leg, for a heartbeat I thought maybe he was trying to act like an old school zombie. Unfortunately, the zees behind him weren't buying it. He was taken down like he'd stolen a mink coat from Saks Fifth Avenue. He'd not had the presence of mind to protect his face as he fell forward. His chin hit first followed immediately by his teeth and nose, both of which shattered upon impact. I'm thinking he didn't even feel it as the zombies that had bowled him over were now feasting on the very leg that had betrayed him.

I quickly pulled the door shut as the third soldier entered. He fell to his knees just clear of the door as I slammed it shut. It vibrated heavily as zombies struck the other side. The soldier who had fallen just outside the door was screaming, a strangled, tortured cry that kept getting higher and higher in pitch until it was mercifully cut off. The three soldiers in the room with us were breathing heavily, trying to catch their breath.

"Thank you," the one by my feet said in between intakes.

"Yeah, just remember that," I told him.

"Who are you?" the soldier that had come in first asked. His M-4 was on his chest held snug by his tactical harness. His hands were resting on it, but more as a place to put them rather than as an attempt to use it. That didn't stop Deneaux as she placed the barrel of her revolver up against his skull. "What's going on?" he asked, placing his hands in the air as Deneaux pulled back on the hammer.

"I didn't let them in just so you could shoot them," I told Deneaux.

"Then why did you? Is this altruism, Michael? These are the very men who would have gladly killed you."

"Michael Talbot?" the soldier with his hands in the air asked.

"You know what, Deneaux? Odds were they had no clue what the hell I looked like. I could have probably told them I was a scientist."

Her eyebrows arched. "Please."

"Okay, janitor maybe. They still wouldn't have known. You, on the other hand, I'm sure everyone knows."

"We should just kill them. We don't know their intentions."

"Maybe I should just ask?"

The soldier with the barrel to his head was nodding.

"Oh, I'm sure you'll get a straightforward answer," she answered sardonically.

I looked at her crossly; if she gave a shit, she gave no indication. "As you already know, my name is Michael Talbot. You've had the pleasure of meeting Mrs. Deneaux, and this is my associate, Tommy, who may not seem it, but is easily the most lethal person in this room. My goal today is to get out of this fuck-fest by just about any means possible. I have no desire to kill any of you, but I will if you stand between my ends and me. You are more than welcome to throw your lot in with us, or you can head back the way you came." I pointed to the door, which was still rattling from multiple impacts.

"I vote for door number one." The man on the ground raised his hand. "Wait, wait, that sounded bad. Option one, definitely option one."

"Me too," the second chimed in quickly.

"Hmmm, let's see," the third with the gaping barrel to his head said. "I can either get shot in the head immediately, tossed to a hungry horde of zombies, or try for my freedom."

"I think I'm going to like this guy." I extended my hand. "Michael Talbot."

"Corporal Jameson. The guy on the ground is my brother, James."

"James Jameson?" I asked.

"What my parents lacked in originality they made up for in humor. My first name is Jim."

"Okay." I mean, what could I say?

"This other guy is Lance Corporal Bukkar."

"Thanks for saving us," the lance corporal said.

"So we're all on the same page?" I asked.

"For the love of God, Michael, do you really believe you have gotten to the root of truth?" Mrs. Deneaux asked as she let the hammer of her revolver down.

"Maybe…maybe not. Fact remains, six have a better chance of survival than three. If we still have stuff to sort out when and if we get through this, we'll take care of it then. Fair enough?"

Deneaux scowled. "Fuck me over Corporal Jameson and I will blow a hole in your head big enough to fit a pack of cigarettes." She strode across the room to sit down and fish out that threat box from some hidden pocket.

"She serious?" the corporal asked.

"She is, and I'm not sure if she's talking to you three or me," I said.

"Whichever," Deneaux breathed out in a ring of smoke.

Tommy nodded solemnly.

"Is there another way out?" I asked as I got closer to the door. The sound of pounding footsteps was increasing as zombies ran amok.

James stood up. "No," he answered after looking around. "We're in the labs. Not necessarily the center of this place, but close enough that getting out is going to be extremely difficult."

"Any ducts or back stairwells?"

"Michael, this isn't some shitty action movie your type likes to watch," Deneaux said through a plume of smoke. "This is a high security building with multiple redundancies built in to ensure that someone just doesn't stroll on in."

"My type? What the hell does that mean?"

"Lower middle-class, uncouth, damn near savages. I'd take a trained monkey over the lot of you."

I'm sure she had more left in her rant, but that was cut short when we heard a crashing sound to the back of us. All of us, and whatever weapons we had, were now trained on the door to our rear.

"What's back there?" I asked.

"More labs," the corporal answered.

"What kind?" Tommy was seeking clarification.

This time it was Bukkar that answered. "Animal."

"Like goldfish?" I asked.

"Yes, Michael, goldfish," Deneaux sneered. "This huge, covert, quasi-government funded facility designed solely to take over the entire human population through nefarious means is studying goldfish."

"Weird, I would have thought their efforts would be better spent someplace else. Maybe figuring out exorcisms or something." I was looking right at her. "Just no accounting for government waste I suppose." I wanted my words to make me feel better, but something on the other side of that door was throwing heavy enough stuff around that I was feeling the vibrations through the cement floor I was standing on. "Please tell me they don't have grizzlies."

The flickering of the lights seemed to enrage the monster. Each flicker brought more violence as whatever it was slamming around came with more frequency.

"Mr. Talbot, sir…" James or Jim started.

"Yeah? And 'Mike' or 'dude' is a perfectly suitable form of addressing me."

"Really, Michael? Dude? I suppose I should say my apologies to the lower middle-class for including you within their ranks," Deneaux scoffed.

"Tell me again why I saved you?"

"Saved me? What a skewed version of reality you house in that drug-addled brain casing of yours."

I had four or five things I wanted to say to her, but most wouldn't have even passed my personal censor, which had a pretty low threshold already. I did not want to get into a verbal altercation with Deneaux. Knowing her, it would end with a bullet in me somewhere. Plus whatever James, or Jim had to tell me looked pressing.

"Mike, these flickering lights are going to present a problem."

"You mean besides being totally in the dark should they stay out?" Yeah, dwell on that for a second if you dare. We were completely underground—might as well be a cave for how much sunlight streams down here. Complete and utter darkness in a maze full of man-eating zombies, well, doesn't that just sound like a barrel of laughs. Hadn't even thought of that. I can't even begin to explain how the fear of that thought began to burrow its way deep inside of my psyche.

"Ridiculous, the back-up generators should keep this place operational for weeks if not months," Deneaux corrected him. I've got to give it to the old bird; there wasn't a hint of a quiver in her voice as she delivered those words. I was wishing I had on brown pants for obvious reasons and she was about as blasé as one can be.

"Normally I'd agree with you, ma'am. The flickering lights are telling another story though. Yes, the generators will keep the place running but they get their instructions from the computer system."

Deneaux and I looked at each other knowingly.

"Go on," Deneaux prodded.

"It's a symbiotic relationship. The computer obviously can't run without the generator, and for safety reasons, the converse is true as well. With that much power running through the system, it has to be regulated. And if it's not, the fail-safe is to shut down."

"How do you know the computer system is down?" I asked. I mean, obviously I knew; but how could he? Just from some lights flickering?

"The flicker of the lights is actually a code. Notice it isn't completely random, there are two quick ones in succession then a three second break and two more. That is a diagnostic pattern to alert engineers that the computers are off-line and a warning to get them back on. Three quick flashes followed by another three quick would mean that the fuel is low. Three quick flashes by themselves would mean maintenance is required on a particular machine."

"All this light flashing is it necessary? Seems like it would be a burden on the personnel here," Deneaux scoffed.

"Only the most important signals are done through the lighting system. The routine ones are done through the computers, ma'am."

"So how much time do we have with the generators on?" I asked.

"An hour at the most. Not any more than that."

"We have an hour to get out of here?"

"That's not entirely true. There will be battery back-up."

The initial flood of dread was quelled somewhat from his statement knowing that we weren't going to be plunged into darkness just yet. "Okay, so how much battery life are we talking about?"

"Close to eighteen hours depending on what's up and running right now."

"Nineteen hours to get a plan together and implement it? Hell, that ought to be a breeze considering most times we don't have nineteen minutes...shit, even nineteen seconds." I was feeling better, not confident, but better. Like maybe the stay of execution had just come through.

Jim was not sharing in my feelings.

"What aren't you telling us?" Tommy asked, realizing the same thing I was.

"When the generator shuts down and the battery kicks in, by default all of the doors that are currently locked will be opened."

"What?" I finally saw a reaction out of Deneaux that did not revolve around scorn. "Whose brilliant idea was that?"

"It was a safety issue so that, in the event of something cataclysmic happening, personnel would be able to evacuate and would not be trapped in their rooms or work areas," the lance corporal explained, his gaze drawn to the floor as if the industrial tiles perhaps housed an answer.

I looked from the door that a thousand zombies could flood through to the other side of the room, where I was certain a pissed off Yeti would come exploding through. Don't get me wrong; the thought of seeing a Yeti thrilled the hell out of me no matter his mental state. That wasn't to say I would not be scared shitless though. Out of necessity, it was he or she we were going to have to deal with. And it came down strictly to numbers. One Yeti is way better than a thousand zombies. We needed to start moving tables and equipment over to blockade our only egress. It was impossible to block the Yeti's door, as it opened into the other chamber. That didn't stop the soldiers from tying their rifle straps to it and then to a bolted down electron microscope though.

"What's the tensile strength on those straps?" I asked James.

"A thousand pounds, at least, I guess. We've been

told they could be used as tow straps in an emergency."

We waited…what more could we do? The gurgles and moans of hundreds or thousands of zombies were compounded by their footfalls. I don't know that I'd ever been so amped up for action and forced to sit on my hands. Could we wait out the zombies? Odds were against it, they were in now and without some sort of reason they weren't going to leave on their own. In less than a day we were going to be trapped with them in these catacombs with the added burden of being completely blind. It was an impotent feeling, and I don't use that word lightly. I sat in a chair, staring up at the ceiling, not really concentrating on anything.

"Can you get anywhere that way?" I asked, pointing to the drop ceiling.

"No, they just hide the miles of cables that crisscross this place. Again no, I know what you're thinking, the holes the cables come in are designed specifically for cables and nothing more. A rat maybe, but certainly not a human," James said.

From time to time, we heard something crash in the lab next to us, but that was more out of the norm. Whatever was in there seemed to know this was a waiting game, and it was in for the long haul. I never much liked intelligence in my adversary since, more times than not, it was me that came up lacking.

The lights brightened and then flickered incredibly fast, it was sort of like watching a film from 1915. Then they popped off. For the briefest of moments we were immersed in darkness as black as the depths of Deneaux's lungs. In the expectant quiet the sound of industrial strength magnets releasing their hold was incredibly loud. The soul-sucking darkness was blessedly replaced by a soft red hue as the emergency lights came on. The effect was chilling; it made everyone look like they were bathed in blood. I could tell by the expressions on others that I wasn't the only one that felt this.

We were all watching the hallway door. It would have been near impossible for the zombies to move it, but that fact didn't stop the dread from flooding in. Just because the odds that the boogey man is real are infinitesimally small doesn't make a child feel any more brave as he or she cowers under the blankets, waiting for an extraordinarily long hand to reach up from under the bed and snatch their leg, pulling them into the underworld and laughing a cruel laugh the whole way down. The zombies kept moving; where they were headed I'm not sure. Odds were they were just milling about, going back and forth. For now, there was not a concerted effort directed on us, and we would have to take that as the positive it was.

It was the nearly imperceptible squeal behind us that really pumped up the fear factor. The handle was twisting slightly back and forth. Either something was testing to see if it was locked, or it was learning a new skill. The rifle slings pulled taut as whatever was on the other side yanked on the door.

The tensile strength on the sling might be a thousand pounds, but I don't think the handle it was tied to was going to match up. That was a thought that came glaringly late. All of our weapons came to the ready, even Deneaux's who'd snubbed out a cigarette to do so. This must be the end, as I don't recall ever having seen her do that. We could hear the fibers of the slings rubbing against each other as they were being pulled to their limits, louder still was the pops and groans of the handle as the metal was being stretched.

"What is going on?!" Bukkar asked, his voice changing pitch.

"Calm down, Lance Corporal," James told his charge.

"Screw this, I watched *Resident Evil*. I know what's on the other side of that door!" Bukkar hissed.

Now I'd watched R.E. myself. Was he right? Was there some giant, genetically-altered, super T-Virus zombie behind that door? If that was the case, we'd be better off in the hallway.

"Corporal Jameson, is he right?" I asked, wishing I didn't sound like a seven-year-old asking his dad to check the closet for a crazed psycho killer clown named Timothy he knew was lurking behind the *Star Wars* toys and dirty clothes he'd told his mother he'd picked up yesterday.

"No, I mean, I don't think so," Corporal Jameson answered without much conviction.

"Well, that was convincing. Six of these bullets aren't going to do anything against that kind of zombie." Deneaux spun her revolver to make sure it was fully loaded.

I don't know what was weirder, that a potential super zombie was behind door number two, or that Deneaux had watched Resident Evil. I wonder if the ushers had tried to kick her out when she lit up inside the theater. My bet was that nobody would have the balls to mess with her.

A loud screech pulled my attention away. Bukkar was pushing furniture out of the way to get to the hallway.

"Bukkar, stop!" Jameson shouted.

"I'm getting out of here, man. We don't have a chance against that thing!"

"Mano, we don't know for sure what it is," Jim said, obviously going to a personal level with someone he knew well. "It'll be alright, man. Just stop moving furniture."

Mano was in full-on panic mode, words alone weren't going to stop him. Tommy wrapped him up tight when Deneaux calmly leveled her revolver on Bukkar.

"Whoa, just stop Deneaux, Tommy's got him." I held my hands up.

"That in itself presents a problem, Michael."

"How?"

"You see, this Lance Corporal Mano Bukkar has now taken Tommy out of the imminent fight, and I can't allow that to happen."

"You can't *allow* it? What the hell are you going to do?"

"Shoot him if necessary," she offered rationally. I mean, rationally at least to her way of thinking, which was somewhere between a cross between psychopath and ogre.

The door to the hallway pushed in just as the handle to the lab door smashed to the ground. We stopped what we were doing, each of us waiting for the pre-conceived notion of our own worst nightmares to walk through. All was quiet. Whatever was on the other side knew it had opened the door, and it knew we were on the other side. It also seemed to know we posed a threat or it would have just charged through. That was good and bad news. Good news, because it felt that it could be killed; but bad news because, again, this showed a high level of intelligence. Tommy let go of Mano, who seemed as rapt as we all were.

The door may have moved a fraction of an inch, or it could have been the play of shadows in the washed out red lighting. Whatever it was, it had a trigger-happy Jim Jameson open fire. Rounds thudded into the heavy handle-less doorway, pushing it open a fraction of an inch at a time.

"Moron," Deneaux managed to get out between staccato bursts from his weapon.

Mano's hands flew up to cover his ears, and I understood the reasoning. The explosion of the rounds in the room was deafening, but it was not the reaction I was expecting from a soldier. He was close to checking out—if the beginnings of his vacant stare were any indication. James finally got Jim under control. A thick cloud of smoke drifted around the room. It happened so fast, I nearly missed it, as the door was pulled open and Big Foot tossed a fire extinguisher. A major league pitcher could not have tossed a baseball faster. The distance from a pitcher's mound to home plate is roughly sixty-six feet, from Sasquatch to Jim's head was half that at best. I don't know if he could have had enough time to blink, much less dodge that projectile. The back of his head exploded in a spray of bone and blood as the extinguisher sheered the top of his skull off.

Mano had dropped down onto his knees, cradling his own head in his hands as if he'd been hit. James was screaming, emptying everything he had into a door that had now been slammed shut. Tommy grabbed Jim's body before it could completely fold onto the ground unchecked.

"What the fuck was that?" James screamed when his rifle bolt clacked open.

I could have just as easily echoed his words. I'd only been half serious when I'd said "Yeti." Now I wasn't so sure.

"Jim, did you see it?"

James had finally turned around to see the damage done to his brother. It was not a pretty sight. Brain matter and blood had covered the far wall in a heavy mist. It was so thick that it looked like someone testing out a paint sprayer had been trying to clean out a particularly nasty jam. We've all seen the movies where the hero picks up a fire extinguisher and smacks the bad guy in the head with it and then within a few seconds the bad guy is up and fighting again. Let me assure you, *that* is Hollywood bullshit. A fire extinguisher weighs in excess of twenty pounds, and when that much steel collides with the comparatively fragile bone of a human skull, metal wins out every time. Jim was dead before the extinguisher hit the ground. Shards of his forehead were still embedded in the part of his brain that had remained in his head.

I thought James was going to join Mano soon as he pushed Tommy out of the way to cradle his brother's nearly headless neck. He was understandably crying and rocking.

"I told Mom I'd look out for you." He was staring into his brother's eyes, which were now as flat and lifeless as a fish.

"Tommy, what was that?" I asked, clutching my rifle.

He shrugged. When a five-hundred-year-old vamp admits to not knowing what he just saw, you could pretty much assume that it is pretty rare.

"So no on the Yeti?" I asked seriously.

He looked over at me with an expression I couldn't easily discern. It was either, "Don't be a dumb-ass, there are no such things as Yetis" or "Don't be a dumb-ass, I've seen Yetis and that was no Yeti."

I guess in the end, it really didn't matter. Whatever was in there, was a killer. Although that wasn't completely fair, there was a chance it was defending itself. Jim had opened fire first. Still, I wasn't going to be the one that tried to reason with it while it was trying to rip my spleen out.

"Help!" Came from behind us as a zombie had come in and fallen atop Mano who had been sitting on the ground. It had bent him forward so far that he was as close to smelling his own ass as he'd most likely been in his entire life. The zombie was draped over him and desperately biting at his boots, pulling on the laces like they were particularly stringy tendons.

"Tommy! The door!" He was closest to the other zombies that were trying to get in and join their brethren for lunch or dinner.

I'd help Mano if it was possible. It was the damn beast though—I could feel its eyes on me from the other room. He was watching through the hole in the door where the handle had fallen out—I knew he was—just waiting for an opportunity to come in and do whatever it is beasts do. Me thinks Tommy had as much adrenaline pumping through his system as any of us; he slammed the door shut so hard he severed a zombie's leg from the rest of him. The only thing holding it to its host was the fabric of its pants. Chinos, if my quick glance was correct. Seemed Tommy had somehow bagged a zombie from 1982.

Mano cried out. It wasn't the falsetto scream of someone who was having their flesh torn free, but it was close. Deneaux and I glanced at each other.

"This is why I like you, Michael. You don't cave in battle."

"Yet you keep trying to kill me."

"Like I said before consider it a compliment. I'll watch this door." She had her handheld cannon pointing unwaveringly at the Yeti's potential entrance.

I nodded. I wasn't a fan of Deneaux, and, at some point, I was going to have to keep an eye on my back before she could bury a knife in it; but shit, when she was on your side, you were definitely better off—though her position changed faster than a crack addict trying to get some sleep. (Pause, let that one sink in for a second...got it?) Mano was folded neatly in half, his nose pressing against the floor. The zombie had ripped through the laces and tongue of his military boots and even into his socks, which were most definitely not Army standard issue green. They were Argyle socks. I wanted to laugh, and maybe I would have if they weren't stained with blood.

Tommy and James were too close to risk using a bullet. I quickly put my gun down on top of a filing cabinet. With my left hand I grabbed the zombie's neck, and with my right I grabbed its shoulder. I pulled her straight up, a small piece of Bukkar's ankle hanging from her lips. This time Mano did cry out in a scream, spiked with painful misery and, worst of all, death. The Black One rode along that sound, reveling in its victory. What he was so happy about made no sense. He always won.

"Son of a bitch!" I was yelling as I ran the zombie into the nearest wall, headfirst.

A carefully placed M-80 shoved in its mouth could not have equaled the damage I did when wall met skull. There was a moment of resistance before the bone plating yielded and the brain smacked wetly against the indifferent cement. Black matter, riddled with a wriggling worm-like infection, coated what was once a dry erase board. If only I could clean up the stain of them as easily. The brackish matter dripped down and pooled onto the small tray that held a myriad of colored markers. I'd used enough force to nearly crush her head all the way down to her mouth; it slightly resembled a spent beer can under the heel of an overzealous drinker. The funny part—if you can call it that—about the whole thing was, as she was falling, her shoulder hit the edge of a chair and spun her over onto her back.

Her shirt was white and surprisingly clean for a monster, the words on her apparel clearly displayed for me on a bosom that I'd imagine would have earned me a smack upside the head from my wife in an earlier time: *Keep Calm and Zombie On.* I wondered if the morning she put that on she'd had some sort of precognition that she was going to end her day as her slogan read, or did it perhaps invoke that particular nasty outcome, somehow swaying the yet unknown fates, like a self-fulfilling prophecy.

"Mr. T," Tommy beseeched. He was still holding the door closed, his shoulder occasionally jumping as something big hit it. The only thing I could think of that would move him at all was a bulker. If that was the case, that door wasn't going to hold for very long.

"Right...sorry," I said, looking up from a girl who could very easily be my daughter's age, tough to say with her face obliterated. Her lower jaw was all that remained on her face. A life cut so short...I hope she'd achieved at least a little of what she'd set out to do.

"Mr. T!" Tommy was actually pushed away from the door by a good few inches, he leaned his shoulder in and moved his feet back to get into a better bracing position.

I think I was getting caught in a loop looking down at that girl, a girl who had parents that loved her. She was the face of all the wrong that had happened, and when I thought of it that way, it made me smile a sick, shriveled little thing that certainly didn't crinkle the corners of my eyes. Deneaux would have been proud. I moved quickly, shoving furniture back into place that the simpering Mano had dragged away from the door earlier.

I had enough things in the room that I could have easily gone from end to end, but that would have entailed getting closer to the Yeti's stronghold; I wasn't game for that. I'd be in reach of his incredibly long arms if he decided to open his door and pull me in there with him. I could just see the fake "Ooops" expression on Deneaux's face as she failed to fire her weapon in my aid, probably even put her hand up to her face, and I could also hear her explanation if I somehow survived. "Why Michael, I didn't have a clear shot, I may have hit you, dear boy, and I just wouldn't be able to forgive myself if that happened." Mind you, this would be coming from the woman that could shoot the balls off a mosquito from thirty yards while she was riding a horse. Do mosquitoes have balls?

"What about him?" Deneaux asked. I was assuming she was talking about Mano, but she never turned to verify this. "You watch the door; I'll take care of it." Now she was pointing with her free hand toward him, confirming my earlier thinking.

Well, if I had any doubt about the bleakness of her heart, she'd just stomped that last vestige out.

"Wait a second before you go blowing a hole in him," I said. This got Mano's attention. He went from whimpering and gingerly touching the skin around his bite to looking directly at Deneaux, his eyes wide.

"Yeah, no holes," he pleaded. "James, help me."

James was still rocking his brother's corpse back and forth, wailing to a deity who right now was not present. The way I saw it, Mano was still technically master of his own fate if that mean looking M-16 sitting on his waist was any sort of indicator. From his position, if he thought about it, he could maybe put five or six rounds in Deneaux before she could swivel his way. I quickly rethought my stance—it was even money. Bookies would have a field day with this if there were such a thing as betting on duels. As it was, Mano had completely forgotten about his weapon.

"Aren't you guys vaccinated or some shit?" I asked, looking for a way to save at least one life in this room of growing horrors.

Mano shook his head. "Only officers and VIPs."

"Michael, if you won't I will."

"He's got a few hours. Why are you in such a rush?"

She shrugged her shoulders.

"Odds are, none of has a couple of hours. I see no sense in adding the mark of his death to our souls."

Deneaux was about to speak.

"Figure of speech, for all of us, I'm thinking," I told her.

She smiled, this one was real. I don't think she believed she'd lost her soul, I just think she thought she'd never been encumbered with one.

"Very well."

"Glad I could get your stamp of approval." I turned back to the soldier. "Would a vaccine help now?"

"Not the vaccines," he gulped. "I know they're working on a cure though." He looked hopeful.

"Working on one? Or have one. They have to have something because they treated and cured my son and friend. Where would they be?" I was beginning to scan the myriad of tables and cabinets.

"Not here." James finally returned from the deep depths of mourning. He gently laid his brother down, stood and wiped his eyes. He was a warrior; he knew if there was time later, he would give his brother the remembrance he deserved. "Hospital would be the place."

"And where would that be?" It didn't matter much—it could be the room next door, but we couldn't get there.

"Other side of the facility."

"Of course it is."

"I can make it!" Mano offered feebly.

Well, if that doesn't give you an indication of how scary Deneaux is, I don't know what will. He was willing to brave ten thousand zombies alone rather than her. I guess that…and the fact he now had the virus in him.

"He tries to open that door, I'll kill him." Deneaux still hadn't looked at him. Her eyes were glued on our other adversary's avenue of approach.

Mano had pulled his pant leg up. I could see thick, black-red tendrils sprouting from the wound, heading to his heart and brain. The virus was spreading and quickly; even as I watched it moved up past his knee and out of sight, buried beneath the camouflage material.

"Get it out!" Mano wailed, looking at all of us. "I've got to go try!" he pleaded.

"You won't make it," James told him.

"I have to try, man, I have to."

"I know you do. I know," James told him.

"Th-thank you," Mano blubbered, heading for the door where Tommy was stationed.

What happened next…I saw it and I barely believe it. Mano had no sooner turned his back when James reached down and pulled his sidearm out, a Colt 1911. He shot Mano with a .45 caliber bullet straight through his spine. Smoke wisps trailed up as Mano fell down.

"I'm so sorry," he told Mano as he shot him again, this time in the head to make sure he was down for good and not suffering. He just stared at the body.

"There's a man that knows how to take charge."

"Not now, Deneaux," I told her.

Even Tommy looked surprised, and I had to imagine he'd seen worse.

"It had to be done." I think James said this more for his own sake than ours, but Tommy tried to comfort him as best he could.

"Then there were four," Deneaux said with her usual cackle. I wondered how many times she'd probably played this little game in her life; and, inexplicably, she always ended up as the last man standing. I wanted to tell her she was a sick fuck, but she'd probably like that.

"Deneaux, do you have an angle on that lock?" I was

whispering.

"Why are you whispering?" Then she added, "Really? Do you really think what is back there can understand you?"

"Are you willing to take that chance?"

"Fine, your game, I'll play until it isn't amusing anymore." She lowered her voice. "Yes, I do. Why?"

"I can feel it in every fiber of my being…that *thing* is watching us. Can you get a shot off and drill it in its fucking eye?"

"From here? I could put the bullet through the center of a penny."

The lock hole was much bigger, more like a silver dollar, according to Deneaux this was like a three-yard field goal attempt in football. Or for you European types, a free kick without a goalie. If I was taking the shot, I would have propped the weapon up on something stable and unmoving, lined it up for half a minute, and most likely would have had my tongue firmly clenched in my teeth as I concentrated hard enough to burst a blood vessel in my eye before taking the shot. I like to think I'm a decent shot, at least with a rifle…and still, the odds I would make this shot under the current circumstances were fifty-fifty; with a pistol that would have dropped down to about ten percent, and that one-in-ten chance would be attributed to sheer luck.

Deneaux took maybe half a heartbeat longer to aim and fire, but that could have been because her exhalation of smoke was clouding her vision. All hell broke loose when that round left the chamber. The beast beyond the door howled in rage and pain when he—or it—was struck. It sounded like the thing was tossing Chevys around the room. I fully expected the adjoining wall to collapse and the thing to come hurtling through at any moment. Even the unflappable Deneaux got off her perch and behind a desk. Not that this was going to stop that thing, for her it was just the perceived safety.

"I think you got him," I said, holding my rifle up

firmly to my shoulder, waiting for it to come.

I wished it would get it over with, as the anticipation was not a good one. I had adrenaline prickles running the length of my arms, shoulders and torso. My body was under the firm belief that I should be getting the hell out of here, and I agreed.

"Whatever gave you that impression?" Deneaux answered wryly.

"Just a hunch." A loud thump to our backs was fighting to grasp my undivided attention. "Tommy?" I asked, not daring to turn.

"Bulkers."

"I love today. How in the hell was I better off in my cell?"

"Oh, dearie, it's just your mind's way of telling you where you belong."

The bulkers were, I believe, attracted to the noise our "friend" was making, and somehow I got the impression that was what it meant to do. A normal, enraged, wounded animal would have charged. That's just the nature of an ordinary creature. Kill what is threatening it; hell, that's a normal human response. Not this thing, no, we had to get a damn animal that had studied the *Art of War*. It knew…it just fucking knew it could not come at us directly, that to do so would spell its doom.

The pile of furniture jumbled as bulkers once again took a go at our door. A cabinet overturned and a chair skittered across the floor, finally resting on the far wall.

"The hinges are starting to show signs of stress," James said.

Tommy nodded when I dared take a quick glance at him for confirmation.

"We need to shut Sasquatch up, he's attracting them," I said, although I had not an iota of a plan to back my words up with.

"I would imagine a good meal would keep him

preoccupied for a while." Deneaux was looking at me.

"I guess that leaves you out," I said, referring to the stringy, tough meat Deneaux would yield.

She got it. For a second I thought she was going to stick out her tongue at me.

Another battering, and furniture spilled like a moving van filled with a homeowner's goods driven by pissed off underpaid employees, so yeah, basically every mover ever. James and Tommy were trying to rebuild our barricade, but that was going to matter little if the door came unhinged. Periodically the Abominable Snowman would screech this ear-piercing sound. I think, if he kept it up, I would have gladly offered myself to it just to escape the din.

For a second that seemed pre-ordained, I mean it had to be, the timing was just too incredulous, the Yeti had stopped screaming. Whatever he had been smashing had finally broken, and there was a blissful second where he was quiet. The bulkers had stopped to regroup before once again attacking the door, so, for just this small window, there was a blaring quiet, if that makes sense. This was shattered with the metallic sound of a door hinge bouncing off the tile floor. All of our gazes were torn to that small, cylindrical piece of metal like it was the key to the universe and technically, for us, it sort of was. Then the cacophony started anew.

"Well, that doesn't bode well."

"How dare you call your son Captain Obvious," Deneaux said.

"I really wish I could figure out how not to always speak my mind. Anybody holding on to an idea…now might be a fantastic time to let the rest of us know."

"Mr. T, I think I can get that door open before the animal can react."

The rest could go unsaid. Once that steel shield was out of the way, we could drill it with as much lead as we could sling. My fear was that it wouldn't be enough. Did Yetis need to be shot with silver bullets? Or maybe it was platinum, I don't know. Never really done my research on the matter. Just because I always wanted there to be proof they existed didn't mean I necessarily wanted to count one as an adversary.

I could hear the machinations in Deneaux's twisted brain already wheeling around. I seriously would not put it past her to put a round or two in Tommy, just enough to slow him down so that the animal could get a hold of him. While it was busy trying to kill the boy, we could take care of it. I mean it was an evilly brilliant plan. Tommy was strong enough that he could put up a viable enough fight while we surrounded and pounded the animal. None of this would portend well for Tommy, but it certainly would for the rest of us, including Deneaux—which, in reality, was all she cared about. There was an animalistic simplicity to her way of thinking. It sure did make going through life a little easier if all you were ever concerned with was your own skin.

"Do not fire until he is clear." I was looking at Deneaux when I spoke. She didn't say anything, but I might have seen the slightest drop to her lip as if I'd caught her. "I've been around you long enough, and yeah, I meant to say that part out loud."

I turned to look over at Tommy. Our barricade was rapidly becoming a pile of rubble. The door now had a noticeable bulge, and the second hinge was holding on for its life. Well, *our* lives really, but the point made is the same. I nodded tersely to Tommy as our choices, which we really had none to begin with, were rapidly diminishing.

"I've got this," James said to Tommy as he took his place trying to hold the bulker door in place.

Tommy had a look of consternation on his face. Just because he was as close to immortal as possible, that didn't mean he wouldn't fear for his safety. A torn off arm was a torn off arm—the bleeding would stop, and the wound would knit itself closed quickly, but the arm, well yeah, that would be gone forever. What happened next was instantaneous.

(Reading it will take longer than what actually happened.) Tommy became a blur as he crossed the room. He pushed so hard on the Yeti's door that I thought there was possibly a chance it would slam against the wall to the side and just as quickly shut again, leaving us back to square one. Although, now the monster would know our plan, or at least part of it, and I was confident it would not allow this to happen again.

Alright...let me try to get the timing right here. Tommy had just shoved the door open, and for a flash of a second, I saw an ape. It wasn't a Yeti, but it could have been if I was just using sheer size as a comparison. The right side of his face had suffered some serious damage from where Deneaux's bullet had struck; a crevice easily as thick as my finger and just as long had burrowed its way from the corner of its eye socket back toward its ear. A yellowish-red pus oozed from the wound. The ape was about to throw what it had in his hands, it could have been a table leg, I'm not sure. I was still completely transfixed by the sight of an ape that was clearly a zombie, but it was more than that.

Deneaux was rattled as well, though she was still able to get a shot off. The bullet penetrated the ape's massive brown chest, leaving a smear of blood. Another concerted attack to our rear sent James hurtling past our location; though I, along with Deneaux, soon found ourselves being shoved along as furniture was spewed about like an erupting volcano filled with office supplies. James was impaled in the stomach with the metal desk leg as the ape fired it past me. Something struck me in the back of the head, spots danced before my eyes. I felt a stream of blood travel down my neck and follow the hollow of my spine. I twisted to see another hinge pin roll to a stop. Anything bigger and it would have made my brain into soup.

James screamed from the insertion of the foreign object. Deneaux was nowhere to be seen. Bulkers had crashed through and were forcing entry into our rapidly diminishing space. A small tsunami of compressed organs and blood were making their way toward us, splashing up against and going around every obstacle in its way. The bulkers, in their desire to get to a food source, any food source, crushed every impediment in their way, squashing them to the point where those unfortunate bastards had popped like overblown zits on a fourteen-year-old Twinkie junkie. The ape was rushing forward, James was his only impediment. The ape seemed to war within itself in regards to destroying or eating the enemy, he seemed to satisfy both urges as he bit through James' shoulder, taking out a chunk roughly equivalent to half a dinner plate. Impossibly large canines shredded through the meat and bone. What was still cognizant within James screamed his final hill-shrilled pitch.

'The ceiling, Mr. T, hurry!' Tommy's in the head voice threatened to complete what the hinge pin had started.

I didn't know what he meant, but that he had an idea was enough for me. I took one stride and hopped atop a table. With one forceful jump and outstretched hands I broke through the pasty dry ceiling shingles. I dislocated two fingers as they struck a heavy metal pipe that looked like something gas or propane would travel through. I grabbed hold, wincing as my fingers wrapped around the metal. A bulker's hand reached up to grab at my thigh, and I quickly pulled my legs up as I struggled to find a suitable enough place to cram the toes of my boots into so that I could hold on…suspended like the world's largest bat.

"You see Deneaux?" I yelled.

Tommy, like me, was clinging to an overhead pipe. He thrust his head over his far side. I could just make out one of her legs. She was on the ground, laid out. Dead or unconscious, either way, she was about to meet one of her two makers, I had my bet in on which one that was going to be as bulkers were within feet of her. On one side of the coin, the world—and my world specifically—would be better the moment she departed this plane. A sort of justice would be paid. On the dreaded flip side, our odds of escape had been greatly reduced, meaning I wouldn't be able to enjoy her demise for quite as long as I would like. Can't have it all I suppose.

The thing that was once an ape bridged the gap between Deneaux and the bulkers. He wrapped his large hand around her ankle, lifting her up effortlessly. A snarl opened up so wide I figured for a second that he was just going to swallow her whole. Instead, he swung her like a club, his goal to bash the bulkers into submission, I guess. Deneaux's head whipped past the first line of bulkers. She narrowly missed having her skull caved in from the contact. King Konglet roared in rage that he'd come up empty. Then something happened that none of us had been prepared for. Deneaux's shoe came off in his hand as she was at the apex of the ape's swing.

You have got to be shitting me was quite literally my thought as Deneaux's unconscious body came flying through the air right at me.

Tommy asked the same question I was asking myself. *'Are you going to catch her?'* I didn't know the answer until I let go with my right hand and snagged her out of mid-air. There was no question I was going to regret this. I was disappointed with myself for saving her. I would have only been marginally more distraught had I let her sail on by, and I was confident I would have been able to reconcile that.

"She's heavier than I figured she would be," I said as I grunted to swing her around so I could keep her as high off the ground as possible. "Would have figured carcinogens didn't weigh as much. She's a fucking rock-solid old lady alright, and I cannot even begin to tell you how revolting it is to be this close to her."

"You did the right thing."

I wanted to ask how he'd reached that conclusion, but the events immediately below us warranted our attention. The ape, deprived of his throw toy and the bulkers, denied their food, now discovered they were enemies. The ape clearly had a case of the zombies, and for some reason, the bulkers weren't picking up on that. The ape was most definitely on their menu, and they were doing all in their power to get at him, teeth gnashing wildly and clacking together like dominoes being slammed down on a table in a particularly rowdy game of Muggins. The ape seemed more than up for the challenge as he slammed bulkers and speeders with his massive fists. If they got too close, he wasn't squeamish in the least about biting off whatever was before him. He opened bodies wide, internal organs sloughing to the floor as he did so, intermingling with the thick layer of viscera already there.

The ape was winning; there was no doubt about that. The bulkers, for all their girth, were not nearly as big as the beast, their advantage lay in numbers. It was a fight to the end, one the ape would finally succumb to. Either way, stuck to this ceiling like a bat or a scared cat was not going to do us any favors.

"The animal lab, Tommy!" I nodded my head over to the open door.

The ape seemed to understand my words and roared his disapproval, not that he was in any position to do anything about it. He was rapidly becoming surrounded. I felt a pang for the majestic animal he had once been, but not this man-tampered abomination. I began to move toward the door. Shifting my feet was easy enough, but I only had my left hand to grasp the pipes. When I let go with it to move, Deneaux and my upper torso came dangerously close to the fight below.

"I'll go first and then you toss her." Tommy had already halved the distance, a few more feet and he could drop down and run in.

There was always the chance I could just "accidently" lose my grip on Deneaux, letting her go WAY too short and right into the mix. Fucking conscience got in the way. Here I am, smack dab in the middle of a war where all the rules of a polite society are thrown out and yet I could not force myself to descend into that chaos. Well, if I'd learned anything from all this, a soul wasn't necessarily tied to a code of ethics, I could still sense what was right and wrong.

"Throw her!" Tommy was standing like a wide receiver in football, waiting for the ball to come his way.

It was comical in a way. Come to think of it, her skin was leathery like a pigskin. This was in no shape, way, or form going to be an easy feat. My feet were pointed toward Tommy, I was upside down and I had to throw a human, well, a being at least. Calling her a human seems to send the wrong message. If I could have gripped her around the waist and thrown her like a traditional football, it would have been a lot easier. It would have been pretty cool to watch Deneaux do a spiral. Now I had to figure out where the best place was to grab her and swing her like a pendulum. I'd thought about grabbing the back of her shirt but there was a high percentage her top would come off and I'd seen enough nightmares in this lifetime that I wasn't going to add to them.

There was her head, good possibility I'd snap it off, but oh well. I settled for under her arm. I had to swing her slightly side-armed to keep her feet from smacking into the heads of zombies below.

"One," I grunted as I swung.

"Two." She had a decent arc going.

"Three." I let her sail.

She slipped a little as I released her and was going to fall short. "Fuck," I muttered as she came within a hand span of hitting the ceiling, thus halting all of her forward momentum.

The back of her head clipped a zombie who looked up. His eyes grew wide like the heavens were dropping him gifts. It was now a race to see who would get to her first as Tommy left the relative safety of the doorway to catch her before she bounced off the floor and was sure to shatter a hip.

Tommy dove, lying out to catch her, he mostly

succeeded. The zombie pounced as well, but Tommy was faster as he whisked her back and up even as he was rising. The bones that shattered were in the zombie's mouth as he bit down hard on tile. Deneaux had once again slipped past her due date.

"Come on!" Tommy offered.

Funny how people think others need encouragement in these situations. I wasn't getting pumped up for a job interview or asking Becky Collins out to the prom; I was desperately trying to save my skin. This was slightly more important than the chance to feel up Becky, slightly. I mean she had really nice breasts for a sophomore. She said 'no' by the way, went with Dennis as a matter of fact. I would have been pissed at him longer if she hadn't drunk so much that night that she passed out before the prom king and queen were announced. She threw up all over the interior of his parents' car. I mean like violent expulsions. There was stomach stew from the windshield to the backseat. The car reeked of gin and bile for weeks.

Add to that, Dennis had to schlep her drunk-ass, passed-out self to her parents' front door. He'd told me he'd thought about ringing the doorbell and just hauling ass. Instead, he had waited with her in his arms as more of what was in her globbed all over the front of his rented tux, which he ended up buying because they couldn't get out the sauce stains from the spaghetti she'd eaten earlier. How could you be mad at someone who had laid out hundreds of dollars for the occasion, ended up grounded for two weeks and basically missed the entire event as he monitored her sickness most of the night? I wanted to tell him it was karma for stealing my date, but even I'm not that big of an asshole. Oh, and to top it off, the bitch had completely thrown his ass under the bus by saying he'd supplied the liquor. I saw her reasoning—she was just trying to mitigate the trouble she was in. Mr. Collins had expressly forbid that they ever date again. Not that it mattered much. At age sixteen, puppy love kind of loses its luster when it is glommed over with vomit.

Wow, random thought as I moved closer to the door. Tommy had slid Deneaux past him and into the zombie-less room—much like one would a shuffleboard puck—before turning his attention on the zombie. He reached out with his left arm to keep it at bay, grabbing the tatters of its shirt while it growled and bit at him. Tommy simultaneously pulled him closer and spun him around. The back of the zombie's head was to him as he wrapped a forearm around its neck and crushed. When the bones were sufficiently destroyed, he twisted the head off. It was vulgar in its savagery. His teeth were gritted as he looked up to me, the zombie falling to the floor, its head still in Tommy's clutches. At some point, as I dropped down, he had gotten rid of it. We both ran into the room and began the task of barricading the door.

This time we were not encumbered with any limitations as we stacked stuff from one end of the room to the other. It would be difficult to get through, but not impossible. We were once again trapped as the din of a battle waged mere feet away assailed our ears. The ape had not yet succumbed. I couldn't be sure, but from the heavy thud sounds, I was fairly confident he was swinging a bulker around like a bat.

"As soon as either of them is done, they're going to come this way."

"Yup," Tommy answered abruptly.

"What's the matter, Tommy? This getting to you? We've been in worse situations." That was partly a lie.

"Did you see the zombie?"

"Which one? There's like a hundred of them in there."

"The one I killed."

"They're not people anymore, Tommy. You of all people should know that. And why now? We've been doing this for months."

"He was a person once."

"Tommy?"

"Mr. T, it was Doc."

I stumbled backwards like I'd been punched in the nose. My eyes watered, my chest pounded, my head swam, and my equilibrium took this moment to lose itself. I staggered to a chair.

"Are you sure?" It was the only thing I could think to ask.

Tommy didn't need to answer. The expression on his face was the only indication I needed.

"Fuck, where's Porkchop?"

"This has got to end, doesn't it, Mr. T? At some point doesn't it just have to end?"

"Of course it does. At some point everything comes to pass." Note that I didn't exactly say how this was going to end, or that the outcome was going to be favorable. But yes, change was inevitable.

Tommy sat just as Deneaux began to moan and stir.

"Well, she ought to make everything better," I said sourly. "And since when did we get back on the menu? I thought as non-humans we were immune to the zombies?"

"There's not much they won't eat and there is a scarcity of food plus..."

"Plus? There's a plus?"

"They're opportunistic, we're here, they're hungry."

"Can't you push them away or something?"

"You already know the answer, with the loss of Eliza we both lost a significant portion of that ability. I'm not sure if I could tell one to close its mouth while it chewed."

"I wish Deneaux would wake up, that's how little I want to talk about this."

Chapter Thirteen – Tracy

"Should have just taken a fucking scooter!" BT said, moving his elbows around trying to find room that wasn't there.

The four-cylinder gas and battery powered hybrid struggled with carrying nearly its own weight in passengers.

"For once, Trip is the smart one in this equation," BT lamented.

Trip had grabbed the saddle off the horse he'd been riding and had, with some redneck ingenuity, fastened it to the roof of the car. With his feet in the stirrups and one hand on the pommel he was screaming at the top of his lungs, "Yeeeee-ahhh!" It was his jumping up and down on the saddle that was driving BT crazy. Every time he did it, the roof would collapse a little more, cramping those inside by incremental degrees.

"Leave him be, he's the only one having any fun these days. And I, for one, find it endearing," Tracy admonished BT.

"You would, you've had sufficient practice riding on the crazy train," BT said sourly. "Why'd he come anyway?"

Tracy shot him a glance that simultaneously seared and froze his face. "You done bitching?"

"Yes, ma'am." He put his hands in his lap.

"Shit, Mom, you rock!" Travis said, truly amazed at the power his mother could wield.

"How many times do I have to tell you? No swearing!" She was looking through the rearview mirror.

"Yes, ma'am," Travis echoed, smiling at BT as the big man turned around to smile at him.

"Oh, my God." Tracy had been about to reprimand BT for egging her son on. When she came in to view of the Demense facility, all of that changed.

It was one thing to see the zombies stream by, it was quite another to see that many all congealed in one spot.

"Must be a hell of a concert!" Trip yelled.

Tracy let out an involuntary laugh because from this distance that's exactly what it looked like, a crowd of people trying to get into a particularly hot event.

"Tracy." BT was saying a lot with that one word. Short of a couple of tanks, there was no way they could get through that many zombies. The car came to an abrupt stop.

"Whoa, this horse is trying to throw me!" Trip shouted.

"Mom? Why are you stopping? We can get through that or find a way around them." Justin had wriggled his way up so that his head was next to his mother's.

They were on a small rise, but it was enough to see that Justin's words were only wishful thinking. The building was blanketed with zombies.

"There's...there's thousands," Tracy said, a distant look to her eyes.

Getting to Mike was of the utmost importance to her, yet she would not needlessly endanger those with her in a quest that had a significant chance for failure. Her head dropped down nearly to her chest.

"Mom? Travis asked. "Are we going?"

BT said nothing as he watched tears fall soundlessly onto Tracy's lap.

"Boys, let's get out and take a look." BT urged everyone out so that Tracy could have a moment to mourn her decision. They didn't have anything near to what they needed, personnel or weapon-wise, to get through that many zombies. To go in would mean their deaths. That wasn't drama—it was fact. To stay out, meant Mike's death. If this was a simple life exchange, BT would have charged in no questions asked. Mike, for all his shortcomings and foibles was his brother plain and simple. Obviously not biologically but certainly cosmically.

If Tracy hadn't stopped when she did, BT would have spoken up had she gotten closer. Mike had asked him to look out for their family. To attempt a rescue under these circumstances would have spelled instant doom. He would be doing little to honor Mike if he had his whole family join him in death.

"I didn't think we'd ever see more zombies than we did at Grandma's house." Travis was throwing rocks off the small hill.

"Is there anything we can do?" Justin asked.

BT shook his head tersely.

"Who's going to tell Mom?" Travis asked.

"She already knows," BT replied.

"What now?" Justin asked, a shine to his eyes from tears that threatened to fall.

"Well, just because we can't get in, doesn't mean your dad can't get out."

"You believe that?" Justin wiped at his left eye.

"Most of me says no. No way anyone could get out of there. But your dad isn't just anyone, we all know that. If there's a way, I'm sure he will make it the most difficult, extreme escape possible."

"That a joke?" Justin was rubbing his other eye now, doing his best to make it look exactly like he was not rubbing tears away.

"It's okay to cry. You're no less of a man for showing emotion."

"Yeah you are," Travis whispered in his brother's ear.

Justin pushed Travis. "Ass."

BT marveled at how resilient the boys were. They were able to process and assimilate new information at a much faster rate than any of the adults. He figured part of that was their youth, but a larger, more significant portion had to do with the age they grew up in. The rate they were bombarded with information almost dwarfed anything from the previous generations combined since the dawn of mankind. It was no wonder they could react faster and think through problems with an alarming speed. For some, the mega-doses of information could cause people to withdraw, including his own nephews who wouldn't so much as grunt at him when he would visit. Too engrossed in their video games. These two would mourn and they would cry and they would move on. It was inevitable.

It was Tracy he feared for. There was a good chance she wouldn't recover from this, at least not fully. Shells didn't survive well in this world. They were too brittle for the rough handling they were likely to get. There was no infrastructure around anymore that could spare the time to coddle those who were fragile. Shells were broken and discarded on a daily basis now.

BT walked back to the car while the boys horsed around a little longer. It was their way of dealing with the danger their father was in. Who was he to tell them it was wrong?

"We should get going soon, chief." Trip had dropped down from the car roof. He smacked BT across the chest to punctuate his point.

"Go? Go where?" BT asked, looking at his chest to make sure there wasn't residue from whatever Trip had been doing last. Knowing the man's penchant for drug use, there was no telling.

"The concert, man, the concert. Look, they're filing in. We're going to miss the opening song, man, and that always sets the tone for the rest of the show." Trip was excited.

"He's right," Gary said.

"Not you too." BT shook his head.

"Well, not the concert part, but they are going in. I can't tell for certain, but I'd say at least a quarter of the zombies have gone into that building. They keep going in at this pace, there will be no more of them outside in an hour."

"So?" Stephanie asked. "Inside, outside, what's the difference? Seems like it would be worse. There will be nowhere to run. You'd be trapped." She shuddered and wrapped her arms around herself. She turned to see Tracy looking at her. "I'm so sorry," she said quickly. "I...I was just talking before I thought."

"I'm glad I never do that," Trip told his wife.

BT wanted to tell him that was because he *never* thought. But now was not the time.

"It's alright; it's not like I don't know what's going on." Tracy was staring off into the distance with everyone else.

"You know this is Mike we're talking about, right?" BT offered.

"We'll wait until all or most are inside and then I'd like to get in a little closer. Just in case, I mean," Tracy said.

"Of course," BT answered.

Henry was looking where they all were. His stub of a tail wagged back and forth twice before he sat down.

"I think he agrees with you." BT reached down to pet the dog's head.

Chapter Fourteen – Maine

Ron paced along his deck. He hadn't heard anything from either of his brothers in close to a week. Odds were good that Mike had just destroyed another truck and the radio along with; he'd just have to wait it out. There was a constant roiling within his gut, though. Part of it was the not knowing what was going on, and part was being one of the few adults left at his home to defend in case of attack. The amount of responsibility was beginning to take its toll. When he wasn't on guard duty, he was repairing parts of their home or its defenses. And when he would finally go to sleep, his dreams were littered with the various nightmarish instances that could still befall them.

Unlike Mike, he'd had his shit together before all this apocalypse crap had happened. He had not needed a court order to join the Marine Corps to stay out of jail. He had, instead, stayed in corporate America. He'd risen through the ranks to become successful and then took the money to invest where his expertise in business had really excelled—in real estate. He'd done so well that he'd found a way to build his dream home, with his wife, and retire early. He felt the sweet fruit was his just rewards for toiling the soil so diligently.

And now where had that gotten him? Money certainly meant nothing anymore. His once beautiful home would now be considered an extreme fixer-upper with additional projects. There were enough dead bodies in and around his yard to rival Gettysburg. His father had perished defending the inhabitants.

"It's not a home anymore. It's a fortress. A prison, really." He had his hands on the deck railing and was looking out over the pond. "We were going to travel. See the world. I was going to make it up to Nancy for all those times I had to work late or fly off to who-knows-where to fix who-knows-what. Seemed so important back then. I knew this was the goal I was trying to achieve and for what?"

"Don't be so hard on yourself." Ron's wife, Nancy startled him as he spoke aloud. "No one could have known this was how it was going to turn out."

He waited for her to join him at the railing before he spoke again. "I know, I know, it's just that, for the first time in my life, I feel so wholly unprepared. I love my brother, so don't take this out of context. But growing up, he was a fuck-up. If there was a way to get into trouble, sure as shit, he would find it. Trust me, back then it was nice to have him around, because it always took the focus off the rest of us. Short of stealing a car, I could pretty much fly under the radar. He just did whatever he wanted, daring the consequences to catch up with him. It was sort of amazing to watch from the sidelines sometimes."

"As his older brother you never thought to maybe help him out?"

"We tried, all of us. It was like trying to straighten a spring; you could push and pull as much as you liked, and eventually it would look like he was straight and narrow. But you turned your back for an instant, and he would spiral back to his true form. He just didn't care. He isn't a bad person—he's not mean. I don't think he intentionally goes around with the attitude of seeking out messes. He just doesn't care about what could happen on the other end of his actions. It's like there's a big disconnect there for him. Most of us look at the world and think if I do 'A' to get to 'B' then 'C' is a potential for the outcome. Whereas Mike is like, 'Fucking A!'"

Nancy laughed. "Yup, that sounds like your brother. Sorry," she said when she realized her husband wasn't sharing in her amusement.

"This is serious." His eyebrows furrowed.

"I know." She had to place her hand up by her mouth to hide her smile.

"I knew the day would come when Mike was faced with prison. It was an inevitability. Civilization is not a fan of wildcards. I'm happy the judge gave him the opportunity to join the Marines. I figured it would do him some good, you know? A good ass kicking or three might be exactly what he needed. Not Mike, though. The Marine Corps just gave him new venues to perform in. Then, somehow, he gets this beautiful, intelligent woman to marry him. If she wasn't from the U.S., I would have said it was merely for a green card, but I don't think there were even any immigrants that were quite that desperate. A wife, kids, a job, same Mike."

"So what's the problem, dear?" Nancy asked, wrapping her arm around her husband's waist.

"The entire time Mike is fucking up, I keep my nose to the grindstone, working sixty, sometimes seventy hour weeks. I'm away from our children for work almost two weeks out of every month, and the goal was for this!" His hand goes out to the expanse of the water and trees before them. "I finally get us here, in this place, and this shit happens. And now that the entire world has been flipped upside down, it's Mike that's the better for it."

"I'm not sure I understand what you're saying, Ron. Mike is better off because there's a zombie apocalypse?"

"No, sorry. No one is better off. What I'm trying to say through my frustration is that someone who walked so precariously and carefree through the previous world is now the one most suited to lead us through this one. The majority of his life has been a fuck up and…and…"

"And it's prepared him completely for all of this."

"Yes." Ron sighed. "Somehow he's kept his entire family safe, and I failed our daughter."

"You did no such thing! There's nothing you could have done. I miss Melanie as much as you do, but I in no way hold you responsible for her demise. She was an adult, she was out on her own, and she got bit. I don't think even your brother could have done anything to prevent that. It's okay, hon. I know you're also still in pain over the loss of your father, we all are, and seeing that you're the oldest, you consider yourself the patriarch of this family now. It's alright to have help, though. You don't need to do this alone. Just because he's your baby brother doesn't mean he's a kid."

"I know, I get it, maybe I'm just tired. This just isn't the way I thought things would happen."

Nancy let go a small laugh. "Sorry," she told her husband. "I don't think anyone had this in their future plans."

"Probably right."

"Get some sleep, I'll stay out here." Nancy watched as her husband headed inside. His shoulders, which had been slumped when she came out, were now at least a little more upright. She was just finishing her cup of coffee and was about to head in to refill it when she heard the cracking of a branch not more than twenty feet into the woods on her left.

They hadn't seen a zombie in nearly a week, and she just couldn't imagine there were any left in the entire state. But that didn't mean she wasn't going to keep looking for them. She knew it was those who lost vigilance who were often the ones that died before their time. As the cracking got louder, her eyes grew wider. The first signs of alarm began to track through her body—adrenaline, sweat, and quickening heart rate. She was even unconsciously holding her breath. She nearly screamed out loud when the fawn stepped from the trees. A heavy gust of pent-up air expelled from her lungs.

"Whoo, where's your momma, little guy?" she asked. The fawn seemingly heard her as he looked up at the deck. His head swiveled to the rear and then he bounded off. "Like I need another cup of coffee," she said, looking at her shaking cup-laden hand.

She went in anyway. As the French door slid shut a zombie, that had been following the fawn, came out of the woods. She'd finally caught up to the mother and son pair this morning after chasing them for two days. Last night, her big break had come when the mother stepped into a gopher hole and fractured one of her front legs. She'd kept on for a few miles more before finally collapsing from the pain and exhaustion. The baby had bleated at her to move. He had stayed long enough to watch his mother die. When the life within her left, so did he.

The zombie was halfway across the lawn when she heard a sound to her right. She looked up to the big house and was drawn to it. A baser instinct told her that this was a habitat that her preferred food lived in.

Even as she approached the structure, her eyes looked around for a way into the dwelling. The sounds pulled her to the other side of the house. If she had been capable of a grin, one would have beamed across her face. She saw a gaping hole in the side of the house. The zombie had also found a small opening in the fence that Ron had on his list of repairs. It had been low on the list of priorities because the zombies before it had not made any sort of attempt to seek it out; if they happened to stumble upon it, the thought of making themselves diminutive enough to fit through it seemed beyond their grasp of comprehension. Not this one. She wouldn't be winning any spelling bees soon, but this one had a predatory gaze to its eyes. There was higher brain function than merely to *eat*—she had rudimentary strategies on *how* to get food, not just consume it.

She walked in and sampled the air with five quick sniffs. *Food.* It was here and in abundance. *Quiet,* she thought. She knew enough to be quiet. This food was dangerous. This food fought back, not like earlier today's food. She walked through the entire basement, stopping to sniff every few steps. The food was tantalizingly close, but not here. She heard the thumping of footsteps above her head. She looked up to follow it.

Up, she thought, looking at the stairs. At the top landing, she stared at the door. She had been tempted to hammer away at it. An angry, red color kept flashing in her head every time she thought this, and she knew that red meant danger. She stared at the door handle. Without even consciously thinking about it, her hand was moving toward the handle. She could not understand why. Even as her hand grasped the cool metal, she could only stare with a sort of fascination, as it seemed to perform this function of its own volition. Possibly muscle memory. A crack of light formed when the door opened slightly. The heavenly scent of food wafted out to her. She let go of the handle and blissfully walked in and past the door.

She heard sounds to her side; there was more than one food. *Too dangerous.* She had to find one alone, a small one, a hurt one. Her instincts were solely in charge as she moved.

So hungry.

The constant gnawing pain tore at her stomach, her relentless pursuit of food propelling her. Even as she ate, she was thinking about where and when she would do so again. She found herself in a darkened hallway. Most of the doors were closed, but not all of them, and there was food in there. She moved silently over the carpeted floor, her calloused dirt and blood caked feet made not a sound as she walked.

Quiet, eat soon.

She saw a bed that dominated the room, but it was what was atop that grabbed her attention and would not let go. A small thing stood up and looked at her. The word *cat* flashed in her mind, but it meant little to her. She'd eat it when she was done with the bigger one.

The small animal made a loud noise and jumped off the bed, its claws sinking deeply into the sallow flesh of her face. Pain erupted along every puncture wound and was quickly calmed by her internal machinations. A claw raked across her eyeball, tearing all the way through her cornea and into the iris and pupil. Her vision began to blacken on one side as the animal dragged deeper, shredding the lens. She wrapped her hands around the middle of the cat and wrenched it free from her face. If she were capable, she would have been surprised to note that her eye was now attached to the claw of the little beast. She thought about taking a few bites from the spitting, snarling beast, but the noise was causing the bigger prey to stir.

All that mattered was eating. She dropped the smaller food on the floor and quickly moved across the room. The small animal jumped on her leg. Bites and scratches, which should have caused some distress, did little as she descended on the food, the food that was now attempting to sit up even as the zombie tore into its neck, rending pieces of it into her mouth. A scream issued forth from the food even as it attempted to push her away. She just kept biting, the food's struggles becoming weaker and weaker until finally they stopped. She tore large chunks of food free, barely taking the time to chew as she swallowed hunks whole down her gullet and into the bottomless pit of her stomach. She could never be full, but she would never stop trying. Another small animal came in making noise and was now savagely ripping into her leg that still rested on the floor.

She could hear the approaching sounds of more food. She knew they represented danger, yet she could not pull away from the food, not until it was gone. Her last thought as the bullet entered her brain was, *Hungry*.

"Oh God, no!" Ron said as he looked past the smoldering barrel of his rifle. The zombie was dead as was the girl it had attacked. Blood pooled on the neck of the victim. Ron let out an anguished cry as he raced forward in an attempt to save what was already lost.

Chapter Fifteen – Mike Journal Entry 6

The sounds in the next room began to abate as the ape had either cleaned house, moved on, or had succumbed. My hope was that pieces of it now resided in a few dozen regular zombies. The beast was without precedent, and it was my sincerest hope that the thing didn't live out the day. I had no desire to ever meet up with it again.

"Trapped again," I said sourly as the lights flickered.

"What was that thing?" Tommy asked.

"Fucking man, experimenting with shit again that they should have just left alone. What could possibly compel them to make zombie animals? Is not this current fuck-fest enough? Mankind is in such a dire rush to rid itself of mankind they don't stop to think of the repercussions of their actions. I'm sometimes amazed we've made it this long."

"Oh, shut up your drabbling, will you? I have a splitting headache." Deneaux sat up, one bony hand caressing the side of her head while the other was fishing in her pocket for a pack of smokes or an emery board to file her hooves.

"You're welcome, by the way," I told her.

"For what? Allowing me to nearly have my head split open by a relative of yours?"

"Tommy, remind me again why I saved her?"

Tommy shrugged.

"Where are we?" Deneaux was now puffing away on a cigarette. Must have had aspirin shoved in it, because she seemed to have forgotten about her aching head as she looked around.

"The other half of the lab. For animal testing would be my guess," Tommy told her as he looked around at the rows of cages full of all various sorts of animals.

It was mostly mice and rats; there were a couple of smaller monkeys, rhesus maybe. They didn't look good, and I truly felt bad for them. I had to assume though that they'd been infected with whatever the ape had and could not be released. I was extremely happy to not see any dogs; I think I would have had to let them out just on principle.

"How are you planning on getting us out of here?" She shakily pushed herself up off the floor and sat quickly in a chair. It was nice to see that the crone actually had a little humanity in her and was bound to the same chances of injury as the rest of us.

"I was thinking teleportation device. Of course we'd have to test it with you first, just to make sure there are no kinks in it and that your atoms wouldn't reappear all disfigured and stuff. That would be a shame."

She over-exaggerated a smile at me.

"Did you say the animal testing half of the lab?" she asked after a moment.

She was already standing before Tommy or I could answer. She walked directly over to one side of the room. "Here's our way out," she said proudly.

Tommy and I went over to look. "Furnace?" I asked. "Seems like a one way ticket."

She had pushed the small door open and was looking inside. I stepped back expecting a furnace type blast of heat and fire. "Idiot," she said when she pulled her head back in and saw me retreating. "The incinerator is two floors beneath us."

"How the hell was I supposed to know that?" I defended myself. "Why an incinerator? Is it for trash?"

"It's for the animals," Tommy said calmly.

I guess I knew that on some level; I just didn't want to admit it. Any failed experiment, all the scientists had to do was send the animal's carcass down into the blaze below. The poor thing would be forgotten the moment it passed through the steel opening. Talk about eradicating one's mistakes.

I stuck my head through and was looking down a large shaft. It had a slight angle to it, but there wasn't anything to hold onto once inside. It would be an express trip down.

"This is our way out?" I asked, pulling my head out. I'd swear Deneaux had gotten closer; she also had a very strange expression on her face, like maybe she had just missed an opportunity to push me in. I cautiously stepped away. Who knows what kind of strength a demon possesses. "Seems like a death trap. Maybe you should check it out first."

"I will." Deneaux was on the move. Tommy and I looked at each other.

"Did she really just volunteer?" I asked him.

"Sheets!" she said triumphantly. She was pulling theses strange, gray woolen pieces of material out of a cabinet. "They wrap the animals in these before they send them down. They're specially treated for an even burn.

"So wait, you want us to lower you down a two story shaft with a makeshift flammable rope into an incinerator designed specifically for burning at temperatures hot enough to melt bone?"

She nodded.

"Fine by me," I said as I grabbed one of the oily sheets.

Tommy and I tied, and tested the ten sheets we knotted up. "Just one needs to fail," I whispered to him.

"I heard that," Deneaux said from across the room. I don't know how the hell she heard us as her head was all the way in the incinerator opening, and she was looking down the shaft.

"Why now?" I asked her as we tightly tied a sheet around her waist and up and underneath her arms.

"Whatever do you mean?" she asked me coyly.

"Come on, this isn't your style and you know it. Putting yourself out in front. Taking one for the team. Exposing yourself to danger. Whatever. Pick your cliché, it's not you."

"Maybe it's time."

"Yeah, I believe that like I believe Tommy would forgo a Pop-tart."

"Hey, I'm right here," he said, his words slightly muffled.

"Sorry, wait, what the hell do you have there?" I asked, walking over to him. He tried to angle his body away from me to hide whatever it was. "Oh, what is that smell?" I asked, pulling back and covering my nose.

"It's an onion-and-liver pâté-glazed Pop-tart." His smile was waxen.

"Oh, come on, you're just doing that on purpose now." I made sure I was far enough away before I removed my hand from in front of my nostrils.

I waited until Tommy was done before I let him come anywhere near to where we were putting Deneaux through.

"Well, I guess this is goodbye," Deneaux said tenderly as we began to lower her down.

My expression probably made it look like I was trying to pass gas in church silently. My features were all contorted from trying to figure it out. We had her about halfway down when I damn near pulled her back up to ask her what the hell she meant. Tender was not a word one used at all around Deneaux and she sure as hell wasn't sacrificing herself. No, the biddy had something else up her sleeve.

"I'd hate to see it all go up in smoke." I laughed at my own pun.

"What was that?" she asked, looking up.

"Nothing, nothing."

"Go slow you idiots. There's a pressure sensor down here that triggers the flames, if I can get by that I can shut it down." She knew the switch could be activated by a scientist up top or it could be manually overridden, down below, to always stay on. Something she planned on doing as soon as she was on the ground.

"You know, you could have told us about that earlier and we could have done it instead," I told her.

"It's time I contributed. Don't you think?"

"It's been time for a good long while. Why now, though, you snake?" I mumbled to Tommy. He nodded his head agreeing with me.

"The acoustics are amazing inside this pipe. I'm almost there. Do you think you could pay more attention to what is going on rather than talking amongst yourselves?"

"We could just let go." I was looking Tommy in the eye, part of me was kidding, but a part wasn't.

"We'd lose the sheets," he answered seriously.

He was right. That was the only part worth saving.

"Careful!" Deneaux shouted up. It was the first time I'd heard something like alarm.

"How big is it?"

"Normal male question," I heard her hiss.

It was slow going from there as we lowered her an inch at a time. After ten more minutes or so, we finally got the 'all clear' from her. The sheet-rope became slack as she undid herself.

"Give me a minute to disable the incinerator and then you can come on down!" she shouted. She could not be seen due to the angle of the shaft, but we heard her just fine. We pulled the rope up.

"I'll go next, Mr. T," Tommy said as he started to fit the makeshift harness around himself.

"Are you sure?"

"All clear." Drifted up from below.

"Alright, we'll be down in a minute," I answered her.

Tommy was just finishing up and getting ready to climb though the doorway.

"Hold up," I said, grabbing the back of his shirt. "This smells worse than that thing you were trying to call a Pop-tart."

"She's trying to help, Mr. T, so maybe she's seen the light."

"The only light she's ever seen was from the end of

her cigarette. Take the harness off."

"Hurry up!" she called from below.

I went over to the cages and grabbed a small goat that had died relatively recently. "Sorry," I told him. I quickly tied him into the harness.

"Is this necessary, Mr. T? We're wasting time." Zombies were once again hammering at the doorway to our retreat.

"Oh yeah, most definitely necessary," I answered as I gently placed the goat into the shaft. "Tommy is on his way down!" I shouted.

"Good, good." The second good was muffled halfway through as if spoken through a doorway.

We were at just about the same point on the sheets as when Deneaux had us go slow when we felt intense heat blaze up. We both pulled back as a blast of super-heated air flowed past us. We let go of the rope when we realized fire was consuming the sheets at an unnatural pace.

"Fucking bitch tried to kill me!"

I had to laugh, hearing swears come out of Tommy was almost as rare as watching him eat a normal Pop-tart. "Don't feel bad, I'm pretty sure she was hoping it was me."

We both found ourselves now staring at the closed door marked with a warning sign and the word "Incinerator."

After a few moments, we both heard Deneaux's voice drift up. "Michael, are you well? I'm sorry about your friend, but I believe I've figured out how to shut this off now."

"You know I'd love to give it a try, but now the rope is gone."

"Pity. I'd like to wish you good luck, Michael, but I wouldn't mean it. *C'est la vie.*"

Tommy was about to shout something when I placed my index finger over my mouth. "She thinks you're dead, let her think that."

"Fucking heartless bitch," Tommy was muttering as he walked away.

I shook my head. It was like listening to a toddler swear for the first time; simultaneously hilarious and frightening. Frightening, only because you hoped your spouse wouldn't come home while the baby you were tasked with watching was now running around the house shrieking at the top of her lungs, "fucking shit, fucking shit!" after mimicking your earlier outburst.

It was one time—I can't be held accountable for that...

The Red Sox had just given up the tying run in the top half of the ninth and I was stressed out. This gets worse because Nicole wouldn't stop, no matter how much I cajoled her or tried to bribe her...or even scold her. Probably because every time she said it, I would giggle uncontrollably. There is just something endearing about a baby swearing. Maybe it's because they have no idea what they're saying, or maybe it's just because of the sound of their infant voices saying something so scathing.

Who knows? But if Tracy came home and her daughter was running around screaming that profanity, I was going to end up sleeping at a friend's for the next couple of days. Which ultimately made no sense since she swore like a sailor on drunken shore leave her own self. Nicole wouldn't stop. Most babies move on quickly to their next point of distraction. Not Nicole, she held onto that phrase like a Bible thumper to the scripture. "Shit, shit, shit." I was running my hands through my hair. My eyes were looking down to the bathroom and the medicine cabinet. Nicole followed me down that hallway swearing the entire time. I'm sure it didn't help that my shoulders were rising up and down as I laughed.

"Stop it," I admonished her, turning around and sticking my finger in her face as I got down to her level.

"Fucking shit," she answered me.

"Wonderful." I stood back up and went to that medicine cabinet, hoping we had what I was looking for.

"Bingo," I said as I grabbed the bottle of Nyquil. "Want some cherry-soda?" I asked her. With my small swearing machine in tow I headed to the kitchen. "I'm going to burn in hell for this," I said as I dumped some of the cold medicine into her sippy cup with some cola.

Her face wrinkled up as a taste she enjoyed was very much tainted with the bitterness of the medicine. Apparently the pull of sugar was stronger than the repulsion of the sour drug, because she drank everything. I washed out her cup to get rid of any residual smell. I thought my plan was going to backfire for a moment as the sugar coursed through her body; she ran around like she was hopped up on pack of Pixy Stix. Then, as if I was watching a wind-up toy on its last few turns, she began to slow and finally crash.

" 'Bout fucking time," I said softly, and with a sigh of relief, as she laid her head down on the floor on top of her stuffed giraffe.

The Sox were in the bottom of the twelfth just as Tracy pulled up. I could hear the car in the driveway. I looked over to Nicole who was still sleeping peacefully, her mouth moving as if she were chewing or maybe saying something in her dream. I'll swear to this day it looked a lot like "fucking shit."

"How was everything?" Tracy asked as she came in, placing her keys on the small table next to the door. By the way, this was a concept I had yet to grasp no matter how many times I lost my own keys.

"Great," I said softly, pointing to Nicole's prone figure. "Holy shit!" I yelled as Wade Boggs lifted a ball up and over the Green Monster.

"Mike, you know how I feel about you swearing in front of her. Kids pick that stuff up." She walked to the kitchen to put down the bag of groceries she was carrying.

Nicole had one eye open and was looking at me, a knowing smile across her lips.

"You little shit," I said quietly.

"Mr. T, what now?" Tommy's question pulled me from a much more happy time.

"Sorry, just took a little trip down memory lane," I said.

"Don't worry, it wasn't enough medicine to even make her go to sleep."

"When this is over, you and me are going to have a little talk. Forget it. I don't even want to know how you knew. Whether you were in my head or watching I don't want to know. What we're going to do now I'm not sure."

Chapter Sixteen – Mrs. Deneaux

"Never thought I was going to get rid of those twits. One down, one to go," she said.

She looked through the small viewing port as what she believed to be Tommy ignited from the inferno designed to reduce all manner of organic material. This would then quickly be sucked up into the specially designed filtration system.

"Too bad it wasn't Michael, or that they had both come down at the same time. That would have been perfect." She smoked a cigarette and waited for the incinerator to cool down to acceptable levels so she could yell up at Michael.

She closed the door and hit the automatic button to the side of the door that lit the incinerator up manually. What Dixon hadn't told her when he had brought her on a tour of the facility was that it had a fail-safe and would only blaze for fifteen minutes before automatically shutting down in order to avoid overheating.

"You get through that and I'll truly be impressed." She was staring into the vortex of blue-red flame. She knew she wasn't out of the woods quite yet, but she was a lot closer now than she had been. If she were to escape with Michael and Tommy, the time would invariably come when he would ask her the questions he'd been meaning to; in all likelihood, that was the only reason he had even bothered to bring her with him. It seemed he always felt the need for closure. She felt a momentary pang of regret as she walked out of the room, but only because she had lost a protective layer from her most immediate threats.

"On your own again, Vivian. Well, it's not like it's the first time."

She poked her head out and looked up and down the corridor. When she realized she was alone she headed quickly for an emergency door that could only be opened from inside. It had a two-man guard station that had been under video surveillance. To go out this way not during an emergency involved multiple clearances and a thorough pat down to ensure no valuable data or equipment was leaving with you. The guards were long gone, and with the computers out of commission, so was the camera's feed. She flipped it off anyway. She swept her keycard past the reader. The light stayed a steady red until she also entered in a seven-digit code that even the guards wouldn't have known.

She stepped into the escape corridor. It was impossibly long, measuring over three football fields. She could barely make out the far end, but what she could see from here looked clear.

"Now what?" she asked herself in a rare moment of self-doubt.

If she let the door shut, there was no way to open it from this side. The chances of Michael following were slim, but that didn't mean there weren't other personnel in the bowels of the facility looking for an exit—or even a few hundred zombies for that matter. If, for whatever reason, she couldn't get the far door open, or something was already in the dim hallway with her, she would have no avenue for escape. The trepidation had her frozen for a moment, and that angered her to no end. In her mind, inaction was far worse than a wrong choice. She dragged one of the guard's chairs over and wedged it in between the door and the frame.

"I still have this," she said, pulling her pistol free from its holster. "Hell or high water…let's get going."

She plodded a slow and steady course, keeping a constant vigil ahead and behind her. When she got to the far side, she let out a small laugh as she looked at a regular door with a push bar, the same as any door you'd find in a school or public building. There was no keycard or codes necessary. Her fear was unfounded. She pushed it open and stuck her head out into an underground garage. There were a few government vehicles and not much more. She came back in and looked the way she had come. Now she was wishing that she'd had enough faith to go on with the escape door closed. She took a step as if to go and undo what she had done and thought better of it.

"Always forward, Vivian, never look back. What's done is done." She stepped out into the garage.

Chapter Seventeen – Mike Journal Entry 7

"Man, that's hot," I said for the tenth time.

"How many times are you going to touch the door and pull your fingers from the heat?"

"Probably just a few more times." I winced as I once again yanked my scorched digits away.

Tommy just shook his head. "She was going to kill me." He'd said that about as many times as I'd touched that damned door.

"I told you, I'm sure she was really hoping it was me."

"That doesn't make me feel any better."

"No? I mean, because it would make me feel better if it had been you she was trying to kill more than me."

"Really?" he asked so forlornly.

I lied and told him, "No, not really."

I placed my hand against the door again, this time feeling that it wasn't as hot. "I think it's running out of fuel or something." I was pretty sure that I burned my eyebrows off as I opened the door to investigate. That is, if the smell of burnt hair was any indicator.

"Is that smell you?" Tommy was blocking his nose.

"I would think that odor would be right up your alley after some of the crap you eat," I told him as I slammed the incinerator door shut. "Think I might wait a while before I try that again."

"I give it a minute," Tommy replied.

"Do you think the incinerator goes off with the power?" I asked, staring at the door. The pull to open it almost overrode the chance of getting burned again. Almost.

"I don't know…maybe."

"She said there was a pressure switch. That has to be electronic, right?"

"Not necessarily, it could just open up a valve that allows forced gas to shoot in and be ignited by a pilot light."

"You think? It's got to be an electronic ignition, doesn't it?"

"Is it worth taking a chance with your life?"

I wasn't seeing a whole bunch of options. We had to wait until the batteries ran out; we'd be bathed in a complete and utter darkness. Then I was going to get into a tube that would hurtle me two floors down into a potential blaze. Even if I survived the fall, and there was no fire, I'd be in an area with which I had no clue of the layout. There could be zombies all around and I'd never know it, except for the smell, and that wasn't going to tell me specifically where they were, just a general location. Fucking Deneaux was probably halfway to a beach house in Malibu by now, sipping a margarita. There was a high probability that, even if we made it down, we'd wander around the basement like we were in ancient catacombs, forever searching for a way to escape. That was the kind of crap legends were made from.

"Bunsen burners!" I shouted out loud.

"Is that some new sort of swear word, Mr. T?"

"This is a lab, right? They have to have some sort of thing to heat up test tubes and stuff to light them with, right? We're going to need them soon, 'cause I don't want to end up lost in some catacombs like in *Zelda* when Travis had to help me out."

"Catacombs? *Zelda*? Are you talking about a video game?" Tommy asked.

"Maybe. Just help me find something that makes a flame."

It didn't take too particularly long until we came across what we were looking for. The benches set into the walls around the far side had the burners built in and these were attached to a gas supply—probably the same one that burned the stuff that went wrong. We eventually found the older equipment in one of the tables we were using as a stop against the zombies. In it were portable burners and small containers of propane.

"Oh, thank you," I said, kissing the bottle and looking up. "Don't look at me like that. I'm scared of that kind of darkness, it'd be unnatural not to be."

"I didn't say anything. I don't like it either. I once was under Paris in the catacombs for almost two weeks."

"Did you mean to be?"

"No, I was chasing Eliza during World War I."

"In the catacombs?"

"She would drag victims down there so she could take her time feeding, ended up being dozens of them."

I shivered involuntarily as a crawling spider sensation traveled up my spine and settled at the base of my neck. "How'd you get lost?"

"She caught on that I was following her, so she grabbed a young woman right off the streets in broad daylight and dragged her kicking and screaming into that hellhole. She knew I would follow and do all I could to help that poor woman. My sister knew her way around that maze like she'd built it. We made turn after turn to the point where I couldn't even begin to recollect how we had got there. My mind was so preoccupied with the cries of the woman, she was slowly bleeding. When she felt she had lured me in far enough, she ripped the body of that poor soul wide open. My senses had been completely overwhelmed by the smell and the sight. I did all that I could to save that poor girl, but there was little I could do except hold her head as she died. By the time I laid her on the ground, Eliza was long gone. I stood and looked around, realizing I was in a convergence of tunnels and each and every one of them could have been the one that brought me to my present location."

"I thought Deneaux was bad. You were in there for two weeks? How? How did you get out?"

"The hunger. I caught a few rats, but the longing, it was almost more than I could bear. I thought my stomach was going to rip through my midsection. Some teenagers came down into the maze-like crypt on a dare, even back then they were dumb and did all sorts of stupid things. I smelled them, and at first they were so incredibly far away. I stumbled toward them like a drunk to a blessed bottle. They were smoking stale cigarettes and drinking cheap wine, daring each other to go further. One of them named Pieter did. He had an old lighter he was using as a torch. I felt his fear as it illuminated my face. He was too frozen to cry out, to run, to defend himself. I'm so ashamed." Tommy turned away.

I'd seen the beginnings of tears watering his eyes. I knew how the rest of this story went even if he didn't finish it.

"He was just a kid, Mr. T, younger than Travis. I couldn't control myself." His hands were now shaking.

"It's okay, Tommy. You don't need to continue."

"I do, Mr. T, because it didn't just stop with him. His blood coursing through me triggered something animalistic, something barbaric. His friends were calling out for him when they could no longer see his small torch. They were coming closer, laughing and shoving each other, even as I drank deep. Pieter's eyes were fluttering as I drained him of his essence. His mouth was moving, I believe he was trying to warn them. I didn't care…I wanted them to come closer. There were three more boys. I didn't stop until they all became permanent residents of those confines." Tommy was crying like I'd never seen before.

What could I tell him? Wasn't like I could pull out the standard, "Well at least no one died" line that I had used countless times with my daughter's myriads of dramas as she grew up. He'd killed four youths, and even if they were dumber than shit for going down into that vast underground wasteland, they sure didn't deserve to become a vampire's meal.

"Why are you telling me this, Tommy? It serves no purpose."

"Because…" He attempted to compose himself.

"Because I would rather that incinerator be on than to have to go through that again."

That I could understand. Was it even conceivable that we could be lost for that long? How long does a Bunsen burner burn? I needed to distract Tommy from his present dark mood. He seemed to be spiraling even further down the rabbit hole that he had dug for himself.

There were no other dead animals, and unless it was a cat, I wasn't tossing a live one down the chute. Okay, okay, I wouldn't toss a live cat down there either, but I'd be more tempted. I grabbed some miscellaneous stuff around the lab and tossed it in.

"Glass? You're throwing glass down there? If the incinerator is off, you do realize we're going to have to land somewhere, right?" Tommy wiped his nose with his sleeve.

I was about to answer him that I hadn't thought it out that far, when a blast of heat whooshed up toward me. "I guess that isn't going to be a problem."

"Just lucky."

"Tell me again how lucky I am," I said sarcastically, holding my arms out. The zombies started to stir again, and then I realized why. The heat from the incinerator was blowing by me and out to them. Must have smelled like a human barbecue in here. No wonder they wanted in so bad. "I guess we're just waiting. If you had to take a guess, how much longer do you figure we have until the lights go out?"

"Eleven hours, forty minutes and thirty seconds give or take."

"That's, umm, pretty specific."

"When you have as much time as I do, you learn how to mark it with precision."

"Makes sense."

We sat there in silence for a few minutes, the zombies having seemingly forgot about us for the moment. "Are you going to kill Deneaux if we catch up to her?" Tommy asked, breaking the silence.

"Almost seems like a disservice to man if I don't. It's just easier said than done. I mean, if she's pointing a gun at me or at someone in my family, it goes without question that I will do whatever it takes. Cold blood, though? That's a different story. Right now I'd like to do that Middle Eastern method of killing someone."

"What?"

"The whole death by a thousand tiny slices. I think one for every sin she's ever committed."

"Somehow I think you'd come up short."

I laughed. It was a gruesome notion, but there was humor in his response. "Yeah, you're probably right. She'd so deserve it, though. Anything but a prolonged painful death for her would be to spit in the face of everyone she has harmed, Paul included."

"Are you sure that was her?"

"I am. I don't know why I am. Maybe not directly her fault. Paul was my best friend and wholly unsuited for an apocalypse. I get that. But even he wouldn't go out shoeless and without a weapon, add to that there were signs they were together before his death. He found something out, or Deneaux suspected he'd found something out. Or…who knows—maybe they only had one bottle of fucking water and she didn't want to share. Not something I would put past the woman. I have never hated a person as much as I hate her. Even your sister—she was almost as much a victim as she was a culprit. She was striking out for all the wrongs she perceived had been committed against her. Shit, even Durgan was just a dumbass trying to impose his will on everyone.

"But Deneaux, as far as I can tell, was a rich, entitled bitch from her very first demented breath. What she wasn't given, she took with merciless cunning, not caring who or what she laid to waste. She's as cold and calculating as they come. There's no passion in what she does. At least Eliza and Durgan thought they had causes. Not Deneaux. There is no line she won't cross or alliance she won't make or break if it is for her betterment. She's worse than a rabid dog. With a rabid dog, you know exactly what it is going to do, and you have to put it down before it does you some damage. Deneaux…you just don't know why and when she is going to strike. She's like a trusted loyal family dog until she just snaps. I fucking hate her, and she deserves to be put down, I just don't know if I'm the one to do it."

"I'll do it," Tommy said solemnly. "My hands are already stained too deeply to be washed away with the waters of absolution, I'll try though."

"I'm not asking you to do that, Tommy."

"I know you're not. It is still something that needs to be done."

"I don't want you adding to your immorality."

"In the eyes of God, one murder is the same as a hundred thousand."

"How is that possible?"

"It's not that he values the loss of a hundred thousand so insignificantly, it's that he values the loss of the one so highly."

"Oh."

That was a point to ponder. I was certainly responsible for the deaths of many. So, at what point were they considered justifiable? Was there such a distinction with God? Did he give a shit? Or was the death of a person a murder no matter what the circumstances? All I could hope for at this point was that Hell would fill up and they'd have to have an early release program.

We sat there for hours, barely talking, both off in our own worlds waiting to be plunged into darkness; although we would have a few hours of light with the burners. If Tommy died going down the chute, I would be left to rot in this room. My guess was that, eventually, I would pull the zombie barrier away and give it a go that way. I was never one to sit idly by for too long with my thumb firmly entrenched in my ass. Just way too uncomfortable. Definitely going to do the trial-by-combat instead of giving the fire a go, figured I'd have all of eternity to mess with the flames.

Tommy was circling the globe's religions, praying and chanting in Latin, English, Navajo and others I couldn't identify. Why not? No clue if God was listening, but even a cardboard shield makes you feel better heading into battle. Nope, scratch that...that's a lie, because you know the falsehood of the protection you wield. He had to believe in it, or why bother. I had mistakenly assumed that the lights were going to go from on to off. We nearly missed it. I had been focusing on a pattern on the floor that looked something like George Clooney when I realized it was becoming harder and harder to see the image. I stood up quickly when I realized what was going on.

"The lights are dimming, Tommy. It's almost time. Help me light these burners." My hands were trembling as I set the equipment up. The impending bleakness had me rattled. There are things I can deal with, and there are things I cannot. Not being able to see ranks right up there; just below losing a family member.

Tommy took the equipment from me and, one by one, set them up and lit them. Compared to the existing light, they barely registered. In a few minutes they were going to look like miniature suns in the comparative gloom.

Both of us turned to watch the lights as they pulsed, offering their dazzling brilliance only a little while longer. Bright, dim, bright, dim, off.

"Shit," I muttered. The Bunsen burners did their job admirably, but their sphere of influence wasn't more than a couple of feet. We still loved them for their effort.

"I guess it's time." Tommy's shoulders were sagging as he headed over to the incinerator opening.

"Hold on, killer." I'd meant it as a jest, to halt him before he did something irrational. "Sorry, wrong usage of words. Let's toss something down there that's a little less valuable first."

Tommy looked at me. "That'd probably be a better idea."

"Wait, really? You *really* (I stressed really) didn't think of that? And they say I'm the one that doesn't think things through."

"There's a first for everything, Mr. T."

"Good one. Okay, let me toss this stool down there." The noise was horrendously loud in a building where all function had stopped. Ball bearings in a running dryer at three am in your bedroom while you were trying to sleep would have been quieter…and more preferable. The noise ended in a flash. The brilliance of the jetted flames would wreak havoc on my night vision for the next half hour.

"Probably a good idea you did that first," Tommy said as he rubbed his eyes.

The zombies began to once again hammer at the door. I wondered if they cared about the dark. With nothing else to focus on, they were working extra hard on that door. Probably the whole wall that separated us in reality, but we couldn't hear them smacking the cinder block bricks. The door, however, sounded like Gabriel was blowing his horn. We could hear the handle twisting back and forth as one of them was trying to open it.

"This sucks," I said, my gaze riveted on a door I couldn't see.

"Look at it from my perspective," Tommy said.

"Huh?"

"I'm stuck here with you."

"Really? Now you joke? We've been stuck here for twelve hours and you haven't said so much as a how do you do and now you're telling jokes? I wish we had more—" I smacked my forehead.

"What? What's going on?" Tommy asked.

"Let's light the burners that are fixed to the stations."

Within a couple of minutes we had the whole room lit up like the Sistine Chapel. A little Barry White, a bedroom, my wife, no zombies or Tommy, and this would almost be an idyllic setting.

"Now what?" Tommy asked.

I knew what he was referring to. Our best escape avenue was blocked. The zombies were plan "Z". (See what I did there?) Going that route was so horrendous that it was the last, last ditch effort. There was no way we could fight effectively and hold the small flames, and we sure as hell couldn't go out there without them. We'd be just as lost and have the added difficulty of not being able to see them. This was worse than "suicide mode" on your favorite video game. I was so bad at vids that I would play in "Bambi mode" and still get slaughtered. I was not liking our chances.

"We fight, I guess. I can't imagine staying here and waiting to starve to death. Or watching you start looking at me like I'm a man-sized pile of roast beef."

"Not funny, Mr. T."

"It wasn't meant to be. Let's get locked and loaded and we'll pull a Butch Cassidy and Sundance Kid."

"I'm truly sorry, Mr. T."

"For what, Tommy? This isn't your fault."

"The whole thing I guess. I've second-guessed everything that has happened. I was pretty sure from the convergence of events that something momentous was about to happen. I should have gathered us all up beforehand and found us a nice island to wait it out on."

"If you came to me even an hour before my fateful shower and subsequent stepping into Henry poop fiasco, I wouldn't have listened to you. I would have believed you to be some crazy religious zealot or doomsday word spreader. I'm not sure what you could have done that would have changed anything. You've done all you could and more. Hold your head up…we're not done yet. We may not have souls, but I don't think we're quite forsaken just yet."

"So you say."

"Come on, kid, you're usually the eternal optimist.

Don't have that fail on me, or we'll be in a world of hurt."

He "hurumphed" or something much like that, and then hefted his gun up after checking the magazine. I took a deep breath in the hopes it would quell my nerves; it didn't work. I started picking up furniture and began to move it as silently as possible. I didn't want to give the zombies any advance notice as to our motives. I'd moved enough stuff that I could open the door and really get the party started.

"Ready?" I asked, although I'm pretty sure it was more intended for me. And by the way, I wasn't.

I looked over to Tommy in true stalling fashion. Just because you know the end is near doesn't mean you literally want to go running into it headlong. His expression was dour and also jumpy, but not jumpy in the traditional way. Shadows were playing across his face, giving it movement where there was none.

"What are you waiting for?" he growled.

"Good game face. Hold on." I pointed to the burners at the stations, they were sputtering.

He got it quickly enough. "They're running out of gas."

He said it just a wee bit louder than I would have liked, and more things happened in that instant than my mind could process. A zombie that must have been at the top of his Brain Eating 101 class turned the knob and pushed the door open. My attention was on the small fires around the periphery of the room, and I was slow to react as the door swung open, hitting me hard in the knee. I moved forward to shut it, but the press of zombies on the other side prevented that from happening.

"They're in!" I punctuated those words with a burst of rounds.

My last couple pinged into the ceiling above us as I was pushed over a chair. The room went incredibly dim to the point where it looked like we were only receiving the illumination from a crescent moon through a pair of sheer curtains.

"Mr. T!" Tommy screamed in alarm.

"I'm okay!"

I'd dropped my flame and was scurrying backwards, pushing with my legs and one free hand. The zombies seemed less hindered by the dark than we were, as they were using their sense of smell to hone in on Tommy and me. I put a round in the knee and thigh of the one closest to me. I had to pull back quicker or I was in serious trouble of having his face fall directly in my lap. I'd shattered his patella and a fair amount of ligaments if the backwards bending of his leg were any indication. He fell to the side, saving me from becoming a eunuch.

Tommy's lone light in the abysmal sea of death and dearth should have instilled hope, a beacon of life. Not so much, it just allowed enough radiance to let us know how hopeless the current situation was.

"I'm coming," I heard him say.

I could not pull back far enough to feel confident that I had the time to stand. I thought all was lost when I felt hands on my sleeve. Tommy almost got a gut full of lead for his troubles. My feet were off the ground and swaying much like a four-year-old being whisked out of a toy store for throwing a world-class tantrum.

"Gotta hurry!" Tommy yelled. I don't know whom that was for. I was right next to him. "This might hurt!"

I didn't even have the time to ask what was going to hurt when I found myself airborne. *What the fuck did you do?* Was my thought as I hit the incinerator opening and found myself falling at an alarming rate. I was going headfirst down the tube, and for a few flittering heartbeats, I did not believe I had enough room to move my arms up to protect my noggin. I was thinking I would pull a Humpty Dumpty as I flew to the floor below, and that's of course if I wasn't instantly flash fried. Just because the gas burners upstairs had petered out didn't mean this oven was empty.

I was like Superman, arms outstretched over my head as I hurtled through space. Unfortunately, my Kryptonite was either propane or concrete. The carnival ride only lasted a couple of seconds. Then the walls of the chute were gone and I was floating in free space. The smell of gas became overpowering; I felt a fine mist of it cover my body like I was a car in a car wash. I waited for the brilliance of a fire to quench all that I was or all that I would ever be. Instead, I was rewarded with the snapping sound of my left wrist folding in on itself. It was broken and I smelled like the flooded engine of a '57 Edsel. I rolled away, harnessing my broken wrist against my body. The pain would have been blinding, but that didn't matter much as I couldn't see anything. I could have poked myself in the eye with my own hand.

I stood up, gritting my teeth from the pain in my arm. With my right, I cradled the injury. Then what? I couldn't go anywhere. I would end up smacking into unseen things nose first. I thought of shuffling slowly and letting the tips of my boots run into obstacles, but where was I going to go? I'd only been in the dark for less than a minute and I was already barreling toward the throes of a serious panic attack. How had Tommy done this for two weeks? I'd come to a new appreciation of the depths of his resolve and courage.

I could hear Tommy's gun firing. He was screaming as well, it was difficult to tell whether it was in pain or outrage. Then there was nothing but utter silence to go hand-in-hand with absolute blindness. I'd been in some serious scrapes in my life, and certainly recently, but nothing had prepared me for the desolation I was feeling now. There was a possibility I'd even take Trip's rock-raping excursion through his escape tunnel over this. Luckily it was completely dark, and no one could see just how much I was startled when something big found its way down the chute.

It was quite possible a zombie had fallen in from the press of so many of its brethren; or worse, followed me down. I winced as I let go of my broken wrist and moved the rifle to my side, holding it tight. Aiming was going to be a bit tricky with only one arm, but I couldn't even begin to imagine resting the barrel on my forearm. The vibration from the recoil would be more than enough for me to drop the firearm from pain. Whatever was in the chute was soundless as it made its quick descent. I could hear the gas jets hissing, though nothing came out this time and the clicking of an ignition system that was not receiving the necessary spark to ignite the propellant. There was the sound of shoes hitting cement and nothing else. I was doing my best to hold my runaway breath to hear something, anything that would let me know if I should start firing.

"Mr. T?" It was said so softly that I thought it might be my overactive and protective imagination making it up. "I've got a lighter."

That I heard. "No!" I told him, stepping back. "I'm covered in gas." Not that it made a difference lighter-wise, but I told him that I'd broken my wrist as well.

"You're going to have to take off what you can so that I can see your arm and set it. It will heal faster if it doesn't need to move on its own. I'll help you."

"Nothing against you, Tommy, I'm just not comfortable with another man helping me undress."

"That's not a very progressive thought, Mr. T."

"No, I guess the way I said it isn't. I wouldn't feel any more comfortable, probably worse so, if you were a woman that I wasn't married to. How's that? Is that better for your delicate sensibilities?"

"Just hurry, I think the zombies are going to figure out soon enough how to get down here, and we need to figure out how to get out."

That was all the motivation I needed. In a minute or two, I was down to my boxer briefs and socks. I tossed my soaked clothing as far away from myself as possible.

"Alright, I'm ready."

The lighter flashed, the flame so bright comparatively that I had to squint. Tommy held the lighter high over his head and advanced. When he got close, he brought it down to my arm. The area around my wrist had already swollen to nearly double its size and was the angry purple of a Barney gone rogue. (Old kid's show if you ever had the good fortune to not see it.) It had snapped so far that my fingers were actually touching my forearm. It would have been a sickening site to behold on an NFL star as I watched from the comfort of my couch. On myself it was horrifying.

"Ouch," Tommy said.

"You don't say?" I wanted to look away. My eyes and my stomach were both in agreement on this. My brain though was still trying to wrap itself around what had happened and would not yet yield its thoughts on the whole thing just yet.

"Damn." The flame went out. "Burnt myself," he said as he sucked his fingers. "Can you hold the lighter while I work on your wrist?" He didn't bother to hear my response when he thrust the hot metal top into the palm of my hand. It sounded like boiling-over water did when it fell onto super-heated stove coils. "Sorry," he said immediately, and good thing too—otherwise I was going to try and press the thing against his cheek.

I waited a few seconds until it cooled sufficiently and flicked the lighter on.

"Ready?" he asked again not waiting for me to respond.

His hands were already on the move before the flame had come on. I cried out as his left hand grabbed my forearm and his right hand wrapped around my fingers. I dropped the lighter as he first pulled my hand further away from my arm and then guided it back in with his left. His squeezing was gentle as he felt the bones to see if they lined up, but right now it felt like each pinprick of pressure was delivered with a ball-peen hammer. Tommy steadied me as I rocked a bit on my heels.

I gurgled some sort of swear words together. Came out something sort of like "Mucking futher wick sticker."

"Maybe we should have done this with you sitting down. Feel better?"

To respond would have meant opening my mouth again, and I was already willing down the minimal contents within me. If by "feel better" he meant I wanted to cave his fucking skull in with a cannon ball, then yeah, I felt worlds better.

We stayed that way for a bit, my wrist braced in his hand. I didn't dare move, because I knew he wasn't going to.

"Mr. T, you need to hold your hand in place so I can find the lighter."

"Fuck the lighter," I said through gritted teeth. Again we stayed this way a few more minutes.

"How about now?"

"The lighter can kiss my ass."

"Well, we're making strides toward improvement."

"Get it, I'll be fine." I wasn't sure how long my legs were going to support me. Tommy guided my hand into place.

"Hold it tight."

"I feel like I've just Super Glued something together, and if I don't hold it into place long enough it will just fall off."

Tommy was on the ground feeling around for the lighter. "That's exactly what will happen if you let go too soon."

Chunks of bile-encrusted somethings rose up into my throat. I was fairly certain I could not go through the placement of my wrist again. I stood steadfast.

"Got it," Tommy said triumphantly. "Okay, Mr. T, I know you're not going to like this part one bit, but you need to do it."

"Worse than having a bone set without a pain killer?"

"To you? Yes."

I was at a loss. "What, Tommy?"

"We need to have your wrist heal even faster."

"Okay, you got some super healing juice I can drink? I mean, I really don't know…no…no fucking way," I told him when I realized just how close to the truth I'd inadvertently come.

"Mr. T, I'd splint your arm in a heartbeat if there were another way. First, we don't have any medical supplies, and second, you're going to need to be a hundred percent to have a chance of getting out of here. It won't take more than a few seconds. We could already be done."

"Do you even have a clue how repulsive I find this to be?"

"There is no other way."

I would have argued more, probably until my wrist could have healed naturally, if not for the sound of something else coming down the chute. It was a zombie. There was nothing else it could have been. We both turned to look as this one landed very much like I'd been afraid I would, headfirst. Its skull cracked open, spilling its contents all over the floor.

"Clean-up, aisle eight," the words tumbled out of my mouth eons before my brain thought to retract them. Which in itself is pretty funny. I mean, really, it's your brain that comes up with the process of speech, so why does it take so long for the appropriate filters to be put in place before thought becomes vocalized? Yet another design flaw in humans.

Tommy pressed his forearm into my face. I got a heavy whiff of gas, sweat and liverwurst Pop-tarts. I would have turned away if the chute wasn't once again populated with a zombie; and, from the sound of it, more than one. I punctured his skin and drank a small sip at first…and then the nature of the beast took control as I pulled deeply like I was sharing an alcoholic drink for two with three friends and wanted to make sure I got my money's worth. Tommy pulled his arm away from me. Pain blistered in my stomach from the loss, and then an intense heat radiated out from my middle, spreading like wildfire through every part of me, including my extremities.

Tommy once again turned; we could just make out a zombie slowly getting to its feet. It landed headfirst as well, but had the safety of landing on the failed test dummy. The muzzle flashes lit up the room like the world's loudest strobe light.

"You ready to move?" Tommy asked as a third and a fourth zombie hit the floor. The cracking of bones, teeth, and jaws reverberated off the walls. It seemed that only the first one down was going to die by contact in its attempt to follow us.

"My clothes." I didn't want to die naked, screw that noble savage shit.

"Good idea." Tommy ran to my pile of clothes grabbed my magazines and then lit my clothes on fire, tossing the burning material into the zombies.

"Not really what I meant," I said as Tommy turned me to the incinerator access door.

At least a couple of zombies were now ablaze, and we had the added benefit of having a zombie candle to light our way. I was just thrilled the doorway was open, surprised Deneaux hadn't locked the access door behind her. I could only assume it also used the magnetic type locks, otherwise, she would have been stuck in here as well. The incinerator may have been a nightmare, but at the moment, it was lit up like Times Square during New Year's. Heading out to the greater room that housed it and the hallway was terrifying. We were going from the horrors we could see to the terrors we could not.

Tommy would flick his lighter occasionally, but we were running—the flame never held. All we would see was the momentary flash of the flint. Try to assemble an accurate picture of your surroundings with a quarter second of light over an ever-changing landscape. Zombies were chasing us. How did I know? Well, Bobby Blaze was one of them. He didn't seem to care in the least that he had become the human torch. His clothes were completely burned away, his hair burning a brilliant orange. I thought that he must've had some sort of hair product in it before he'd become a zee. He had been burning with so much intensity that his skin had caught fire. Large swaths of charred flesh were hanging from his thighs and chest. It was his manhood that sickened me the most, the tip of it burning and, as the flesh melted, flaming pieces fell away to the floor as he ran. I couldn't help thinking it looked like the worst burning case of gonorrhea in recorded history. I was pretty sure a shot of penicillin wasn't going to do him any good.

I noticed our light source was starting to fade. Bobby Blaze must have been boiling his brain or perhaps he'd burned through the muscles on his legs. Either way, it was getting dark again.

"You know where you're going?" I asked Tommy as we ran.

He seemed so sure of his turns. I should have known better—this was just purely escape mode. We needed to get away from the zombies first and find a way out second. Even over my labored breathing I could hear the heavy footfalls of pursuit. More than once I had turned and fired, the muzzle flashes illuminating the nightmare behind us. My wrist was feeling better, but it was far from healed. I was shooting with one arm—and not my natural arm either—while I was half turned around and on the move. To say they were less than successful would be a vast understatement, unless of course some of the rounds that hit the walls miraculously ricocheted off and into a brain or two of the ones that followed. If that were the case, then I was a friggin' crack shot.

"You smell that?" Tommy asked.

"You're kidding, right?"

"Smells like hot dogs."

I almost vomited thinking about Bobby Blaze's Burning Bobbitt. I pleaded with a deaf god for that to not be what he was referring to. The visual, along with the olfactory input, would just be too much.

"Beans, too."

That was it. I dry heaved. Now I had to add Bobby Blaze's Blueberries to the equation. I nearly tripped over my own feet with my head hanging so low. I figured I'd lost some precious lead time, so I turned and fired again. This time it would have been impossible to miss. The zombies were within five feet; I could clearly make out the twisted snarls of their mouths as they hunted us, their arms outstretched, long streamers of drool hanging from their death dealing teeth. Their eyes would narrow when they would catch a glimpse of us.

"Gotta run faster," I grunted to Tommy, turning back to the front.

It was then that I caught a sliver of light from an opening door. I knew two things right then. One was we were not alone; and the other was Tommy was quickly pulling away from me.

"Mr. T, come on!" he shouted.

He was beginning to act a lot like my son, Justin, in the Captain Obvious respect. Really, what were my choices? Not hurry up and be eaten? I'd rather go shoe shopping with the missus. I nearly fell when I stepped on one of my shoelaces, talk about instant karma. I ended up coming in hot, stumbling headfirst past Tommy and in. I winced as I used my arms to keep myself from crashing into some steel shelving. Tommy slammed the door shut and threw a decent sized slide bolt to lock the door. I thought that strange, but who was I to complain if it kept the zombies out.

"Hi, Mr. Talbot."

"Porkchop?" I turned to see the boy as he moved to sit in front of a small propane camp grill.

On one side he had boiling water with hot dogs and on the other was a pot full of beans. The room was lit up by three flashlights, strategically placed to keep as much of the shadow back as possible.

"Are you alright?" I asked. Seemed funny to ask that of a kid who was sitting down to a meal, and I was the one covered in gore and gas, nursing an injury and nearly nude.

"Doc is dead," he said, having a hard time looking me in the eye.

"Whatever happened, Porkchop, it wasn't your fault." I moved closer to him, as did Tommy.

Porkchop shied away from Tommy. I can't say I blame him. He was well aware of what the other boy had done, and he'd been listening to the ravings of his adoptive father for a long while now. Tommy immediately moved away to give him space.

"He saved me," Porkchop sniffed. "I was in the cafeteria. I have a job as assistant to the assistant potato peeler. It's great. I only have to peel when I feel like it, and I usually get some cake before they put it out for the meals, so I always get the corners where there is more frosting. So, on the nights I know they're going to have chocolate cake, I peel potatoes."

"Seems like a fair trade to me," I told him. He nodded.

"It was Red Velvet night today…or was it yesterday?" He looked over to me.

I was about to respond and he continued on, in the end I suppose the time of day was unimportant in the recanting of the story.

"I love cream cheese frosting, Mr. Talbot, maybe more than fried chicken. So I decided I'd peel some extra potatoes, only they weren't having potatoes, it was carrots. Those are even easier to peel."

I had to disagree on a personal level. More than once I'd nicked my fingers with those barbaric peeling devices.

Nothing like bloody carrots and cucumbers to go with your meal. Adds iron so I'm told. Screw knives…between cheese graters and peelers I'd spilled way more blood than any kitchen disaster that started with a blade.

"I was on my thirty-third carrot when I heard screams coming from the far side of the cafeteria."

I looked at Porkchop strangely. I hadn't known he was OCD like me. Counting peeled carrots was exactly the type of thing I would have done. Poor kid, depending on if we got out of here or not, he was in for a life relegated to counting just about everything from steps to tooth brush strokes.

"It was Mr. Springer."

"As in Jerry?" I had to interrupt him.

"Who?" Porkchop asked.

I shook my head. "Sorry."

"Mr. Springer the janitor. He was always nice to me. Sometimes my job was to help him gather trash bags. But usually he just let me ride around on the cart. This is one of his secret locations."

That explained the old-fashioned slide bolt on the door. "What's so secret?" I asked, looking around the room for a stash of booze or a cot.

It was more like a mini-fire department, which made sense. Wasn't like if this place had caught on fire they could call the local fire station. Against the far wall were heavy jackets and pants. Immediately below them were heavy rubber boots, to the side, hanging on hooks, were helmets with fire-shield glass in front. I'd like to admit that bells were going off in my head right about now, but all I could think about was how heavy and uncomfortable all that crap looked like it would be to wear. A small unused card table with some chairs resided in the corner.

"You thinking what I'm thinking, Mr. T?" Tommy asked.

"I doubt it." I'd moved on to wondering if the jacket

would chaff the hell out of my nipples if I donned it without a shirt.

"Mr. Springer liked to come down here and read." Porkchop had gone back to answering my question.

"Why is that a secret...oh," I said when Porkchop got up and walked over to a small row of lockers. Opening one up, I saw it was full of books with men wearing kilts for covers. He was a closet romance novel reader. I had to smile a little at that.

"He was also a volunteer firefighter."

That made more sense. That was why he would have had keycard access to this place and even more of why he would want to hide his addiction. Tough to be a manly fireman with a *Romancing the Highlander* novel in your back pocket.

There was a heavy banging on the door we'd entered. It appeared that the zombies were also romance-reading fans. It was a hope of mine anyway.

"Mr. T, we should really be finding a way to get out of here."

I held up a finger and silently shushed him. This was a small room; there was a bench in the middle—I would imagine to help in donning fire apparel...or reading in this case. The lockers and the hose were mounted on the far wall, along with an axe. There were no holes in the floor, walls, or ceiling as far as I could see that would allow for some miraculous escape. At this point, I'd love to tell you that all of this was coming together in my head.

It wasn't.

I was blank slating. I think maybe it had something to do with being nearly naked and the damn burning itch in my wrist as it healed at an impossible rate. Right now, as far as I was concerned, we were trapped, might as well hear Porkchop's story out. He would recite it whether we were listening or not, and this would give me plenty of time to claw at my crawling irritation.

"I stood up from my duties to look through the opening that went from the cook area to the serving area. From there, you can see out into the cafeteria. Mr. Springer was swinging the end of his mop back and forth in the face of a zombie. Then he stuck the handle into the zombie's mouth and drove him backwards into the wall. Left a huge blood splatter. It was pretty gross."

I had a newfound respect for the sometimes fireman and secretive romance-reading janitor.

"It was when more zombies came in that he started to lose the fight. He killed two more, and would have had another if one hadn't bit his shoulder from behind."

"He killed three zombies with a mop?" I asked.

Porkchop nodded.

"Damn, I wish he were here now. I'd help him carry his books." And I meant it.

"I couldn't move, Mr. Talbot. People were screaming and running all over the place, but I couldn't move. I kept watching as more and more zombies just tore him apart. He was still fighting with five of them on him. He saw me once, it was across the cafeteria, but I heard him tell me to run. I couldn't, though, he needed saving and I did nothing."

"Porkchop, there's nothing you could have done. If you had gone out there with your potato peeler you would have been dead, too." I tried to calm him down. He was crying now, fat tears falling to the floor as I helped him back to the bench.

"Dad, I mean Doc Baker, came in from the other side. He was looking around like crazy for me. I couldn't even call out for him. I was like peas."

"Huh?"

"Frozen."

"Gotcha."

"So he finally spots me, and he's waving for me to come and follow him, but I can't."

"Because you're peas," I say as I put my arm around

his shoulder.

"Because I'm peas," he echoes. "So he comes to me."

He was crying now, a full-throated keening coming from him. This sound seems to be a siren song for the zombies as they redouble their effort on the door. The bolt looks solid enough, but I'm not sure how long it can hold.

"He...he grabs my hand and we...we start running the way he came in. It was too late though." He had to stop his narration while he exhausted his supply of tears. "If I had gone when he waved to me, we might have made it."

"You don't know that, Porkchop," I tried to console the boy.

"He told me to get somewhere safe. And that was it. The zombies started biting him. I ran that time. I came here. It was the safest place I could think of, and I knew Mr. Springer had food and a stove down here. We used to come here to go "camping". Mr. Springer said he sometimes felt trapped in this place, and he wanted to go topside and see the stars again. He tried, but the people in charge said he couldn't, so he did this."

Porkchop was pointing to the stove, hotdogs and beans. He then did something I had not been expecting and was honestly frightened of. He stood and walked over to each flashlight and turned them off. I think I may have been shivering by the time he got to that third one. I was going to plead to his sense of compassion to leave it on. He had his reasons I suppose, and if worst came to worst, I would wrestle one away from him.

"Look up," he told us.

"Holy shit," was the best I could come up with on short notice. Mr. Springer was the Michelangelo of glow in the dark paint. He had recreated the constellations in painstaking detail. Even Tommy was amazed.

"Aries, Andromeda, Cassiopeia, there's hundreds here. They're perfect." I could see Tommy's jaw had grown a little slack. "I swear, if I look at it long enough, I can see it move."

I sighed in a sort of sadness and cold longing, with an edge of desperation, as Porkchop turned the flashlights on. For a brief moment it had felt like we'd escaped and were no longer trapped levels beneath the earth.

"He held the zombies off long enough for me to get away. So I came here."

"I can see why." The door rattled again. I'd swear I saw the bolt bow out a little.

"We used to talk a lot, me and Mr. Springer, mostly about our homes and food, sometimes zombies. He told me once that he didn't think zombies could bite through the fireman gear. I didn't really believe him. I haven't seen anything yet that stops them, not even concrete walls."

I looked over to the uniforms, my feet quickly taking me to where my eyes had been looking. I gripped a sleeve of the protective clothing; it was thick and heavy. I was more inclined to agree with Mr. Springer. Especially after I read the tag that said the material was woven with a Kevlar mix. Anything that was designed to stop a bullet should be able to stop zombie teeth and fingernails. I put the jacket on, might as well have donned a piece of clothing consisting entirely of knitted together mosquitoes. If the zombies didn't kill me, the incessant scratching would.

"These could work," I said, fidgeting about, trying to get into the impossible position of having the material not touch me.

"There's a shirt in the locker," Tommy said, noticing my discomfort.

I thought I was going to do a happy dance at the possibility of putting a layer between the torture device and me. That was of course until Tommy pulled out the wadded up ball of clothing.

"It's dirty," I told him.

"So," he responded evenly. "Stop being a prima donna."

"You want me to put on dirty clothing from someone I don't even know? And that somehow makes me a prima donna?"

"Would it matter if you knew them?"

"No," I answered honestly.

"And that most definitely makes you one. What's the worst that could happen?" he asked.

"Scabies, maybe."

"I don't think you can catch scabies from a dirty shirt."

"What about flesh-eating bacteria?"

"I guess…I don't know. Porkchop, did Mr. Springer complain about any large skin lesions?"

Porkchop just tilted his head, not getting the question. Tommy seemed to thoroughly be enjoying himself. "Just put it on." He tossed it at me.

The end of a sleeve landed in my mouth. That alone would have been enough for my gag reflex to kick into gear, but the wafting stench that followed it completed the job. Before the zombies came, I'd smelt jock reek during my youth having played sports, and I remembered that acidic stink of testosterone along with sweat and a teen's innate ability to let it age for a few days at the bottom of a locker. This was easily one of the worst funks I'd ever had the displeasure of smelling. But this shirt had all of the above ingredients along with what could only be described as essence of boiled skunk nards. The resultant putrefaction was tearing up my eyes and clawing through my olfactory senses.

I was like a cat trying to avoid water as I put the shirt over my head, all stiff-armed and clearly agitated.

"What's the matter with him?" Porkchop asked Tommy.

"He's afraid of catching leprosy."

"What?" I ripped the shirt off. "Can you really catch that from a shirt?"

I should have known by Tommy's smile that he was

full of shit, but I was having a hard time distinguishing things clearly through the haze of odor. Plus my eyes were nearly closed tight. The door rattled again, I didn't need to have my eyes open to hear a screw fall to the ground. The sound was small, but the actual event was monumental.

"Porkchop, get some gear on," I told him.

"I tried, it's too big. I can't even walk in it."

"Well, it's your lucky day, because I'll carry you."

"Then what, Mr. T?" Tommy asked.

"Well…see…now I've got this all figured out."

"Oh no," Tommy and Porkchop said in unison.

"*Et tu?*" I asked the smaller boy.

"My name is not Brutus and you are no Caesar," he told me.

"Impressive." And I meant it. "Fact remains I have a plan. Come on, let's get your stuff on. You too, Tommy. Looks like we're joining the volunteer force."

I'm not going to say I got over putting that gross ass shirt on, but it helped that I was assisting Porkchop in getting dressed. Once I placed the heavy jacket on, it hid a fair amount of the smell, kind of like locking it in Tupperware. Although there was some sticky fluid around the collar of the neck that about made me freeze in motion every time I turned my head and felt the material adhere to my skin. "It's nothing, it's nothing, it's nothing," became my chant.

"He going to be alright?" Porkchop asked Tommy. I was down by his feet pulling his boots on, and Tommy was doing the straps in front of the boy's jacket.

Tommy shrugged. "Mrs. T is really the only one who would be able to tell us."

"You two crack me up. Porkchop, I'm going to turn around. Will it be alright if Tommy helps you get on my shoulders? I want to do a sort of dry run here and see how this is going to work out."

Porkchop looked to Tommy quickly, then me, and nodded. I went down on my knees as Porkchop stood on the narrow bench. He looked like he could go swimming in that suit. The kid might like to eat, but he'd been losing weight fast since I'd met him. Tommy picked him up and easily deposited him on my shoulders. It wasn't too bad, felt like a small backpack. I grabbed my rifle and maneuvered around. Tommy caught Porkchop before he fell over.

"You realize that you need to hold on, right?" I asked him.

"I did not realize that," he said, flustered.

"You ever done a piggyback ride?"

"Technically, Mr. T, a piggyback ride is where he would wrap his legs around your mid-section and his arms kind of around your neck. This is more of a shoulder ride."

"Always one in the crowd," I grumbled.

"I've never done either." He looked down as he said it.

I would have questioned him further, but I remember him telling me that his father was a world-class d-bag. Well, maybe not with those exact words, but the sentiment was the same.

Tommy propped Porkchop back up.

"Okay, kiddo, I'll hold on to your legs with one arm, but you're going to have to hunch over and grab hold of my shoulders. Okay?"

"Okay," Porkchop answered, but he looked far from thrilled about it.

I got him back up there. I bounced a little and made a couple of quick movements to my right and left. Porkchop's arms encircled my neck much like I thought they would. The kid was strong enough to choke out a bear. I tapped his arms. But apparently the universal signal for "ease up" was not one he was familiar with.

"I think you're killing him," Tommy said to Porkchop as he looked into my reddening face.

Porkchop finally relaxed. "Shoulders," I moaned, grabbing my raw throat. "Hold on to my shoulders."

"I was," Porkchop countered.

"Hold on, Mr. T. There's a strap here. Lift your arms, I'll connect it around your chest, and then Porkchop can put his legs under it so he can't fall off. That way he won't have to hold on to your shoulders as hard."

"Sure, anything that keeps him safer and me with more air is fine with me. You good with that?" I asked Porkchop. I was smiling at him, attempting to keep him at ease, but my insides felt like they were liquefying, and I could pretty much squirt out everything within me. I know it's gross, I'm just letting you know how I felt. Keeping him safe was the only thing that mattered in this whole equation.

"How do you want to do this? I won't be able to watch your back and cut a trail."

Tommy had still not seen the shining path I was laying out before him. I motioned with my face toward the wall.

"Yeah, what about it? It's an axe."

"What's next to the axe, Tommy?"

"A fire hose. What do you want me to do with that?"

"Really? How old are you? Fine, let me make this *real* clear. What's the fire hose hooked up to?"

"I would imagine high...OH, I get it! That's actually one of your better plans. There's only one thing."

"Yeah, go on, killjoy."

"The hose is only two hundred feet. What do we do after that?"

"Well, let's just hope we've found the way out by then. We'll have Porkchop holding the flashlights, so at least we'll have light. That hose, when turned on full blast, should be able to send those smelly bastards careening down the hallways like a particularly thick loogey down a drain."

"That's gross even for you, Mr. T."

"I know, I kind of wish I hadn't said it." I was looking at the hose. It would buy us some time while we looked for an exit. Then it was going to come down to the rounds we had and the axe, which I was going to take.

"I know the way out," Porkchop said as Tommy helped him get his legs under the straps.

"You do? Are you sure?" I asked. I don't know why I didn't just trust him, and it wasn't because he was twelve. I would have asked the same question to my wife, although she would have punctuated her answer with a punch to the shoulder.

"I said I did." I could just about hear his eyes rolling in his head as he spoke. "Mr. Springer showed me the way. We couldn't ever go because it was guarded, and you needed a keycard, but he said if I ever needed to get out...that was the way to go."

"Why did he think to show you a way out, Porkchop?" I was curious.

"He said stuff like this taking over the world shit always went to hell, and that I needed to be prepared to run from it while the getting was good."

"Smart man." Whether someone from the inside wanted to significantly increase his or her pay grade or outside influences wanted to end the reign, this place was a magnet for trouble. "How close is it?"

"About three-quarters of a hot dog."

I wasn't sure I'd ever heard that sort of measurement. If we were talking about how fast Henry could get through three quarters of a hot dog, then we were already outside and this was all a wasted exercise. If we were talking about Nicole when she was around six and wouldn't eat anything that didn't come out of a Doritos bag, we were pretty much going to waste away inside these walls. Porkchop, I think, was a perfect blend of the two. We were three or so minutes at a regular walk from getting out. Of course, we'd be running if we could; but more than likely, a few dozen zombies stood in our way.

Porkchop was leaning back as far as he could, testing the tensile strength of the straps that held his legs in place.

"That's not helping my shoulders any, kid," I told him.

"Yeah, be careful, he's old." I appreciated that Tommy was trying to lighten the moment, but not at my expense. Talk about the M1A1 Abrams Main Battle Tank calling the AH-64D Apache Longbow Attack Helicopter green…or something like that.

I knew my limitations. I hoped Tommy knew them as well when I asked him a question. "You going to be able to handle that hose?"

"I should be fine." He grabbed the business end and pulled out a good ten feet or so. "It's not like it's hooked up to a fire hydrant."

I walked over to the door and put my hand on the bolt. Tommy had a hand on the large red valve. "Wait, before I open this door, are we sure it's going to do more than just get them wet? I mean, I'm not trying to baptize the fuckers here. I want this thing to slam them against the far wall."

"I don't know about slamming them against walls, as it's only a three inch diameter hose. It will keep them away though."

"This sounded way better in my head."

"Mr. T, all of your plans sound better in your head."

He was being serious. I could only grunt in agreement.

"You ready?" I asked Porkchop.

He had his helmet over his head and was leaning over, his head next to mine. His glove-covered hands were draped over my shoulders and were grabbing anything that felt sturdy. I'd thought he would be able to hold a flashlight so he could be our light source; that was, of course, until he once again rolled his eyes at me and showed me that the helmets, which we all had on now, had built in lights. Each one of us was now covered in heavy gear, wielding traditional weapons, and now potentially had a secret weapon. We knew the way out in theory, and we were three-quarters of a meat by-product from escape. This is the best I'd felt today about our chances of escape.

Porkchop rapped on the side of my helmet with his fist. "I said I was ready, Mr. Talbot." I looked up at him. He was smiling.

"Yeah, I was asking more for myself," I told him.

I turned and nodded to Tommy. He slowly turned the wheel. It squeaked loudly as water began to dribble out the front of the hose. I had stopped pulling back on the bolt. I'd seen kinked garden hoses with more pressure than this fire hose was displaying. He kept cranking the wheel. I kept waiting for the point when he would stagger back from the pressure. There was a decent stream coming out; if we were going up against some fire ants we might stand a chance.

"It must run on a pump!" Tommy had to shout as the water was hitting the metal lockers and making a loud splashing noise.

"This blows. Back to 'Plan B' I suppose."

"You have to flip the switch first." Porkchop was still smiling.

"The switch? What switch?"

"There's a pump switch over by where the uniforms are."

"Were you going to tell us any time soon?" I asked him.

"I forgot. I'm only twelve, I can't be expected to remember everything."

"What do you think, Mr. T?" Tommy, Porkchop and I were all nearly head-to-head-to-head, looking at the innocuous black switch that could very well spell the difference between life and death.

"Well, I guess we'll never know if we don't try." I cautiously reached out and moved the button to the 'up' position. It was at this point that I noticed the hose was pointed directly at my midsection. Water was dribbling out and landing on my boots. "That nozzle closed?" I asked as I pushed it away.

"Mostly. I don't think it worked."

Maybe off in the distance I heard machinery whirring, it was possible that was wishful thinking. Then we both watched as water swelled the hose like a snake eating a body-length sausage.

"How?" I wondered.

"It makes sense that it could be on another redundant generator in a different locale in case of a fire in the main generator room. Does it matter?"

"Not really. Want to do a test run?"

Tommy seemed to exert some strain as he hefted the now filled tube away from us. He opened the nozzle up, a jet of water as thick as my forearm rushed out. The force of the water was enough to send chairs and the table skittering along the floor. In many cases if they were hit right they would spiral out of the way. Tommy had to actually brace himself as he wielded the water cannon around. It wasn't as powerful as the ones used for various crowd control measures but this was no gardening hose either. Tommy quickly closed the nozzle.

"I think it works!" He was smiling.

"You good with this?" It seemed superfluous even as I said it, as he was already moving toward the door with his new Super Soaker Supreme. "Your job is to just hold on, Porkchop. You got it?"

I knew he was nodding because each downward tilt slammed his helmet into mine.

"Ready, Mr. T?" Tommy was standing with his legs apart facing the door, one hand on the nozzle.

This had sounded so much better before I had my hand on the lock. The water stream was strong, but was it strong enough? Were we merely going to give the zombies a nice shower before they sat down to eat? We were about to find out. I slid the bolt back, pulling the door open as I moved out of the way. The water works were almost instantaneous. The zombie that had been right at the door looked a little road worn. His gray, sallow skin hung loosely from his cheeks, neck and eyes, giving him a "droopy dog" expression. Tommy nailed him straight in the face. I noticed, before the zombie was pushed back, that the skin from his face was being ripped away like stuck gum on a hot driveway. How many times had I told my kids to not spit their gum out on the driveway when they were younger? Used to spend an hour of every weekend out there with the hose, my thumb over the business end, trying to get the perfect stream consisting of high pressure and a thin line of water to pry the offending sticky substance off the ground. It looked just like that, but instead of black pavement underneath, there was the glistening red and white of muscle and bone.

For a second, the zombie let his face take the brunt of the punishment before he began to get pushed back. As the floor became soaked, he lost traction and was thrust hard against the wall. I'd love to say he was slammed up against the far side of the hallway hard enough to smash his fucking skull…but no such luck. He was down, but certainly not out, as his feet slipped from under him. More zombies were trying to fill the void but were kept at bay and repelled as Tommy moved forward.

"Time to go, Mr. T." He was grimacing. It could have been from the macabre work he was performing or the exertion the hose was having on him.

I fell in behind, letting him clean the way. Once a zombie fell, it was easy to send him sliding down the hallway, much like a makeshift Slip 'N Slide from my youth. He was keeping a good ten-foot push to the front of us, the rear was going to be my responsibility. Porkchop groaned as the M-16 went off. I should have thought to get some padding in his ears to help muffle the sound. He shifted his head to my other side to get away from the noise. I was careful to not step on the hose as I walked backwards. There were a few dozen zombies to our back, a lot, but not nearly as many as had been upstairs. I didn't dare check out our front. As long as Tommy was still moving forward, that was a good thing.

"Two magazines," I shouted to Tommy as I let one fall to the ground.

I could feel Porkchop twist in his seat, considering the "seat" was me, it wasn't too hard to tell. "Next right!" he yelled.

Tommy grunted. Our pace was slowing. I hoped it was the accumulated weight of the hose as he pulled it along with the occasional zombie riding atop.

"How's it going up there?" I asked.

He grunted again. It had to be gruesome. I was stepping in the human residue left over as the hose was stripping zombies clean like a pressure washer. The flaps of skin that had no definition were bad enough, but when you started to see the odd nose or tattered ear float by, well, that was sickening. The gray tiled floor was slick with water and blood. Mr. Springer would have had a hell of a time trying to get this cleaned up.

"Another right!" Porkchop yelled.

"One magazine!" I'd thinned the herd to the back, but I knew now that one more magazine wasn't going to do it. It seems I'd slightly underestimated the strength of our enemy or, more likely, they were getting reinforcements attracted to all the noise as they came down the chute. My ass hit Tommy's as he stopped.

"What's up?" I asked him as I hit the bolt release button and took out the closest zombie, adding what could only be described as a third nostril, albeit bigger than the other two and not quite symmetrical…but yeah, a third nostril.

"Out of hose."

I hadn't realized that the thing was about knee high as he'd tried to stretch its length even further by force. "How much further, Porkchop?"

"Half an order of small french fries."

"Kid, you can't go changing the measuring device mid-stream, this is how spaceships are lost. One side of the design team uses metrics, the other Standard Fast Food fare. It's a mess. In terms of that hot dog you were talking about, how much further? And this isn't one of those stadium foot longs, is it? Probably should have discussed this earlier."

I'd fired off two more bullets since I'd asked the question. The zombies had initially rushed us, but when we held them off—Tommy with the hose and me with the gun—they'd sort of retreated to a safer distance. We had a good twenty-foot bubble to our front and rear. They were waiting, they were patient, they had all the time in the world. Not like they were going to die, at least not without a little help.

It's that predatory shit that really scares me. Mindless, eating, chewing machine is one thing, but to pause and reconsider needlessly injuring yourself in the pursuit of food, well, that's an entirely different animal. I hated their progression. Although, right now, their caution was giving us more precious seconds of life. Sure, it was terrifying seconds of life, but it beat the tranquil quietude of eternal nothingness or in mine and Tommy's case, endless wandering.

I was going to save my bullets for as long as they would let me. Every time they looked like they wanted to take a step nearer, I dropped one. They would snarl in anger but would come no closer.

"What's going on up there?" I asked.

"They're staying out of effective range. From where they are, I'm sure it's just a refreshing splash of water."

"A quarter of a hot dog!" Porkchop blurted out. "I was retracing my steps as I ate, I remember thinking that maybe I should go back and get another one, because if the trip was any longer, I wouldn't have any left. I had ketchup and mustard all down my forearm and Mr. Springer said we were just about there as I licked it off."

I could only hope Porkchop liked to eat that one last piece in one mouth-crowding bite, as opposed to taking littler and littler portions as he got to the end in a desperate bid to make it last longer.

"My left side pocket, Mr. T. I have an extra magazine. I'd get it for you, but my hands are full."

I took a shot and then turned to reach for it.

"Other side," Tommy said.

"They're moving!" Porkchop warned.

I turned and fired, wasting a bullet on the breastplate of the closest zombie. She staggered back as her body absorbed the round. Of course it had to be a woman and why not go just a little further. At some point she'd lost her shirt, probably ripped away by Tommy's hose, and to make it just a little more therapist worthy, she was a liberated, free-spirit without a bra. I wasn't overly concerned for myself, as I'd seen a breast or two before. But Porkchop? This shouldn't be the way he was exposed to some of the finer things the fairer sex had to offer. The kid was probably going to become a monk after this traumatic experience. Then it dawned on me that I seriously doubted it would be an exposed breast that sent him over the edge, not after all the devastation he'd born witness to.

The bullet had clipped the edge of her sternum, broken bone bits protruding from the top of the wound as viscous, thick, sticky blood dripped from the bottom. It was as black as coal in that hole. I may have seen something whitish pass over the gap from the inside, but I quickly turned away. Porkchop did not. This I knew because his helmet light never wavered. At least not until I put a bullet in her head.

"She was pretty once," he said. "She looked a lot like what I expect Rachael would have if she'd had the chance to grow up."

"I'm sorry, kid."

"It wasn't her, she's already dead." I turned and

started fishing in Tommy's pocket again.

"Mr. T, your other left," he told me when I started looking in the original pocket he'd told me that had not contained what I was looking for.

"Right, right."

"Left!"

"No, I was just agreeing with you."

"Mister Talbot!"

I knew that warning. The zombies were pressing their luck again. This time, I made sure to drop two for their troubles. They once again pulled back and may have even added a few inches onto their initial perimeter. But they knew something was up; we were no longer moving, and as far as they were concerned, we were cornered. This time I turned the right way and fished the magazine out.

"I'm going to turn the hose off, Mr. T."

I almost thought about telling him to leave it on. It could be used as a fair barrier as it whipped back and forth. I actually thought better of it when I realized it would be shooting us in the back and could very well propel us into the arms of the awaiting zombies.

"Hold on for a second. Porkchop, which way is out?"

He was silent for a second. I had a minor panic attack that perhaps he had forgotten or, more likely, hadn't really ever known. Then, much to my relief, he spoke.

"There's a water bubbler coming up, which I thought was weird, because it doesn't even have cold water come out. Looks like a small sink with a handle on the side. Water barely came out any higher than where you put your mouth. It was hard trying to wash my arm, and even though I was thirsty, I didn't want to drink it because it was warm like bath water, and that's just gross. Nobody drinks bath water, right?"

"Probably not, at least I hope." I was having an internal struggle thinking about someone drinking dirty bath water. The boy nearly sidetracked me as I got hung up on

Mark Tufo

that detail. "So once we see the fountain, we can get out?"

"Almost, the next left is a short hallway that leads to the guard station, and that's the door out."

"A quarter of a hot dog you say?"

He nodded again, his helmet reverberating off of mine.

"Here we go. Okay, Tommy, on three, shut the hose off and we'll start running at them."

"One," he started. "Two."

Damn, that came fast. I was sort of hoping he'd do that, two and a quarter, two and five-eighths, two and whatever; but no…he moved right on to three without hesitation. I was already turning to the front when I heard the hose hit the floor with a clang. He was firing, and I joined a moment later, brass hitting the floor at an alarming rate; faster than the zombies to our front.

"They're coming!" Porkchop was looking over both of our shoulders.

I turned, and for a fucking second it was like the deadliest game of Red Light. The zombies seemed to all try and stop their forward movements, like they were hoping to not be detected and thus sent to the back of the starting area. Going back in this game meant a bullet, though, as allowing one to get to the "goal" meant we would become zombie droppings.

I unloaded almost the remainder of my magazine to keep them second-guessing their desire to come up from behind. Tommy was shooting so fast that it seemed he had his selector on automatic. I kicked his newly discarded magazine into the feet of a zombie.

"There's the fountain!" Porkchop's outstretched arm was pointing. It was close enough that I could even see the left he was talking about. Could it be possible? Could we get out of this? Hope did that whole surging thing, and then it was pretty much swept out from under me. No, I mean literally. I felt my body being torqued to the side and backwards as something grabbed a hold of Porkchop. He was screaming so loudly I thought he might shatter the safety glass on the helmet.

"He's biting me!" Porkchop was flailing from side to side trying to escape its grasp. As I turned, so did the zombie. Porkchop's legs were nearly all the way out of the safety strap, only the toes of his boots were still entrenched, and those not firmly.

"Tommy, I need some help!"

There was another huge burst of ammunition from his gun then he turned. All I saw was the meaty end of the butt stock coming for my head. He threaded the needle between Porkchop and me, striking the zombie. The bone-jarring and shattering hit sent the monster sprawling. I ejected hot brass in a bid to make some much-needed room between them and us. I don't know if the zombies sensed we were close to escape or they were forgoing all caution in an effort to thwart their constant hunger.

I watched as Tommy was swinging his rifle like a club, skulls disintegrating under his attack. When he got a few feet of clearance, he tossed it at a zombie and quickly retrieved the axe he had by his side. This was going to get real interesting real quick. We'd both be swinging axes in a hallway not much more than six feet across. If we didn't kill each other, I'd consider that a moral victory.

My bolt popped open and stayed that way. I was out. I grabbed my axe as well. The hands of a zombie were almost on my jacket when I drove the edge of my weapon with extreme prejudice almost completely through his head. I could see the blade through his open mouth.

I tried to keep as much of an up and down motion as I could so that Tommy and I wouldn't interfere with each other, but the damned zombies wouldn't get with the program. More than once, the sharp, barbed point of my blade had come within inches of hitting Tommy on my backswing. I knew this because his had come dangerously close to me as well. Our axes were blurring blades of death, looked a lot more like a snow blower ripping through a Nor'easter than it did fireman tools cutting through zombies.

I lost the axe completely at one point when it stuck heavily into the shoulder blade of a zombie. I'd overshot his head and drove deeply through his back, the heavy bone holding fast. That, combined with the gore-covered handle made me lose my grip. I ripped up and was rewarded only with my hands in the air. For a second, it looked like I was at a hip-hop concert. You get the reference, right? Hands in the air and all that?

Luckily, my zombie buddy didn't head out with my axe. I was able to get my hands back on it and get a better grip. I placed a foot in his gut as I pushed away and simultaneously wrenched the blade free. "That was fucking gross."

"Fucking gross," Porkchop echoed. I could hear it in his voice as he tried to hold back the heaves.

Tommy and I were spinning slowly in a counterclockwise direction as we shuffled forward to keep the zombies at bay in a complete circle. It was effective for the most part, right up until I got bit. This wasn't a 1970's karate movie where the hero is being attacked by fifty bad guys, but only one at a time; these zombies had either not seen those movies and didn't know they were supposed to fight that way, or they had seen them and learned from it. They were bumping and stumbling over one another in a bid to get to us first.

The axe was a great tool for caving in a door, and maybe a hostile or two, but a mad rush of them in a closed-in environment was not optimum. My left leg buckled as a zombie Tommy must have killed crashed into the back of my knee. I had been in mid-swing, and this was my plant and support leg, so I went all the way down, my knee striking the tile floor before I could recover. I was pushing back up when a zombie from my blindside struck.

I don't know if zombie jaws were evolving, or possibly that I'd just never really been bit by a person, but when that thing latched on to my calf, I cried out. I mean, it was a manly cry, full of deep overtones and grunts. But shit...that thing hurt. My leg buckled in on itself again as he clamped down on the muscle, not allowing it to completely flex.

"I'm bit!" was the only thing I could think to yell. Really, it was the only thought I had at that moment.

Tommy spared a glance, but no help was coming from that way as he was being swarmed. If I didn't deal with my attacker in the next second or two, he would be joined at his dinner party by a table of twelve or thereabouts.

"Smash him in the head!" was Tommy's sage advice. The pain was so blinding I was hoping that's why I hadn't come up with the solution on my own.

"Yeah, smash him in the head," came Porkchop's terrified echo.

We were both staring at the zombie who was shaking his head back and forth in a tearing motion. I quickly turned my axe upside down and drove the head of it down into the zombie like I was purging a clogged toilet from the world's largest shit. Impossibly, he bit down harder, I think in a purely reflexive action, because when I brought the axe back up, it was covered in a fresh layer of brain.

It took two more hard jams before the zombie finally fell away. I was horrified to see four teeth stuck in the heavy material of the fireman pants. I brushed them away; I did not, however, have the luxury of checking the wound to see if he had broken skin. There were more zombies coming to finish off what the other had started. I fought with anger; whereas, before, it had been a mixture of survival and fear. Now it was pure unadulterated rage. Rage that I could potentially even now be dying from the bite, rage that I would never see my family again. Rage that some zombie asshole had the audacity to bite me.

I was swinging the axe around like a kid would a baton trying to hit a fly. I didn't care what I hit as arms flopped to the ground, the hands still opening and closing. Breastplates were shattered, exposing internal organs, genitalia rendered from their hosts. Skulls were caved-in, heads were decapitated. Grisly did not even begin to scratch the surface of what I was doing. Humans thrown into a cement mixer would have looked less horrific.

Eyeballs shot from sockets, intestines fell like ribbons thrown from rooftops during a holiday. I was heavy-chopping zombies, cutting straight through them when Tommy shouted.

"Mr. T, they're gone, they're gone!"

For a moment, my primal mind could not conceive of why the enemy would up and leave so close to their target. They hadn't left though, not in the traditional way. Piles of dead zombies were strewn about the floor. Some were moving but due to some various injuries like a severed spinal cord or amputated leg they weren't going anywhere.

"We did it," Tommy said, I think maybe trying to bring me back off the edge he thought I was on. But I wasn't, not this time, the anger had clarified everything. It had burned away the guilt, the self-doubt, the regret. It was a cleansing, making ash of the burdensome feelings we as humans carry around with us. Not going to lie, it felt good. I knew at some point I'd start to feel those things again, but right now it was fantastic.

"The door is down there." Porkchop was pointing.

The escape from the building had been brutal. We'd had a betrayal and a rescue, and yet I could not get it out of my head that we were not done. We'd earned it, so I just couldn't place why I felt the way I did. As we got closer to the door, the more my concern built up. That the damn thing was propped open didn't help either.

I was expecting a dozen shock troops with riot gear and fully automatic weapons or a few dozen bulkers just waiting to smash stuff. Or...shit...if I'm going to go down that path, why not just have it be Eliza and Deneaux standing there hand in hand. That would be enough to stop my heart from beating.

I cannot even begin to tell you how much I wished I had some ammunition. To be able to push the door open with the barrel of my weapon and have rounds speeding to clash with the opposition I was sure was out there in some form. It was right there, a threat, just not one I could have foreseen. Tommy took the lead, the only way I could have been closer peering over his shoulder was if we were sharing the same suit, and that would have just been plain awkward on many different levels. We were looking down a narrow corridor. It was impossible to say how long it was as our flashlights only penetrated so deep, like a carrot in a whale's ass. And no, I have no idea why that analogy popped into my head, it just did.

"You watch the door, Mr. T. I'm going to move a little further in."

I was about to tell him we needed to stick together, but right then, I was realizing why rage wasn't the greatest emotion on the planet. It used up gallons of adrenaline, and the result of burning adrenaline was extreme fatigue. My legs felt washed out, my arms like wet noodles unable to support even the axe handle. Porkchop's added weight on my shoulders was threatening to drive me face first into the ground.

"You're going to have to get off for a minute," I told him as I got down on my knees so he could hop down. He looked around, and I don't think he was too thrilled with his new vulnerable position.

I'd been so busy trying to keep from collapsing that I had not at all watched our six for any incoming bad guys, and I'd lost track of my twelve. Tommy's flashlight looked like a birthday candle from however far away he was.

"Looks clear!" Tommy had shouted.

"Can I take this stuff off?" Porkchop asked.

I wanted to nod, but the energy required to do so seemed insurmountable. Something like "Un," escaped my lips. He took that as a yes and proceeded to tear off the oversized pants, boots and helmet. The jacket he kept on.

He picked up his helmet and was directing the beam of light to where the zombie had bit me. "There's blood, Mr. Talbot, and you don't look so good. You've got kind of that same color I had when I once put a hamburger with cheese and sautéed onions in my ice cream."

"Why would you do that?" I asked in a measured cadence as I struggled to regain my breath.

I was severely suffering the after-affects. How much longer could I have fought before my heart just exploded? Not long by the look of it. Although I was more concerned why he would take two great foods and, by mixing them together, ruin them both.

"Look at me," he said as he lifted my helmet off. Just having access to cooler air made me feel better. Porkchop didn't think so. "I think you're becoming a zombie."

Shit, who knows, maybe I was. I had no idea what it felt like to turn, and right now I was feeling specifically like a piece of discarded fecal matter.

"I'll make this quick." Porkchop stood up and grabbed the axe out of my hands.

"You think maybe we could talk about this for a second? I mean, I did just carry your ass to safety."

"I guess I owe you at least that much."

"Appreciated."

"But no funny stuff."

"No funny stuff. I promise...if I'm a zombie, I'd appreciate you killing me."

I sat back so I was resting up against the wall. I pulled my gloves off and reached down to pull my pant leg up as far as I could, which was almost to my knee, easily far enough to see the ring of teeth marks the zombie had made on my leg.

There was some serious bruising from the pressure, but he had not broken skin.

"I think I dodged this one, Porkchop."

"Are you sure? I mean, I'd hate to do it, Mr. Talbot, but I would."

"I know you would. Hate to do it, I mean. I'm mostly fine…just out of steam."

"What's going on here?" Tommy had come back and Porkchop was still standing over me, the axe at nearly the ready.

"Porkchop here was concerned I might be becoming a zombie, and he was going to help ease my transition into the next world."

"In his defense you do look pretty bad, Mr. T."

I wanted to come back with some caustic remark, but I was tapped. "Just need to sit for a minute."

"Sure." Tommy stood and gently took the axe from Porkchop. "He'll be okay. I don't know how long this thing is, but there are no doorways or intersecting corridors along the way, so I'm pretty sure this is the escape route."

"Can you be certain?" I asked, raising my gaze up to his with some considerable effort.

"Completely."

"A hundred percent completely?"

He nodded.

"How?"

"There's a cigarette butt every fifty yards."

"Oh." If Deneaux was here, than we could rest assured it was a way out. "Wait, are you positive she's still not in here with us, like a vengeful wraith?"

"I think we're okay. I didn't smell any new smoke."

"How about you and me make sure nothing is coming from the building, and we'll let the old-timer get some rest."

Porkchop looked from me to Tommy and nodded. That was one resilient kid. I don't think they moved more than ten feet away; I was out when they had hit half that distance. It really couldn't have been more than five minutes. They were next to the door just keeping an eye out for anything coming. It was enough to do a little bit of a reset on my system. I'm not going to say I felt a hundred percent, but I also didn't feel like I had thickening sludge running through me anymore either.

"They're coming, Mr. T." Tommy was helping me to my feet.

"The British? What?" My sleeping mind was struggling to find meaning in his words. Then the realization hit like it always does. Zombies. I stood up. I was a little dizzy and tired but not enough to hinder my escape attempt. "How much time?" I was looking over at Porkchop. "Can we barricade the door?"

"Way ahead of you." Tommy had the chair, which had earlier been holding the door open wedged under a small lip of metal in the middle.

"That's not going to hold."

"Way ahead of you. Porkchop, I'm going to carry you."

"I'd rather run. My bum is still hurting from my last ride."

"Go, I'll be right behind you," I told him.

"What are you doing, Mr. T?"

"Nothing legendary, I'm just going to hold this door shut to give you guys a head start."

"I'll stay, too," Tommy said.

I looked from him to Porkchop and frowned.

"Oh, okay. Well, hurry up then," he told me and left.

"How long is this thing?" Porkchop asked with trepidation, referring to the length of the corridor.

"About two hot dogs."

"We should get going then."

Their lights started bouncing wildly down the shaft. The chair skittered away as a heavy impact hit it from the other side. Luckily, I'd had my shoulder up against the door or I would have joined the chair.

"You okay, Mr. T?" Tommy's voice trailed up from ahead.

"Fine!" I answered.

I was bumped a couple of inches away from my perch as the zombies regrouped. One unlucky bastard was going to be called Lefty from this point forward as he mistakenly thought putting his fingers in the ensuing opening was a good idea. I slammed the door shut so tightly that the stinking little finger sausages were severed from the zombie. I conveniently ignored the fact that they were slender enough to belong to a woman. I don't know why that should bother me more, but it did. Monsters are male-based, at least in my head. The Boogie Man, Swamp-Thing, Dracula, Frankenstein, even the phonetically confusing monster named Mummy was male. Zombies just needed to be male— it made it somewhat justifiable to kill them. I'd always been brought up to never strike a woman, much less put a bullet in her head. This was a constant war within my psyche.

I was just going to have to accept the fact that the *man's* fingers I had just chopped from *his* body were super skinny, and had long nails and he liked to paint them with red nail polish. Who am I to judge what a person does with their body in the privacy of their home?

I placed my back against the door and braced my feet out in front of me. The walls to either side were close enough that, with my arms outstretched, I could use them to help hold myself in place as well. Tommy and Porkchop were making decent time, I'd decided that once I could barely make their light out I was going to make a run for it. That was the plan anyway. If you've read any of my previous journals you'll realize that it never really works out.

I think maybe a bulker had found his way downstairs to this lowest level, because no way could one of them fit down that fire chute. I wish one of them had tried early on, it would have clogged up the works for the rest of them. It would have been like Santa minus his magic dust going down a chimney. Nothing would have come out that incinerator for a week and maybe longer without a little assistance.

The bulker hit the door so hard, I was airborne, flying through the air like a superhero, at least for a second, before I scraped my palms up using them as improvised landing gear. My days as a living door lock were over. My feet were already propelling me into the upright position. I didn't bother turning around, I was going to run flat out until I hit the far door. Good thing too, because the thing that hit that door the second time ripped it clear from its large steel hinges. I knew I wasn't dealing with an ordinary zombie when I heard the heavy metal door slam to the ground not more than five feet from my retreating form. As it was, it kissed my heels as its forward momentum made it slide another twenty or thirty feet. I was catching up to Porkchop and Tommy.

"RUN!" I screamed at the top of my lungs.

I maybe should have used the psychic connection Tommy and I shared. But it was still like a second language to me and I wasn't comfortable enough with it, especially in a crisis situation where I reverted to my *native* language. I was close enough that I saw the look of horror on Porkchop's face when he turned to see what was wrong. That was all the incentive I needed. Whatever it was, it was huge, fast and fucking scary. Adrenaline pumps, I was positive, had shot themselves dry were pumping out pure crystalline power, and I was like a junky demanding more and more. I scooped up Porkchop like he was a bag of leaves rolling around the yard on a blustery New England fall day.

"Don't let me go, Mr. Talbot." I had him clutched to my chest and he was looking over my shoulder.

"How we doing?" I managed to ask him.

"Don't slow down."

I swear, like an image in a mirror, I could see what

was coming being reflected in Porkchop's eyes. It was huge, black and silver. Our zombie ape had found us. Tommy kept stealing glances back.

"Whatever happens, Mr. T, do not stop."

"I wasn't planning on it." That was when the alarms should have been going off in my head. Not sure I can be held too accountable, kind of had my own thing going on.

Then he was gone, not literally—he didn't dematerialize. He just reached up, shut off his light and dove to the side. He was as invisible as if he were the tip of a feather being dipped into an inkwell. Even after his words, I almost stopped…damn near couldn't help myself. He had his reasons, I could only hope he knew exactly what he was doing. We hadn't gone another ten feet when I heard a sound I hope to never have the misfortune in life to hear again. Accurately describing it would be like trying to explain what love was to a cat. I mean, to love something besides itself. I'll give it a shot, though. Picture a Yeti using a nail gun to build himself some shelves to go inside his cave. Now think of the sound it might make if its hand got in the way of one of those nails. It was a wail like no other. It was so loud that Porkchop dared to release his death grip on me to cover his ears. I did not have that same luxury.

I swear I could feel my eardrums being driven inward; a few more decibels, and they'd tear in half from the force, I was sure of it. The sound was primal and full of not just rage but hatred. Only from hatred could a sound so malevolent be born.

"Run, Mr. T!" Tommy was on my heels. Any closer and he'd be giving me a flat tire if that were possible in boots.

I'd like to think I had another gear or two to offer up to gain some speed, especially since mine and Porkchop's lives were at stake. Tommy's as well, considering he was stuck behind us. I didn't feel an answer was necessary; first, because I couldn't spare the breath; and second, I was already doing it.

"Hand me Porkchop!"

"Don't let me go, Mister Talbot." Porkchop clutched tight like a toddler prone to nightmares will a favorite teddy bear.

"I can run faster than you, Mr. T," Tommy beseeched.

Where was he getting all this extra air to exhale on words? I was laboring; the thought of speaking was difficult.

"He'll throw me to it, Mister Talbot." Porkchop was crying.

I was surer than Ivory Soap's claim of purity that Tommy would not do this, yet, that the boy believed it was enough for me to keep running with him like I was a momma kangaroo and he was my offspring. If the transition from myself to Tommy wasn't perfect, there was a good chance we would all go down into a rolling heap of food-like substance for the zombie ape.

"Can't," was all I could get out to Tommy.

I'd no sooner got the word out of my mouth than I was thrust to the side. The over-sized monkey may have started the process, but the unbelievably heavy concussion completed it. I was pretty sure I could feel sticky blood running out of my ears and down my neck. I'd later learn it was actually Porkchop's sweat, but right then, I thought I'd broken something internally in my head. Although my wife would have you believe that something has been broken in there for quite some time. My struggling lungs were now filling with dust as the entire structure was being shaken on its foundation. I knew the sound for what it was—ordinance, but that didn't stop my fantasy prone imagination from thinking that it could possibly be a vengeful god taking out his wrath on this desecrated ground.

So much dust was swirling around that our flashlights were as useless as car high beams on an extremely foggy night. Visibility was reduced to inches. The building above us was not dealing well with the explosives raining down on it. Our feet were involuntarily leaving the floor from the concussions…and then something happened that I really hadn't been expecting. My legs were moving, but they were no longer touching a solid surface. I was flying! Or rather, Tommy had unbelievably lifted me (and thereby Porkchop) clean off the ground.

"This is very emasculating," I told him when I was finally able to do so without hitching.

"You can bring it up at your annual Man-Card Holders convention in Spokane."

"Not bad." Actually, pretty outstanding under the circumstances. "Door!" I warned.

Tommy was going so fast that, if the thing were locked, we were all about to become a smorgasbord of conjoined, congealed parts. Tommy slowed up a bit and gently placed me down. I swear the heels of my boots were smoking and made a squelching sound like a jumbo jet does when it lands. I just hoped Porkchop didn't adjust like overhead luggage did, according to flight attendants anyway. I'd yet to see someone get smacked on the top of the head by a wayward carry-on. I turned slightly to the side letting my hip hit the push bar. As long as Deneaux hadn't blockaded it, this should work out fine. Then I was through. We were through. The air was fresher and I could see some ambient light not dependent on my underpowered helmet beam.

I kept running. I wasn't quite sure where to go, but just because we were out of the building didn't mean the ape or the regular zombies wouldn't follow and eat us. Zombies had no boundary issues. Tommy should have still been on my heels, especially since I had slowed a bit to a speed that I thought wouldn't shatter my hip and pelvic bones should the door have stayed shut.

"The truck!" Tommy was shouting from about twenty feet away.

I didn't see what the hell he was talking about. I heard

fists of fury striking a solid steel door though. Sounded like Thor himself was attempting to break it down.

"Flipped the lock," he told me as he raced up, grabbed my shoulder, and just about drove my face into the military truck I'd had a hard time seeing.

The ground was shaking as rounds kept pounding into the building. There was a fairly good chance our miraculous escape was going to end under countless tons of concrete. The glow plugs took an inordinate amount of time to heat up. It's amazing how long a second can drag out when chunks of building are falling all around you and a crazed zombie ape is trying to peel your flesh like a giant banana. I don't think it was more than fifteen seconds, but my mind was racing so fast that I think I could have read *War and Peace* in the interim. Well, not really, that book is friggin' huge, and I've already proved over and over that I can't sit for much longer than a Dr. Seuss book.

When that truck started, I was elated. It soared up there with some of my most memorable moments of my life. For example, the day I got married. (Okay, covered that one. If that wasn't here and she read this, I would be up that smelly creek everyone ends up on without a paddle. Not sure why anyone would put their canoe in a creek named that anyway, I suppose it's not really relevant right now.) The birth of my kids being another, and how could I forget the 2004 Red Sox World Series. Depending on if my wife and I are having a disagreement, the Red Sox status moves up or down. I wonder if I should just scratch that out?

Tommy was shouting and pointing to where we needed to go, but it was easy enough to see. There was only one roadway out and there was daylight. We were so fucking close, so fucking close. My head slammed off the steering wheel as the truck was tossed up into the air, or the ground fell away, not really sure. As I looked up, all I saw was a fireball, not off to the side or in the distance—we were immersed inside of it. The air was wrenched from my lungs as the fireball consumed all the oxygen. All I had to do now was wait for the searing, blistering heat, something I was all too familiar with.

"Fuck."

Chapter Eighteen – BT

"How big is that place?" Tracy asked as she saw the last of the zombies straggle into the building. "We can get a little closer now, maybe offer some help if we hear anything."

BT could see the falsehood of hope Tracy wore like a protective shield. There was no way out of that building. The zombies would be so thick, it would be impossible to elude them.

Travis came up to his mother and grabbed her hand. Justin, on the opposite side, took her other one.

"Mom?" Justin asked.

BT (in fact, everyone save Trip) knew that one-word question was infused with much more meaning. He might as well have said, "Mom, he's dead, we should get going."

"He's alive. I won't risk anybody's lives going in, but dammit, we are going to be out here when he comes."

Justin glanced over to Gary who looked like he wanted to be anywhere but here.

"We're not going in? Why'd I get a ticket then?" Trip asked, ripping out a handful of lint from his pocket and shaking it around. Pieces of it fluttered to the ground.

Tracy turned, her eyes glistening. She let go of her boys' hands and headed back to the car. BT grabbed Justin before he could follow.

"She just needs to be alone for a while."

"BT, we need to get out of here. When those zombies finish…" Justin gulped when he realized exactly what he was saying.

"I know, boy, I know, but your mom needs a minute to say her final peace."

Justin hugged the big man. "BT, he died for me. He died trying to find a cure for me, how am I ever going to live with that?"

"Proudly. You will live proudly with the fact that

your father loved you enough to sacrifice his life to save yours. Something he would do a thousand times if he had to. He has handed you...both of us...a second chance, and it's what we do with it now that will honor him. You hold your head high. Just remember, there isn't anything that man would not have done for any one of us. Even Trip for some strange reason."

"Thank you." Justin detached himself from BT, wiped his eyes and walked away a few steps to be somewhere more private with his thoughts.

"You okay?" BT was looking at Travis who was staring steely-eyed at the building.

"I'm going to kill them all," he said before turning away.

A chill ran up BT's spine. "I believe you." Something in the tone of his voice convinced him.

"I believe him, too." Dennis said after he watched Travis walk away. "I've seen that same damned look on his father, but it was on the football field. Identical results though."

BT nodded, the only one that seemed completely unaffected by the current events was Henry. He would alternate between lying down and sitting up. Occasionally he would let out a bark-like sound. Sometimes his tail would wag, at other points, his fur would bristle and his ears would pull back, and always without fail he kept a vigil on that building.

"Not gonna lie, dog, you creep me out a little sometimes. Is Mike the dog-whisperer, or are you the human-whisperer?" BT asked him as he stroked the dog's massive head and then moved on to scratch the sweet spot on his chest. "I wish I could see what you do." Henry promptly sneezed all over BT's forearm in response. "Thank you for that."

BT would wait as long as it took for Tracy to come to the realization that Mike was gone. He would not be the one that took that from her, unless of course they were in danger, then he'd suffer the consequences if need be. He sat down next to Henry and draped his arm over the dog. His butt had no sooner made contact with the ground than it rumbled.

"Really, dog? You wait until I sit down to do that? Come on, man, I thought we had some sort of deal in place?" BT started scooting away, knowing that the toxic emissions were mere moments from assailing his nostrils.

"Tanks!" Travis shouted.

"I don't know if I should feel relieved that it's tanks and not you," BT said as he started to rise. Dennis stuck a hand out and helped him up.

"Thank you," BT told him.

"Are they coming to help?" The look in Tracy's eyes was breaking BT's heart.

Even if they were, he figured they were too late to change the outcome. A squadron of twelve tanks aligned themselves in a loose arc to the northwest of the facility. Joseph and a few of his officers were sitting atop specially trained horses on top of a small hill overlooking everything. BT noted they were closer to their group than to the tanks. He, and those around him, stepped back as they felt the heavy percussions even from their distant vantage point.

"NO!" Tracy and Trip screamed as they watched rounds impact the building.

"I had front row center." Trip fell to his knees, his head in his hands.

Tracy jumped into the car. BT was slow to react and might not have made it in before she raced off if not for the fact that she had to go around Trip.

"At least he's finally good for something," BT muttered as he just about dove into the passenger's seat. Tracy didn't look at him, nor say anything as she barreled down the road. BT struggled for long seconds attempting to shut his door. He'd just pulled it closed as she drove off road, making a straight line for Joseph and his men. BT had one hand on the roof of the car, the other on the door. He was doing his best to not be thrown around like a beach ball. The car was making loud thumps as she seemed to continually bottom it out or hit a protruding rock.

BT thought about warning her in regards to destroying the car, but he knew she wouldn't care. The horses whinnied and danced about as the car headed straight for them. BT noticed that one of Joseph's men was aiming a rifle at them. He also saw that Joseph told him to stand down or something along those lines, because the man reluctantly put the weapon down. Then the big man witnessed something he still had a difficult time believing happened and that he'd actually seen it. Tracy had to be doing seventy miles an hour over uneven terrain—the car, more times than not, air bound. She had turned the wheel hard to the right whilst simultaneously slamming on the brakes. BT thought they were in serious danger of overturning a few times if the g-forces he was feeling were any indication.

Without missing a beat, the car still slightly sliding, she slammed it into park, opened the door and stepped out, striding toward Joseph. It was not each individual event that had blown BT's mind; it was the fluidity in which she had performed those actions. It was smooth and seamless. He, however, was still bouncing around like an epileptic on Red Bull. Tracy was already shouting at Joseph while BT was having a difficult time finding the door handle.

"Stop those tanks from firing!" Tracy shouted. She could be heard clearly even though the explosions in the background were deafening.

"I will not," Joseph said as he tried to calm his horse.

The animal had not seemed all that disturbed by the tanks, but rather from the waif of a woman that was yelling at its rider. Joseph was pulling on the bridle as the horse danced nervously.

"My husband is in there!"

"Even if your husband was alive, which I do not

believe is possible, this is much bigger than he is. If he were even half the man you convinced me that he has become, he'd understand this needs to be done. The Demense Group, along with the zombies we sent in there, must be pummeled out of existence."

"I know the man," BT bellowed as he got free from the car, something he hoped Tracy had damaged beyond repair. If he never had to get in a car piloted by her again, that would be too soon. "Yes, he would understand why you were doing what you were doing, but no, he would not appreciate you bombing him. I think it's safe to say I can guarantee that."

"It matters little now." Joseph's face looked like a cross between pained and consternated that he was being bothered during his biggest victory over the forces that he perceived to be evil.

"My husband is a good man! You cannot end his chance of escaping like this!"

Joseph's horse whinnied and reared back from an explosion that rivaled all the others combined.

"Cease fire! Cease fire!" Joseph yelled into his radio. Chunks of debris were still raining down when they got their first glimpse of the crater that used to house the Demense Group.

"Ammo supply or fuel, tough to say," one of Joseph's men stated before the commander could ask what had caused the massive explosion.

It looked like a meteor impact respite with sloped crater walls ringed by black smoking material.

"I'm sorry," Joseph told Tracy before he turned his horse around and rode away.

Tracy stared at his back for a moment before turning to the wreckage before them. BT walked over and wrapped his arm around her waist. She leaned into him. Neither said a word. Even if Mike had somehow found a safe haven within the tempest, he could not have avoided the destruction of the gigantic detonation.

"We have to go down there." She looked up at BT and he nodded. Although the chances of finding anything left of her husband...his friend...were beyond imaginably slim.

Joseph sent men to bring a reluctant Tracy and BT back to where the others had set up camp. There was more than one relieved face when they returned.

It was more than twelve hours before the fires abated enough that they could begin to think of going down to the crater. By then, the dark had settled over the area and it would be entirely too dangerous to attempt what, ultimately, was merely a body retrieval. None of them could see any sense in the risk of adding to the travesty, except Trip, who was now convinced they were the first men to step foot on the moon.

"I don't even remember the launch," he kept saying around the somber encampment. "You'd think *that* I would remember."

"I'd like to launch his ass to the moon," BT grumbled. "Sorry," he muttered even lower when he realized Stephanie was looking at him.

"Trip, honey, why don't we get some sleep? It's going to be a long day tomorrow."

"Why is it going to be longer? Are we going to approach the speed of light which will elongate the time/space continuum?" Everyone around the small fire was staring at him, no one said anything so he continued. "Or is it going to be made from taffy?"

"Thought we'd lost Trip for a second," Gary said. It was the first words he'd spoken in a long while. He'd been looking over at the hole in the ground where his brother's last known whereabouts had been. "This can't be it," he said as Tracy had grabbed his arm.

She desperately wanted to believe him. However, it was difficult to do so when looking at those ruins.

Tracy awoke the following morning with Trip leaning

over her, his face not more than a handful of inches away from hers. His eyes were open wide and deeply bloodshot.

"Good morning, Trip." She hadn't moved.

"Is it morning already?"

"Umm, Trip, how long have you been like this?"

"Five, six hours maybe." He was still leaning close.

"You've been standing over me like this for five or six hours? What in the world for?" She was trying to sit up, but Trip wouldn't move.

"Bennie said Ponch is alright."

"Who is Bennie, Trip?" Tracy didn't think grasping onto the straw that Trip was showing her was in her best interest, but she couldn't help it.

"The dude on the jet."

Tracy finally maneuvered around so she was able to sit all the way up. Trip was still staring where her head had been. "Whoa, how'd you do that?" he asked when he realized she was next to him.

"Oh, dear God, I should just walk away now." Tracy was shaking her head. "I don't know of any Bennie on a jet, Trip."

"Bennie and the Jets? Is he talking about Elton John?" BT had rolled over and was now watching. "Don't listen to a damned thing he has to say, Tracy."

"You like Elton John, BT?" Gary asked. "Me too."

"Just because I know a song doesn't mean I like it, Gary. Tracy, move away from him!"

Trip was leaning over still, but his head was turned so that he could look at Tracy. "I'm telling you, Bennie said Ponch was fine and so was his friend, Stomach."

"See. Don't listen to him, he's making no sense." BT was slowly getting up to physically move Trip away.

"Who is Stomach?" Tracy asked, searching Trip's eyes for some sort of sign that there was sanity hidden somewhere deep in them.

"You know. His friend, Tummy."

BT had gripped Trip's shoulders. He was about to lift him off the ground and give him that moon launch Trip had missed.

"Wait, BT."

"He's not just a burned-out hippie, Tracy, he's scorched earth. No matter how much you want to believe, you can't. He probably doesn't even know what he's talking about."

"Who is his friend, Tummy?" Tracy asked.

"Does he mean Tommy?" Travis asked.

Tracy gasped. "Could he really mean Tommy? Could he have made it?"

"Tracy, I bet he thinks we're still in the snow-plow."

"Tour bus," Trip corrected him.

Tracy was now standing, looking over towards the smoking desolation.

"Whoa, how does she keep doing that?" Trip was now standing. "Yeah. Ponch, Stomach, the Butcher's son and a Yeti made it out."

"Oh for the love of…" BT threw his hands up in the air and stormed off.

"Mom?" Travis asked.

"I don't know, but we're going to find out."

Tracy, and the rest, headed for the roadway. They hadn't gone more than a few hundred yards when they heard the approach of trucks. They stopped when they reached the group.

"Hop on," Joseph said from the passenger seat of one of those trucks.

Tracy couldn't decide if she wanted to swear at him or thank him so she did neither as she went to the rear and climbed in, followed shortly by the rest. Nobody said much as the truck was already half filled with Illuminati soldiers; plus, the noise of the large diesel engine made communication difficult anyway. The truck hadn't even completely stopped when Tracy jumped out.

"Mom, you're going to hurt yourself that way," Travis said as he followed.

"She'll be fine, apparently she practices this a lot," BT said as he exited.

Tracy ran to the lip of a hole that plunged more than a hundred feet down. Smoke still smoldered in a dozen places along the hundred-yard expanse. A man with a Geiger counter walked around the edge holding his sensor over the lip.

"There was the potential for this to have been caused by some sort of nuclear explosion, and you didn't bother to tell us?" Dennis was livid.

"The probability was low," Joseph said evenly.

"Why the test then?"

"Can never be too careful."

"Yes you can, we could have slept further away."

"We've been monitoring throughout the night. There is no fallout that we can detect."

"Does that mean there is fallout you can't detect?" BT asked. "And if my little friend here is concerned, so am I!"

"We're friends now?" Dennis asked. "And I'm not little."

"United front," BT told him.

"Be with your friend's wife. I think she needs the both of you more than I need to be questioned right now."

BT and Dennis turned to see Tracy had tears falling from her face. Joseph was ordering his men to make sure none of the zombies had survived. Not that it could even be possible. Twisted steel and chunks of concrete larger than a semi were at the bottom of that pit of despair. Tracy walked around the entire outer lip looking for anything that resembled a place where someone could have escaped. Then she did it again.

"We need to go down there," she said when she got back from her second go around.

"You're kidding, right?" Justin asked.

"I mostly certainly am not," she said indignantly.

"Tracy, the walls are nearly vertical, and there are things you can impale yourself on the entire way down." BT was trying to talk some sense into her.

Just then, she saw Joseph approaching. "What do you want?" Tracy lashed out. "Haven't you already done enough?"

"I couldn't help but hear you talking," he said, trying to be as polite as possible.

"This is awesome. I didn't think sound could travel on the moon...without atmosphere, I mean," Trip declared.

"And, yet, we can talk," Travis said sarcastically.

"That's weird too," Trip answered.

Stephanie looked embarrassed as she led Trip away to a different area.

"I'd just like to offer my sincerest condolences for your loss. I cannot, however, allow you to go down there. It is entirely too dangerous. I'm sending some men down on ropes in a few minutes. I have told them to let me know if they hear anything."

BT watched as Tracy's eyes narrowed and her lips clamped tight. She'd seen Mike do enough boneheaded things to earn that look. Carnage was immediately about to follow. "Justin, Travis, help me with your mom." The boys hesitated moving in, when they saw the look she was directing at Joseph.

"I don't want to get involved," Travis said as he prepared to bolt.

"Get your ass over here, boy!"

Travis was weighing his options on who was scarier; BT or his mom. "Sorry, BT. You and Justin are on your own." With that, he left to seek out his uncle, who he hoped could shield him from the coming storm.

Three of Joseph's men got into special safety harnesses that attached to heavy climbing ropes. These were tied off to a trailer hitch on three separate trucks. The men cautiously made their way down the side, slowly crawling among the wreckage.

"What's taking them so long?" Tracy was pacing around nervously.

"It's dangerous, Mom," Justin told her.

She hurrumphed and crossed her arms. "I could have done it faster," she said as the men touched down on the bottom.

She'd apparently said it loud enough that they heard her as one of them looked up. He didn't do it, but BT was pretty sure he wanted to flip her the bird or tell her ass to give it a try.

If Tracy thought their descent down was slow, then the pace they were walking across the debris was about to set her over the figurative edge. "I've seen sloths riding turtles move faster!"

"Listen, lady, you have no idea how dangerous it is down here. Every time you step, something moves! So…me and my team would appreciate it if you would keep your thoughts to yourself!"

"That will be enough, Wilkins," Joseph told his man.

"Yes, sir," he answered, glowering a little longer at Tracy before he turned away.

For over half an hour, the trio scoured the bottom. BT wasn't certain what they were looking for; surely not for the grieving widow's husband. He was saddened for the loss of his friend until he caught sight of Henry who had not come within twenty feet of the rim. He was staring off in a completely different direction, his tail wagging furiously. He would have gone over to the dog to try and see what he saw if not for the next few events.

"Sir, there's nothing here. Definitely nothing living." Wilkins made sure to direct that last comment Tracy's way.

The words had no sooner echoed off the walls of the crater than the earth began to shake as if in protest of his callousness. The ground shook for a solid ten seconds as the unstable pile fell in on itself another five feet.

"Wilkins, let's go. Get you and your men out of there!" Joseph was urging the team.

The importance that the men needed to move faster was not lost on them, but to do so risked injury by slipping and falling on any number of matter both organic and inorganic. The ground shook again, followed by a squelching sound that was similar to two pieces of dry rubber rubbing against each other under high pressure.

"What the hell was that?" one of Wilkins' men asked.

The answer came soon enough as brownish red ooze began to seep up from the ground the men found themselves on.

"What the hell?" Wilkins asked.

At first it was slow and merely making the ground wet. Then, from whatever underground pool this was coming from, the dam had burst, the ground losing definition as the sludge rose.

Gary vomited as a wave of heated air tainted with zombie guts blew up from the pit and over everybody. He was not the only one to fall victim to the stench. The juice from twenty thousand pulverized zombies was resurfacing. Wilkins and his men were in serious danger of drowning in the material.

"Start the trucks!" Joseph yelled. "If it gets over their heads I want you to drive."

"Sir, I can't pull them over this stuff, they'll be shredded," one of the drivers said.

Wilkins stopped to help one of his men who had fallen over. "My leg is stuck!" The man was wrenching at his knee, the inner workings of zombies already splashing above his calf. "Help me!" he begged Wilkins. "I don't want to die like this!"

"Nobody does," Wilkins answered. "Shut up for a second, and I'll make sure you don't have to."

"Wilkins? Can you get him out?" Joseph asked. The question was clear enough, if you knew what to look for. If he couldn't get the man out, Joseph didn't want Wilkins to die pointlessly in a failed rescue.

"Get out of there," Tracy was saying to herself.

As more slush was coming up, the accumulated weight was pushing the precarious pile down. This was compounded by the emptying space where the zombie guts were coming from and gave the illusion that the liquid was rising much faster than it was. What was a minute before at the men's calves was now over their knees.

"Wilkins, let's go!" Joseph shouted.

"Sir, I can't get Heller free!"

"Stand aside, we're going to have to pull him out. Now, Wilkins!"

Joseph directed the driver to move slowly. Heller was at an angle to the truck so that, when the vehicle pulled up, it twisted the upper half of his body. He screamed in pain. There was not a man or a woman in the area not looking down on the events playing out. While Wilkins was seeing how Heller would make out, the third man of the group was about halfway up the lip as three men pulled on his rope to aid his climb.

"A little more," Joseph told the truck driver. Heller's torso was twisted almost a full ninety degrees from his lower half.

Heller screamed again, and Tracy wasn't sure if she could watch much longer. It was clear to her that the man was going to be pulled apart soon, much like those who were drawn and quartered centuries ago. The truck engine revved, Heller's next scream was a high-pitched one, followed by the distinctive sound of bone cracking.

"He's free!" Wilkins shouted, rushing forward to keep a passed-out Heller's head above the muck line.

"I want men on both their lines, slow but steady pulling!" Joseph commanded.

By the time they came to the crater wall, the zombie slush was mid-chest and Wilkins was doing all he could to keep Heller from drowning. The man's head kept lolling back and forth as he slid down into shock.

Fifteen more minutes and both were back on the perimeter. Heller was going to be on light duty for a while, his left leg broken in two places along with a bad case of bruised ribs. Wilkins had suffered some cuts and scrapes, but was immediately cleaned up and pumped with enough antibiotics to flush out an elephant.

Tracy could only stare down at the miasma. Mike's fate lay within the swirling browns, reds and blacks down there. If, by some chance, he had survived the zombies, found a safe sanctuary away from their bites, and then his refuge was somehow strong enough to withstand the bombing, there was very little chance it would be airtight and not allow the pressed zombies inside. Even if by some miracle it was, he would be running out of air by now. She would mourn when she got home. All she hoped for now was that his death had been swift and merciful; something that was not in abundance these days. Even Trip, whose grasp on reality was tenuous at best, seemed to realize the solemnity of the event.

The only one who seemed wholly unaffected by the destruction and loss was again Henry, who had rolled over and was now wriggling around with his legs airborne in a desperate bid to sate the itch he had on his back.

"Are you going to be alright?" Joseph asked Tracy as he came up to her. Travis and Justin kept a close eye on the man and their mom, not really sure which way this was going to play out.

BT had walked away, too distraught to even comfort his friend's wife. Dennis had no such compunction about displaying his heartache in public. He sat down hard on the lip of the hole, his head in his hands as he grieved for his friend.

"I'm going to need a truck," Tracy said, pulling her gaze away from the scene below. "I'm ready to get my boys home," she told Joseph evenly. Her eyes were red-rimmed, and her lip may have held the slightest quiver, but she stood strong.

"I have no trucks I can spare, but we will give you a ride until such time as I can secure you a vehicle," he told her.

Tracy nodded.

Within ten minutes they were heading out. Tracy felt it was unnaturally quiet, although that could have been attributed to the rhythm of her heart, which had been broken.

"A BMW lot? Now we're talking," BT said as they pulled up. It was the only blip of sunshine on an otherwise abysmal day.

Joseph ordered his men to get two SUVs running and siphoned other tanks to make sure the fuel tanks were full. "Ma'am," Joseph told Tracy when she got behind the seat.

"Thank you for saving us. I will, however, never forget that you did not at least try to save my husband."

"I understand, and I am sorry for your loss. Good luck, and I wish you nothing but the best." He spun his finger in the air and pointed back toward the truck. His men jumped on board and left in a black plume of exhaust. The parking lot was much quieter with the heavier diesel engines gone; the purring of the two BMWs not much louder than a person whispering.

Justin helped Henry into one of the SUVs. The dog immediately stretched and took the majority of the second row. Travis got in beside him.

Gary came to Tracy's side. "Do you mind if I ride with Steph and Trip? I don't think I can take any more smell," he said, pointing to Henry who sneezed in response.

"Great. I'll take his spot." BT hopped into the passenger seat.

"That's fine. I wasn't going to sit there," Justin said

sarcastically. "I'll get in with the stoner."

"Great, then there isn't a problem," BT said as he pulled the door shut. He turned to Tracy. "I don't think I could listen to that perpetual pot-head spew one more thing about how he visited Gandhi or some shit."

Dennis moved to the rear of the car, having the entire third row for himself. Tracy hoped he stopped crying soon. It was withering away her resolve to stay strong until such point that she could collapse in on herself, much like the Demense building had.

"I don't think so," Stephanie told Trip who was sitting behind the steering wheel of the other SUV. "The last time you drove, you thought it was a rocket ship."

"It wasn't?" Trip asked as Stephanie gripped his shoulder and gently pulled him out. "Get in the backseat," she told him as she helped him back in.

"Wonderful," Justin said as Trip sat.

"You live here?" Trip asked him.

"Wonderful," Justin repeated.

Gary hopped into the passenger seat. This was the second time he was going home without Mike, and he felt the loss more acutely this time than he had the first. For a few moments he wished he'd died in those first days of the zombie outbreak. *It would have been over a long time ago, and I wouldn't have had to go through any of this*, he thought in a dour mood. The joy and the victories were too insignificant and placed too far away to outweigh the overwhelming losses and defeats that kept piling up at a rapid pace.

Tracy pulled out of the parking lot, hoping to put as many miles between her and Mike's final resting spot before the day was through.

Chapter Nineteen – Mike Journal Entry 8

My head was ringing and my stomach felt like I'd been rabbit punched by the Hulk. Somehow it was comforting to see that Tommy was suffering as well. This is such a strange reaction in humans. Why is sharing misery such a common event? You would think people would try and pull themselves up instead of drag each other down. It really was only a matter of time until man took himself out of the picture. *If* man were to make it out of *this* disaster, which I wasn't holding onto much hope, it would be a century and a half at the minimum before we came off the edge of extinction. By then, who knows? Wolves would probably be running the show.

I couldn't tell if I was in the midst of a severe case of vertigo. Either the building was shifting, or we were actually moving. Tommy was yelling something, but I might as well have been in Tibet behind one of those huge gongs while the monks were performing their rendition of *Moby Dick* by Led Zeppelin. For those of you who may not know, this is a drum solo. It was possible I was as deaf as a politician to the outcries of his constituents. Tommy was pulling his seat belt out, that made no sense to my brain, which had been acting like a ping-pong ball inside my skull.

"Seat belt!" I know I shouted it, because my throat hurt after I said it even though I didn't hear it.

Explosions were going on to the rear of us, the truck lurching forward as the concussions slammed into the back of it. I was just picking my blood-dripping head off of the dashboard when I saw something run past that was huge and on fire. The ape had escaped. If I had the presence of mind and a rifle, I would have shot it. But what were the odds we would ever cross paths again? Yeah, I already knew the answer to that question before I asked it. I could only hope it would be on my terms, not his. And yes, I knew the answer to that statement as well.

Tommy saw it, too, and we moved in its direction, maybe to run it down or maybe just because it was heading out. Most likely, this was the way it came into the facility; and therefore, in theory, it would know the way out.

The ground under us trembled violently. *This* was how I imagined the world was going to end, being split apart by major earthquakes or a meteor strike, not a microscopic virus. Even with the seat belt on, I was in danger of giving myself whiplash and a concussion. The ground movement was so violent that it was impossible to see clearly as the earth was jumping by feet. It was impossible to focus.

I don't know how Tommy was able to drive. His whole body was leaning on the steering wheel, I guess in an attempt to keep the truck from veering. The ground leapt up one more time, higher than all the other times combined. The truck went with it and, for heart-lurching moments, we were in flight before the truck collided back down with the pavement. I stupidly looked into the side view mirror. Ever watch any movie or documentary about volcanoes? You know that pyroclastic cloud that just swoops down the side of the mountain and destroys everything in its path? Yeah, well, that's what it looked like, and it was rapidly gaining on us.

"Faster, Tommy!" I may have audibly heard my words this time. I'd either found a new level of volume, or I'd regained a little of the hearing that I'd lost.

Porkchop was seated between us, alternating looking from my mirror to Tommy's. "Yeah, faster!"

Tommy glanced in his mirror as well, his eyes growing large. He might have been scared, but we weren't moving any faster. I looked to his foot; it was already planted on the floor of the truck.

"Shit." I rolled up my window. Most likely this was going to be as effective as hiding behind lawn furniture when someone shot a bazooka at you, but this was all about perceived safety right now.

I could not keep my eyes off of the mirror as the gray

cloud rushed to greet us. The force was enough to lift the rear of the truck off of the ground. Tommy was struggling to keep the wheels straight, and us, from being broadsided much like the ship in *The Poseidon Adventure*. (Cheesy 70's movie where the ship *Poseidon* turns sideways to a tidal wave and is turned over upside-down.) My daughter Nicole loved that movie, made me watch it a dozen times, which was about eleven-and-a-half times more than I wanted to.

There were a couple of times when the back of the truck was desperately trying to come even with the front, and it was only Tommy's yanking and cranking on the wheel that kept this from happening. I don't know how he knew which way to turn. We were completely encased within the debris cloud. I expected a wall at any moment to jump out at us so we could brutally crash into it.

The cabin was beginning to fill with the foul air. It was a caustic toxic mix of plastics and zombies that threatened to choke the lives out of us. I was trying my best to take short, measured breaths; I wasn't having any luck. It was like I'd just run the fifty-meter dash and was trying to regulate my breathing. When the inside of the cab became as dense with ash as the outside, I figured this was it. Porkchop's eyes had closed. I was afraid he had passed out and was moving steadily toward death. Then, like we were being birthed from the pits of hell, we emerged into beautiful, blissful sunshine. Tommy and I both rolled down our windows as he drove a few hundred more yards before finally stopping. I jumped down and hauled Porkchop out with me. While I was busy coughing up my lungs, Porkchop sat up from where I deposited him.

He stood and patted my back as I tried to get all of the poisons out of me. "Mr. Talbot, you should have really held your breath like I did. I used to win all the time against my friends when we would bet who could go underwater and stay there the longest. I even beat Bobbie Gibbons, who I saw go up for a gulp of air and come back underwater and tried to make it look like he didn't, but I had water goggles on and could see him do it clearer than I can see you. Although he tried to deny it, said I was jealous that he could hold his breath longer, which was funny, because I still beat him, so that really didn't make much sense. You okay? Every time you cough it looks like you're smoking. Can your lungs be on fire?" He was bending over trying to peer down my throat. "I don't see any flames, I think you're alright."

I wanted to thank him for his expert advice. "Go help Tommy," I hacked out. From the sounds of it, Tommy didn't sound much better than I did.

If I thought my throat was raw before, it was absolutely skinned now. It felt like I'd swallowed shaved glass. So even when Porkchop handed me a water bottle that had clearly been drank from, I didn't refuse. At that exact moment, germs could kiss my ass.

We all sat there a few minutes longer, looking to the place we had escaped. More than a city block was laid to waste and now sunken in. It would be hours before the dust settled and the fires went out. I had no desire to be there for it. We'd emerged victorious, but we'd suffered a loss with Doc gone. I was under the assumption my family was safe, though; and we'd saved Porkchop, so I was actually feeling pretty good. That was tempered slightly knowing Deneaux and the damned ape were still out there, and like steel to a magnet, they'd both find their way to me. It was a foregone conclusion.

We were still hacking up lungs as we, once again, entered the truck and departed.

Tommy recovered faster than I did, but by degrees I was feeling better. Some of it was putting distance between our former captors and us, but a big chunk was that I was racing to meet back up with my family.

"I don't know if I thanked you, Tommy," I said, turning to him. He didn't say anything. "You risked everything and I appreciate that."

"We're family, Mr. T. What choice did I have?"

It left him a lot of choices, but I didn't bring them up. "Just, thank you," I said, reaching over Porkchop and tenderly touching Tommy's knee. The gesture, which was meant as one of affection, seemed to cause him pain and discomfort.

He looked over at me.

"What, kid? What do you have to tell me? It's written all over your face, I just don't read vampire so good." My heart started thumping in my chest. Did he know something about my family that he hadn't told me? Were they in danger or worse? If he didn't fucking spit it out soon, I would beat it out of him. Okay, that's hypothetical...or is it rhetorical? Because he could kick my ass.

"There's more coming."

"Huh?" I was expecting something along the lines of Tracy has been kidnapped by a rogue band of Jehovah's Witnesses, not some vague threat. "Zombies? Are you talking about zombies? There will always be more of them coming."

He shook his head.

"That ape? There'll be more of them apes coming?" That was indeed terrifying, and sort of funny in a shtick 60s movie kind of way. I could see the marquee now: *Planet of the Zombie Apes.*

"Rednecks?" He shook his head. "Militant ants hell-bent on the destruction of the planet? What, Tommy? Because I can keep guessing all day long."

"My kind. They're coming."

I shit you not, my response was, "Walmart greeters are coming? What are they going to do? Sticker us to death."

On some level, I knew exactly what he meant; I just couldn't wrap my mind around it. Not yet anyway. We'd just barely escaped with our lives, defeated a shadow government group that wanted to rule what was left of the world, and witnessed the destruction of a fair part of the zombie population in this part of it. My family was supposedly safe and heading home, as were we. This was a time and a cause for celebration, not for gearing up for another conflict.

"Are they just going to have the smiley face stickers, or will they have superheroes, too?

Porkchop asked.

"Eliza and you weren't the only ones?" My head sagged.

"No." His head sagged to match mine.

I probably shouldn't have said her name aloud, because suddenly Porkchop looked like he might be...no, scratch that, he was going to be sick.

"Pull over, Tommy!" I was barely able to open the door and get Porkchop out before he started heaving.

I'd finally caught a break when his first projectile of bile shot over my left shoulder as I was helping him out. As his feet touched down, I stepped to the side. That seemed to be the worst of it as he hunched over like he saw a particularly shiny rock.

"You okay, kid?" Sometimes I could be an insensitive shit.

He'd lost his mom and dad on the first night. Then lost most of his second family to the very vampire I had just mentioned, and now Doc, his surrogate father, was gone as well. The kid probably thought he was driftwood with nowhere to place his roots.

"Sorry." He didn't look up but stayed fixated on that mythical, shiny rock.

"I'm the one that should apologize." I was rubbing his back. "You know you're part of my family now, right? I won't let anything happen to you."

"It's not me I'm worried about, Mr. Talbot." He stood up. I steadied him as he looked a little unsure on his feet. "It's everyone around me. Everyone I care for ends up dying." His pleading eyes were looking at mine.

"I'll make sure we're alright, Porkchop." I tried to be

as sincere as possible.

I truly meant the words, but it was an impossibility to guarantee such a thing. Even if the world was normal, and I had moved them all into the woods, hundreds of miles from people, one of them could get Lyme Disease from a tick and die. There is no such thing as safety, only the obscure illusion of it. Sure, you can take steps to be safer, like maybe don't take up chainsaw juggling, but that's about it. I think in the movie *Jurassic Park* one of the characters was quoted as saying, "Life will find a way." The converse is also true. Death will find a way, and if it's looking for you, there is no place to hide.

"I think I'm okay now." He looked better; however, I don't think he believed a word I said.

He walked toward the side of the road. I was going to ask him where he was going. Should have known the kid was smarter than me. He wanted Tommy and me to finish what we were talking about before he came back in the truck.

"Is he alright?" Tommy asked as I hopped back up into the cab.

"Better than me, I would imagine. Let's not make this like pulling teeth. Tell me what is going on."

Tommy looked like a whipped dog. "When someone as powerful as Eliza is killed, it can be felt. You felt it."

"How could I forget?" When Tracy was finally able to shove a knife into her withered heart I felt that she'd done the same to me, the pain was that acute. For a while I doubted I would be able to go on, and if I did, it would only be a fragmented part of me…like a hollowed out egg…brittle and easily broken on the outside, empty on the inside.

"Others felt it, too. I had hoped that maybe they would disregard it, but that doesn't seem to be the case."

"Is your vamp-dar going off?"

"My what, Mr. T?"

"Your vampire radar?"

Tommy looked at me like most do when I open my

mouth—confused and maybe somewhat disappointed. It was alright. I'm used to it.

"I guess…sort of. Nothing quite as detailed as radar, more like feelings. Her passing was noted, and I'm fairly certain someone will come to check it out."

"Like a vampire bureaucrat? Someone to rubber-stamp her demise? I'm not sure I get what's going on."

"There will be those who want to know how it was done and by whom."

"Is Tracy in danger? Is there some sort of atonement for killing her?" If that was the case, I was going to snag Porkchop and we were going to push this truck as far and as fast as we could until we caught up with her.

"Not really. Vampires are rarely fans of other vampires. They tolerate each other, more or less, as long as boundaries are not crossed. My sister cared little for these staked-out hunting grounds. She went were she wanted to and killed without impunity. She'd kill a vampire as well if it suited her needs or she was confronted. When someone like that is taken down, others will want to know how, why, and for what reason."

"And maybe to see if a threat exists for them as well. Isn't there like a vampire council we can tell that we want nothing more to do with their kind? Hell, it sounds like we did vampire-kind a huge solid. They should be sending us champagne or something."

"You've seen too many movies. There isn't a council."

"What are the chances they'll just find out what happened and leave?"

Tommy shrugged.

"Not to be a dick, but I don't think a shrug right now is the best answer you should come up with."

"I don't know, Mr. T, vampires are unpredictable. Even if they come, see, and are satisfied, they're not going to just hop back on a ship and head out."

"This shit just never ends, it's like an old beginning. There will be no hesitation this time on my part. I will not allow them to live if I'm given the opportunity. Which side of the fence do you fall on?" I asked him.

Eliza would always be his sister. Would he want retribution for her death even at the expense of his adoptive family? Would he take that opportunity if he received help? That made no sense. If Tommy wanted revenge, there would be little we could do to stop him.

"I'm sorry, I'm sorry I even asked that." I went from staring at him to looking out the windshield. "How long do we have?"

"Well, that's one benefit to living forever, you're never really in a rush. Payne will come with others, and they will most certainly take their time. Rounding up supplies and a means of transportation will be no easy feat. Add to that the fact that vampires really don't like to wander too far from where they were turned."

"Pain will come?" I asked, not understanding that part. I was clearly confused.

Tommy had to take a second to figure out what I was asking. "Not pain, p-a-i-n." He spelled it out. "But rather Payne as in P-a-y-n-e." He spelled this out as well.

"Fitting name." He nodded. "And this other part, are you kidding me? You have an eternity to see every nook and cranny of the world and you stay in your own neighborhood? That's crazy."

"Crazy, Mr. T, but true. That's why vampires are such a rarity in the United States. Vampirism started in Eastern Europe and has pretty much plagued that region ever since. Sometimes people have killed them, other times vampires self-regulate their population. Very rarely do they move to different hunting grounds. It could be months, maybe even years before they come."

"I don't know if that's a blessing or a curse. We'll never be able to hold vigil for that extended amount of time.

We'll let our guard down believing ourselves safe. You're sure they'll come?"

"It's in the air."

"Like a foul breeze?"

Tommy snorted. "Not quite, Mr. T. Have you ever wondered why, at certain parts in human history, a huge, earth-changing idea or revolutionary product will be developed by two people at vastly different geographical locations at the same time with neither of them having prior knowledge of the other's work?"

"Um, vaguely." I was lying.

"Some scientists have argued that, once a thought is created, it sends out signals and that these signals can be picked up by others. Philosophers have a slightly different view, but pretty much the same thing. That all of the ideas are out there…it is just a matter of us being in tune to collect them."

"So boiling this down, you're saying you have tuned in to the thought of a vampire and he wants to come see Eliza's final resting place?"

"It's not crystal clear, not like someone made a phone call, but something like that, Mr. T. And "he" is a "she" and there are three of them."

I wanted the more colorful "what the fuck" phrase to come out. I ended up with, "Are you kidding?"

He shook his head, so I had to assume he wasn't. My next thought was to slam my head against the dashboard as many times as I could until the thought fell through my ear hole with the leakage of brain matter.

"The threat is not immediate, Mr. T. I'm just telling you, the thought is out there."

"Why couldn't they just make another cotton gin?" I stepped out of the truck, the sun not feeling as warm or as bright, as if a thin veil had been pulled over all existence.

Porkchop came up to me when he saw me exit and grabbed my hand. "There's a good place to puke over here,

Mr. Talbot." I may have thanked him as he led me away. He was rubbing my back. "It's okay, Mr. Talbot, just let it all out." He rubbed a little more, when he realized I wasn't going to yield any results, he stopped rubbing. "Are you hungry? I'm pretty hungry. I could really go for some corn dogs and beans. Maybe some fried dough, too, that would be great. Been a long time since I've had any of that. We went to Five Banners."

"Six Flags?" I asked, thinking he'd got it wrong.

"Nope, Five Banners. My dad took me there a couple of years ago. Said it was cheaper, and with the money he saved, he could get a better bottle of hooch. I never heard of hooch, I thought maybe it was orange soda, and I was really looking forward to it. When we got to the amusement park, he pulled out a big bottle of his hooch. I knew what it was then. He sat on a bench by the front of the park and drank the entire day. I was really hoping he'd go on rides with me."

Now I found myself rubbing his back again, this time to comfort him for his asshole of a dad.

"I had some money my mom gave me. I think she knew he wouldn't give me any. I rode just about every ride that day and ate everything I could afford. By the way, I don't recommend fried Twinkies, made my stomach cramp up pretty bad. Had fried dough, corn dogs, pizza on a stick, icees, sodas, french fries..."

Porkchop was ticking off all his entrees on his fingers. It was fairly impressive, he had to use some of his fingers twice to get them all.

"...chocolate covered pretzels. I think that's it. I had to wake my dad up on that bench. He had passed out and wet himself. When we got back to his car, it was so hot inside and his pee smelled like boiling cabbage. I can't stand boiling cabbage. I threw up, I threw up everything. There where pieces of pretzel, fried dough, half a Twinkie..."

"I get it." My stomach was starting to roil.

"It was all over the windshield and dashboard. It

started to sizzle in some spots, like it was cooking or something."

"Are you just messing with me now?"

"My dad was so drunk he didn't even realize I had gotten sick, he reached over and grabbed the half a Twinkie to—"

"Heard enough!" I said loudly, walking away with my arms up in the air.

"Okay, you should have just said something," he told my retreating form.

The thought of the vampires took a distant back seat, like they were sitting at the rear of a stretch school bus in comparison to Porkchop's recounting of his dad eating regurgitated fried snacks. It took a long time before I felt comfortable enough with my inner piping to get back into the truck. Tommy and Porkchop were both smiling at me. Porkchop had shared the same story with Tommy, and now they both found it hilarious that the whole thing distressed me.

The truck moved down the roadway in near silence. I caught Porkchop elbowing Tommy more than once to look over at me so they could both grin anew. Still, for the most part, the ride was uneventful and quiet.

"We're going to need gas soon," Tommy stated. I had been dozing off.

"And food," Porkchop chimed in.

"I wouldn't mind stopping for the night, Mr. T. I'm kind of exhausted from all that's happened."

"I can't imagine why. Yeah, I'm pretty tired and beat up myself. I wouldn't mind taking a break either."

Part of me wanted to press on and make sure my family was okay and to thwart this latest threat along with the countless others my over-active imagination hadn't even come up with yet. Tommy, however, didn't seem overly concerned or at least he wasn't letting on. We had time, so it seemed, and Porkchop could do well with a decent meal and night's sleep. It would probably be a good idea to not stray too far from the Demense building before our stop anyway. The closer we stayed, the less likely we were to run into zombies, and that was fine by me.

Tommy pulled off the highway and up onto an overpass. We could see for a couple of miles in either direction north or south on the freeway and even to the east and west the trees had been cleared for the clover of road. Nothing short of the invisible man was going to sneak up on us and why the bastard wouldn't be in some women's locker room anyway was beyond me.

"I'll get some gas," I told Tommy.

"Alone?" he asked. Porkchop was in the back of the truck pulling out some boxes. Some were medical supplies and a couple were MREs. The boy looked absolutely ecstatic at his find.

"Fine dining tonight," I told him, enjoying his happiness. Enjoying the MREs? Well…that wouldn't nearly be fantastic. "Yeah, alone," I told Tommy. "There are no zombies, and you can even see the gas stations from here." I pointed at a small strip of stores about a quarter a mile down the road. Two were gas stations, three were fast food joints that I would have paid a handsome price for anyone of them had they been open. "Eating Fresh" right now would have been many times more preferable than to what Porkchop was digging in to. Looked like something a homeless person may have put together after some particularly bad Dumpster diving retrievals.

"I'll be fine. Just keep an eye out on Porkchop." After being cooped up in that prison, I needed some time to stretch my legs. "I'll call when I get there, Mom."

I left before he could protest or offer to do it himself. I really just wanted some alone time. I'd actually gotten precious little of it since this had started. There was no imminent threat, the day was gorgeous, and I was free. I could feel Tommy's gaze on my back nearly the whole time.

He was taking his guardianship duties entirely too seriously. I waved over my head. The first station I reached was in pretty bad shape. Two of the six pumps had been either pulled or pushed free from their moorings and were nowhere in sight. Can't imagine who would have taken them and for what reason. The covers to the underground tanks were all lifted up. One of them even had a siphoning hose sticking out of it.

"Someone left in a hurry," I said as I walked over to the contraption. There was an electric pump attached to the hose along with jumper cables, apparently having used the car they rode in as a power source. "Hope they shut the car off first," I said. "Your loss is my gain." I grabbed the equipment, although I didn't have a car battery or a container to put the gas into.

If the gas station looked bad, the Subway sandwich shop was destroyed. I'm not even sure the building could have been salvaged. A war had apparently been waged for cold cuts, because bullets holes riddled the entire structure. And by the sheer number of holes and the line of damage they did, someone wasn't playing fair; it was easy to see they'd had a machinegun and a shitload of rounds. Whatever, or whoever, had been in the shop had long departed either physically or metaphysically. I thought about going in to see if something edible survived, but I'd swear that building swayed in the breeze. I wasn't going to chance it.

The second gas station looked similar to the first. This one at least had a smattering of cars in it, and not all of them had holes in their gas tanks. I walked up to the plate gas windows, unsure how this one could still be intact considering the damage suffered just next door. How one stray round from the thousands shot had not hit this building was fairly impressive. The sun was glaring, I had to cup my eyes as I peered inside.

"Well, hello there," I said as my eye spied something worthy of my attention.

I looked for a few seconds longer, wondering if it

were a mirage. I mean, how this particular treasure was overlooked was beyond me. Of course the paranoid part of me thought it could be some sort of elaborate trap.

"Fuck it. Not the first trap I've walked into knowingly."

I was just about to pull my face away from the glass when a zombie ran headlong into it at a full sprint. I thought that I'd broken my nose as I was thumped off the pane.

"That'll get the old adrenaline pump working. Cheap thrill that was!" I muttered.

Still, I really wanted what was inside. It was then that I realized I wasn't armed. I looked around at the cars. I wasn't fond of a tire iron as my primary weapon, but it would do in a pinch. The first car was a cheap foreign model, the iron tool inside it having about as much heft as a loaf of bread. I tossed it to the side. Next to it was an old T-Bird, looked like the owner of the garage was, at some time, going to restore it. When I found the tire iron that belonged to it, I figured if the metal got reworked it could become a broad sword.

"This'll work."

I walked back up to the storefront. Murph, an employee I gathered by his name-tagged shirt and pimply face, was waiting not-so-patiently for my return. He was pressing up so tightly on the glass his pimples were bursting like tiny volcanic pustules, smearing white, thick oil all along the interior. I tried not to look because it was gross; it looked like he was coating lard all over the place. I went to the door and pulled. It was locked.

"Dammit."

I wondered briefly if there was a rear entrance right as I brought the curved edge of the tire iron down on the glass. My arm reverberated heavily for my effort. The glass mostly held—it was still up, but now there was a large fracture line running north and south for a couple of feet.

Murph, the pimple popper, had come over to

investigate my work, his head tilting from side to side as the crack elongated on its own. He knew what was happening. As I began to wind up to smack the glass again, my new buddy had other plans. He backed up. For a second, *my* head may have tilted as I was trying to reason out what the hell he was doing. I stepped back quickly when I finally caught up to his actions. Murph had lowered his head and was running straight for the glass. It sounded like a rifle shot as the glass exploded. I think he should have waited a bit for the crack to get bigger or me to strike it again, because he was pretty dazed, looking like he had just gone a couple of rounds in a prize-fight boxing match and had been more on the receiving end than the giving.

I did not give him a chance to recover as I brought the full weight of the tire iron to bear on the top of his skull. My arm shook almost as violently as it had when I struck the glass. It was possible Zitty Murph had always been known for a thick head, and that was why his career had stalled at gas station attendant…or he was just a new-and-improved variation on zombies, one of the skullers. I brained him again, and two more times, before I finally heard the telltale sign of bone cracking.

"Motherfucker, you're going to give me carpal tunnel!" I yelled at him as I brought the iron down again.

This time I was rewarded with brain matter. Murph fell to his knees, his teeth chattering like he'd been locked in a meat freezer. He pitched forward face first and was still.

"So worth it," I said as I stepped over his body and headed in.

My eyes still adjusting to the gloom, I almost missed the movement of my next obstacle. It couldn't have been much older than five. His teeth were bared, and he had a rapacious look on his face, yet he was cautious, as if he knew just how dangerous I was. He wanted to eat; he just didn't want to die more. He ducked behind one of the aisles.

Are you kidding me? I thought. He was going for

stealth mode. I get that he was at a distinct size advantage, but when did zombies figure that out?

"Listen, you little fucker, get your ass out here!"

A can of peas rolled down an aisle toward me. I swear I could hear eerie mood music playing in the background. You know the kind they play in the movies, it masks the sound of the monster sneaking up on the character that is about to get filleted with a machete or, in this case, have the back of his knees ripped out. My prize was tantalizingly close. Was it worth it? I felt for the kid that had lost his childhood and thus his life, but the thing running around here wasn't him…not anymore. If I didn't kill him, I was just adding to the problem now that I'd allowed him a means of escape.

He might have been shooting for stealth by hiding behind things, but his brain had not quite figured out the part about heavy footfalls. I could hear him running like he was caught playing video games after bedtime and was now stomping back to his room in a huff. I had a good sense where he was, but this cat-and-mouse shit was unnerving, especially since I wasn't convinced I was the cat.

I walked quietly down the small aisle I was fairly certain he was at the end of. When I turned the corner, he looked about as surprised as I did. I cocked my arm back, hesitating when he placed his arm in front of his face and head in a defensive gesture; that was a human motion. He had me second-guessing my intent, and it was nearly my demise. I don't know if the zombies have only the mind they have taken over to use as their host, or if they operate independent of it, but I think if this kid had been older I would have been screwed. He looked to the side and past me. He saw something, and a five-year-old just can't play that stuff off. They don't have the experience.

I wheeled to see the boy's mirror image. "Twins!" I shouted just as I brought the point of the tire iron straight down.

The kid had gotten that close, his feral rage twisting his face into a mask of hate and hunger. I pulled the point out of the top of his skull and thrust the kid away. I didn't even bother to turn and see if his brother was coming; I knew he was. I swung for all I was worth. I was a little low, the blow catching him on the edge of his shoulder, glancing off to hit him just below the ear. It didn't kill him, but it did have enough force to send him skittering away, giving me some room. I spun to check on the status of his brother, but he was having a serious disconnect between body and brain, as half of his body was moving while the other side was drooped in disuse. I brought the tire iron down, ending the life of the world's youngest stroke victim.

I moved quickly to the other one. He was dazed. I did a quick check to make sure he wasn't a triplet or some crazy octo-child thing. When I came up to him, iron raised, his hand went up again in defense.

"I'm not falling for that this time." Then the little bastard's mouth moved. Sound didn't come out, but I would've had to have been blind not to see the word "please" being formed on his lips. "Fuck you!"

I swung for the fences, his pleading instantly turning into the more familiar sounds of hate. Maybe I put something more into that swing than I thought I could, or perhaps I was so disgusted that the monster inside of the boy was using him in such a way as to make him appear more human so that killing him would be more difficult. Like I needed any more guilt in my existence. Whatever the case, that tire iron went three-quarters through that little boy's skull. His head fell in on itself in an attempt to fill in the space.

"Nature abhors a vacuum!" I spouted insanely.

All manner of matter sluiced from the gigantic wound, coating my weapon, the lower parts of the boy's face and his torso. I let the iron go, allowing the thing in front of me to fall. I kicked him in the midsection, sending his remains to the wall and away.

My chest was heaving like I'd been doing wind sprints. I'd almost forgotten why I'd come in at all. I walked over to the side of the store and bent down. "Still worth it," I said as I picked up the case of beer.

I didn't even wait until I got out of the store before I cracked one open. It's tough to call warm beer in a can the nectar of the gods. But as I stepped out into the warm embrace of the sun, blue sky and birds chirping in the distance—yeah, I could say that. I tilted my head back and just poured the entire contents down my gullet. It tasted something like wet metal shavings mixed with donkey piss, and it was heaven.

I downed another one before I moved a foot. I almost started heading back to Tommy and Porkchop when I remembered what the hell I was doing down here in the first place. I rummaged around for the span of three more downed beers before deciding I was not going to be able to find a gas can. Another idea popped into my head, most likely fueled by my beverage. I checked the eight or nine cars in the lot to first see if any of them would start; that was a no go. I then decided which one was the lightest and pushed it over to the seemingly untapped underground gas tanks. I went over and grabbed the siphoning kit. I knew the battery in the car had some juice in it, because the dome light had come on when I opened the door.

"Come on, baby, do me right."

I had placed one end of the hose down into the well, the other into the fuel tank of the VW. I hooked up the terminals to the battery, flipped the switch and stepped back. I was not at all certain how this was going to turn out. The little motor was spinning, so that was a good sign. Then I saw the hose moving. (I, umm, had to do a quick adjustment when I realized I'd set the thing up backwards and was pulling gas from the car and sending it into the ground. Hey! It wasn't like anything was labeled.) A minute later, I was back in business. It wasn't a fast process, and I was able to down another beer as I waited. When gas started falling onto the ground, I stopped, unhooked everything, and stuck it in the back seat.

"It would be cooler if you started."

I stuck what remained of the case of beer on the front seat. Out of habit I turned the radio on and was assailed with static nearly as loud as a jet taking off. I lowered the volume and looked around. The car itself was worth about five hundred bucks, but the speakers and amp installed had to be double that. What was weird, though, was the stereo he had in place. It looked like something pulled from salvage. It had knobs and a cassette player. Who still has a cassette player?

"Who does this?" I asked aloud. "Well, if there's a cassette player, there has to be cassettes."

I checked everywhere...nothing. It wasn't until I shoved my fingers down into between the cracked leather casing around the emergency brake that I got my first hint of success.

"Please be Zeppelin." My tongue was firmly entrenched between my teeth as I desperately maneuvered my fingers around trying to get a hold of the wily cassette.

I finally pinched a corner between middle and index fingers. "Gotcha!" I pulled it out between the thin opening. "Oh, come on." I was looking at the artist's name on the front. "Barbara Streisand? Really?" Shrugging, I popped it into the player.

I grabbed the steering wheel with my right hand as my left grabbed the frame of the door. I started pushing, every few feet taking a second to wet my whistle. Let's just say that, by the time I was within earshot of Tommy and Porkchop, I was lit like a cheap cigar and singing *The Way We Were* at the top of my lungs.

Tommy and Porkchop came down and helped those last few hundred feet.

"You alright?" Tommy asked, looking at the fair amount of gore I was wearing.

"I am now," I said, raising another beer to toast. After I told him all that had happened, he almost soured my mood a bit.

"You realize, Mr. T, we could have driven the truck down to the gas station and filled it up, right?"

Actually I hadn't realized that, but now I had to play it off like I had. "Yeah, but then I wouldn't have been able to listen to *Send in the Clowns*." That was the only title I could remember, because I actually had to fast forward past it. I can't stand clowns.

We filled up the truck from the car. Well, Tommy did. I was doing my best to polish off the case. They say drinking alcohol doesn't solve any problems, well, neither does drinking milk. At least with booze you can forget for a little while. Horrible reasoning or genius; depending on whether you had just started or were suffering through the after-effects.

We stayed on that overpass the rest of the day and night. We pulled the truck's canvas roof back so that we could see the stars as we laid down in the back in relative safety. Tommy didn't mind standing watch—or he didn't trust me to stay awake. Either way, Porkchop and I did some serious stargazing under a brilliant sky. I'd just been looking up at Orion, or maybe Lupus, when I felt a heavy push on my shoulder. I expected to have limited sight due to the darkness, I immediately had to shield my face from a nearly noon sun.

"What the hell?" I said, rolling to my side, doing my best to hide from the sunlight's intense scrutiny.

"We should get going, Mr. T," Tommy told me.

"Beef stew! Me and Tommy went back to the gas station and found it!" Porkchop was holding up a spoonful of something that looked and smelled pretty much like Henry's wet dog food. "Want some?"

"I'm good." I sat up, debating which was the worst enemy: the sun or the food thing Porkchop was eating. I waited until the boy was done before I got out of the truck and sat down next to him. I was in pretty decent shape considering how much I drank but definitely not at a hundred percent.

"You hear that?" Tommy came from around the other side of the truck.

"Sorry, probably my stomach gurgling."

"It's a car." Porkchop was holding up a pair of binoculars that looked like they could be used to view Mars.

"Where were those?" I asked, scratching my head.

"Back of the gas station," Tommy answered.

"How long have you guys been up? Forget it. We should probably hide." We had no weapons that would be worth a damn in a firefight. "Let's go, kiddo." I picked up Porkchop who was still looking through his over-sized field glasses.

***

"What's gotten into this dog?" BT was grumbling. Henry was uncharacteristically jumping from one seat to the other while also barking. He finally made the leap to the front, landing squarely in Tracy's lap.

"Ooomph. Oh, Henry, I've told you before…you're not a lap dog," Tracy admonished, but he wasn't listening. His back paws were firmly dug into her midsection with his front paws on the dash. His stubby tail was furiously going from side to side. "I've only ever seen him that happy when he sees Mi—"

"Truck!" Travis said, pointing up to an approaching overpass.

"Military." BT's eyebrows furrowed.

Henry was barking now.

"Stop the truck," Tracy told BT.

He'd taken over the duties after Tracy had nearly driven off the road while she was wiping her tearing eyes for the fortieth time. Tracy struggled to check her weapon with

Henry in her lap. With the truck stopped and confidence high that she was ready to fire if need be, she opened the truck door. Henry gingerly, but quickly, found his way down, although Tracy did her best to stop him. He ran about fifty feet further down the roadway, then proceeded to sit on his butt, look up at the overpass and bark.

***

"Henry?" I was seeing the dog I was just having a hard time confirming the reality of it. Alcohol hangover can give you a sort of disconnect from reality as you recover.

"BT's in the driver's seat," Porkchop said, but I was already running to the cloverleaf so I could get down to the roadway. It was not easy running in fireman gear.

***

"Is that Tommy waving to us?" Tracy asked, shielding her eyes. "And…and Porkchop, I think." She had exited the truck along with everyone else. "What are they doing?"

"Fast roping, it's a way to exit a helicopter quickly," Trip explained. "I used to have clients do this from time to time, and not always because they had to."

Tracy gasped as Porkchop came over the guardrail and headed down. Travis and Justin had gone up to greet them. Tommy came down next.

***

I was running for all I was worth. When I came down off that spiral of roadway, I was nearly dizzy. Then my eyes found Tracy. Any discomfort or hangover was blazed away as I picked her up and swung her around.

"We have got to keep meeting like this," she said as

she stroked the side of my face and kissed me even as we twirled.

Henry was barking in excitement, BT was grinning, my boys were walking back to me with Tommy and Porkchop (I don't know how they beat me down). Gary was crying. Trip, I think, was tripping (if the way he was chasing an imaginary butterfly was any clue) with Stephanie in tow. She waved quickly before resuming her guardian duties.

"Good to see you!" Dennis said.

I hadn't been this happy since maybe the day I got married, or the birth of each of my kids, or maybe even the day Henry allowed me to adopt him. The world right this very fucking second was a sparkling jewel and I loved it. Even if Deneaux was still out there, even if a Yeti-like animal was roaming around, and especially even if a Vampire tribunal was coming. Right fucking now, everything was fine and I was going to savor each and every second of it, even if it was damned.

Epilogue 1

Tommy and I had a brief respite. The lab wasn't necessarily the best place to have a heartfelt conversation, but if I'd learned one thing it was this. We might not get another chance. Simple as that. Death hovered around the living like it never had before. Sure we're all born knowing what the inevitable outcome is, but we'd never had it so violently thrust in our faces before. If Death got paid by the collection of souls, then he had indeed become a very wealthy entity. Maybe some good could come from this—maybe he'd just retire to an island in the Bahamas, sipping Mojitos with little umbrellas in them. If nothing else, it was a semi-comforting thought.

"I'm ready to answer your questions, Mr. T."

"Huh?" I asked, staring up at the ceiling. Chunks of ceiling tiles were clinging to their supports, defying gravity to the last. Some not so successfully if the area we had to clear out to sit down was any indication. The ape had done some serious damage during his stay.

"Questions. I know you have them."

"I don't even know where to start, Tommy. I mean…I guess I'd like to know why you were using Ryan Seacrest as a spirit guide or maybe not. Wait, I've got it. How many Talbots have you been in contact with?"

"All of them."

I sat up, the ceiling tiles suddenly losing their luster. "All of them? Over the last five hundred years? How is that even possible? And why?"

"You realize it's impolite to ask questions one on top of the other, right?" He was smiling.

"Yes, because my biggest concern is being polite. How long have you known me?"

"Longer than you know."

"Wait, what?" You mean even before the zombies came?"

"I first saw you the day after you were born."

"Are you shitting me?"

"Nope. When you were born, there was a mix-up in the nursery."

"Wait, let me try to understand what you're saying. So either I'm not really a Talbot, or I almost got to go home with a different family and live a semi-normal life away from the craziness that comes along with being a Talbot?"

"You nearly went home with the Murphy's."

"I could have been Irish? Weird."

"They would have treated you well enough, however, in all likelihood you would have died at the age of twenty-two."

"War? Or was I saving someone?"

"Slipped on ice and fell into a culvert."

"Really, that's it? Was I at least saving someone when it happened."

"You were trying to recover a cd you'd dropped."

"A compact disc? I died for a compact disc? Was it at least Widespread Panic?"

"A Celtic Christmas."

"I give up."

Tommy shrugged his shoulders. "It was an easy enough fix. I just switched the tags on the beds and no one was the wiser."

Now I felt somewhat guilty that baby Murphy died in a culvert some twenty or so years ago. "The Murphy's...how did they take their son's death?" I needed to know.

"Oh, he was much more cautious than you, he was nowhere near the culvert that day. He grew up to be a pretty successful broker."

"That's good, I guess." I wanted to know how Murphy, my near half-brother, made out. Odds were it wasn't good. Tommy wasn't clarifying, and as far as I was concerned, the man had already cheated death once. I was going to let it stay like that. "Why though? I mean...I know why your sister was tied to us, I get that, but what could you possibly hope to achieve by interfering?"

"When I was a child back in what is now Germany, Lizzie and I realized that I'd been cursed with the gift of foresight. She did everything she could to keep that a secret from our father, but I didn't have all my wits. I think a lot of that had to do with how many 'realities' lived in my head. I couldn't keep them all straight. At first, my father thought I was mentally challenged, although those weren't his exact words. Then, when I started predicting the weather or when this or that person was going to die or get married, he thought differently. Possessed is what he said. I think he would have killed me for either offense. But then he would have had to tell the other villagers why he'd done it, and he didn't want his good name..." he nearly spat that out, "...dragged through the mud by having sired a dummy or a demon."

"I'm so sorry. I can't even imagine what that must have been like for you growing up."

"It was as close to a living hell as can be achieved on this plane. And even that miserable existence paled in comparison to what Lizzie went through. Being a dirt-poor peasant back then was horrible enough, add in that she was a female to an abusive, uncaring father. And even though she was going through all this, she still took on the brunt of punishment my father meant to dole out to me. You have to see why I did what I did in the hopes I could one day get her back."

I did and I didn't. The Eliza he'd known had long ago departed to parts unknown. What remained was an evil that dwarfed anything her father, a mere mortal, could have aspired to. She was responsible for the deaths of thousands and that was before the zombie apocalypse. Her existence as a human was rife with misery and for that I was despondent. The moment she accepted Victor Talbot's bite, she'd gone on a crusade to eradicate all humanity. Guilty, innocent, young, old—it made no difference to her. Everything that wasn't her, was the enemy, plain and simple.

"Your silence is very telling, Mr. T."

"I'm sorry, Tommy. I didn't know Lizzie, I only knew Eliza. It is tough to feel compassion for someone who has a personal vendetta against everybody you love, including myself."

"I can understand that. Can you understand the guilt I felt about her?"

"Guilt? For what?"

"I didn't protect her like she protected me." He was near to tears.

"Tommy," I said as I wrapped an arm around his shoulders. "I don't think you were in any position to help. You were...what? Like eight years old, right? Your father was the real curse in your family, it was his actions and his alone that spawned what your Lizzie was to become. We can only hope that he is paying for his past sins."

"He is," Tommy said with such certainty a shiver went up my spine. I sort of wanted to know how he knew the whereabouts of his father but the larger and wiser part of me refrained. "I'm sorry." Tommy started anew after he collected himself and his thoughts. "I've strayed a bit from where we started."

"That's probably because you've known me for way too long."

Tommy smiled, and I'd swear it was like someone had turned on a hundred watt bulb in that dingy, dirty place. Maybe that wasn't such a good thing. Who wanted to see the rats that could potentially be scurrying in the corners?

"The Talbots. Why did I follow the Talbots? At first, it was because of Victor. He was the key. All the legends I could dig up said that if I killed him, Lizzie would become human again."

"And what of you?"

"I would have stayed in my half-vampire state. A life in near eternity without her would be a small price to pay to have her back for that short span of human life."

Again I got a heavy ripple that rode through me. Most times I just simply could forget that I would long survive all I held dear. There just wasn't much time for reflection; simple survival took up the majority of my existence. That was a good thing, no, that was a great thing. Thinking that I could potentially go eons without those I loved was unfathomable. I'm pretty sure most times my feeble mind couldn't even conceive of the concept. Tommy thankfully ripped me from thoughts that would have invariably spiraled down to despair and depression.

"After she killed Victor, I knew almost the moment she had done it. My visions changed. They'd become more powerful when Eliza changed me, but when she killed Victor, they became more focused as well."

"On the Talbots?"

"On the Talbots. Someway, somehow, one of the Talbots was going to be involved in a fight for the very survival of man as a species."

"You didn't know who?"

"No, my visions don't work like that. It's not like watching a television show."

"I didn't say that."

"You were thinking it."

"Now you're the Thought Police? Might as well put me in jail now."

"Sometimes my 'sights' are nothing more than a feeling, other times I catch glimpses of what can potentially happen. At times, it is like someone shattered a mirror, and I can only see shards of what was once reflected, so I have to piece it together as best I can. Then there are the offshoots that can spell disaster if I do not step in. Sometimes, for some reason, I'm shown things that will never come to pass, at least not in the universe I travel in now. And I'm left to wonder if I need to do anything with these sights, are there things I need to do here and now that can prevent or mitigate them."

"You manipulate the future? That sounds pretty dangerous, Tommy."

"I just told you about how I switched you back at birth. Did that not ring a bell within you?"

"Sorry, seemed anecdotal at the time."

"No, there are times I have to step in because, if I do not, the outcome trends toward disaster."

"How many times have you done this? I mean step into someone's life and alter it for them and all around them? And what gives you the right?"

Tommy looked up.

"Really?! You're going to use *Him?* Convenient." I said that last word softly though, just in case it was true.

"It is not easy, this life I have. It has been a heavy burden. I am constantly confronted with apocalyptic scenarios and the many ways that they can come about."

"Who was your first? Who was the first Talbot's life you altered?"

"Do you really want me to answer this?"

"It's my lineage, I think I have a right to know." I was being obstinate.

"I don't think you're going to like how this ends up."

"I'll be the judge of that."

"Mr. T, you're not fully realizing how I 'see' things. I am given five to ten second visions and have to piece everything else around them. Sometimes my vision can be decades maybe even centuries in the future. Sometimes they may happen within moments of me seeing them and I have to decide on that limited amount of information how I should act or what I should do or say to those around me."

"Are you expecting me to change my stance?"

"Not really. I was merely hoping."

"Okay, so who was the first?"

"Just remember you asked. The first was Linus Talbot."

"Wait. Linus?'"

"Linus Talbot, sort of an obnoxious, loud-mouth drunkard."

"Glad to, umm, see we've evolved away from that." I coughed. "What? I don't drink much...anymore."

"Can I get back to the story?"

"Sure, sure."

"Linus was a blacksmith's apprentice outside of what is now Liverpool. He was heading home to his pregnant wife. I'd been shadowing him for three months. I'd seen him involved in different threads throughout my visions. It seemed he was to play an important role in a number of them." Tommy paused. "I think maybe we should just stop. I don't think this is such a great idea, and I'm pretty tired."

"You barely sleep."

"*That*, you have to remember? Dammit, Mr. T, I really don't want to do this."

"It was like five hundred years ago, right?"

"Close enough."

"I promise I won't hold a grudge."

"You're lying."

"Your visions tell you that?"

"No, just experience. Okay, Linus was heading home, I did nothing more than steer him away from a particular street."

"Sounds benign enough. So what would have happened?"

"He would have won a small fortune by that day's standards playing dice."

"See my face, Tommy? I'm pretty confused."

"If he had won that money, his next stop would have been to the tavern where he would have drank away all his winnings and his earnings. He and his wife would have become homeless."

"Idiot. No...no I meant Linus. But wait, why didn't you just let him win and then stop him from going to the tavern?"

Tommy paused. "I...I guess I could have done that. It had not occurred to me at the time."

The audible slap as I hit my forehead echoed throughout the cavernous laboratory.

"You weren't there. I had mere moments to make a choice."

"Okay, okay, let's move past this part, what happened to Linus?"

"He was run over by a runaway ox-cart two weeks later."

"What? I thought you said he was somehow involved in getting the best of some great calamity."

"I never said that. He would have been the cause of it."

"What the fuck, Tommy?"

"After he lost his home, he would have been living out on the street where he would have gotten bit by a disease-riddled rat. His genome was perfectly aligned to accept the disease where he would have passed it on to half the continent causing what would have become known as the Sharts."

"Now you're fucking with me. The Sharts?"

"It's not as funny as today's vernacular would have you believe. It was actually the liquefying of the bowels. Everything, and I mean everything, was destined to leak out. The death was a prolonged agony and misery, with one's innards dragging behind them. It would have dwarfed the Black Plague. If mankind survived, their numbers would have been drastically reduced to a population that would have teetered on the brink of extinction for years."

"That's just gross, man. I could have done without the visual. What happened to his wife? She must have lost the house after Linus became road kill."

"She actually became a very successful blacksmith."

"That was allowed back then?"

"Not really, after her husband died she donned his clothing and went to work in his steed."

"The blacksmith didn't notice anything strange?"

"Mrs. Talbot was an, umm, robust woman, handsome in her own way I suppose."

"Did she ever marry again?"

"No, and she also used her maiden name when she opened up her own blacksmith shop. Towns were much smaller back then, the Talbot name was not necessarily held with the highest regard. Probably saved her and the baby's life though. Had Eliza discovered a Talbot life she would have snuffed it out."

"And what of the baby, what happened to him?"

"He grew up most of his life with the Murphy last name."

"Murphy again?"

"Just serendipity, no true causal relationship."

"You sure?"

"Mostly…anyway, after his mother passed, he found some letters she had packed away among her things, basically telling him all about the life she was reluctant to share when she was alive. He changed back to the Talbot family name at that point. Lived a fairly decent life as he took up his mother's blacksmith shop, married and had three children. Fairly uneventful as far as your surname goes."

"Well, at least that turned out well, I suppose. What about me? Did you ever alter anything in my life besides the crib thing?"

"Haven't you heard enough?"

"There is, isn't there? Tell me!"

"You're not going to like it."

"Add it to the long list of things I don't like."

"Do you remember when you applied for that job with AmeriCorp?"

"Sure. I'd been laid off for months, it was my first big break in a long while. Had two interviews and was told I'd be doing a third. Figured the job was mine at that point and now we were just going to hammer out the details. Never heard from them again...why?" I asked, suddenly suspicious. "What did you do, Tommy?" He stood up, probably to get out of harm's way. I stood up with him. "Tommy. Tell me, man. What did you do that kept me at that shitty pothole-filling job? I could have made some money, moved the family to a better area."

"If you got the job, odds were you were going to be away on business. Minneapolis, as a matter of fact."

"What's wrong with Minneapolis?"

"Nothing in and of itself, other than you would have been there on December 7th."

"The day of the outbreak." I sat down heavily, barely noticing the lump of tile that was attempting to get intimate with me. "Wow, that's pretty heavy." I was thinking of what might have become of my family if I'd been a thousand miles away. All roads led to disastrous followed immediately by horrendous. "What did you do to prevent me from getting that third interview?" I was only curious. How could I be mad when he'd saved my family's life, again.

"I'm sorry, Mr. T. I called their HR department, pretending to look for a contact number. I told them I was your probation officer and you had missed your last check in."

"Probation officer? What crime had I committed?"

"You were a habitual driver-while-intoxicated."

"That was enough to not give me a chance to work for them?"

"I also said you tended to pass out nude."

"Oh, *come on*, you couldn't have said I robbed a bank or something?" Then another thought dawned on me as I moved a piece of debris away from underneath me that hadn't even the common decency to take me out for dinner before it went exploring. "Tommy."

"I'm done Mr. T. I've answered your questions."

"Not quite. What if…okay, let me rephrase this. You said yourself that not everything you see comes to pass, or maybe you don't quite understand it. What if the zombie apocalypse had never happened?"

"My guess is you'd still be filling in holes."

And right now, somehow even that most pedestrian of life-styles sounded like heavenly bliss.

Epilogue 2 – The Pull of Mike – As told by Joseph DiPaolo – Knight of the Templar and Rhodes Scholar

The paths of most of our lives, if mapped out with string, would look a lot like Nikolai Rimsky-Korsakov's *Flight of the Bumblebee*, as we flitted from random event to random event, making chance encounters with countless numbers of people. Not Mike, though, nor others like him. His path would be as straight as the spoke of a tire; his life trail is inexorably straight, always. He has no choice but to walk this line. Oh, there's no rule to how one must walk as Mike has proved over and over. As the crow flies is more than just a phrase in his case. Some might think it would be easier to have a path already laid out before you. But I can assure you that is not the case. Have not all of us at certain times in our lives avoided a particularly nasty or distasteful event, person, place? Insert noun here. These are not choices Mike can avert. The crow may be able to fly above the din, but Mike has to plow through it.

Most people intersect with others at various points along their lives and move on, but when our route comes in contact with someone like Mike we are pulled to him, almost drawn. We can't help it. There is something in the simple honesty of his path that we crave, a way to escape the chaos of life. When I talked to Tracy about this she laughed. I don't think she was a believer, and neither was BT.

"I hated Mike when I first met him. Thought he was arrogant as all hell," she'd told me. "I sure wasn't 'drawn' to him like you say."

"I second that," BT had added.

"There's resistance at first. As much as we want order, we also want to have freewill, and we certainly don't want to walk to anybody else's tune."

"Especially Mike's. Probably has the soundtrack to *Pretty in Pink* running through his head." BT nearly snorted at his own joke.

"I've been with Mike for over two decades. I've never seen the man walk the straight and narrow," Tracy said.

"Like I've said, it's not how he goes through life, it's the events themselves he has to follow. In this life and every other one."

"There's more than one Mike out there? Is this some sort of cosmic joke?" BT was not looking too amused.

"Does he know this?" Tracy asked with a true measure of concern.

"On some level he may."

"That could explain some of his behavior," BT joked.

"Indeed it could," Joseph said, turning the conversation serious. "There are some 'spokes', if you will, that cannot handle the strain, and they shatter like the breakable spirits they are."

"Come on, you're talking about alternate realities and multiple lives. Do you really think me…we…will believe this?" BT questioned.

"Ask yourself this. Do you feel a strong pull to Mike?"

BT nodded unconsciously as did Tracy, though she knew she was doing it.

"That's because you've both known him, and were meant to be with him through all time, every time."

"And what about Trip? He's a part of this grand design you're talking about?"

"My string was in knots before Ponch came along," Trip said.

"Well, see that's the first thing I've heard that I believe." BT was smiling at his own wit.

"Probably not going to like this part then," Joseph said. "Trip is like a shepherd."

"That's why I can smell things so good!" Trip said, touching his nose.

"Not a German Shepherd, honey." Stephanie put her

hand on her husband's shoulder.

"Come on, Joseph. Him?" BT looked disgusted.

"There are some like Trip who can see the tapestries we all weave, the fabrics of our existence. Sometimes he gently guides us to where we need to be or, in my case, pulls a person kicking and screaming."

"You really expect me to believe this?"

"I'm not trying to make you believe anything, BT, but that you, that all of us are here... well, that's proof enough."

"That we're here in this field?" Gary asked.

"No. That we're here, at the end," Joseph said solemnly.

"Dun-dun-dun!" Trip sang out for dramatic effect.

Epilogue 3 – S.S. Crossbearer – Destination: New York, Port of Origin London

The ship creaked and groaned as it cut through the swells. Heavy winds cracked the canvas sails, billowing them out to catch the might of the blustery weather. Sheets of ocean mist broke over the bow spraying a lone figure who seemed oblivious to the less than favorable weather conditions. Her hair as red as a bonfire at night, she was her own lighthouse; the crew avoided her as the ship would avoid deadly shoals. To approach meant certain swift death. Always she peered forward, expecting to see what she was seeking at any moment.

The men who had been doing their best to steer clear of the woman at the bow shrunk back even further when they realized another was moving swiftly past them, paying them no more mind than if they were ants upon a sizzling roadway. The raven-haired woman was of indeterminable age and had a beauty beyond reproach, even with the hard set of her eyes and the tightly closed lips. A sailor taking more than his rations of rum had learned just how savage she was. When the woman had walked by, he had catcalled and attempted to smack her on the ass. She had turned and caught his hand before he made contact. With one fluid motion, she had separated his shoulder and thrown him overboard. When the other sailors started to launch a rescue, she had told them that the first to aid him would find themselves in the water with him. The man had screamed for help before losing his battle with a swell of seawater. The three mysterious passengers had watched silently.

"Payne, I have prepared your dinner."

Payne turned slightly as the woman approached.

"There is more going on here, Charity."

"This ship? These men are sheep."

"No, with Eliza. This was no ordinary death."

"Are you concerned?" Charity asked coolly.

"Intrigued perhaps. I knew Eliza was cruel, even for our kind. When she killed my poor Victor, I should have hunted her down then and there, and yet I didn't, for she intrigued me then as well."

"You had your reasons. I wish you had let Sophia and I take care of her, though. Victor may have been your offspring, but he was our sire. We had a duty to him."

"She would have killed you." Payne did not say the words as a slight, only as a truth. Charity wisely stayed silent. "It seems her brother is in the New World as well." Payne was once again staring off into the distance to a spot only she could see.

"The half-ling?"

"He is no longer a half-ling."

"That is interesting. I wonder her reasons for finally completing his turn."

"I see so much, yet not enough to get a clear picture. There was a witch involved, a powerful one and, another, a medicine man. Somehow I feel a piece of Victor himself was implicated in her death."

"How can this be? My sire has been dust for centuries," Charity asked in wonderment, showing some emotion for the first time since they'd started the voyage.

"I have been wondering this as well. We will find our answers soon. Come, we will dine together." Payne locked her arm around Charity's. The crew quickly found duties to perform that would not have them anywhere near the women's return trip back to their cabins.

The smell of iron-rich blood beset their senses as they walked into Payne's room. The meal was naked and tied to a bed by his wrists and ankles. His chest was heaving in fright, lines of blood streaking his arms and legs as a third vampire lightly dragged a knife across his skin, not enough to cause true damage, but with enough force to make blood weep to the surface.

"I see you are eager to feed, Sophia." Payne's canines

elongated, her eyes taking on a glazed appearance. She swiftly crossed the room and sank deeply into the man's neck. Charity and Sophia found their own spots.

The crew did their best to block out the screams of the forsaken.

I hope you enjoyed the book. If you did please consider leaving a review.

For more in The Zombie Fallout Series by Mark Tufo:

Zombie Fallout 1

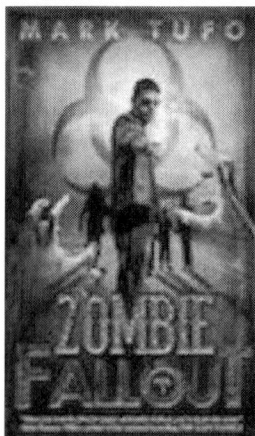

Zombie Fallout 2 A Plague Upon Your Family

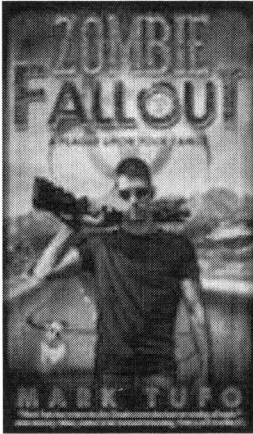

Zombie Fallout 3 The End....

Zombie Fallout 3.5 Dr. Hugh Mann

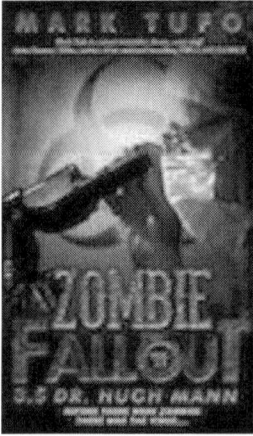

Zombie Fallout 4 The End Has Come And Gone

Zombie Fallout 5 Alive In A Dead World

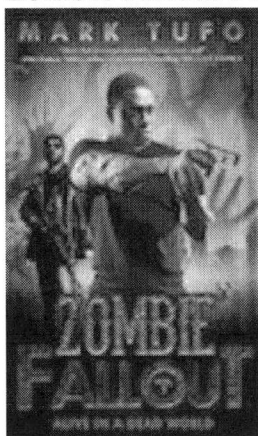

Zombie Fallout 6 Til Death Do Us Part

Zombie Fallout 7 For The Fallen

The newest Post Apocalyptic Horror by Mark Tufo:

Lycan Fallout Rise of the Werewolf

Fun with zombies in The Book of Riley Series by Mark Tufo

The Book Of Riley A Zombie Tale pt 1

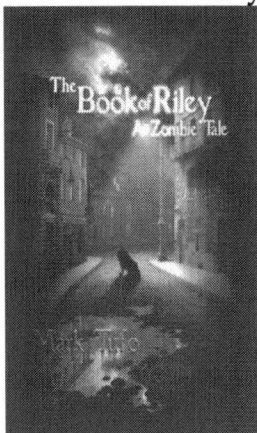

The Book Of Riley A Zombie Tale pt 2

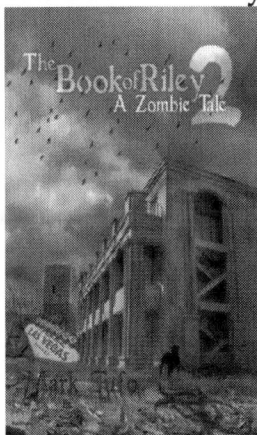

The Book Of Riley A Zombie Tale pt 3

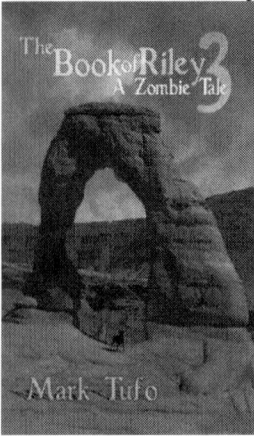

The Book Of Riley A Zombie Tale pt 4

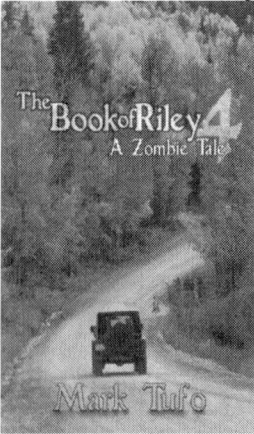

Or all in one neat package:

The Book Of Riley A Zombie Tale Boxed set plus a bonus short

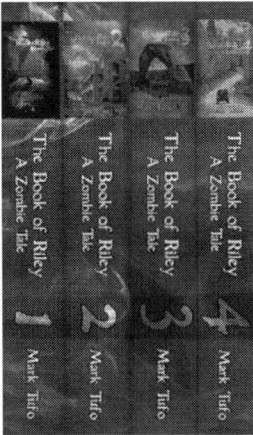

Dark Zombie Fiction can be found in The Timothy Series by Mark Tufo

Timothy

Tim2

Michael Talbot is at it again in this Post Apocalyptic Alternative History series Indian Hill by Mark Tufo

Indian Hill 1 Encounters:

Indian Hill 2 Reckoning

Indian Hill 3 Conquest

Indian Hill 4 From The Ashes

Writing as M.R. Tufo

Dystance Winter's Rising

The Spirit Clearing

Callis Rose

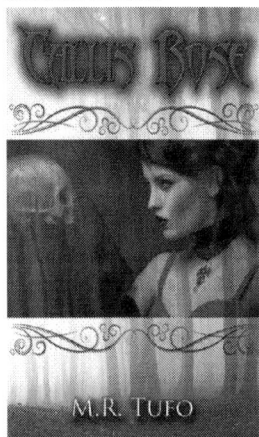

I love hearing from readers, you can reach me at:

email
mark@marktufo.com

website
www.marktufo.com

Facebook
https://www.facebook.com/pages/Mark-
Tufo/133954330009843?ref=hl

Twitter
@zombiefallout

All books are available in audio version at
Audible.com or itunes.

All books are available in print at Amazon.com or
Barnes and Noble.com

7597717R00188

Printed in Great Britain
by Amazon.co.uk, Ltd.,
Marston Gate.